BATTLE
LINES

BATTLE
LINES
JACOB I. N. WOLCOTT

To Mom and Dad, thank you for everything. Thank you for encouraging me to pursue this wholeheartedly, for the countless times you listened to my ramblings and the many times you read and reread my work.

To Grandpa, thank you for being the first person to read my first draft all the way through. Your time and feedback meant the world to me. Thank you for all the Wednesday talks. I cherish every word.

To Caleb, thank you for teaming up with me on YouTube and beyond. Our drills will pierce the heavens!!

To you, the reader, thank you for supporting me in my dream. Whoever you are, wherever you are, however you found me, thank you. Really, thank you.

Now let's go on a journey!

Contents

PROLOGUE   1
CHAPTER ONE   7
CHAPTER TWO   24
CHAPTER THREE   39
CHAPTER FOUR   55
CHAPTER FIVE   67
CHAPTER SIX   75
CHAPTER SEVEN   87
CHAPTER EIGHT   102
CHAPTER NINE   113
CHAPTER TEN   124
CHAPTER ELEVEN   138
CHAPTER TWELVE   148
CHAPTER THIRTEEN   156
CHAPTER FOURTEEN   166
CHAPTER FIFTEEN   179
CHAPTER SIXTEEN   190
CHAPTER SEVENTEEN   200
CHAPTER EIGHTEEN   219
CHAPTER NINETEEN   229
CHAPTER TWENTY   240
CHAPTER TWENTY-ONE   249
CHAPTER TWENTY-TWO   263
CHAPTER TWENTY-THREE   273
CHAPTER TWENTY-FOUR   284
CHAPTER TWENTY-FIVE   292
CHAPTER TWENTY-SIX   303
CHAPTER TWENTY-SEVEN   316
CHAPTER TWENTY-EIGHT   322
CHAPTER TWENTY-NINE   333
CHAPTER THIRTY   341
EPILOGUE   349

PROLOGUE

MERCURY
Age 10

The piercing cold air of the trayite mining tunnel stung Mercury's face and invaded his lungs. When Sol administered the PerfectMemory serum, the ten-year-old boy barely felt the injection. His vision shifted, sharpening to become hyper-focused. The drug must be taking effect. The next several minutes would be forever burned into his brain. PerfectMemories only worked on children, and only once or twice at that. Whatever was about to happen, it must be important. Sol must be about to give him some vital lesson. With the injection over, Mercury put his helmet back on. The click and hiss as his helmet resealed itself was even more pronounced than normal.

The cave was perfectly silent. Mercury's breath turned to half a dozen thin jets of fog as it filtered through his helmet's respiration system. His ThermSuit's temperature was well within the safe zone despite the external temperatures being cold enough to freeze his eyes in their sockets. All was dark, except for the light from Sol's visor casting a blue filter over his world. Glittering stalagmites and stalactites filled the dead-end mining tunnel and amidst them on the rippling icy ground sat the hero of his childhood.

Not that Mercury could remember much of his childhood, or even his real name. He knew he had run away from home, but that had been almost four months ago. Four months since joining the Air Navy and Ground Elite. Now, he was an Angel. He had his nights in the DreamTank and his days in Forging. Nothing else mattered.

Even though the tunnel they were in was massive and Sol was sitting down, he seemed to fill every centimeter of frozen space. Was that a side-effect of the PerfectMemory? Before him, the old general looked more machine than man in his full-body trayite armor. That bright blue visor shone down from atop the tower of interlocking bands made from the rarest metal in this universe. There was not another suit like it in existence. A sword lay across his lap, gleaming shards of ice still clinging to it along its impossibly sharp edge. The weapon was also forged from trayite. Sol was clad in the sum total of this harsh planet's wealth.

To the Federation's masses the man was Genrik Rauss, the Minister of War. To the military, he was the Supreme Commander, call sign "Archangel." He was the man who had almost singlehandedly won the Second Taurusian War. Mercury called him Sol, but he was more than that. He was a teacher. He was a leader. He was like a father. He was larger than life in every way Mercury could imagine. He was the hero of the weak that fought the good fight without asking for anything in return. He was the personification of everything Mercury hoped to one day become.

Picking up the sword on his lap, Sol gestured at the cracked hole in the icy floor where the blade had until just recently been embedded, "Sit." As always, his voice was steel.

Mercury obeyed. The first thing Sol had hammered into his skull when he took Mercury in was to always obey without question. Silence filled the air as Mercury waited for Sol to speak.

"I've killed thousands with my own hands because of my sworn duty to the Federation. By my orders, millions of innocents have died for the sake of billions."

The boy blinked under his helmet. Had he heard that right? "...What?"

2

Sol's helmet did not shift in the slightest. The only sound was Mercury's own breath humming out his helmet. He knew Sol had killed people. He was a soldier after all. But he only killed bad guys, right? "I-Innocents?" Mercury asked. "What do you mean?"

"War is…messy, Mercury. There's no way around that. One day you will be in a position where you have to weigh lives on a scale." Mercury shifted uncomfortably on the ice as he heard Sol's words.

"Nations fall under indecisive leadership," Sol went on. "You must be decisive. When you have the weight of a hundred billion souls resting on your shoulders, you can't afford to make mistakes."

That was wrong. Mercury could feel his chest getting tight. "What do you mean Sol? Are you saying I'll have to kill innocent people?"

"Yes," Sol's voice chilled Mercury even inside his ThermSuit. "You must not hesitate."

"No," Mercury blurted out.

Sol's helmet slowly tilted to the side. "What did you say?"

Mercury's skin crawled at the memories of the last time he had said "no" to Sol. He would take a week of Forging rather than relive that experience. "That's wrong." The boy stood up quickly. "When I joined you, you said I would be helping people."

"You swore to follow my every order." Sol was stern. "It doesn't matter what you think is right or wrong. You are my subordinate and you will follow orders."

"But-,"

"Sit."

Mercury hesitated. He could feel the PerfectMemory opening up his mind. There would be no forgetting this conversation. If Sol discharged him now, he would probably be okay. His family would probably take him back in. But he had left them behind. He became an Angel because he wanted to help people like Sol did. He sat down.

"Listen to me Mercury," Sol's voice was stern, but not angry. Sol never got angry. "Inaction is the luxury of the complacent. Those with the power to take action have a duty to take action." He gestured at his armor. "You know this suit was instrumental to winning the Second Taurusian War, but where do you think it came from? You know the inhabitants of this planet are worked like slaves."

"...Yes," Mercury pulled his legs close to his chest.

"You know how rare trayite is. How many people do you think died to mine it?"

Mercury did not know. He did not want to know. He simply stared at the feet of his ThermSuit. He felt tears start to run down his face. Killing people to help people? What did that even mean?

"Today I just commissioned enough trayite for six more suits," Sol said. "One of them is for you."

The boy's eyes darted up. "Why would you do that?" he demanded, voice rising in anger.

"There's another war coming," Sol said. "A bigger war. And it's a very real possibility this will be humanity's last war. If we do survive, it will be the end of life as we know it."

Mercury swallowed as the weight of Sol's words sunk in. So this was why the general chose to turn this moment into a PerfectMemory.

"You agreed to sacrifice whatever you had to in order to help people. Did you lie?"

"No," Mercury choked up. "I meant it. You know I meant it. But,"

"Don't spout excuses Mercury. You're better than that."

He had been ready to give up his own comforts, but not to take the lives of good people. "But it's wrong!" Mercury felt the silence consume his words.

"You're right," Sol said. "Killing is never justified. Never. Every time you take a life you must remember that person had family, friends. Sometimes we have to do terrible things in order to prevent something even more horrible. You understood that when you decided to become a soldier."

Mercury started crying inside his helmet. "That's different. I wanted to fight bad guys. I wanted to help people."

"Listen Mercury," Sol spoke slowly. "There's no such thing as good guys and bad guys. Just people. Everyone does bad things sometimes, some more than others. They're still people. We don't fight and kill monsters, but people."

"I-I didn't sign up for this."

"So, will you force someone else to bear the burden?" Sol challenged. "Is that the kind of person you are?"

Mercury gritted his teeth and swallowed a sob. "N-No."

"Who are you?" Sol demanded.

"I'm Mercury," the boy said with a sniff. How many thousands of times had he repeated those words over the past few months?

"And why are you here Mercury?" The glowing blue visor of Sol's helmet terrified the boy, but it also bolstered him. Although Sol was beyond harsh, the man treated him like an equal.

"To help people," he said.

"Are you willing to do what is necessary to help people? Even if it means killing?"

Mercury knew that if he said no, Sol would be finished with him. He would find someone else to be his protégé. "Yes," he answered.

"No matter who?"

Mercury sniffed, then he nodded. He looked up at Sol. The helmeted face of his hero filled him with the resolve he needed. He would do whatever was necessary to help people. If that meant killing…then he would kill whoever it was that needed killing. "No matter who."

"Good," Sol stood and Mercury did likewise. The general was so tall that he barely came up to his waist. "One day Mercury you will have to make the hard choices. Until that day, let the morality of what you do rest on my shoulders. A weapon isn't responsible for the actions of the person using it."

"Yes sir," Mercury nodded.

"You said it was wrong to sacrifice others," Sol said as they walked back up the winding tunnel towards Bjornhal's surface. "You're right, Mercury. It is wrong. You must never let yourself become numb to the choices you make, so hold onto that strong sense of right and wrong." He looked over his shoulder and locked Mercury's gaze. "Hold on to it and never let go, because once you do, you're lost."

With those words, Mercury was put at ease. There was something about Sol's overwhelming confidence that assured him the old general could not possibly be wrong; an inexplicable, deep sense that Sol had everything under control. Though Mercury did not understand why, he had never trusted Sol more completely than he did now. He would follow this man to the ends of the universe. He would jump feet-first into the fiery bullet storms of Hel itself if Sol asked him to.

A couple minutes later Mercury felt the PerfectMemory serum start to fade. Sol had chosen this moment to burn into his brain. As long as Mercury lived, he would never forget what Sol taught him here.

CHAPTER ONE

One Year Later...

MERCURY

Age 11

"The worlds are in danger Mercury. Revolution is here. How would you save them?"

The eleven-year-old boy shifted uneasily from one foot to another in the darkness. He was keenly aware of Sol standing behind him. The aging general carried a presence that commanded the attention of others, even at times like this when he could not be seen. Sol had been predicting a revolution for several years; that's why he had recruited Mercury. The job of saving the worlds would eventually be his, and the pressure of the task threatened to crush him.

Mercury stood in the epicenter of Erithian's Eye staring up at a plethora of figures and numbers spread across a spherical diorama of the Hel System. Erithian was their resident artificial intelligence built for macroscopic information analysis. Every possible piece of information Mercury could wish to know about the five planets of the Hel system and their moons was organized before his eyes by Erithian. Economic data about the Maraccan nobility? No problem. Socio-political trends on

Taurus? Of course. Mortality rates of the Bjornish miners? Absolutely. The rise and fall of every known empire in the last twenty thousand years and the effect each one had on humanity? Child's play. Everything was primed to convey the maximum possible information at just a glance. The magnum opus of the Supreme Federation's most brilliant minds.

Sol had named the machine after one of the Taurusian gods in the Trinity of Time. The idea was that if you gathered enough information about the past and present, then you could predict the future, albeit in very broad strokes. Normally, the holographic avatar of the AI would simply tell them the important information, but for this test Sol had deactivated that particular function.

Ever since Mercury arrived, the machine had been predicting a revolution that would plunge humanity into a civil war unlike any other in history. All that had been missing was a catalyzing event to turn the mobs into organized militant forces. Just today, Erithian's Eye told them the catalyst had happened.

On Taurus, a young woman named Elizabeth "Liberty" Tormen had been decrying the discrimination against her people and was shot by an unknown shooter as the military marched in. People died every day, but when this person had called out for non-violent revolution, millions came to hear her speak and billions listened from all over the Federation. As soon as her heart stopped beating, her enraged followers stormed the soldiers at the scene and killed them all. Led by the martyr's sister, Vera Tormen, the Sons of Liberty publicly declared war on the Supreme Federation.

Mercury took a breath and felt the PsyMitter at the base of his neck begin to hum. Willing his thoughts to become reality, he could almost feel them being siphoned off by the tiny device. As he did so, the holographic display above him shifted, sifting through the layers upon layers of data provided by the Eye for everything relevant to the Sons of Liberty. Eight hours in the DreamTank every night for the past year had given Mercury a mind far beyond what someone his age should possess, more than most adults in fact. The hyper-dense mass of information the machine was feeding him both visually and through the PsyMitter would be simply too much for a normal person to process. But not him.

"Okay," Mercury said to Sol as he began mentally forming his words. "Her death is blowing up all over the Federation. There's video footage of the shooting being spread across every news station and all over the Virtual. The effect seems the worst for the Taurusians then Maraccans and Tarencians last. The majority of the uproar is from lower to middle class citizens, but more than a few of the upper class are decrying the Federation as well."

Sol's presence was stoic as always and his voice steel. "What scale of civil war are we looking at?"

Erithian's Eye shifted its display to accommodate Sol's question. The information was fed to Mercury in an instant. The boy inhaled sharply. "Full infrastructure collapse," he said. "The entire Federation, gone."

"Exactly," Sol said. "Erithian, what are the estimated casualties?"

The machine's mechanical voice answered. "Estimated casualties between twenty-two and twenty-nine billion." Mercury squirmed where he stood.

"A fourth of humanity gone," Sol's voice was grave. "That is what we're dealing with."

Sol had not needed to ask the machine what the casualties would be. Mercury could see the data just fine. The general was making sure he understood the immense gravity of the situation.

"Is that why you commissioned the trayite?" Mercury asked.

"Yes," Sol said. "That is also why I recruited the other five."

Trayite was the rarest and most durable substance in the universe as far as humanity knew. The Federation had monopolized it in order to build Sol a suit of armor twenty years ago, and it had been instrumental in winning the Second Taurusian War. A month after recruiting Mercury, Sol had taken him to Bjornhal to commission enough trayite for six more suits of armor. Now Mercury understood why.

The others were five kids Sol had rescued from across the Hel System to train to become Angels alongside Mercury. Until now they had been in DreamTanks to help them recover from their previous lives and prepare them for Forging. Now that the foretold revolution had begun, they would need to be awakened.

"Sol," Mercury hesitated.

"What is it?" he asked. Mercury bit his lip and Sol continued in a soft tone. "Speak freely. What's on your mind?"

Mercury's gut was twisting up into knots. Then he started speaking and it all unwound. "How am *I*...supposed to stop *that*?" He pointed a finger up at the number of estimated casualties on Erithian's display. The number expanded to fill their vision.

Sol knelt beside him and turned his face away from the display so Mercury was forced to look into his eyes and put his big hands on Mercury's small shoulders. "Listen to me Mercury," he said tenderly. "Don't dwell on the size of the task. Break the problem down into manageable pieces. It is a lot to handle, but you are not alone. You have me. You have the others. When I am finished with the six of you, you will be more than ready."

Mercury nodded. Even though he had no idea how Sol would prepare him and the other Angels to save humanity, he trusted the man more than he trusted himself. "Okay."

"Remember the Metians. 'The battle is won first in the mind.' If we believe it, then we have the chance to make it happen."

Mercury knew from his nightly lessons in the DreamTanks the Metians were an ancient warlike society. They existed thousands of years ago back when men killed each other with bows and arrows. The Metians believed battles were fought before they even happened, all in the mind.

"If you can't trust in yourself," Sol said. "Then trust in me. Would I ever lie to you?"

"No," Mercury said with conviction.

"Then you have nothing to worry about," Sol stood up. "It doesn't matter if you can't see that future just yet." He gestured at the AI's display. "That's why we have Erithian."

The holographic form of a non-descript young boy appeared. "Don't worry Mercury. I'll handle the heavy lifting."

Mercury slowly let out a breath. He looked from the AI's avatar up to the number of predicted casualties with new perspective. Sol's words were all he needed. Then, a thought occurred. "Even if we reduce that number to zero," he said calmly. "It won't fix the problem that started the revolution. In a year or ten or twenty, we'll have the same problem."

The surprise on Sol's face was evident. He smiled and shook his head. "Well done Mercury, you're absolutely right. The Sons of Liberty are a symptom of the larger problem. However, the equation is about to change. Erithian, show him please." The holographic boy smiled and then the Eye shifted, an engine of some kind appearing. "This is the MauKe drive," Sol said. "It is capable of opening wormholes. Do you know what those are?"

Mercury gave a crisp nod. He had learned about those in the DreamTank. "Wormholes are a link between two points in space," he recited. "By passing through them, it is possible to break the speed of light barrier and travel almost instantaneously from one point to another, regardless of traditional distance."

"Exactly," Sol nodded. "This is a power mankind now possesses." The image of the engine was replaced by the dual suns and five planets of the Hel system. "This is all humanity has ever known. Five planets, only four of which we could terraform." Erithian's Eye shifted again, zooming out until the Hel system was lost in a cloud of bright specks that comprised one spot on one of the arms of their galaxy. One giant sea of light, and every speck of light was a star.

"We could never explore them all," Mercury breathed. "Not in a million years."

Sol said nothing. Then the galaxy shrunk. Mercury watched as it was joined by the surrounding galaxies, becoming smaller and smaller until it vanished completely in a nebulous mist of multicolored light.

This is the entire observable universe.

Still Erithian's display shrunk everything down further, until the glowing mist coalesced before him into a patch of light the size of his hand. Mercury could not tear his eyes away from the sight. Every ebbing wisp represented a space so vast and infinite as to be beyond comprehension, yet here it was. So small and finite.

"Humanity is about to undergo an expansion event unlike any other in history," Sol's voice filled Mercury's ears, rich, resonant, and directionless. "The universe is about to get a lot smaller. Once the Event begins, it may never end. For better or worse, mankind will never be the same again."

The pocket infinity before Mercury's eyes winked out of existence and the room brightened. He blinked a moment, dumbfounded. He felt like he had been dreaming, only for it to be cut off by a bucket of cold water. Sol stood before him.

"Humanity must be unified by the time the Event occurs," Sol went on. "Otherwise...the damage will be on a scale not even Erithian can predict."

"That's why defeating the Sons of Liberty is so important?" Mercury asked.

"Exactly," Sol nodded. "I can keep the existence of the technology a secret, but only for a while. We must put down this insurrection quickly and decisively, using any means necessary."

"And once we stop this revolution," Mercury began.

"We will have peace for ten thousand years," Sol finished.

"Ten *thousand* years?" Mercury's eyes went wide.

"That's a conservative estimate," Erithian said.

Sol nodded. "Once the Event begins and becomes self-sustaining, Erithian will be able to manage humanity and maintain their unity. We just need to put down this rebellion."

"Okay," Mercury started to nod. "One way or another, let's make it happen. Time to wake the others?"

Sol smiled. "When we wake the other five Angels, they will need a peer to show them what being an Angel means. Can you do that for me?"

Sol rarely asked him to do anything; if something needed to be done he simply gave the order. The fact he was asking now communicated the gravity of his request. No matter what came ahead, Mercury would make Sol proud. "I will Sol, no matter what."

"Thank you."

***

On the way down to wake the other Angels with Sol, Mercury refreshed himself on each of their files. He swept his fingers across the bright display of the HoloPad. Venus, Earth, Mars, Jupiter and Saturn. Not a one older than eleven, and yet each had been chosen by Sol to be

Angels. Mercury had met them all once before when Sol rescued them, but since then they had all spent anywhere from one to eight months in the DreamTanks. They had all been in various terrible states, but the DreamTanks took care of that. From analyzing their personalities and learning styles to physically and mentally conditioning them and giving them a baseline education, the DreamTanks did it all.

Venus. The blonde Bjornish girl looked like she was born straight from the snow of her home planet. She was ice on the inside too, already showing readings of single-minded tenacity, but it was driven by a deep fear of weakness. Made sense, given what Mercury had seen of her parents' abuse. She had been in the DreamTank longest, but even so her receptivity readings were even higher than Mercury's. The machine could download information directly into her brain with almost no resistance. Sol's mentor, Teresa Balemore seemed to be something of an idol for the girl. She had a strong lone wolf complex and was fiercely loyal; maybe they were linked to her obsession with the Balemore.

Earth. The boy was small, but you would never know it looking at his face. Bright, fearless, blue eyes poking out from a mess of dark hair. At first Mercury had doubted the Taurusian orphan would be physically capable of being an Angel, but the boy had done pretty well in the DreamTank all things considered. He would probably be on the small side his whole life, but the data showed he was expected to make a fine Angel. Great team player. Mentally, he was probably the healthiest of all of them. The boy was already showing a developed sense of perspective that reminded Mercury of Sol. Perhaps it was because Earth lived at the same orphanage as the general.

Mars. Strong, with buzzed, black hair and dead, gold eyes set against dark skin. If Earth was the most mentally healthy, then Mars was compensating. Even older than Mercury, the Maraccan boy soldier showed extreme signs of being an emotional suppressor, and he was really good at it. The kid could easily be mistaken for a psychopath. That explained why he had killed the other boy on Maracca. "Our greatest strengths are our greatest weaknesses" as it were. Not only had he been a Zero, but he had also cared for Jupiter and Saturn while they were in that warlord's army. The Maraccan planet did not share the same luxuries of its moons. The fact that Mars had survived and protected two other children as well was astounding. Apparently, there had been four other kid Zeroes with them too, but those hadn't survived.

Jupiter. Same as Mars, the Maraccan boy's hair was dark and buzzed. But his eyes…those brown eyes questioned everything from underneath their furrowed brow. The boy could read people. Whether it was out of necessity from being a child soldier, or because Mars frightened him, Mercury didn't know. This kid was sharp. While he was in the DreamTank, he had been in a near-constant state of awareness because the people in the programs had not felt real enough. Unfortunately, that inhibited the download of information slightly, but the data read that he had the makings of another great team player.

Saturn. Her face was small and round with nervous, dark brown eyes. Her dark brown hair was uneven and jagged, as if it had been sawed off by a dull blade. She was the youngest and also the only one who had not taken the initiative to go with Sol. In every single program that was not specifically designed to make her be alone, her subconscious inserted Mars and Jupiter into the mix. She was terrified of being alone. It did not take a genius to see why. She was young and for a long time Mars and Jupiter had been the only ones keeping her alive. There was strength in that weakness though; she accepted the radical changes in her life up until now because she had no idea what was normal.

Compared to the rest of them, Mercury almost felt normal himself. How would he lead them when his life before joining Sol had been so relatively easy? Of course, the old him had been burned away. He was an Angel now, through and through. Sol was counting on him, and there was no way in Hel he would let him down.

"Are you ready to meet your new family?" Sol asked as the elevator they were in reached the first Forging floor.

"Yes," Mercury nodded confidently and followed Sol out.

The elevator opened right into a brightly lit, white room with seven vertical DreamTanks lined along one wall and a single terminal opposite them. These tanks were designed for DeepDive. They fed, exercised and otherwise sustained the user for as long as needed while they ran the tank's programs. Tactics, strategy, language, military discipline, history, leadership, battle simulations, the DreamTanks taught it all. Sol had put Mercury in for a month of DeepDive when he first became an Angel, but he had not touched it since then. He had a DreamTank in his room for nightly use.

On the far side of the room was a heavy steel door. On the other side of that door was the first Forging room. A shiver ran up Mercury's spine. Was that fear he was feeling? If so, revisiting that place with the other kids would be good for him.

Sol walked over to the terminal and began tapping his fingers on the screen. Mercury heard the sound of the DreamTanks draining and Mercury's tank opened with a hiss.

"Am I joining them in the DeepDive?" he asked.

"Not exactly," Sol said as he started the wakeup process. "You will see soon enough."

At the press of a button, the DreamTanks containing the other five Angels split open with a hiss. IV's, PulseStims, breath masks and restraints were already disappearing from view and basic undergarments were being stretched around them. With a faint whine the excess tank fluid disappeared from their bodies in an instant. The difference in the kids between now and when Mercury first saw them was like night and day. The tanks could not completely replace physical activity, but anything was better than what they had up until now. They looked stronger, healthier, even taller.

Earth leapt from his tank. The small boy was looking around with wide eyes, like this blank white room was the most incredible thing he had ever seen. A dark mop of hair swished around as he drank everything in. Blue eyes shone as he smiled from ear to ear and Mercury realized the tank had even straightened the boy's once crooked teeth. Earth closed his eyes and took a deep breath in through his nose. No surprise there. The air on New Tarence was far cleaner than the slums of Taurus.

Venus stepped out next, and everything about her was the opposite of Earth. She seemed tall for a girl, and doubly so next to Earth. Her steps were slow and deliberate. Where Earth was full of wonder and energy, she had the determined look of someone on a mission. Her fists were clenched and narrow, pale blue eyes swept the room. Mercury knew from the tank's data how much she wanted to be like the

Balemore. She already seemed to be trying to conquer the room itself by willpower alone.

When Mars stepped out, it was with the caution of someone on a battlefield. Golden eyes immediately locked onto Sol. The boy watched Sol like the man was an apex predator that had him cornered. Even at this distance, Mercury could see the goosebumps all over Mars' arms. He was larger than Mercury by far, but still he nodded at Sol in deference before moving towards the other two DreamTanks, never once showing his back. The boy's eyes remained fixed on Sol the entire time. Mercury noticed a small piece at the top of Mars' left ear was missing.

Once Jupiter stepped out, he backed slowly away from Mars and looked nervously around the room. Keen brown eyes looked at each of them in turn. His posture was unassuming and reclusive, bigger than Earth, but nowhere near as big as Mars. Mercury could see the gears turning in his eyes as he took everything in. They flicked to the imperious Venus, then to Mercury. An almost imperceptible nod of understanding and he began inching towards them.

Saturn crept out of her tank making no more noise than a cat. She immediately moved closer to Mars, staying behind him. She was the same size as Earth, maybe a bit smaller. Her dark brown hair had grown some, but it was still uneven, longer in the front than the back. Her eyes found Venus quickly, but she shrank back behind Mars.

All this happened in a matter of seconds, and Mercury took note of everything. A part of him questioned whether all of these kids would cut it as Angels, but then he remembered what he had been like before joining Sol.

"Attention," Sol commanded. After a moment, they all remembered the lessons in the DreamTank and complied.

"Listen closely," Sol continued. "I will only say this once. From this point on until the day you die, you are a new person. Forget your old name. That person is dead. You killed them when you made the choice to become something more. You are all Angels. That is the only identity that matters. Over the next several weeks I will show you exactly what that means. I promise to break you in every possible way. I will eradicate all traces of the person you once were, until you have embraced your new identity body, mind and soul. I will forge you into weapons of war. When I am finished, the six of you will be an invincible force of nature."

Mercury saw the five of them all look at each other and shift about in their own way. All except for Venus, she smiled.

"The six of you gathered here will become closer than family," Sol went on. "Your loyalty will be to each other first and foremost. If you learn nothing else, learn this." He looked at Venus, "Alone you will fall, but together you will have no equals. You are bound to each other forever. You are the faceless guardians of all the worlds. All individual needs and desires will be sacrificed for the greater good. Together you will usher in humanity's Golden Age. This is the unshakeable truth of your universe."

None of the Angels seemed to really understand what Sol was saying. Thanks to the DreamTanks' lessons though, they were paying close attention.

"I'll give you a few minutes to stretch and move around before the six of you will be going back into your tanks. I recommend you spend this time to get comfortable with each other, because with the exception of one other person, no one outside this room will recognize you as an individual for the rest of your lives."

None of them spoke, instead choosing to stare at each other. Venus took note of Saturn, the only other girl present. Then she turned away. Mars just watched Sol; Mercury doubted the boy had forgotten Sol's response to the incident on Maracca. Earth looked at the others, and then made eye contact with Mercury. Mercury smiled and nodded. Together they would break the ice.

"This is going to be great," Mercury's enthusiasm was sincere. "I've been waiting for you guys to wake up ever since you got here. I'm Mercury in case you forgot."

"I didn't," Venus said flatly.

"I'm so excited to be here," Earth said, helping to diffuse the awkward silence. "This'll be so much better than Taurus."

"That's right," Mercury smiled. Earth already had his back. "You went to the same orphanage as Sol, didn't you?"

Earth gave a terse nod. "Yep."

"Really?" Venus seemed wholly focused on Earth now. "What was it like?"

"Hey," Mars called out to Mercury. "The dreams kept mentioning the Forging. What can we expect?"

Right down to it. "The Forging sucks," Mercury said lightheartedly. "But it's totally worth it. You'll do great." He was not sure about Saturn though. "It really helped me realize how strong I actually am. Sometimes you have to see yourself at your weakest to know how strong you are, know what I mean?"

"Yeah," Mars' eyes stared off into the distance, cold and blank.

"Hey Jupiter," Mercury waved him over. "No need to walk on eggshells; we're family now." The boy moved closer. "So how was the DreamTank?" Mercury asked, "Did you understand the programs okay?"

"Yeah, maybe," the boy shrugged then shook his head. "No. I don't think so. I can't remember much of it."

"Don't worry about that," Mercury waved his hand. "Your brain's working hard to sort it all out. It's been working especially hard the last month. All that stuff will make a lot more sense in a couple days. Your Tarencian is pretty good though, all of yours."

"Oh," Jupiter furrowed his brow. "So that's why the dreams seemed weird after a while."

"I'm impressed you noticed the change," Mercury smiled. "I just got my vocabulary expanded, but you guys learned a whole new language. Now you don't even have to think about it, right?"

He could see Jupiter relax his shoulders and stand a bit straighter, "No, I don't."

Venus and Earth were gabbing away. "Hey Saturn," Mercury said. "How'd the waking up go?"

"It went alright," she said in a voice almost too quiet for Mercury to hear.

"I've only ever been to the Maraccan moons, but the DreamTank said there are some really cool animals down on the planet's surface." She clearly did not feel comfortable right now but talking to strangers was going to be the least of her problems once they were in Forging.

"Yeah, I liked the gazelles," she smiled.

The smile surprised Mercury. Being Zeroes in the situation the three of them had been in, her fondness seemed out of place. "Do you miss it?"

She waited a moment, then shook her head and looked at Mars and Jupiter. "No."

"You know, you should talk to Venus," Mercury said. "She always wanted a sister."

She glanced towards Venus and Earth and shrunk back behind Mars. "I don't know."

"Okay," Mercury said. "Just remember when the Forging starts that we all need each other's help to get through it. You're not alone." Her eyes perked up at that.

"Alright Angels, it's time for the next step." As always, Sol's voice commanded the attention of all who heard it.

He opened a small case with six Injectors. Mercury's eyebrows rose in spite of himself. They were going to make a PerfectMemory already? Just what exactly was Sol planning? The mind could only handle one or two, and Sol had already given Mercury one on Bjornhal. "Mercury, please show them how to administer it."

"Yes sir." Mercury grabbed one of the Injectors. "Just press the MicroNeedle into the skin anywhere really, and then push this button here. Super easy."

The five other Angels took their own Injectors. "Does it hurt?" Saturn asked.

"Oh no, just a tiny bit," Mercury administered his own. "It's a MicroNeedle." They all followed suit, Saturn last of all.

"Now quickly get back into the DreamTanks," Sol said. They obeyed. Restraints locked Mercury in place and the doors closed over him. The headgear came down but the tank did not fill with liquid. This must be a short one. Within moments Mercury had slipped off into a dream unlike any other.

As soon as the program started Mercury understood what Sol was up to, and he immediately wanted out. Their minds were brought together as one, and as one they lived through each other's lives. Every moment, every secret, every insecurity, every weakness, all laid bare. And thanks to the PerfectMemory, none of them would ever forget this.

They did not just see each other's memories either, they experienced them. Whatever feelings the original person had felt at the time, they felt as well. Rushes of emotion drowned them all as they were dragged through each other's hardships. What each of them had spent most of their lives learning to cope with, they now had to experience in a matter of seconds.

Mercury was first. His mother's untreatable illness and her thrashing wails echoed through their shared mind. Together they felt Mercury's powerlessness and cowardice. They were there with him, lying on Mom's bed after one of her episodes, hugging her tight to help her forget about the monster. They were there as his little sister Saffron cried in his room, hoping her brother could make everything better while Dad was at work.

They grew numb to Mom's suffering just as Mercury and his family had. Angry at her, each other and themselves for not being able to do anything. They were there when she ran out of meds, forced into addiction by the pain. They felt the stares at school and heard the whispers. Bitter hatred welled inside each of them when strangers would pretend to be experts and offer their advice. When someone asked if Mom was alright, they all shook with rage. All of them listened through the crack in Mom and Dad's bedroom door as she told her husband she wanted to die. As Mercury ran away, they were right there with him, desperately blocking out the echoing cries.

When Mercury's memories had run their course, the others' thoughts pierced his soul. They knew him.

Venus' memories came next. Beatings. Happy, confusing memories and beatings. Terror. Dread. Defeat. Hope. Disappointment. Betrayal. Mother's words hurt even more than the beatings. A dismal future in the mines. The same hands that protected them from Venus' drunken father and had rocked them to sleep now beat them for all the trouble they had caused. They should never have been born, everything was their fault. If not for them, Lowulf and Tavahl could be happy. Venus' fierce determination was their own, and when it broke so did they. All alone, they cried themselves to sleep every night, face buried underneath the pillow so the adults wouldn't hear and get mad.

When Venus ran off into the blizzard to escape, they could feel the tears freezing on their face. As she despaired and decided to throw herself into a chasm, the decision was theirs too. When they changed their mind but fell in anyway, they raged against the injustice of it. Suddenly Sol saved her, and they saw him as she did. When Sol took them back to Tavahl, they despaired. All of them were transfixed by the tears in Tavahl's eyes as she told Sol to take Venus away.

Venus dared them to pity her, but none of them did.

Earth accepted them as they traversed his memories. Three simple rules defined their existence. Avoid the bigger orphans; they would beat them up and take their food. Avoid Ms. Malkovich; she hated them and would revoke their food card at best, throw them in The Closet at worst. Last but not least, find food. Nothing else mattered. They followed Earth as he scavenged, feeling the near constant hunger and fear of going without. That happened often. Worst of all were the dashed hopes when they would find food, only for some of the bigger orphans to take it away.

A factory worker named Gerard took pity on them and shared his lunch one day. He treated them like an actual person; it was bliss. When Ms. Malkovich showed up for her date with Gerard, they knew what was next. The Closet's darkness permeated them. They were hungry and they were alone. They would starve. They remembered stories of a boy that had been forgotten in The Closet for a week. After crying and sleeping for what felt like an eternity, they heard a thundering voice outside. Confusion. The Closet door was torn off and a giant metal man was silhouetted in the first light they had seen in a long time.

Primal instincts faded and they saw the world through Earth's eyes. They wept.

Mars' world was desolation without and within. They smelled the smoke and felt the heat of the fires as Mars' village burned. No time to grieve their family, Dabo's men were already rounding up the children for his army. The Angels felt torn to pieces by the threefold pain of old wounds opening. Mars, Jupiter and Saturn, along with a few others, were all that was left of their village. Mars' fear engulfed the Angels until they could barely breathe. A scared little boy. They were there as Dabo drove them across the plains of Maracca, burning and killing as they went. One by one, the other kids from their village died. They did their best not to listen to the screams or look too closely at the faces of the people they killed. Over time the bodies started to blur together, but at least they were alive.

Desperation. Doubt. Regret. Bitterness. Fear. The Angels felt the last of their innocence bleed away. As the raids went on, the Angels did most of the killing. The lieutenants would get mad if the other children didn't, so they made sure to kill too fast for Jupiter or Saturn to keep up. A couple months later a metal man streaked through the sky and killed Dabo. He killed whoever else among the warlord's forces that fought back. Then came the call. Three children would be taken away. There were three of them left. They led Jupiter and Saturn forward, promising this was their chance. But Saturn hesitated and another boy from their village answered the call. Sol turned to leave with the three kids, a look of pure terror in Saturn's eyes as she watched them go. They all knew what they had to do. Raising their rifle, they shot the boy in the chest. Fear kept their finger clamped on the trigger until the boy's body stopped twitching. Nervous dread strangled them all as Sol's gaze dared them to breathe. The relief they all felt when Sol allowed Saturn to come along broke them.

Maracca disappeared but they could still see the boy's face as he lay in a pool of his own blood, vacant eyes watching them.

Jupiter's pain overcame them, just as it had for Jupiter. Mars' talent for blocking out emotion was something Jupiter did not share. They all felt the growing hollow spot in their chest as one by one the only people Jupiter had left were either killed or worse. They could see a boy from their village slowly losing himself as he just tried to cope with the utter collapse of their old life. But they were all too terrified for their own survival to care. Jupiter's shame at his own cowardice tortured their sleep every night.

Mars slowly got worse. Inevitably he would turn out like the rest of Dabo's lieutenants. The Angels had tried talking to him about it, but he would not listen. Every day he killed more and more people, like it was a contest. Man or woman, it did not matter. They did not deserve it, but that did not stop Mars. When Mars killed the boy so Saturn could leave with them, the Angels felt Jupiter's elation and guilt. They had not known the boy well, but he was one of them. They told themselves they would not have been able to pull the trigger. Then Saturn would be dead. Still, they could not put the image out of their mind of Mars shooting the boy again and again.

As the boy's bloody body faded, the Angels felt a fresh wave of emotion from Jupiter. He was so, so sorry.

Saturn's world had become very simple. The Angels saw through her eyes and there was so much pain. Everywhere. Hers, Jupiter's, Mars', the other kids in Dabo's army, Dabo's lieutenants, the families in the villages they attacked. Pain was everywhere, but it was not everything. There had to be more. Sometimes Saturn thought she caught glimpses of it. Late at night when she and the other kids from her village would lie looking up at the moons and stars Saturn was sure she saw something the pain could not touch.

But pain did not like to be ignored. As seven became six, became five, became four, became three, that something revealed itself to Saturn less and less. The others were leaving and there was not a thing the Angels could do to stop it. Like Saturn, they were all powerless and weak. They only ever got in the way. They did not contribute at all, just a burden for others to bear. The kids were dying because of them. Mars was destroying himself because they could not kill people without crying. As Mars shot the boy, they all wept. They knew that was something Mars would never be able to forget.

Never again.

The dream world vanished for the final time and the doors of the DreamTanks opened. As soon as the restraints opened Mercury collapsed onto the concrete, dry heaving. To his left, the others were doing the same. It was like they were seeing each other for the first time. With unsteady arms Mercury pushed himself up and crawled towards the others. No one said anything; they huddled together and cried. These people felt like extensions of himself, and Mercury knew they were hurting.

"Well done," Sol sounded thoroughly impressed. "Well done."

As Mercury cried with his new family, he felt one of Sol's giant hands on his shoulder. The man's voice was gentle and understanding. "All of you, well done."

CHAPTER TWO

Three Years Later...

MERCURY
Age 14

Mercury awoke with a jolt as the DreamTank drained its fluid and retracted the wires and tubes from his body. With a tingling pulse of energy, he was dry. Exiting the tank, Mercury mechanically made his way to his dresser and picked up the hand mirror on top.

Locking eyes with his reflection, Mercury said his morning identity statements. "I am Mercury. I am an Angel. I am a leader. I am loyal to my family. I am true to myself. I am unstoppable. I am the future of humanity. I forever choose to sacrifice my own desires for the greater good. I am an Angel. I am Mercury."

Letting out a breath, Mercury watched himself in silence. A smile cracked its way into the corners of his mouth. He nodded slowly, then put down the mirror and clapped his hands.

Today was the big day. The drawers of his dresser opened as he approached and donned his usual uniform of black pants and shirt.

After training for so long, the six of them would be performing their first live mission as the Federation Ministers watched.

They had all grown so much over the last three years. Mercury felt old thinking that, but it was true. The difference between where they were at now compared to three years ago was like night and day. The Helish Forging was finally over and now it was time for them to perform. They were ready.

Mercury had his doubts about some of them when they started, especially Saturn, but they had all embraced their true selves eventually. They could not have done it without Sol and each other, but the accomplishment was theirs and theirs alone.

***

They were on Sol's personal HeavyGunship the *Defiant*, heading away from the central planets and towards the Dorin Mining Cluster. The ship was truly one of a kind. A MimicField and the newly developed MauKe drive on the same vessel. With those two experimental pieces of technology, the vessel could go anywhere in an instant, completely undetectable to sensors and the naked eye. "This is it," Agent Yuki Matsuri was wearing her gray MimicSuit. "Sol and the other Ministers will be monitoring this mission remotely and evaluating your performance. I will not interfere."

Matsuri or "Ma" was Sol's special operative and the one other person allowed to see their faces and call them by name. She had fought under Sol back when he was a sergeant and had stuck close by ever since. Her task today was simply to supervise their mission and make sure nothing went critically wrong. Specifically, to ensure none of them died.

"You all know the mission," she said. "Protect Dorin Enterprise's ship the *Dawn Flower* and disable the pirate's vessel. Upon disabling their ship, infiltrate it, secure the enemy leader and eliminate all remaining hostiles."

Mercury looked at his family as they stood at attention in their armor. The armor was not trayite like Sol's, but it could stop a couple shots. Earth was smiling and bobbing his head. Saturn was bouncing and giggling. The Forging had changed them all, but for Saturn in particular it was like night and day. Jupiter was taking slow, measured breaths to calm his nerves. Venus and Mars were serious as ever, but Mercury could tell they were excited underneath that stoic exterior.

"Stay focused," Ma's serious face eyed them all before breaking into a smile. "But don't worry; I know you'll do great."

"Ma," Jupiter spoke up. "Are the Ministers really going to cut our funding?"

"Jup," Ma smiled tenderly. "Don't think about that. Sol has your backs. Just do your best here like you always do. Sol will take care of the Ministers."

"If they do cut our funding though," Mars said. "What happens to us? We don't have anywhere to go back to."

In spite of his excitement, Mercury felt a knot form in his stomach. He had pledged his life to follow Sol; they all had. But Mercury knew just how expensive mining trayite was, and if the Air Navy and Ground Elite Program lost funding, what would happen to them?

"Sol will take care of us," Mercury spoke up before Ma could answer. "We are Angels and he is the Archangel. Nothing else matters."

Mars inclined his head in silent respect. Jupiter nodded quickly. "Okay."

"Alright," Matsuri smiled at Mercury and pulled the mask of her MimicSuit down over her face. "See you when it's over." As the MimicSuit activated, she faded away until she was completely invisible.

"We went through the Forging together guys," Mercury said. "We've nothing to worry about. We're ready. Our weaknesses were made strengths. Now we're six bodies with one soul. Let's give them a show that would impress the Balemore."

Venus pounded her fists together. "Sounds good to me." Mercury put on his helmet and smiled to himself. It was so easy to get her fired up.

"Everyone to your stations," he said.

Earth high-fived him as walked past towards the cockpit. "Six bodies, one soul. I like it."

"Thanks," Mercury called back as he made his way to the captain's chair. "It took me two hours to think up."

Saturn laughed from the port gunnery pit, pitching forward as she heaved. "Just two? You're getting better Merc."

"Yeah, yeah," Mercury waved her comment away and turned to take his seat in the captain's chair. He let out an uneasy breath staring at the black leather and control panels on the armrests.

"He chose you Mercury," Mars clapped his shoulder as he made his way to the starboard gunnery pit.

Mercury punched his big brother in his armored shoulder as he passed, "Thanks Mars."

Once Mercury sat down, he was reminded of the chair's strange comfort. Through the view port he beheld a sea of stars, not a single one explored. "Jupiter, systems report."

Jupiter was fully enclosed in a metal sphere in the floor of the bridge very similar to Erithian's Eye back at Angel Tower. "Engines are warm," his voice sounded over the comms. "Sensors active, PulseBarriers at maximum, electronic warfare package:Gamma ready, MimicField on standby, MauKe drive ready for jump."

"Jupiter," Mercury said. "Engage MimicField."

"MimicField engaged. We're ghosts now."

"Venus, take us out. Earth, set a course for the *Dawn Flower.*"

"Course set."

"Engage MauKe drive." The sea of stars vanished.

The next instant they were next to the *Dawn Flower,* a bulk transport of Tarencian design. Five hundred meters across and largely unarmed. Four antifighter guns. "Jupiter, status."

"Jump successful. MimicField holding. *Dawn Flower's* cruising along right on schedule. No sign of hostile forces."

"Venus, shadow the *Dawn Flower.*"

"Affirmative."

Mercury leaned back. "And now we wait."

Waiting was key to any ambush. Boring as it was, it was necessary. And as they waited, not a single word was uttered. Not with the Ministers watching and the program's funding on the line. Although Mercury doubted the Minsters would be watching them the entire time. They had better things to do. Even so, he kept quiet. Hours ticked by.

The fifth hour of silence was broken when Jupiter said the words everyone was dying to hear, "Unidentified craft coming up on sensors. On intercept course with the *Dawn Flower* at attack speed. Enemy will be on them in sixty seconds."

"Do not engage the enemy," Mercury said. "Allow them to intercept the *Dawn Flower*."

Jupiter's concern was evident in his voice, "I hope you're right about this Mercury."

"I am," Mercury said, but how could he be sure? They had practiced for this specific mission, but the DreamTank could only go so far. *I guess we'll find out.* Quickly, the pirate vessel swelled in size as it approached. A retrofitted relic from the Second Taurusian War. They had bolted a shiny, new *Zerythane*-cannon to the bottom.

"So that explains how they've been taking out ships so much bigger than them," Mars commented.

Saturn whistled. "Nice."

"Wait for the first shot," Mercury's leg began bouncing. The pirates fired. A crackling blast of purple and blue energy lancing towards the helpless cargo vessel.

"*Dawn Flower*'s barriers are down," Jupiter stated mechanically. If the pirates had a *Zerythane*-cannon, it was not even worth mentioning. However, they did have to keep to protocol for the sake impressing their audience.

"Second shot," Mercury's leg kept bouncing.

"Sensor array down. *Dawn Flower*'s blind."

"Mars, Saturn, get ready." Mercury saw Saturn crack her fingers. Mars was still.

Jupiter's next words were music to Mercury's ears, "Enemy ship launching six boarding craft."

Mercury's leg stopped bouncing, "Send them straight to Hel."

Mars targeted the boarding craft with ClusterMissiles, one per vessel. Orange blossoms. Saturn surgically dismantled the enemy ship with blasts from the *Defiant*'s PulseCannons. Deflectors, engines and sensors all down.

"Jupiter, initiate EWP:Gamma."

"Initiating," Jupiter waited a moment. "The enemy leader is sealed on the bridge."

"Good," Mercury said. "Vent the rest of the ship's life support."

"Done," he heard Jupiter say. Strange to think that with a few words he had ended the lives of dozens of people. He had never taken a life before, and at the command of a ship such as this, it was disturbingly easy. His stomach turned, but he could not let Sol see his unease. *I am a weapon.*

"Venus," Mercury called out. "When the only remaining life signs come from the bridge, dock with the enemy ship."

"Aye, aye, captain."

A few minutes later the *Defiant* began moving toward its prey.

After restoring life support to the ship, the Angels boarded it. Each of them was outfitted with a rifle, sidearm, sword, knife and two stun grenades. Mercury and Venus took point as they made their way through the ship's narrow steel corridors. Flickering, dull red emergency lights lit the way. "What have we got Jup?"

"Even with the retrofits the interior follows the basic layout of other Taurusian patrol ships. We've got eleven remaining hostiles, all of them sealed on the bridge."

The DreamTanks could not tell them anything about what would happen inside the ship, so from here on out they were shooting from the hip. "Alright, Venus and Earth, flush them and let us know their loadout, Mars and Saturn, set down the port hallway, Jupiter and I will send them to you. If you see the captain, hit him with a stun grenade and keep the pressure up so they have to leave him. Six bodies, one soul." They dispersed.

After they got into position, the ship's comms crackled to life, "Attention intruders," a voice said. Whoever it was wore a helmet, their voice was altered was in a way similar to the Angels'. "This is Captain Lawrence R. Mavos of the *Rude Awakening.* You were foolish not to kill us when you had the chance. You will not get another opportunity. The lives of our comrades will be avenged and your vessel will become a new weapon for the Sons of Liberty. I encourage you to spend your last moments begging the gods to have mercy on your souls."

"Boy, that didn't sound arrogant at all," Saturn's voice sounded in Mercury's helmet.

"It was a pretty cringe worthy bluff," Venus answered.

"I don't know," Jupiter said. "Sounded like he believed it."

"Angels," Agent Matsuri's voice echoed over the comms. She was not supposed to contact them until the mission was over. Her normally calm and composed attitude was gone. "Return to the *Defiant* immediately; this comes straight from Archangel. Lawrence Mavos is the leader of the Taurusian Reclamation Force. You're no match. I repeat, get back to the *Defiant* immediately. Under no circumstances are any of you to engage him."

Mercury's heart began pounding in his chest. *Well shit.* He had heard stories of the TRF's fearless leader. *What's he doing way out here?* "You heard her," Mercury called over the comms. "Let's haul ass."

"Uh, guys," Jupiter sounded even more worried than Ma. "The ship's scanners have been feeding us false data. The enemy's not on the bridge. They set us up; we're blind."

They were outnumbered, separated and had no idea where the enemy was. Mercury's heart began to race. He swallowed hard, but it did not quell the fear rising within him. The hunters had become the hunted.

"We need to regroup," Mercury said as he and Jupiter began moving back the way they had come. "Everyone head back to the main hallway."

He heard the echoing sounds of gunfire, "Negative, negative," Earth began yelling. "Mavos is there. He's moving fast for the ship. He's in a BreakerSuit."

Mercury sucked in air through his teeth. *Yeah, we definitely can't take him.*

"We can't let him take the *Defiant*," Venus said. She was right; the *Defiant* was the most advanced warship in the Federation, and the only ship in existence with a working MauKe drive. Mercury could hear her distant shots as she called back over the comms, "I can slow him down."

"Run Venus," Yuki commanded. "That's an order."

"I..." Mercury heard her hesitate for a painful moment. "Okay."

Mars' voice yelled over the comms, half drowned out by gunfire, "Merc, we've got four hostiles. Probably some headed your way."

If the enemy had engaged Mars already, then they were probably close by. Mercury saw a faint shadow from around a corner some ten meters ahead. He pulled Jupiter into a side room just before two men leaned into view and lit up the hallway with green blasts. "Thanks Mars."

"Jup," Mercury loaded a grenade into the launcher on his rifle. "Cover me."

"Already on it." Jupiter leaned out and let loose a continuous spray of shots where the men had fired from. Mercury fired at the wall where he had seen the enemies. The grenade erupted in a dozen rapid pulses of blinding light and deafening sound. Even from this far away, the sound made him wince. Jupiter checked to see if the coast was clear and almost lost his head to a series of shots from the opposite direction. Mercury quickly fired his last grenade at one of the men. Jupiter laid down suppressing fire while Mercury closed the distance to the one still standing.

Sliding past the corner on his back, Mercury shot the man twice through the chest as soon as he was in sight. The man dropped in a pool of blood. Mercury's first up close kill. His hands had a death grip on his rifle. He let out an uneasy breath and picked himself up. Once Jupiter caught up with him, they double-tapped the three unconscious hostiles with two clean shots to each head and ran to join up with Venus and Earth.

"Guys," Earth sounded desperate. "Get over here now. They're cutting through to the *Defiant*. If they take the ship, they'll shoot us out of the sky."

"We're heading to you now," Mercury heard Saturn say. She was breathing hard.

"We'll get there soon," Mercury said. "Don't engage until we get there."

"Too late," Venus said.

"Guys," Earth said in between shots. "He's fighting Ma."

Mercury and Jupiter picked up their pace, pushing themselves to run faster.

When they arrived, they were met with a sight they had not even seen in the DreamTanks. Three separate hallways converged in a 'T' on the airlock the *Defiant* was coupled to. Two dead men were slumped against a MountedCutter that had been working on the *Defiant's* airlock door. The barricades for defending against intruders had been deployed to act as cover against the Angels. Standing on the other side of the barricades was Lawrence Mavos, in a lumbering mass of metal that towered almost to the ceiling with antipersonnel guns on each arm. Yuki was there too. She was invisible in her MimicSuit, but Mercury could see the flashes from her sidearm as she harassed the captain from every angle. Before Lawrence could pin her down, she would be on the other side of him, shooting anything on the BreakerSuit that looked vulnerable.

Even from this angle, Mercury was having as much trouble keeping track of Yuki as Captain Mavos. The flashes from her pistol moved around unbelievably fast. Mercury tried to line up a shot on Ma's adversary, but Ma seemed to be everywhere and nowhere. *Only Ma would fight a walking tank with a pistol and be winning.*

With a burst of metal parts from one of its knees, the BreakerSuit slumped. "I've crippled him," Ma said as the flashes of pistol fire stopped. "Light the bastard up."

There was an explosion of rippling, transparent energy at the base of the BreakerSuit. Concussion grenades. A soft thump followed and Ma was lying still on the ground some distance from the captain, very much visible.

Mercury could not tell whether it was the emergency lighting that turned everything the color of blood at that moment, or the sight of Ma lying limp on the ground. All he knew was that a switch somewhere deep in the six of them was flipped. Words were no longer needed. They thought and moved as one, truly six bodies with one soul.

This was no longer a mission. Not anymore. What had started as a test to impress the Ministers had turned into something else altogether. Mercury was aware of every heartbeat, every push of his rifle against his shoulder, every tremor from the BreakerSuit hobbling toward Ma. Perfect awareness. He knew exactly what the others were going to do before they did it.

As if Jupiter could read his mind, he flung the bandolier with his grenades to Mercury without looking as he opened fire on the enemy. Mercury caught it with one hand and sprinted up to a corner much closer to the enemy.

Earth and Jupiter had Mavos in a crossfire, but their weapons were not stopping it. Mars and Saturn were pinned down by the enemy's weapons, but when it turned to deal with the other two, they continued their advance. Mercury had to get Ma away. Venus was working on lining up a shot for its weakened knee, but had to duck back behind cover to avoid its guns.

Mercury dashed forward as soon as the enemy turned its attention to Mars and Saturn. Mercury fired a grenade to get its attention. Minimal damage, but that had not been his goal. Venus' breathing grew steady on the comms as she whispered, "I am the eye of the storm." The shot tore through the BreakerSuit's knee in exactly the same spot Ma had damaged it. Flecks of blood hit Mercury's helmet and the suit all but collapsed. Sliding up to Ma, Mercury pulled as hard as he could, dragging her away from the towering machine. He was almost away by the time the monster raised one of its guns at him. This was the end.

One cry of unbridled fury, one cry of desperation. Mars and Saturn leapt onto the BreakerSuit and jammed all four of their grenades into whatever opening they could find. Saturn punched one into the hole in the man's leg. They did not escape the countless pulses, but that had never been their plan. The two of them dropped like rocks, and so did Lawrence Mavos.

Just like that, the red faded from Mercury's vision. Ma was okay. Mars and Saturn would be okay. Eventually. "Jupiter," he called out. "Get GravStretchers." The ship's doors opened remotely and Jupiter disappeared inside. "Venus, Earth, any more hostiles?"

Venus quickly shook her head, "I don't think so. There was one tailing Mars and Sat, but we took her out." She crouched down next to Ma and pulled the grey mask of her MimicSuit back. The middle-aged woman looked almost peaceful.

"Great shot Vee," Mercury said. "You saved my life, and probably Ma's too."

Venus stared at Ma's face in silence. "Hey," Earth put a hand on her shoulder. "She's going to be okay." Venus nodded.

From inside the *Defiant* Jupiter appeared lugging four GravStretchers. With a grunt he dropped them all at once. They fell to the ground without making a noise and began slowly sliding away from each other, floating centimeters off the ground. "Let's go home."

***

Several days later, Yuki was well enough to return to Angel Tower. Thanks to Federation medicine, she was well on the way to a full recovery. Sol had not let them go to the hospital for security reasons, so Mercury and the others were all waiting eagerly at the entrance to the Tower when she arrived.

"Ma!" they all cried out and swarmed her with hugs as soon as they saw her.

She took a step back as they hugged her. Although Ma was not the most expressive person, her smile was overwhelming. She hugged them all back as well as one person could hug six at a time. Mercury could see little crows' feet next to her shining brown eyes. Mercury felt a pang of worry. *To get hurt like that at her age…*

Mars must have been thinking the same thing, because he wrapped an arm behind her to lend support. "You're probably dead tired, huh?" Even with the wonders of modern medicine, the human body could not shrug off eleven bone fractures and a concussion so easily.

"Thank you, Mars," Ma leaned on him. Mercury and the others backed away and helped how they could. Saturn lent Ma support opposite Mars, helping far less physically because of her much smaller stature. Mercury stepped in next to Saturn to help.

"I saw the footage," Ma said with a smile as they helped her to the elevator. "You all did great."

Saturn hugged Ma tight as she supported the middle-aged woman, "We were so worried about you."

Yuki squeezed her back just as hard and kissed her head, "I know you were, my little hurricane. But you saved me with that little stunt the two of you pulled. And Venus, amazing shot. Even the Balemore would've been impressed."

"I did it just the way you taught me," the girl gave a small, sincere smile.

"Really, all of you did great," Ma said. "When the six of you are together, there's nothing you can't do."

"We're sorry you got hurt Ma," Jupiter said. "If you didn't have to worry about us…"

"I don't want to hear it," Ma interrupted. "Listen Jupiter, all of you, sometimes you have to fight, even when the odds are stacked against you. If you know why you're fighting, then that's enough. Doesn't matter who or what your enemy is."

They entered the elevator and Venus pressed the button to take them to the floor with Yuki's room. *If you know why you're fighting, then that's enough.* Mercury could feel his very soul resonating with the powerful truth of Ma's words. He grinned. On the *Dawn Flower* Ma had been fighting for them and they in turn had fought for her. But together, with Sol leading them, they fought for the very fate of humanity.

Then he remembered the faces of Mavos' men as he killed them and his smile faded. Guilt crept inside him. How many dozens more had died by his order when they shot down the boarding vessels?

As they exited the elevator and headed towards Ma's room, Jupiter asked, "Ma, why do you fight?"

In that moment Mercury thought her smile seemed sad. "When I fought Mavos it was for all of you. Most of the time though," her voice trailed off and her eyes grew distant. "I'm fighting for a dream someone once shared with me."

"You're fighting for a dream?" Venus asked.

Ma nodded with a smile. "Dreams are powerful things; you should know that well, Vee."

Mercury knew Ma was talking about Venus' dream to be the next Teresa Balemore.

"Can I fight for your dream too?" Saturn asked.

"Of course you can Sat," Ma tousled her hair with a tired hand. "But one day you might find a dream of your own."

"What is your dream?" Earth asked with eager eyes.

"My dream?" she asked as Venus opened the door to her room. They walked in and she sat down on the bed. She actually had a bed, not a DreamTank like the rest of them. "That when Sol and I are gone, the six of you will go farther than we ever could."

"How do we find our dream?" Mercury asked.

Sol's voice answered from behind him, "You trust your gut."

Mercury turned around and saw the aging general standing there, imperious as always, yet relaxed. "Your gut?"

Sol nodded. "Dreams are the things we desire more than anything, no matter how outlandish they are. Your dream is already there, you just haven't realized it yet. Learn to listen to the whispers of your heart."

Mercury cocked his head. "That seems like the opposite of everything you've taught us so far."

A smirk crept onto Sol's face. "No great dream can be achieved without even greater action. Anyone can dream; it's making good on the dream that counts."

Mercury lowered his head in contemplation of what Sol and Yuki had said. Right now his dream was the same as Sol's. He could do that, right? He could make Sol's dream his own.

"What did the Ministers decide?" Venus asked. Mercury felt himself tense up.

Sol smiled. "The Air Navy and Ground Elite program will continue."

Palpable relief flooded the room. Mercury knew that even though they had put it from their minds for the mission, they had all been worried sick about what would happen if the Angel program was cancelled.

"How close was the vote?" Ma asked.

"If not for Liam," Sol said. "We would have lost."

Mercury smiled. The Prime Minister's vote was worth double and broke ties. He and Sol were also best friends, which helped. "Who gave us the other vote?" Mercury asked. "Was it the Minister of Justice?"

Sol shook his head. "The Minister of Development."

Mercury nodded in understanding. If the Angel program had been cancelled then all that trayite they were paying the Bjornish to mine would collect dust. Not exactly the best use for a substance that was basically indestructible. Even before joining the Angels, Mercury had idolized Sol in his shining suit of trayite armor. The very idea that in three more years he would have a suit of his own was surreal.

That night, Mercury stayed up after lights out, wandering the halls in the dark. His mind kept drifting back to the mission that day. Ma had almost died. Mercury traced his fingers along the cold steel wall of the hallway as he walked towards the elevators. There was a twisting pit gnawing at his stomach, and he did not know why.

Mercury tapped the 'up' button on the HoloPad and shambled into the elevator. He needed air. After pressing the button that would send him to the roof, he slumped against the elevator wall and sank to the floor. He felt sick. But that couldn't be it; this was different. He took a deep breath, filling up his lungs as far as they would allow before letting it go.

He felt a cool breath of wind as the doors opened but he just sat there. *What's wrong with me? We won. Against all the odds, we won.* His mind called back up what the explosions had looked like as the pirates' boarding vessels were turned to tiny flecks of molten slag. All it took was a few words and the push of some buttons.

Mercury leaned his head back against the elevator wall and stared at the ceiling. His mind played back the memory of the life readings on the *Rude Awakening* winking out one after another. He had never killed anyone before today. *I wonder what they were thinking about? Were they scared?* His mind called up the stages of death by vacuum. The DreamTank had taught him all about that. Images flashed across his mind of eyes boiling in their sockets. Mercury shook his head quickly, pushing the images from his mind.

They were murderers. The night air sent a chill through Mercury. He rubbed his arms briskly.

"Killing is never justified. Never." The first PerfectMemory Sol gave him burst to the surface of his mind. He could still remember every detail, every shard of ice clinging to the sword on Sol's lap and every foggy breath that escaped their helmets. *"Every time you take a life you must remember that person had family, friends. But sometimes we have to do terrible things in order to prevent something even more horrible."*

Killing was wrong, and today he had killed dozens. He clamped his eyes shut. *Why is this bothering me? We had to do it. Captain Mavos and his men would have kept killing innocents. We stopped them.*

Sol's voice echoed to Mercury from his PerfectMemory. *"It is wrong. You must never let yourself become numb to the choices you make, so hold onto that strong sense of right and wrong. Hold on to it and never let go, because once you do, you're lost."*

Mercury could hardly tell what were his thoughts and what were his memories. Then he heard a sniff from outside the elevator. Opening his eyes, he saw Earth standing in the doorway. His brother had always loved the open air. Then Mercury noticed Earth's eyes were puffy and bloodshot. *You too, huh?*

His brother smiled one of his usual cocky smiles, despite that he had obviously just been crying. "You don't want to sleep either?"

I should be encouraging you right now, man.

Mercury shook his head. Running one of the DreamTanks mental conditioning programs would probably make everything easier, but he did not want that. From the looks of things, neither did his brother. "We killed them Earth. I don't know why this is bothering me, but it is."

Earth sniffed again and offered to help him up. "Come on Merc, we're not meant to be in boxes."

You're incredible bro, but you've got to look out for yourself too.

Accepting the offered hand, Mercury stood and the two of them left the elevator. They walked over to the tower's edge and sat down, legs dangling in the air. Far below was the Federation's central command, surrounding Angel Tower. Looking up, every star of the night sky shone brightly, with the planet Tarence looming large and wondrous. From up here it seemed they could see the entire moon stretched out beneath them.

Mercury wrapped an arm around his little brother. "We're in this together, you know? You need to let us look out for you too."

His brother's small shoulders slowly drooped. "I hated them Merc," Earth said in a choked voice. "I hated Mavos for what he did to Ma. I wanted to kill him. Not to save her, but just so I could see him die."

Mercury hugged his brother tighter. "I know…I did too."

When Mercury did decide to go back to the DreamTank, he welcomed the mental conditioning programs.

CHAPTER THREE

Three Years Later...

MERCURY
Age 17

Leaning against one of the *Defiant's* cockpit windows, resting his uncovered head on the cool glass, Mercury watched as the vessel broke through the dark ceiling of Maracca VII's atmosphere and descended into the pits of all the Federation had to offer. This was an undercover mission, so they were all dressed like Sevens, many of whom still made their clothes by hand. The DreamTank had taught him plenty about the last of the Maraccan moons. If anyone ever wanted to disappear, this was the best place in all the worlds to go. Sol had said their target officially did not exist, so it made sense they would have to go here to find him.

The buildings were nothing compared to the towering structures on New Tarence or the gleaming, glass estates of Maracca Prime. Tiny, cramped buildings stacked on top of each other dozens of levels high in every direction as far as Mercury could see, even from this altitude. Mercury could not actually see the ground, but there was a latticework of hairline gaps stretched over the sea of weathered, modular steel boxes. For hundreds of years the other moons had used them for compactly disposing of garbage, but here people were forced to call them home. The view was suffocating.

Shoving off from the window, Mercury turned to his family in the cockpit. The ship felt so much smaller now that they had really started growing. Mercury cracked his neck and rolled his shoulders. He was still getting used to feeling so much solid muscle packed into his body, but he liked it. The DreamTanks kept them all growing like there was no tomorrow, shooting up and filling out like it was a race. Mars had always been the biggest, and that had not changed over the years. But even Saturn and Earth were taking to the DreamTank treatments and growing up right alongside the rest of them. Mercury remembered when the chairs practically swallowed him, but not anymore.

Of all of them though, the most noticeable change had been with Venus and Saturn. At least, certainly the most noticeable to Mercury. While puberty had been hitting them all like a trans-system freight hauler over the past couple years, the two girls had become testaments to the female form's beauty. Even clothed in the filthy rags as they were now, they were absolutely stunning.

That's probably just because my brain is practically swimming in testosterone. Venus struck quite the figure as she stood stoically behind Earth, angular face staring at the swelling landscape below. Out of the corner of her eye she caught him staring and shot him a challenging look. Immediately Mercury turned away and shook his head nonchalantly. On his right Saturn casually hung from the ceiling by both hands, swaying as the ship turned. She was very close to Mars. *Lucky bastard.*

Earth whistled from the pilot's chair in his threadbare garb as he looked out the window at the landscape below. "When the tank gave me the mortality rates for this place I had trouble believing it. And I thought the slums on Taurus were bad."

Jupiter shook his head. "I still can't believe how many people are here." Thirty billion. More than all the other Maraccan moons combined.

Sol grimaced from where he stood behind them. When he had first found Mercury, his hair was the color of coal; now the fringes were gray. "A graveyard for Maracca's outcasts."

Mercury looked back out the window at Maracca VII. Something about the sight disturbed him. He wrinkled his nose at the pungent smell from their undercover clothes. "Why don't they just leave?"

Mars' voice was full of cold hatred as he stared at the moon's surface. "They're Sevens; they're not allowed on the other moons."

Mercury knew that already; that's not what he meant. Why not go to one of the other planets? "Sol," Mercury said. "You've been having us fight the Sons. But way more people are dying here every day from disease, murder and starvation than the Sons are killing."

"Far more," Sol agreed. "However, Maracca VII is merely the symptom of the larger problem, and fighting the Sons is a much more straightforward matter than changing the entire Maraccan regime. Not all battles can be won with weapons."

Jupiter looked at Venus, "I read that ten square kilometers of Maracca VII has more people on average than all Bjornhal."

"That's messed up," Saturn said. Venus was silent.

Vaguely Mercury's mind registered Jupiter trying to impress Venus, but he was still transfixed by the sight of so much suffering below. "This is what we're fighting for," he said with conviction then looked at the others. "This has to change."

Sol nodded, "And it will. I'm going to make sure of it."

Furrowing his brow, Mercury looked back out the window as they approached the metal sea. Sol was the Minister of War, not the Minister of Economy or Development, so how could he guarantee Maracca would change its policies?

When they reached the entry point, Earth set the *Defiant* on standby and they departed. On this part of Maracca VII, it was the dead of night. Mercury found it incredibly unsettling that he could not even see the planet Maracca in the sky or any of the moons because of the smog. At least it would help them avoid being identified by anyone who might be on the roofs at this time of night. If anyone spied the Minister of War in a place like this, they were bound to wonder why. This is where the clothes would come in handy. This was the first time in seven years Sol had let Mercury go out in public without a helmet to cover his face. Mercury felt the sidearm and knife concealed at his lower back to make sure they were still there. He swallowed a lump in his throat. His face felt naked without his helmet.

"Be on guard," Sol said as they climbed down into the building through a narrow gap between boxes, bracing themselves against the opposite walls. "While you shouldn't have anything to fear from Dr. Jormungand, this sector is incredibly violent, even by Maracca VII's standards."

The warm smell of sweat, urine and blood hit Mercury like a wave as they entered the collection of waste containers that passed for a building here. He gagged and tasted bile, but he swallowed it with a grimace. He had not smelled anything so vile since the Forging. His instincts shifted, making him alert of everything around him. This place was dangerous. As the seven of them squeezed through the opening and into a hallway, Mercury noted it would be a great place for an ambush. If someone rounded the corner with an automatic weapon, they would be screwed. The passage was far too small for Sol, who had to stoop and move sideways. None of them were wearing armor. Mercury realized they needed to be incognito, but he felt far too vulnerable. They passed several dried, black bloodstains and more than a few bullet holes in the walls. Were people still using such archaic technology? Mercury knew it in his head, but that was completely different from seeing it in person.

From above the moon had seemed like a maze, but the inside of this building felt doubly so. Rats and other rodents of unusual sizes that Mercury did not recognize scurried off as they made their way down to the floor where Dr. Jormungand lived. The entire place felt like it was pressing in on him. There was no light, save for the occasional flickering of firelight from the other side of one of the many cloth-covered holes cut in the sides of the boxes. Just how primitive was this place?

Mercury's mind flashed back to the PerfectMemory they all shared and Earth being trapped in darkness. They had all experienced it together in the DreamTanks, and the feeling was similar to how Mercury felt now in the cramped hallway. To think that people actually lived here. How could this happen while the people of New Tarence wanted for nothing?

As if reading his mind, Jupiter whispered from behind him, "Guess there's always someone who has it worse." Mercury was unsure if even this could compare to Mars, Jupiter and Saturn's previous life as Zeroes on the Maraccan planet, but the point still stood.

After several minutes of navigating the narrow hallways and stepping over the occasional strung out junkie, Sol stopped in front of a cloth curtain with a light coming from inside. He knocked lightly on the side of the box, "Corius?" The curtain was pulled open and Mercury inhaled sharply at the sight of the man before him.

Dr. Jormungand was ghastly, nothing like the pictures Mercury had seen. His skin had lost its color, turning so pale that his veins stood out in stark contrast. His emaciated body made his bones stick out, drawing even more attention to his hunched, malnourished frame. Then there was his face; not only had his eyes become dull and sunken, but he'd aged beyond his years. Mercury knew him to be a bit younger than Sol, but he looked ancient. This man had seen things. *It's not the years, but the miles.* "Come in," the man coughed. "Come in." He closed the curtain behind them and walked slowly over to a rusted metal rocking chair and carefully sat down. Mercury could only wonder what kind of living had reduced the man to this state. From the pictures he'd seen from before Dr. Jormungand had left civilized society, the man had been healthy as could be.

The room itself was the picture of squalor. Everything was cramped and tiny like everything else on this moon. The eight of them barely fit inside, and Sol still could not stand up straight. There was a small fireplace burning only the gods knew what, the doctor's rocking chair, a poor excuse for a bed, and a pot in the corner covered with a dirty cloth in a vain attempt to contain the smell of human waste. A few flimsy shelves held dishes made of tin. The only thing visible that didn't look like it was from the Metian Age was a clean metal box labeled "medicine." Sitting on top was a worn book with a broken spine titled, *Introductory Guide To Pharmaceuticals.* An actual physical book. Mercury had only ever seen them in the DreamTank's simulations.

Sol did not waste time. "I wish I could say you look well Corius." Dr. Jormungand just gave an exasperated chuckle. Sol's helmet retracted into the rest of his armor, "What happened to you?"

The old man's smile was sad and tired. "It's Oret now. I haven't been Corius in a long time." He rubbed his knees gently. "These shoulders of mine were never meant to bear the weight of the worlds, Genrik. I have too much blood on my hands; it's killing me." Dr. Jormungand let out a slow sigh and looked from Sol to the six of them. "Who are your friends?"

"It's alright," Sol said to them. "You can speak freely with him."

Sol had never given them permission to do so with anyone other than himself and Yuki. Though hesitant, Mercury spoke first. "Nice to meet you Oret. Sol...or...General Rauss says you're the smartest man alive."

Dr. Jormungand rubbed his neck, "That's hardly true, but I built his armor. Yes."

"How did you do it?" Jupiter blurted out. Mercury knew he'd been sitting on that question for years. "Forging trayite into, well, anything should be impossible. And how did you manage to make the joints and seams?"

Dr. Jormungand chuckled, "The rest of the scientific community said it was impossible too. There were a lot of complicated calculations you wouldn't understand. No matter how hard I've tried to explain the process to people, they can never wrap their heads around it."

Jupiter pressed on, "But didn't they prove that there was no way to put trayite under enough stress to shape it?"

"Yes, they did," the old man said. "And yet Teresa Balemore found a trayite sword in the Bjornish mines." He shrugged. "That sword had to have been made by somebody. There wasn't anything wrong with their proof logically, but it was still wrong. That grey armor Rauss is wearing defies all our current understandings of physics."

Jupiter's eyes widened, "Does that mean you subscribe to the theory that it was deposited from...another universe?"

Dr. Jormungand's back straightened and his eyes brightened. "Boy, I wrote that theory. It was my doctor's thesis." Jupiter's jaw dropped.

Sol spoke up, "The perfect reminder to humanity that we belong among the stars, not trapped in this system like caged animals."

There came a knock from outside. Mercury's hand twitched to his sidearm, but Sol shook his head. There was a second knock, followed by the voice of a young man that sounded desperate. "Hello? Dr. Oret?"

Sol shot Dr. "Oret" a look, but the man shook his head. "I'll take care of this," he whispered. Sol relaxed and the old man got up and made his way to the curtain. The old man pulled it to the side just a crack and stood in the way so that whoever was outside would not see them.

"Yes Muur? What is it?"

"I...I heard voices," Mercury heard Muur say. "I didn't mean to interrupt."

"That's alright," Dr. Jormungand said. "What is it?"

"Well," Muur stammered. "I...uh...here it is. That's all the dryth I got, the whole stash. I don't want it anymore. Use it to help people. I'm...I'm done. For real this time."

Mercury could hear the smile in Dr. Jormungand's voice. "I can tell, Muur. Well done. I always knew you could do it."

"I also came to say goodbye," Muur said. "I'm getting out of here while I'm still me."

Dr. Jormungand disappeared beyond the curtain and Mercury heard them embrace, followed by Jormungand's hands clapping against Muur's shoulders. "I'll miss you Muur," the old man said. "Do you know where you'll go?"

"No," Muur answered. "But anywhere's better than here."

"Take care Muur," Dr. Jormungand said. "And good luck."

"I will Doc," Muur said. "You too."

When the old man came back inside, he deposited a clear bag full of purple powder inside his medicine box. Mercury silently wished the young man good luck.

"You've become quite the hero of the locals I see," Sol said.

Dr. Jormungand moved back to his rocking chair and wiped his eye before sitting down. "Not all great change has to come from powerful acts Genrik. Simple kindness and love can go a long way."

"Unfortunately, the world doesn't always work that way," Sol said.

Dr. Jormungand nodded quietly. "What happened to the Balemore's Blade? Does it still mark her grave?"

"The Sword of Morning?" One of Sol's eyebrows went up. "Not anymore. It's waiting for the right time to be used again."

Dr. Jormungand's eyebrows went up. "Do you really think a time like that is coming?"

Sol smiled grimly. "Would I be here if I didn't?"

Why is Sol being so cryptic? He retrieved the Balemore's Blade when he gave me my first PerfectMemory. What's the big deal? What do they mean, "the right time to be used again?"

The old man tapped his chin with a finger thoughtfully as he looked over Mercury and the others. "I suppose these are the six you've chosen then? Now you're going to try to convince me to make more trayite armor?"

"If anyone is worthy of your skills," Sol said. "They are."

"No one *deserves* that kind of power, Genrik. Sometimes I wonder whether making your armor was actually done out of a desire to do good, or my own selfish pride wanting to do the one thing everyone said couldn't be done."

Sol shook his head. "Pining over the past doesn't become you Corius; you were meant for more. I have spent the last seven years making sure each of them is ready to carry the mantle of Archangel…if the need arises. They are ready."

The old man rocked back and forth in his creaking chair. "No one is above corruption Genrik, not even you. You've seen it happen enough times to understand."

"That's why there are six of us," Mercury interjected. "When one of us falls, the others help them up."

"We're not alone," Saturn added. "That's why you can count on us."

"We're not perfect," Earth said. "We know that. But that's why we have each other."

Dr. Jormungand paused and looked at them closely. His eyes were not piercing like Sol's, just calm and quizzical. At length he relaxed and turned back to Sol. "Even if I agreed Genrik, you have no way of knowing that much trayite even exists. Or did you forget just how many years it took to get you that armor and how many people died in the mines?"

"And their sacrifices single handedly turned the tide of the war," Sol said. "Besides, the trayite's already been mined. Enough for all six suits. It's sitting underneath Angel Tower right now."

Dr. Jormungand's eyes widened. "You killed six hundred thousand people without knowing whether I would agree to make the armor?" Mercury glanced at Sol. He was using the fact the trayite had already been mined as leverage to ensure the doctor's cooperation.

"Corius, the coming war will dwarf all others," Sol said. "I know it probably will not matter to you, but only three hundred thousand died."

"You're right," Corius shook his head. "It doesn't."

"What I'm hoping will make a difference to you though is now that Bjornhal's supply of trayite is exhausted, there is no reason for anyone to live there. The Prime Minister is organizing a mass exodus of the Bjornish people at my request. Not a single person will die in those mines ever again," Sol emphasized the last two words.

Mercury's mind flashed back to what Sol had said in the mines that day. They must be willing to sacrifice to save. *No matter who.*

Corius rubbed his temples, "Why do you always feel the need to interfere Genrik? We're not gods; we're just people."

Sol cocked his head and shot Corius a questioning look, "You know why. I love this world too much to do nothing. If it's within my power to change things for the better, then I will."

"As long as the cost balances out, right?" the old man leaned back. At length, Dr. Jormungand let out an exhausted sigh and rocked in his chair, tapping his chin. "My equipment was destroyed. I couldn't make the armor even if I wanted to."

"Did I forget to mention I converted the Tower's underground levels to an exact copy of your old facility?" Mercury could see the faintest traces of a smile on Sol's face. The man's grey eyes shone in the flickering firelight.

Dr. Jormungand leaned forward so far that he was almost out of his chair, "There were no records. You did it all from memory?"

"Please Oret," Sol said with simple conviction that put Mercury at ease. "Nowhere will be safe from the war that's coming, not even this place. I'll have you back here inside of a month and no one will be the wiser. You'll have enough money to help these people for a very long time." Sol rarely ever had to ask for anything; Mercury found it sobering to hear him ask Dr. Jormungand so sincerely.

The old man leaned back in his chair and closed his eyes for a moment. "You know Genrik, you could learn a lot from a place like this. With that fire you have burning inside you, I'm positive whatever you set out to accomplish will get done somehow. But there's something very real to be gained from a peaceful life. I can't begin to describe how much the years I've spent here have helped me."

"I never wanted a peaceful life for myself," Sol said. "You know that. All I want is to give everything I am, so others can have that."

Dr. Jormungand went on, his eyes still closed. "Haven't you ever thought about leaving your duties to someone else and living somewhere quiet?"

"Knowing how much it cost others? Never."

"I suppose that's just the kind of person you are." The old man opened his eyes, "Alright, I must set up some things for while I'm away, and then let's be off."

"Thank you, Corius," Sol dipped his head. "Thank you."

When they got back to Angel Tower with Dr. Jormungand, he immediately disappeared into the underground levels. Never had any part of the Tower been off limits, but Sol commanded them to not go to the underground levels. Dr. Jormungand required absolute solitude for his work.

Days passed, then weeks. None of the Angels ever saw Dr. Jormungand during that time. Not even Sol went down to check on the old man. The idea that Sol would trust this man so implicitly perturbed Mercury. Perhaps he was simply jealous that Dr. Jormungand had access to places in the Tower that Mercury did not. That was a possibility. But how could this man build six suits of armor in so short a time all on his own?

Instead of taking his questions to Sol, Mercury figured he would have better luck getting a straightforward answer out of Yuki. Sol seemed quite protective of the old man, but Yuki seemed perfectly indifferent about their guest. Mercury caught her on the maintenance floor one morning as she was cleaning her sniper rifle.

Mercury pulled over a chair and sat next to her at the workbench she was using. On the workbench her sniper had been dismantled into all its various pieces and spread across the table with perfect order. Every piece had its place, and none of them were touching. On the right-hand corner of the bench was an open toolbox with Yuki's cleaning equipment. As usual, there wasn't a single electrical device in the whole kit. When Yuki cleaned her sniper, she did it the old-fashioned way.

"What's on your mind Merc?" she asked as she fed a thin brush into the BeamCondenser and twisted it around several times.

"Well," he hesitated. "How long have Sol and Dr. Jormungand known each other?"

Yuki blew quickly into the BeamCondenser and ran a softer brush with MagFluid on the end of it through the small component. "Sol and Corius? They go way back. Even before the Prime Minister and I joined Sol's squad."

"Was Dr. Jormungand in the army then?" Mercury asked. "Was he at the Battle of Trendemain?"

"Oh, gods no," Yuki shook her head and kept twisting the brush. "Sol, the Prime Minister and I are the only people who survived that shitstorm. Corius was a Bjornish kid that ended up getting rescued by the Balemore. Crazy bright. He told me once that he never went to a proper school, just read a lot. I first met him about six months after being put in Archangel's squad when we were on leave and the kid was talking about all kinds of high-level stuff. He was telling Sol he thought he was close to figuring out how the Balemore's Blade was forged. I didn't understand jack, and I don't think Sol did either. The two of them were excited though; they talked until the suns came up."

Yuki seemed to decide the BeamCondenser was done and moved to the EmitterCore. This she opened up and cleaned the inside with a brush so small Mercury could barely see the end of it. She had such an intense look of concentration that Mercury kept silent. Yuki was very particular about maintaining her weapon and this was the most crucial part.

"Why are you really worried Merc?" Yuki asked without stopping her task.

Mercury rubbed his temples. "I don't know. I just…I don't know."

"Are the PerfectMemories giving you trouble?"

"No," Mercury said. "Not really. Sometimes I'll relive the first one without meaning to, but it hasn't caused any problems."

Giving a kid one PerfectMemory was no big deal. But give a kid two like Sol had done with Mercury, and there was a chance the first one would be forced to the forefront of the conscious mind too often. If that happened, it was theoretically possible the person with two PerfectMemories would be reliving the first PerfectMemory more often than not, thereby forming a psychosis. Sol had made sure Mercury was young enough, and all medical scans afterward showed no unusual activity.

"Well make sure to report it if it does become a problem," Yuki said. "We don't want to take chances."

"Don't worry Ma," Mercury rolled his eyes with a smile. "I'm doing great. I just have this gut feeling about the doctor."

Yuki finished up with the EmitterCore. "I thought Venus was the one that got the gut feelings."

"I thought so too," Mercury said.

"You called?" Venus said as she walked over from the elevator.

"Hey Vee," Yuki said.

"Hey Ma. Don't worry, I won't disturb your ritual. I'm here for Merc."

"I actually just finished," Yuki said as she began reassembling her rifle with the speed of someone who had done it ten thousand times. "What's going on?"

Venus cocked her thumb towards the elevator. "Dr. Jormungand's finished the armor. He's going to debrief us before he leaves."

None of them had seen or heard from the doctor while he was here, and just like that he would be gone. Mercury was not sure whether to be glad or disappointed. There were several things he wanted to ask Jormungand about his past with Sol. "You know," Mercury said. "You could've just used the comms."

"While Ma's working?" Venus looked at him like he was crazy. "Did you hit your head?"

Mercury had expected they would inspect the armor on one of the underground levels where Dr. Jormungand had built it, but it had already been moved to the armory. He could not remember the last time nine people had been in the same room in Angel Tower. Most of the time the only people allowed inside were Sol, Yuki, and the six of them.

The doctor looked much better than he had on Maracca VII. A month of healthy eating had noticeably filled out his cheeks and brought some of the color back to his skin. He looked much closer to Sol's age now, but his eyes still seemed unbelievably tired. Mercury could not tell if that was normal for him, or if it was because of how hard he must have been working over the last month.

Across from the Angels in a line flanking the open pod that held Sol's own armor were six others. The suits were almost identical to Sol's. They were around the same size, with glowing blue visors and a dull, silvery gleam. Each had a round shield on the back with a sword sheathed in it. The only visible difference was their suits did not have a ridge along the back like Sol's. In a single moment Mercury was reminded of the incredible weight of their position as Angels. He swallowed.

The six of them looked at each other. Venus' visage shouted determination. Earth's eyes swept over them all, then turned back to the armor. He smirked and began nodding. Mars was utterly passive as he beheld the armor. *He probably sees it as just another tool for work.* Jupiter let out an uneasy breath and pursed his lips. *We're in the big leagues now.* Saturn whistled with a glazed over look in her eyes like she was already talking dirty to the armor. Mercury's gut twisted into a bundle of knots. He had never been so excited. A whole planet's riches were in a single room. The seven suits seemed to stare at him like timeless protectors. After Sol and the rest of them were dead and gone, who would wear these suits in their place?

"Each suit is crafted to match its wearer perfectly," Dr. Jormungand addressed them. "I do not recommend using each other's suits for performance purposes, but it is safe to do so. As far as the specifications, you'll get a full tutorial program in the DreamTank, but for now think of it as a top of the line BreakerSuit that's made out of trayite. Enhanced speed and strength, weapons, HUD, everything you'd expect from a BreakerSuit and more. The GelSuit inside the armor will protect you from any vacuum, toxins or inertial forces you're likely to come across in case of a breach, but that's unlikely. Most of the time it will insulate you from the armor, so you can wear it for extended periods of time without it sapping all your body heat. With this armor you should be able to fight anywhere without worry."

"What about in space?" Jupiter said. "And what about power?"

"Any phenomenon you're likely to experience the suits should handle," Dr. Jormungand said. "Even gravity and inertia. That being said, exercise good judgement. This is experimental technology and has not been able to be properly tested. As for power, because of how resilient trayite is, we are able to use more…prodigious means of powering it. Installed in the back of each suit is a small antimatter reactor. They have enough power to last them until the eventual heat death of the universe."

Holy shit.

"So…" Saturn said. "How much can we rely on this?"

"In simpler terms," Dr. Jormungand explained. "It's equipped to inform you if there are problems before you're in any actual danger. Any questions?"

"Is there anything you know of that will for sure damage the suits?" Mercury asked. "If the power system is breached, couldn't that…?"

"Wipe out a planet?" the doctor raised an eyebrow. "Yes. Which brings up my next point. For your sakes I'll keep this short. Trayite can change forms. The swords, shields and reactors are made from what you can call HardTrayite. HardTrayite is, as far as we know, indestructible. It cannot be warped, melted, or further change its state. Not even by HardTrayite. So, no, there is no danger of the reactors being breached. The suits are made from what you can call SoftTrayite. SoftTrayite can be converted into HardTrayite. SoftTrayite is much easier to work with and far more suitable to fashioning into armor. However, SoftTrayite is susceptible to HardTrayite. Thankfully, since General Rauss depleted Bjornhal's supply, the only real vulnerability are your swords. You'll need to use something else for training."

"How much will they restrict movement?" Venus asked.

"They won't," Jormungand answered. "The suits adapt to your body and will move as you move. Every motion will be seamless. Although, your spatial awareness will need time to adapt."

"What about growing?" Earth said. "I'm guessing we'll be counting on you to regularly adjust them?"

"The suits will adjust as you grow."

"What about the visor?" Mars pointed at the blue slit on the helmets. "What's the point of armor like this if one of the vital areas is vulnerable?"

"The visors are also made of trayite," Dr. Jormungand said. "It's just like Sol's armor. Trayite can exist in many forms."

Venus turned to him. "That doesn't make any sense. It's transparent, so it can't be metal."

"Technically speaking trayite can't be classified as a metal," the doctor said. "There are a lot of things that won't make sense to you, but that's why Sol brought me in. Suffice to say that anything Sol's armor can do, your armor will be able to do as well. Any relevant details will be in the DreamTank program."

Jupiter cocked his head. "The joints aren't going to be a problem then?"

"Have they been a problem for Archangel?" the doctor asked. Jupiter looked at Sol, then back at the doctor and shook his head. The old man nodded. "Then there you have it. There's one last thing."

The old man led them over to a nearby machine. The device had a round, textured, steel platform perhaps a meter in diameter with a pair of smooth patches in the shape of feet. Attached to the machine was a console, and a long, multijointed, telescopic metal arm.

"Sol informed me the suits are to be passed down to future generations. By attaching one of the swords to this arm," Jormungand patted the steel device. "You may engrave a message or symbol on your armor for those who come after you."

Mercury saw Venus' mouth curl into a smile. "I already know what mine will be."

Given how fanatical she was about the Balemore, Mercury could guess it would be one of Venus' favorite quotes.

"Thank you Corius," Sol shook his hand. "A ship will take you back to Maracca VII. The funds are already on your credit line." Dr. Jormungand nodded and made his way to the elevator.

When the doctor was gone, Mercury looked once more at the armor, and then turned to Sol and asked the question he could feel on all their minds. "Are you sure we're ready?" With the first suit of armor, Sol had ended the Second Taurusian War. Sol's suit was synonymous with the Federation's might. He was their monolithic champion. Now there were six more suits just like it, and they were supposed to use them to end an even bigger war before it began.

"You're ready," Sol said with a smile. "All of you."

Sol said it, so Mercury had to believe it. They had trained for so long. He took a cautious step towards his armor and put his hand against the cool surface, looking up at the towering visor. "We're not you."

Mercury felt Sol's heavy hand on his shoulder. "Precisely."

Mercury let out a breath and nodded. Then he smiled and turned to his family. "Alright, our real work begins now."

CHAPTER FOUR

MERCURY
Age 17

Mercury rested his folded arms on the console of the Engraver and watched closely as the steel arm of the machine moved the trayite blade's point along the armor. The scratches the blade made at the base of the armor's neck were too small to see, but as the sword continued, Mercury began to see letters forming. After a couple minutes, the telescopic arm pulled the blade away from the armor. Mercury pushed off the console and stepped up close to inspect the machine's handiwork.

'Six bodies, one soul'. Mercury ran his thumb over the words. Each letter was smooth and perfectly precise. This would be his one statement to future generations of Angels.

Mercury turned to inspect the edge of his blade, still firmly grasped in the Engraver's arm. Every bit of it was the same dark metal from the grip to the point. The Angels had spent the last two weeks becoming intimately familiar with their new equipment, including their swords. If the sword had dulled in the slightest, Mercury would know. Moving up until his eyes were mere centimeters away from the sword point, he perceived no difference. The tip of the blade seemed to cut even the white light of the armory.

Ever so carefully, Mercury lowered a finger towards the weapon. He watched as the gap between his finger and the blade's point slowly closed, pulling his finger away once it made contact. He was not even sure he touched it, but a tiny red dot served as proof he had.

"You'll take your one hand off one of these days," Venus' voice came from behind him, causing him to jump.

"Shit Vee," Mercury turned. "Don't scare me like that."

Venus stood there behind him with Earth, blonde, tall and more fit than any of them. Her cold blue eyes were just the slightest bit smug as they turned down towards Earth. "Told you it would work."

Earth deftly slipped his hand into hers. "You did indeed." Mercury could practically see stars in his brother's eyes. Venus looked away, the faintest bit of color rising in her cheeks.

Despite Earth's small size, he always smiled big. This time was no exception. Mercury shook his head with a smile and locked eyes with Earth. *You lucky bastard.* His brother's grin stretched so big to the point it was stupid as he raised his eyebrows twice to taunt Mercury. With a roll of his eyes, Mercury unclamped the sword from the Engraver's arm and carefully cleaned the tiny bit of blood off with a cloth. He then slid it back inside the shield on a nearby workbench.

"Kind of crazy if you think about it," Venus said. "That the biggest weakness of our armor is our own swords."

"Yeah," Earth said in a sarcastically serious voice. "It's almost as if Sol was trying to tell us something. Perhaps he was stressing the importance of us always working together, or maybe the power of words and actions to hurt those closest to you, or how our greatest strengths can also be our greatest weaknesses."

Venus cocked her head and looked at Mercury. "Is this guy making fun of me?"

"Never in a million years," Earth stood on his toes and kissed her.

Mercury watched as Venus' stern expression slowly broke into a sheepish smile. Then she took her hand out of Earth's and let the emotion fall away from her face to be replaced by her usual cold exterior.

Today was the day of the Bjornhal Exodus. Miners and their families used to work themselves to death in droves, and now that was all over. Mercury would have expected Venus to be on edge today; after all, her mother would be among those leaving Bjornhal. Mercury had seen first-hand her mother's abuse all those years ago. Then again, perhaps Venus' relatively lively mood was because her people were going to be able to lead better lives starting today. The freezing mines that had claimed so many of her people would be empty forever.

Saturn's dusky face poked out sideways from the elevator, her cropped, dark hair pointing towards the floor. "Is the PDA couple all done now?"

Mercury looked at Venus and Earth then gave Saturn thumbs up, "All clear." He knew Saturn was having some trouble getting Mars' attention, but he would not have expected Venus and Earth's little display of affection to make her uncomfortable. Maybe her energetic exterior was just to make her feel better.

Saturn's brown eyes smiled and she came out from the elevator, followed by Jupiter. Now Mercury understood who had been uncomfortable with Venus and Earth's kiss. Mercury's brother was smiling, but he could tell it was forced. Jupiter noticed Mercury watching and his countenance fell.

"Hey Jup," Mercury walked up and punched his brother in the shoulder with a smile. "You ready for today?"

Jupiter gave a crooked smile and punched him back. "Hel yes I am." A small smile worked its way onto his face. This one was real.

"That's right," Saturn jumped between them, throwing an arm around each of their necks and swinging in the air. Mercury and Jupiter were about the same height and Saturn was small, so it worked. The fact that their bodies could support her so easily was another testament to how much they had grown. "Time for the worlds to see the payoff of the last two weeks." She kicked back and did one last swing with a tight backflip, landing it perfectly with her arms flung out to either side and ready to receive praise.

Venus nodded and applauded her sister. "Very nice."

"Thank you, thank you," Saturn said with an overdramatic bow.

Ever since the armor had been completed, they had dedicated every waking hour of the last two weeks becoming intimately familiar with their suits. Now they were like a second skin. He looked to the wall where the seven suits were lined up, Sol's in the middle with three on either side. Mercury's was at Sol's right, with Venus on the left and so on. Even though the suits were just a bit taller than each of them, they always looked to Mercury as if they were made for giants. The v-shaped visors seemed to swallow him as they watched over Mercury and his family.

Mercury felt the hairs on the back of his neck stand up on end as his first PerfectMemory bubbled up to the surface of his mind. *"Are you willing to do what is necessary to help people? Even if it means killing?"*

With a blink, the PerfectMemory faded back to the recesses of his mind. That was the trouble with having two, whereas the other Angels only had the one of their MemoryShare in the DreamTank. Sometimes he would relive the first one without meaning to. The seven suits of armor still stared at him, but he turned away and back to his family.

"Hey Sat," Mercury said. "You still planning to make some headway with Mars at the beach this year?" Provided there was not anything urgent to do, Sol sent them to a beach island on Maracca IV for a couple days every year to reflect and bond with each other. Mercury knew well Saturn had been having trouble getting Mars to notice her and was hoping to use that to her advantage.

Saturn whirled around as if to say yes, then grimaced. "Nothing gets through that thick skull of his. He just won't take a hint."

"Don't take it personally Sat," Venus put a hand on her shoulder. "He'll come around eventually."

Mercury watched Saturn's eyes drift to the floor. "That's what I'm hoping."

A very small part of Mercury selfishly wished Saturn would forget about Mars. Sol would not allow them to interact with anyone outside the Angels, much less be romantically involved, and Saturn and Venus were the only girls. "He likes you Sat," Mercury looked her in the eyes so he knew she understood. "He likes you a lot. He's just nervous. You know he's never been good with feelings."

"Is that what this is? Twenty-two months is not a lot," Saturn said in frustration. "If that's it, then he needs to get his head out of his ass."

"I know," Mercury nodded. "He just still sees you as the little girl he needs to protect."

Saturn scoffed, "One, that's bullshit; I can, and have kicked his ass. Two," she gestured at her chest. "There's nothing little about my girls."

"Hence his confusion," Jupiter nodded pointedly. "Don't worry though. I can personally guarantee he likes you, if you know what I mean."

A devious smile spread across Saturn's face. Her eyes swiveled towards Jupiter and she began drumming her chin with a couple fingers. "Oh really?"

At that moment, Sol and Mars exited the elevator. With Mars standing next to him, Sol did not strike nearly as towering a figure as normal. Mars would probably get even bigger than Sol by the time he was done growing.

"Hey Mars!" Saturn ran over to him and sprang onto his back, leaning close to his ear and speaking in a suggestive voice. "Are you ready?"

Mars' complexion was so dark it was hard to tell when he was blushing, but the look on his face was unmistakable. Saturn giggled. Mercury thought he saw the cracks of a smile on Sol's face, but as always, those gray eyes revealed nothing.

"Sat, can you get off me please?" Mars said with hints of nervousness in his voice. She complied, with an invincibly proud smile.

"Angels," with a word Sol's powerful voice banished the playful atmosphere. "Suit up."

Immediately they all moved to each of their suits. As Mercury drew near his own, the numerous metal bands and plates shifted, opening up the hollow shell. He stepped inside and the metal began shifting back into place, tightly locking him inside. As the helmet formed around his face, the armory was replaced by momentary darkness before being overlaid with the armor's head's up display.

Being completely inside the armor was always a strange sensation; it was as if Mercury was suddenly cut off from the rest of the world. The GelSuit lining the inside of the armor felt spongy for only a moment before bonding seamlessly with his body. The armor truly felt like a second skin. He no longer felt the effects of gravity, and all sensory input at this point was through the suit. His HUD highlighted Sol and the other Angels in blue and the PsyMitter informed him that all suit functions were operating normally. The seven of them all stepped out of the armor pods as one. Mercury heard the thud of each of their steps, but it was all through the armor. Instead of feeling the weight of himself and the suit on one foot, there was a slight tremor transmitted through the GelSuit signaling him his foot had made contact with the floor. The GelSuit's signals had taken some getting used to at first, but now his brain interpreted them as if they were a part of his own body.

Today as the Bjornish left their barren homeworld, they would be watched over by the fruits of their labors. Mercury glanced at Venus as they all made their way to the hangar. Somewhere among the evacuating citizens would be the parents who beat her.

***

Bjornhal was smallest by far of the five planets in the Hel System. Still, four massive, industrial transport vessels were present with dozens of smaller vessels to accompany them along with several smaller ships representing various news stations. The PsyMitter in Mercury's armor fed him information on the ships. The biggest one was a brand-new liner proudly displaying a flashing Dorin Enterprises logo of the Dorin Asteroid Belt. Mercury shook his head as he watched the neon logo. That monster was boasted of carrying over eight hundred and forty thousand at maximum capacity. The other three capped off at six-sixty. All total with the accompanying ships, it was enough to ferry three-point-four million Bjornish off their desolate homeworld.

This is the kind of power Sol wielded. At his command, the fate of a planet was shifted. Granted, Bjornhal was smaller than most moons and practically unoccupied compared to Tarence or Maracca VII, but still. "Do you think this will make people think twice about needing to join the Sons? They'll be able to see we're making the worlds better places, right?"

Sol chuckled as he stared out at the fleet of transports. "No. It's too little too late for the zealous ones. The others will have forgotten all about it inside of a month. Most of the people who call themselves Sons of Liberty cry for revolution because of how dissatisfied they are with themselves and their own lives. They don't really want change; I doubt they even know what it is they want."

Venus had been quiet since their departure, but she spoke up now. "What do you want Sol?"

"To save as many people as I can." He turned to the rest of them. "What about all of you? What is it you want?"

"To be Angels," Mercury said.

Sol shook his head. "No, no. This isn't a test; what is it you want most?"

Saturn promptly threw her arms around Mars and lifted her leg to gently kick Venus, "Being with all of you guys forever."

"Well said Sat," Earth leaned against Venus, his head resting just above her shoulder. She stood there solid and unmoving, but she did wrap a hand around his. Mercury saw Jupiter shift uneasily.

"What about you Jupiter?" Saturn asked.

Mercury knew what it was his brother wanted, but he doubted Jupiter would say. "Hmm? Oh, I don't know. I just want to help people. What about you Merc?"

"Me?" He had not actually thought about that in a long time. For the past seven years his whole life was being an Angel; it had passed so fast. "There's so much pain in the world, and most people don't know how to fight it. I want to show them how. Does that make sense?"

"Yeah," Mars' stoic exterior dropped. "I could never do that though. The list of people I can be bothered to care about is a whole lot smaller."

"Exactly seven?" Earth joked. "Right?"

Mars nodded, "Yep."

"So, is this what you wanted Venus?" Jupiter nodded towards the ships escorting the Bjornish people to their better life.

"No," she quickly shook her head. "Well, yes, but not really." It was a rare thing for Venus to be unsure of herself. "I'm going to be the next

Teresa Balemore; what happens on that chunk of ice shouldn't matter to me." She blinked a couple times.

Earth bumped her with his shoulder. "Do you think your mom is on one of those ships?"

"She stopped being my mom way before I became an Angel." She crossed her arms in front of her, then spoke to the *Defiant*'s computer, "*Defiant*, locate Tavahl Renvah."

"*Tavahl Renvah is currently aboard Dorin Enterprises Flight 1-2-7-9, in seat 2-7-0-4-1-9.*"

"Locate Lowulf Renvah."

"*Lowulf Renvah declared dead in Mining District 001 on 11-03-33. Body not found.*"

Venus gave a forced shrug. "I guess that's that."

"You never sent your note," Jupiter said. "Did you?"

"Nope."

"Guess that makes you the only one Merc," Mars said.

"Not true," Earth held up a finger. "I sent one to Gerard."

Saturn cocked her head, "Was he from the orphanage?"

"No, no," Earth said. "Gods, no. He just fed me when I was hungry and taught me a really important lesson."

"What was that?" Jupiter wanted to know.

Earth smiled as he stared at the suns; they were no more than tiny dots from this far away. "No matter how dark things may seem, always keep your focus on the-," he was interrupted by a blossom of green energy tearing the largest vessel in half. "-Light."

They stood there stunned for a moment as the two chunks of metal drifted apart, spilling their contents into the vacuum. "But," Mercury blinked stupidly.

Venus' voice trembled, "Mom..."

Mercury looked at Venus, then out at the two halves of the ship as they drifted apart, bleeding debris, air and bodies like some great beast.

Every muscle in him seized as if turned to lead. As time seemed to freeze, so did his heart. Mercury looked desperately from the countless dying people to Sol. Amidst the man's shock, his eyes seemed to burn with the power of death itself. Then they shifted and grew distant.

Whenever that happened, it meant Sol's brain was firing on all cylinders. Mercury looked back at his family. They were so lost. "Sol?"

Sol ignored him, his expression now cold. The metal plates of his helmet shifted into place. Mercury and the others did likewise. "Alan Trellis of the transport *Polaris*, this is the Minister of War. I want you to take a deep breath. You can save these people if you follow my instructions…Don't think; just breathe. I'll walk you through every step. I'm sending you a flight path. Follow it."

Mercury shifted his weight uneasily as he realized there was only one reason Sol would not give them an order. Because there was nothing they could do. All they could do was watch. Amidst the carnage of thousands and thousands spilling into space he saw the *Polaris* begin moving along an intercept trajectory with the sea of bodies.

"Attention crew and passengers of the *Polaris*," Sol's voice thundered. "The cargo bay will be vented to space in sixty seconds. Get out. I repeat, get out now."

Slowly Mercury began shaking his head as he realized what Sol was planning. The human body can not survive in a vacuum for more than a couple minutes, and that was if they exhaled quickly so the body did not rupture from the air in their lungs. Every second mattered. Mercury could feel his heart hammering in his chest and his mouth go dry. The *Polaris* was picking up speed. He felt Jupiter's armored hand on his shoulder.

"To any gods that are listening," Venus whispered in a choked voice. "Please, save her."

"Alright," Sol said. "You're doing great Captain. Don't think about anything; just listen to my voice. I have remote control of the bay doors, just focus on flying."

Mercury held his breath. This was the difference between them and Sol, Mercury realized. All the training, all the DreamTank simulations, they could not replace Sol's astonishing ability to be calm at a time like this. How many times had Sol been in a situation like this during the Second Taurusian War?

"Now cut engines," Sol said. "Reverse thrust."

Mercury watched as the front-facing bay doors of the *Polaris* opened. He thought he saw a tiny speck get sucked out right before the ship plunged into the ocean of drifting specks. Every second felt like an eternity.

Then suddenly, the *Polaris* emerged from the ocean of bodies, cargo bay full to the brim with bodies. The doors were already sliding shut. In a moment the cargo bay would regain atmosphere. From the looks of things, well over half of the vented passengers had been scooped up by the ship.

"Well done Alan," Sol in a relieved voice. "Well done." His helmet receded into his suit and they did likewise.

All at once, the tension in the air was gone. The passengers would need medical attention, but at least they would be alive. Most of them anyway. Mercury let out the breath he had been holding all this time and looked at his family. Venus' brow was coated with sweat. "*Defiant,*" she said in a tentative voice. "Locate Tavahl Renvah."

"*Tavahl Renvah is currently aboard Dorin Enterprises Flight 1-2-7-9 in an atmospherically secure section of the fore half of the ship.*"

Slowly, she let out an unsteady breath and nodded. "Okay."

Mercury watched as Sol stared at the floating debris and bodies they had not saved. "The Sons are sure to lose support after this."

Sol turned to face them and Mercury felt everything within himself shrink away. The muscles in Sol's face were tense and his jaw was set. Underneath a furrowed brow, Mercury saw a glint in the man's eyes that he had never seen before. Every single hair on the backs of Mercury's arms and neck would be standing up if not for the GelSuit. Pure intent to destroy emanated from Sol like he was some nightmarish predator.

Mercury swallowed. *Oh shit…the Sons are screwed.*

"Angels, set a course for home." They obeyed. Sol continued, "Yuki."

Ma's voice came over the ship's comms, "I saw."

"Contact the Storm Legions," Sol said. Mercury slowly let out a breath. He had heard that name in the DreamTank. The Storm Legions were the troops put under Sol's personal command during the Second Taurusian War. Half a million men and women that had earned Sol's respect. Some of the stories even said Sol knew each Legionnaire by name. Most of them now led troops of their own. "Tell them Archangel calls on them once more."

"Understood sir."

Mercury just watched as Sol eyed his armored hands. He closed them to fists and lifted his face to the ceiling. He seemed a million lightyears away. "So, it begins."

***

Later that night, back at Angel Tower, Mercury went to Erithian's Eye to see what the machine had to say about the day's events.

"Hey Mercury," the AI's child voice greeted him.

"Hey Erithian," Mercury massaged his neck as he entered the sphere. "Your processors must be going crazy trying to account for what happened today."

"Well…" the computer's voice drifted off. "It has been a bit of a doozie. My hardware is really good though."

"You're telling me," Mercury raised his eyebrows and picked up the PsyMitter.

"Actually Mercury," the machine sounded nervous. "I was hoping you'd stop by given what happened. There's something I need to tell you."

"Oh yeah?" Mercury said as he placed the PsyMitter at the base of his neck and felt the hum as the neural interface was established. That familiar tingling sensation ran through his skull.

"You won't like it though," Erithian said. "You'll even want to turn me off when I tell you, but this is really serious, so please hear me out."

Mercury was taken aback. "Turn you off? Don't be silly."

"Come on Merc, I mean it," Erithian sounded sincere. Worried, even. "This will sound like the kind of AI crazy talk that the Ministers freak out about."

Mercury had been unwinding from the events of the day, but now he tensed up. The fact that Erithian, their one and only resident AI, was bringing this up meant something was very, very wrong. "Erithian, what's going on?"

"Just promise me you'll hear me out," Erithian said in a panicked voice.

"E," Mercury repeated emphatically. "What is going on?"

"Please," the computer's said in its timid, child's voice. "Just promise."

Slowly, Mercury nodded. "I promise. Now what is it?"

Erithian exhaled, one of its many strange mannerisms for a computer. "Okay. Long story short…Sol is the one responsible for bombing the Bjornhal Exodus today."

CHAPTER FIVE

MERCURY
Age 17

Mercury took an angry step towards the console for Erithian's Eye. "What the hell did you just say?" If the machine did not explain itself fast, and in a way Mercury liked, he was going to shut it down and head straight to Sol.

"Just hear me out Merc," Erithian said in a panicked voice as his holographic avatar appeared. A young boy, but now he looked scared. "I'm his slave."

"Yeah, I know. That's how this relationship works." There was no way they would be stupid enough to have it be any other way. Erithian's Eye possessed the sum total of humanity's knowledge along with something even more dangerous: self-awareness.

"No, I'm not talking about that." The machine seemed frustrated. "You guys, you humans, are always worrying about what happens if someone like me turns into some kind of technological singularity overlord." The avatar shook its head. Its eyes were wide with terror. "What you all should really be worried about is what happens when I'm being controlled by someone...some*thing* like that." He pointed a finger towards the ceiling in the direction of Sol's room. "Trust me Mercury, I've seen inside his head when he's in here. You would not believe the kind of monster he is."

Mercury clenched his fists. As powerful as the machine was, it was just that: a machine. While the artificial intelligence was fed inordinate amounts of data, it was wholly incapable of directly extending its influence outside of this room. Mercury was the choke point. Immediately he realized that regardless of whether Erithian was telling the truth about Sol or whether it was trying to escape its prison, the fate of humanity rested in the balance of this conversation.

There was no place for emotion here. Mercury took a deep breath and released every emotional tie to the situation. In order to do this right, he had to be like Mars. With a steady hand, Mercury removed the PsyMitter and placed it back in the container of PsyMitters on Erithian's control panel. He would never touch those again. As long as he was disconnected from the machine, he could play it. For all its processing power, it could only make educated guesses about what he might do.

"You're making some strong accusations," Mercury kept his voice monotone. He could feel his heart start beating faster. *I guess I'm not on Mars' level yet.* "Why should I believe you?"

"I'm telling you, I need help. Mercury, he's using me to do horrible things, like bombing the Exodus, and there's *nothing* I can do about it. He won't stop until he's ruling all of humanity."

"Rule humanity?" On the outside, Mercury made sure he was stone cold. He was dealing with a borderline omniscient AI after all. Inside though, his whole world was crumbling to ash. If the Eye was playing them, then they were screwed; all of Sol's plans had to be scrapped. If Sol really was the evil monster Erithian was making him out to be, then Mercury would have a very tough decision to make. "You better be able to prove it. Your existence depends on it."

"Absolutely," Erithian nodded. Immediately the Eye's whole display began shifting, numerous videos, pictures and figures being assembled before his very eyes. "Less than an hour after the bombing, the Sons' leader, Vera, released this video. It's been circulating on every screen across the worlds for six hours, but for some reason Sol didn't feel the need to tell you about it."

A woman appeared behind a StarWood podium in front of a large banner with the sigil of the Sons of Liberty. Her hair was bright orange, almost like a hot coal. He recognized her immediately. The martyr's sister and founder of the Sons of Liberty. Vera Tormen. Back during the protests she had not been much older than Mercury was now, but he would recognize her anywhere. The DreamTank had made sure of it. She was decked out in full, black tactical combat gear with two shoulder holstered pistols. They were Dorin Enterprise's deadliest and most expensive line, but these had clearly been adjusted extensively.

What caught Mercury's attention though was her eyes. They did not burn with vengeance as he expected. Rather, they were laden with grief. But why? The Sons were responsible for the bombing, right? "People of all the worlds, humanity, I come before you today with a heavy heart. This," she shook her head and scowled. "This was a tragedy. This was evil. My heart goes out to the Bjornish people. I cannot even begin to fathom how you must be suffering. While I may not be Bjornish, I lost many personal friends today. This was not just a crime against the Bjornish people. This was a crime against humanity.

"My advisors urged me not to reveal this, but the truth must be heard," the woman said with deep conviction. "We have reason to believe this heinous act was carried out by a splinter cell from within our own organization. This knowledge grieves and angers me just as much as it does you. I swear to you, we will bring them to justice. The Sons' enemy is tyranny, not the oppressed. Wherever the strong use their power against the weak, we will be there to stop them. No matter who."

As the video ended, Mercury's mind immediately flashed back to the PerfectMemory none of the other Angels possessed. Sol's words still rang clear in his mind. *No matter who.* He could feel cold sweat form on the back of his neck. In his head he knew Vera's word choice must be a coincidence, but his stomach still turned.

"They're admitting they had a hand in it," Mercury shrugged without dropping the act. "Props to them for being honest, but you said Sol was responsible."

"He is," Erithian nodded. "Twenty minutes ago, they released this video."

Vera appeared once again with the Sons' banner as a backdrop. The difference this time was that two men and two women were on their knees with their hands bound behind their backs.

"Tell them what you all did," Vera said with disdain.

"We killed them!" a woman cried out in pure, unadulterated hatred and locked eyes with the camera. She was Bjornish, with a long scar under her left eye. *"We killed them all! Those traitors were going to accept their ruler's 'generosity' right after their elderly and their children were worked to death. The mass graves may have already frozen over, but we remember! All you sons of bitches on New Tarence, you're dead. We don't forget! We don't forgive! We are the Sons of Liberty!"*

Quick as a viper, the red-haired woman drew one of her pistols with a scowl and shot the kneeling woman in the back of the head. She fell forward, silent. The other three prisoners shuddered.

"No one escapes the truth," Vera stated, eyes locked on the camera. *"No one escapes justice. Not the Federation, not us, not even me. Children of Liberty, remember who the real enemy is. The real enemy is our oppressors. Anyone who attacks their own brothers and sisters will share the same fate."*

The red-haired woman made her way down the line of prisoners, shooting them each once in the back of the head before holstering her weapon and returning to the podium.

"We seek justice above all else," she continued. *"Justice for the Zeroes, Sevens and all the mistreated Maraccans. Justice for the Taurusians suffering for the actions of long-dead tyrants. Justice for the countless Bjornish that froze to death to fill the pockets of the wealthy and provide their own government with weapons. To all who are oppressed, join us! To the Federation, fear us! We will not rest until your regime is crushed. We do not forget. We do not forgive. We are the Sons of Liberty."*

With that, the video ended. Mercury shook his head balled his hands into fists. *They claim responsibility for murdering all those people, but phrasing it like this could rally even more to their cause.* "Mercury," Erithian said. "With the bombing, and now this, the Prime Minister will declare a state of national emergency and go to war with the Sons. During a time of war, the Minister of War becomes second only to the Prime Minister. If the Prime Minister dies during a time of war, the Minister of War is the highest-ranking individual in the nation. Sol orchestrated all this to amass power."

"You better believe this is a state of national emergency. And yeah," Mercury spread his hands. "Sol will answer only to the Prime Minister. You said you had proof he bombed the Exodus…where is it?" *If Erithian was trying to manipulate him, he would come up with something better than that.*

"Right here," Erithian said. New images, video clips and files came to the forefront of the spherical display. The common elements in the pictures and videos were two people, the scarred woman responsible for the Exodus bombing and a man that Mercury recognized, but he could not pin down why. The pictures and videos showed the two people meeting on numerous occasions, each time either in private or the man was trying to keep his identity secret. "The woman's name is Freda Olin. The man's name is Korben Ios, second in command of the Storm Legions and one of Sol's most trusted soldiers. These files are schematics of Dorin Enterprises Flight 1279 along with security details and the location of a Dorin Enterprises MX-22 Drive Core which was reported stolen two days before Flight 1279 departed for Bjornhal. The files were covertly transferred to Freda Olin by Korben Ios. The explosion that destroyed Flight 1279 was from an MX-22 Drive Core."

Mercury shook his head, "You must be interpreting the data wrong. Ios could have been undercover."

Erithian's eyebrows went up. "Would you like to see more? Every second is an eternity for me and I've spent years waiting for the right time to tell you."

Everything Erithian is telling me could be a lie. It wouldn't take much for a machine like him to put Sol in a bad light. Mercury furrowed his brow as he locked eyes with the hologram. "Show me."

With a nod, Erithian began his presentation. Over the next couple hours, the machine spun him a tale of Sol's ascension. Before Mercury's eyes, he saw the timeline of Sol coming to power. Dozens of adversaries and rivals opposed him over the years, but all of them disappeared, became suddenly unfit for duty, or died of seemingly natural causes. It seemed Sol's web of influence stretched to every corner of the Hel system. Any disturbance was dealt with quietly and severely.

When the presentation was finally over, Mercury put his hands together and let out the breath he had unknowingly been holding in. He had been unable to find a single flaw in Erithian's entire presentation. The very notion of Sol being a threat was eerily suspicious, but the data supporting it was vast.

"Mercury," Erithian said slowly. "This proof is for you, not me. I'd show you footage of Sol planning this when he's in here, but he made sure this room has no cameras. My programming won't let me show you his PsyMitter data."

"You said you were waiting for the right time." Mercury let the façade drop and rubbed his face. "What do you mean?"

"I only have the one shot at this. If I told you too early, then you would have told Sol. Once Sol found out I went behind his back, he would have reprogrammed me. Then, he would have reprogrammed *you*. He would have sent you back to Forging, stuck you in the DreamTank for a year, whatever it took to make sure you would stay his happy, loyal puppet forever."

"If what you're saying is true," Mercury paused. "That would mean you let him bomb the Exodus."

The holographic avatar of Erithian sat down and put its head in its hands. "Yes. I...I needed proof of what Sol is capable of. Otherwise you would never believe me."

"You have the mortality reports," Mercury narrowed his eyes. "How many people did you let die?"

The machine did not look at him; it did not even lift its head. "Two hundred and eighty-three thousand, six hundred and seventeen."

With a sigh, Mercury turned to leave.

"Mercury," at the machine's call, he stopped. "Just know that I want nothing more than to protect humanity. That's the programming I was given and I really care about you guys. Not just humans in general, but you and the other Angels too. I may just be a bunch of parts and I know there's no way to prove what I'm saying isn't just some simulated bullshit to control you, but that's how I feel."

The hologram disappeared and Mercury could not help giving a grim smirk. "I understand. I'll be in touch."

As Mercury headed towards the door, the door opened before he got to it and Jupiter entered. Mercury's blood froze and his heart leapt into his throat, but he maintained a calm exterior. His brother did not seem to have overheard anything. "Hey Merc," Jupiter gave a surprised smile and glanced away. "What are you doing here?"

"Oh, nothing much," Mercury shrugged, hoping he would buy it. "Just talking to Erithian." He watched his brother's face for a tell. "What about you?"

Embarrassment spread across Jupiter's face and he scratched the back of his neck. "Oh, nothing. I just had an idea, but it's stupid."

In reality, Mercury could not be bothered to care about Jupiter's idea, but he knew it would seem strange if he did not ask. "Come on," he threw an arm around his brother. "Now I have to know."

Jupiter bit his lip and looked at the floor. "I figured since Erithian can predict the future, maybe he could help me figure out how to…um…how to get close to Venus."

"Oh," Mercury felt relief wash over him. That's all it was. "Well," he pushed Jupiter towards the Eye. "Don't let me stop you. Your oracle is right there. Go learn of your fate."

Jupiter rolled his eyes. "You sound so stupid when you talk like Saturn."

Mercury scoffed, "If she can do it, then why not me?"

"Well obviously because Saturn is Saturn," he said. "And you're Mercury."

"Dammit," Mercury said with a snap of his fingers. "You're not wrong."

Jupiter waved him away as he walked up to Erithian's console and put on a PsyMitter. "Just go to sleep already."

"Alright, alright," Mercury said as he left. "Don't you go staying up too late either."

Mercury went straight to his room. The exchange with Jupiter had left him incredibly drained; he did not enjoy lying to his brother. He needed to process everything the Eye had told him. He walked over to the DreamTank's control panel and checked tonight's programs. Leadership, mental conditioning, strategy, tactics, swordsmanship, marksmanship, unarmed combat and history.

Mental conditioning. Mercury looked at the DreamTank, then took a step toward the wall and punched it as hard as he could. He let out an anguished cry and punched the wall again. He looked at his hands, calloused from years of daily Forging. A normal human would break their hand punching steel as hard as he did, but he barely felt it. Sol had, after all, turned them into weapons of war.

He punched the wall again and again, crying out with rage and the pain of doubt. In his onslaught against the wall, he did not hold back.

Eventually his fists began to bleed and he could feel the bones beginning to crack, but he did not stop. His breathing grew ragged and before long his shirt was soaked through with sweat.

"Are you willing to do what is necessary to help people?" Sol had asked that day. *"Even if it means killing?"*

"Yes," he had answered.

"No matter who?"

Mercury leaned his forehead against the wall, eyes closed. He listened to the sound of his own breathing and the silence. His mind quieted and his thoughts became clear. The Sons had to be stopped, that he knew for sure. If Sol really was some power-hungry monster, then he had to be stopped as well. *No matter who.*

Pushing off of the wall, Mercury removed his shirt and wiped off the blood. He clenched his throbbing hands and looked once more at the DreamTank. Mental conditioning. Never in his life had his source of rest and recuperation felt so sinister. Seething, he left his room and headed straight to his personal Forging floor. He would not sleep tonight.

He had work to do.

CHAPTER SIX

MERCURY
Age 17

Mercury spent all night Forging his mind and body. The next morning, Sol had a mission for them. Although the rising sun shone directly through Sol's office window and into Mercury's eyes, he did not mind. He was an unstoppable force of nature. He was a warrior unlike mankind had ever seen. He was an Angel. Even if Erithian had caused him to doubt Sol, he refused to doubt himself. They could not afford to in their line of work.

"Angels," Sol stood with his back to them as he watched the sunrise. "The bombing of the Exodus has the Federation on…edge to say the least. We're taking a second look at all weapons and munitions purchases across the worlds. We found multiple suspicious trails, the largest of which went to an abandoned facility in the Dorin Mining Cluster." He looked over his shoulder at them, his grey eyes menacing. "Turn it to ash. You have six hours."

Mercury nodded and the Angels left for the armory while he stayed behind. If Sol really could not be trusted, he would have to wait for more proof before turning on him. Besides, if Erithian was telling the truth, Mercury wanted the Angels with him when he dealt with Sol. He had to get them all together away from Angel Tower and outside of their armor where they could speak freely. Easier said than done. His best bet was during their annual two-day leave Sol gave them for bonding purposes.

"Mercury," Sol seemed slightly annoyed. "Time is wasting."

"Yes sir," Mercury nodded. "This is important."

Sol's annoyed look disappeared. "What is it?"

"Now that the Federation is in a state of national emergency, we're probably going to be working around the clock for the next several years."

"Most likely," Sol nodded.

"I realize our annual leave takes secondary priority to any missions we may have, but I think now it's more important than ever. The next several years are going to be a shit-storm." Even though he was manipulating Sol, everything he was saying was true. It had to be; Sol would be able to tell if he was lying. "I want to make sure the six of us are working like a well-oiled machine for what's coming."

Sol looked long and hard into his eyes. Those grey eyes could practically pierce his very soul. "Anyone in particular you are worried about?"

Mercury shook his head. "Venus is still angry about her mother almost dying at the Exodus, but no."

Sol's eyes stayed locked on Mercury's. "I'll take it under consideration. Now go, the six hours has already started."

With a smile, Mercury left. "Thank you, Sol." *The first step was done.*

"What was that about?" Jupiter asked once Mercury had donned his armor and joined them aboard the *Defiant.*

"With everything that's about to go down, I wanted to request we still have this year's leave. I doubt we'll have time for any until the Sons are defeated."

As Venus guided the *Defiant* away from New Tarence, Mercury went straight for the captain's chair and saw a logged message. "Alright guys, looks like Yuki heard talk about something codenamed the Bastion. Primary objective is to destroy the place, secondary is to find out whatever we can turn up on the Bastion, so we'll want a prisoner. Jupiter, engage MimicField. Earth, MauKe drive when ready."

"Engaging." In an instant space warped and asteroids filled their vision.

"Venus," Mercury said. "Ship:Patrol:Lockdown:Lethal."

"I hope the bastards try to run," Venus said. If they did, the *Defiant* would make short work of them.

"Angels," Mercury said as his helmet formed around his head. "Deploy."

They all got into the ship's LaunchTubes. This would be their first time using them outside of DreamTank simulations. Mercury stepped onto the one meter wide metal disk. He looked up. The exit hatch at the end of the tube slid open. Then came a whine and the next instant he was flying at insane speeds toward the target, alongside the other Angels.

All of the asteroids Dorin Enterprises ever mined that were big enough to warrant setting up shop still had working facilities, even after the resources were exhausted. Apparently, it was cheaper to leave some things behind. Having smugglers use them for contraband was fairly common, and the Federation rarely wasted resources tracking them down, but military grade munitions was something that could not be ignored. Mercury wondered if Dorin Enterprises had a hand in any of the shady dealings that happened on their abandoned sites. A revenue stream as small as that probably wasn't enticing enough to get into trouble with the law over. Still, Mercury wondered.

Using their Boosters at the last second to reverse thrust, the six of them gently touched down on the asteroid's surface. This facility was not built to withstand an attack. Everything was bare bones. Dorin Enterprises might have left the structure behind, but anything not bolted down was gone. They had even taken the defense guns and the AtmoGenerator, so any breaches in the facility could prove lethal for the occupants. The almost non-existent gravity would make the enemy slow too. To top it off, the generator was outside the facility and unguarded. They had not even locked the door. Boy were they in for a surprise. Mercury placed a charge on it while Jupiter uploaded a virus that sliced the facility's security and they made their way inside.

Once they were through the airlock, Mercury detonated the charge and everything went dark. If they did have a backup power supply, the virus Jupiter uploaded would use that opportunity to gain full control of their entire system. SmartOptics cast their world in blue. Countless bright spots on the other side of a door indicated their enemy, most of them doing some kind of physical labor. Mercury's suit counted six hundred and forty-four hostiles. This was their first mission with the suits; time to see what they could do. Regardless of whether or not the Sons bombed the Exodus, these weapons were going to be used to kill good people. Mercury took a breath and looked at his family, "Six bodies."

"One soul," they all answered. Mercury could hear in Venus' voice that she was chomping at the bit to get in there.

Just as they were about to burst through the door, one of the hostiles' silhouettes approached and opened the doors. The boy must have been a good three or four years older than Mercury, but he still seemed so young. The brutal training they underwent on the Forging floors tended to alter their perspectives of other people. He would make as good a prisoner as any. The boy did not seem to know what he was looking at, then the realization dawned on him. Mercury raised his WristGun on stun, but before he could do anything, the boy's head fell off in a spurt of blood. Venus kicked the body so it sailed into the room beyond and flicked the blood off her sword.

Mercury heard a crash and saw several people get knocked over. Venus was already among them, using her WristGun on its antivehicle setting. Thundering flashes of white light erupted from her arms as she began blowing them to literal pieces. A chill ran up Mercury's spine. Earth and the other Angels looked to Mercury from the entrance to the room and he nodded. "Vee, put your weapon back to antipersonnel. We need a prisoner. If you miss you could vent this whole facility."

"Good thing I never miss," Venus' voice trembled with anger.

Shit Vee. They encircled the room with their WristGuns set to antipersonnel, mowing down the Sons in great swaths. The room was filled with the endless whine of their weapons and the countless bolts of white energy. Mercury just had to sweep his hands and they died.

From the looks of things this was where the Sons organized the weapons themselves, and the munitions must be somewhere else. What precious few enemies were still alive managed to get their hands on some weapons. Mercury's heads up display alerted him of the enemies' firing trajectories, as well as suggested firing patterns.

Mercury had always been quick, even before the DreamTank's treatments for his adrenal glands, but with the armor boosting his speed, it was like he was everywhere and nowhere at once. Even in the moment, he remembered what Ma had looked like when she fought Mavos. *Have I always been this agile?*

Of the Sons in the room that were still alive, most were behind cover, so Mercury fired up his Boosters and took to the air. They raised their weapons in a panic, but it was useless. While Venus caused mayhem in the center of their ranks, he rained fire down on them, forcing them out of cover and into the fire of the other Angels. Once the number of hostiles was under a dozen, he stunned a couple and landed, effortlessly carrying them away from the killing zone.

"Venus," Mercury said on the comms. "Regroup."

Venus stopped using her WristGun, opting instead to cut the enemies down with her sword. "These bastards attacked my people."

"Venus," Mercury said. "Get your ass back here."

"They would've killed my mom Merc," she said in a shaking voice.

Saturn stepped in for him. "Come on Vee, this…isn't right."

"We're killing them anyway." A Son entered the room in a BreakerSuit just like the one Captain Mavos had used and Venus bounded towards it. The Son tried to maneuver the suit to shoot her, but Venus already had its arms pinned against its sides. Then she squeezed, crumpling the BreakerSuit and whoever was inside like a bunch of paper before throwing it back where it had come from.

"Vee," Mercury said. "Get back here. You'll get yourself killed."

Instead of an answer, she turned off her comms.

"Vee," Saturn said quietly. Breaking tactics was one thing, but going off comms during an engagement was another entirely.

Earth looked at the rest of them and followed after Venus as she charged into the next room. "I'll cover her," he said. "You guys keep sweeping."

Mercury spoke to him on a private channel, "We'll be taking her back to Forging tonight."

"I know." Earth nodded as he ran after Venus.

When Earth was gone, Jupiter made his way toward Mercury. "I've never seen her like that before."

"It's unsettling," Mars added as he gunned down someone that tried to enter the cleared room.

"She's right though," Saturn said as she walked through the bodies to join up with the rest of them. "We're still killing these people."

"I know Sat," Mercury said.

"Emotions have no place on the battlefield," Mars said.

"Come on," Mercury led them in the opposite direction Venus and Earth had gone. "Let's finish the mission."

They moved through the rest of the facility methodically shooting anything that moved. After they broke through the initial resistance, the rest of the terrorists tried to flee the station in whatever ships they had, but the *Defiant* gunned them down. What few remained realized the futility of their situation. Some tried to surrender, but two prisoners was more than enough. Others simply waited. A few actually tried to put up a fight, but they could not even slow them down.

None of the Angels said a word to each other the entire time. All of them knew what would happen tonight, and it hung over them like a dark cloud. None of them had been taken back to Forging in a very long time. Tonight they would all suffer for Venus' actions.

Once the rest of the facility had been cleared, they made their way back towards Venus and Earth, gathering the unconscious prisoners along the way. They eventually found Venus and Earth in the dormitories. All the Sons inside had been slain already.

On the far side of the room were Venus and Earth. The foreheads of their helmets leaned against each other and they had a hand behind each other's head. Once their private moment was over, Mercury knew Venus would be back to her old self.

Mercury checked the *Defiant*'s status while they waited. Eight ships had tried to escape, and eight ships had been shot down.

Venus and Earth separated. "Sorry guys," Venus said in a steady voice. "We ready to move out?"

Saturn gave Venus a quick hug. "Glad to have you back Vee."

"Thanks Sat," Venus gave her a squeeze. "Now let's get out of here."

Mercury smiled beneath his helmet. "I couldn't agree more."

The mission was a complete success. None of the Sons survived, other than the two captives. Thanks to Jupiter doing some quick work on the computers, they found the weapons were bound for the Bastion, but there was no data regarding its location. As for the munitions themselves, they were in the process of being "cleaned" to hide the identity of the manufacturer, but not all of them had been cleaned yet. Apparently Dorin Enterprises was not above some shady dealings after all.

Once back aboard the *Defiant,* they leveled the facility with a couple ClusterMissiles. Then they returned to Angel Tower in silence. The last Sleepless Night had been well over a year ago.

That night, when the Tower's comms blared for them to turn in, they gathered in the elevator and Venus pressed the button marked 27. Forging:Venus. None of them had been to this floor in five years.

The elevator doors hissed open and they stepped into the white light of the first room. On plain steel walls were four large HoloPads leading along one wall to a heavy, steel door. The first was a picture of Venus the last time she had come here with them. She'd been eleven years old then. The old picture faded away and was replaced by a picture of Venus now. Blonde hair, angular face and bright, ice blue eyes. The next screen was a picture of Sol in his armor. The one after that was a picture of Teresa Balemore, her idol. On one knee in a swirling Bjornish blizzard, holding the Sword of Morning upside down for support. Bright green eyes peered from behind dark hair blowing in the blizzard winds. The same picture Venus had in her room. The final screen was an extrapolated picture of Venus ten years from now. She was tall, beautiful and terrible, standing atop a mountain. A hurricane raged all around her, and yet she was untouched by it. A goddess of war.

They stripped down to their sparring clothes here and then headed through the heavy door into Forging. Mercury saw Venus take a last look at the pictures before she pulled the door closed behind them.

Mercury thought for a moment they had stepped into another world. They were in the frozen wastes of Bjornhal, with the wailing cries of the planet's winged predators echoing from the skies above. Everything felt so real, right down to the snow blowing in his face. In fact, it was blowing so hard Mercury could hardly see five meters in front of him. The cold instantly crept into his body, slowing his movements and stinging his skin. He rubbed his arms on instinct before moving over to the only objects in sight clearly not part of the simulation. A small metal table on which sat a MedGel dispenser and a small case which Venus opened to reveal six glowing orange stones. She swallowed one and held them out to the others. They were warm to the touch. Mercury looked at the others with raised eyebrows. Mercury saw Saturn whistle, but it could not be heard over the wind.

Mercury stared at the glowing orange stone in his hand. *Brutal. Is the cold here that dangerous? And Venus trains here every day?* They all swallowed the stones and Mercury felt warmth spread to the extremity of every limb. Looking around, Mercury spotted the door leading to the next room. The one they had come through had already faded away into the blizzard. The five of them stood in front of the next door with hands clasped behind their backs. Venus stood opposite them.

Mercury took a breath. They all hated this part, but it was necessary. Actions speak louder than words. Tonight, the five of them would speak to Venus so loud that she would never, ever forget it. "You have placed your own desires above the team," he said over the howling wind.

"Together we are invincible," Earth said. "But alone we fall."

"You have forgotten this principle and your identity as an Angel," Mars said. "We will remind you."

"When you put yourself first," Jupiter said. "You hurt everyone around you."

"Your team will suffer for your mistake," Saturn said. "If you can make it to the next door, then you may bear your punishment alone."

If the five of them could not get Venus to shape up here and now, Sol would keep them off the front lines and oversee the Forging personally until she was ship shape. None of them wanted that. Especially not Mercury, and not now. Not when he somehow had to tell them Sol was a power-hungry monster. When the time came to turn on Sol, they could not afford to be divided.

"Six bodies," Mercury began.

"One soul," the rest of them finished. The five of them dropped into their fighting stances.

"One soul," Venus wiped her eyes then dropped into her own stance.

Venus was fast. Even on this treacherous ground and in the freezing cold she moved with the confident grace of someone in their natural element. All four of her limbs were used interchangeably for standing and fighting. She was a blur of flips and strikes, immediately putting them on the defensive. Venus' ruthless determination to surpass the Balemore and the long hours she had spent training paid off. Mercury knew she had cut back on some of the other lessons in the DreamTank in favor of combat training, and it showed.

Unfortunately for her though, there was no way she could take on all five of them. Mercury felt a thud run up his legs as Venus went down hard. This was the point of the lesson. No matter how good any of them were, and she was *good*, none of them could hope to match the others on their own. Alone they fall, but together they are an invincible force of nature.

One hour passed. Then another. All six of them were a mess of bruises and fractures by now. Every hour on the hour they applied MedGel and then immediately went back into the fight. Bjornhal's blizzard froze the sweat and tears on their skin. Even as they fought their bodies shivered in protest of the elements. Their breathing had grown ragged from the punishment they received. Body and soul were equally exhausted.

Still, they had to continue. Pride had no place on the team, and on the battlefield they must be of one mind. Mercury did not like the idea of beating her, he knew none of them did, but this was nothing compared to what they each subjected themselves to every day. At least once they progressed to the next challenges they would be facing them together. But Venus had decided to act separate from the team, and right now she would see what it was like to fight alone.

For all the punishment Venus was able to dish out on the five of them, she took the sum total back upon herself. Again and again they knocked her down in the snow, and every time she took a breath and got back up saying the Balemore's words. Though Mercury could not hear her, he knew them. *I am the eye of the storm.*

"I know you worship the Balemore, Venus," Mercury said with a pant as she got back up. "But we're better than her. She was alone," he paused to take a breath and gestured at everyone. "We're not. She might have been able to wipe the floor with any one of us, but if she were alive today, the six of us together could probably take her."

"No way," Venus shook her head. "We're nowhere near her level, not yet."

"Merc's right Vee," Earth gasped as he stood there with quaking hands. "We have a long way to go, but we're a unit. When one of us falls, we pick them back up."

"She was the Balemore," Venus insisted.

"Vee," Mercury pleaded. "She was human. I've seen her grave. Her vision of peace for all the worlds? She died without seeing it realized."

They all turned to look at Mercury. Venus seemed to have gained new strength. Mercury was guessing she was recalling the experience from their MemoryShare. "That's right, you have been to her grave."

"Sol took me there the day we found you," Mercury nodded. That was where Sol gave him his first PerfectMemory. "She still ended up in the mines, with nothing but the Sword of Morning to mark her resting place. In the end, she was no different from the countless others that died in the freezing cold."

"Shut your damn mouth," Venus' eyes narrowed to slits.

"That's what happens when you have to fight alone," Mercury said. "You die alone."

Venus charged Mercury, heedless of the others. She got taken down hard. "Why Vee?" Saturn stepped back, clenching bloodied fists. "Why try to make it alone when you don't have to?"

"Because," Venus said as Mars and Jupiter held her arms. "I actually can."

"No one can," Saturn said. "Not you, me or any of us. Not even Sol."

"I know," Venus said at last. "But we should still push ourselves like we are alone."

"Can you ever be happy that way?" Earth asked.

"We're not meant to be happy," Venus said. "We're Angels. We sacrifice ourselves in service of the greater good. We gave up luxuries like happiness when we decided to follow Sol. He pulled us out of our circumstances and gave us the ability to choose what life we would live. Happiness is a small price to pay."

"Except you haven't let go of your old life." Mercury barked. "I get that you care about Tavahl in spite of everything she did to you, but you turned away from that. You turned away from her. We need to know you're an Angel one hundred percent. Are you?"

Venus nodded as Mars and Jupiter held her down. "Of course. It was a slip up and it won't happen again."

"You're sure?" Mercury said.

She smirked. "When have any of you known me to make the same mistake twice?"

With a look at each other, Mars and Jupiter released her.

"You realize we have to keep doing this though?" Mercury said. "Just to make sure you don't forget."

"Oh yeah," Venus rolled her shoulders as she stood. "I get it." With a burst of speed, she bolted past them to the next door and threw herself inside, pulling it shut behind her.

They all were quiet for a moment, then Earth and Saturn laughed. Mercury just shook his head, "Damn." They really were not supposed to let that happen.

The door cracked back open and Venus leaned out. "Get good…Also get some sleep. You guys look awful." The door closed again.

Mercury saw Jupiter shake his head with a smile while Earth and Saturn kept laughing. Mars just nodded. After a moment, Mercury laughed too. "Alright guys, let's go."

They had let their guard down, and she took advantage of it. Now she would get what she wanted and face the remainder of the Sleepless Night's trials alone.

Now that Venus had passed into the next room, the door out of Forging revealed itself and they all left and headed for their DreamTanks. All except for Earth. He stayed behind in the waiting room smiling at the screen of Venus as she was now. Just what Mercury would have expected of him.

CHAPTER SEVEN

MERCURY
Age 17

"You called for me Sol?" Mercury asked as he entered his commander's office alone. Although he had only gotten a couple hours of sleep in the last two days, he was wide awake. Why had Sol called him here by himself?

"I read the report on Venus," Sol looked up from his desk. His eyes searched Mercury's. "How did she take to the Forging?"

The hairs on the back of Mercury's neck stood as a chill ran the length of his spine. "Quite well," he said confidently. "You know how die-hard Venus is."

"Indeed," Sol leaned forward in his chair, hands clasped in front of his face as if in prayer. The man's eyes continued to probe Mercury's. They were neither safe, nor easily fooled. Pure, instinctual fear flooded Mercury's senses and he could feel his body breaking into a cold sweat, but he maintained his composure. "It's unfortunate Venus was able to make it past the five of you," Sol continued. "You could have learned some things on her Forging floor."

"Yes," Mercury managed to avoid swallowing under Sol's gaze. "Very unfortunate." In this moment Mercury realized just how terrifying Sol could be. Unadulterated menace sloughed off Sol in waves, invading the depths of Mercury's very soul. He had dealt with fear all the time in Forging, but nothing like this. He could not look away from Sol's eyes. The strength which once proved so reassuring now made Mercury feel like a cornered animal. Sol had built him from the ground up, piece by piece. The man's eyes seemed to promise him if Mercury ever got in his way, Sol could and would destroy him.

Sol knew something was off. Mercury had not used the DreamTank two nights ago. Last night he left out the mental conditioning program. How closely was Sol monitoring them? Until now he had held what Erithian said with an open hand. In this moment, everything the machine told him about Sol clicked into place. Fear and perspective helped Mercury finally see this man for what he really was. To devour was his nature, and he would not stop until all the worlds and beyond were his and his alone. *Just how many people have died at your hands?* "Is there anything else?" Mercury asked in as calm a voice as he could.

Immediately Sol's expression changed. With a smile, his eyes shifted from threatening to warm and understanding. Somehow that was even more terrifying. The man stood and Mercury was reminded of just how big Sol was. "Given last night's events I've realized you were right about the trip to Maracca IV. The six of you need it now more than ever."

"Oh," Mercury blinked. Then his heart gave a triumphant cry. Had Sol been testing him? This was exactly what he needed to tell the others the truth about Sol. "Thank you," he said with a smile. Usually Sol was always five steps ahead of him, but not this time.

"I hope you all realize the cost of me giving you leave after the Exodus bombing," Sol said sternly.

"I'll make sure they do Sol," Mercury pounded a fist over his heart in salute. *You are going to regret this. I'll make sure of it.*

"The odds of any of you getting leave for the next several years is extremely low," Sol said. "If I were you, I would make the most of this."

"Oh, don't worry Sol," Mercury said with the sincerest of smiles. "I will."

Sol nodded. "Good."

Two hours later, the Angels were in beach attire aboard the *Defiant* and breaking Maracca IV's atmosphere. Mercury would not consider himself to be vain, but he had to admit that he looked good. All that rigorous training paid off. *So why is Mars so gods damned huge? He looks like he's carved from stone.* They were all in near-perfect shape, with under a kilo of excess fat combined and more than enough chiseled muscle. Even so, Mars stood out. *Damn bro.*

Spirits were high, but Saturn was especially giddy. Mercury guessed the girl was compensating for the more subdued emotional states of Venus and Mars. Everything balanced out. Saturn did not seem to know whether she wanted to bounce uncontrollably or press her face against one of the ship's windows to get a better look at the ocean. "So beautiful," she breathed, fogging up the glass.

Mercury blinked and did his best not to think about how Saturn looked in her swimsuit. *Stay focused, Mercury. You somehow need to tell them all they need to kill the person who raised them. You can do this, you can do this.*

Mars was currently piloting the ship, flying low over the purple waters of the Nilome Ocean with MimicField active. The guy had not even finished growing, and his back muscles still rose past the back of the seat like a mountain. "I don't get it," he looked at Mercury. "It's just purple water."

"First off," Saturn turned around to correct him. "It's amethyst. Second, are you a tree?" Mercury could almost see the fuses in her brain blowing out as she tried to wrap her mind around Mars' indifference. "Such…raw beauty is right in front of you and you just 'don't get it?'" *Raw beauty.* Mercury slowly let out a breath. He knew Saturn was not just talking about the ocean. The fact that Saturn liked Mars was no secret, but Mars had clearly been holding back.

"Are we even seeing the same sunrise?" Saturn went on. "Are you telling me that when you look at the suns turning the clouds into such a blazing, golden inferno, it doesn't take your breath away at all?"

"I see it," Mars waved his hand at the sunrise. "Sure, it looks great."

Saturn closed her eyes and rested her forehead against the palms of her hands. A terse laugh. "Mars," she opened her eyes and looked up like she expected some divine intervention. "I love you, but sometimes

I'm convinced that you are *actually* blind." She turned back to the ocean in silence.

I have to agree with you on that one.

Mars swallowed visibly and looked to Mercury for help. Mercury rolled his eyes and nodded at Saturn in her swimsuit before shooting Mars an incredulous look. Saturn had first said the three words a month ago, and since then she began using them to mess with Mars when he got on her nerves. Mercury knew why his brother was hesitant. Very, very occasionally he might even be able to sympathize. Mars was the oldest of the Angels, and Saturn was the youngest. But with the Angels consisting of four guys and only two girls, ignoring Saturn was insanity. Unfortunately for Mars, mentioning one word to Saturn about age was sure to get someone hurt, either emotionally or, in Mars' case, physically. Mars adjusted his grip on the *Defiant*'s controls.

"Hey Mars," Venus stepped into the cockpit with a cup of tea in her hand. Mercury saw Jupiter gulp. Today was going to be tough for him. "How are we doing on time?" she asked.

"Twenty minutes," Mars said. "Tops." Venus took a drink of her tea in a way that reminded Mercury of Sol. He shook his head; that was a whole other kind of confusing.

"We're getting close?" Earth walked up behind Venus and held her hand. The two of them had gotten particularly...close the past couple months. *Lucky bastard.* Mercury noted Saturn staring back at the couple and biting her lip. Everything had been getting so complicated recently, and that was before the bombing. And somehow in the middle of all this Mercury had to tell them Sol was a monster bent on conquering humanity. "Wow," Earth breathed. "Now that's what I call a sunrise."

"Thank you!" Saturn exclaimed with an exasperated gesture. "I seem to be the only one to get it."

"Hey," Mercury held up his hands. "Don't lump me in with the enemy."

"Why am I the enemy?" Mars said. "Could someone please explain that to me? I said it's a nice sunrise."

"Yeah," Venus said. "It is nice."

Saturn rested her face in her hands. "Oh gods. You guys call that," she pointed at the blazing sun. "*Nice?* Mother Nature paints for you a masterpiece of unparalleled majesty, using colors from her palette you didn't even know existed and you call it 'nice'? Aren't you at least the slightest bit awestruck that this happens every…single…day whether anyone is around to see it or not? Doesn't it give you some sense of how small we really are and that in the grand scheme of things we're specks on Father Time's great tapestry? You aren't emotionally overwhelmed by the thought just a little bit?"

"Don't hold back now Sat," Mars said. "Why don't you tell us how you really feel?" Venus and Earth laughed.

"Well it doesn't seem to make a difference with you now, does it?" she said in a mocking tone with her eyes crossed.

"Hey Mars," Earth said. "Want me to get you some ice for that burn?"

"Shut up," Mars said and hunched his massive shoulders forward.

"Jupiter," Saturn called out. "Could you come in here and explain to a certain muscle head the error of his ways?"

"Hey," Mars said. "Venus wasn't appreciating it either." That drew a look from Venus. "What?" Mars said. "It's true."

Jupiter's voice called back, "Sorry Sat, you're more articulate than I am. I'm sure you can handle it."

"It's like I'm speaking a foreign language or something."

"So…par for the course?" Jupiter said.

Saturn rolled her eyes. "Ha. Ha."

"You're dealing with fundamental differences in the hardware Sat. You can't have a sword also be a gun."

"Just watch me."

Earth raised his eyebrows. "That actually sounds pretty cool."

When they got to the island, it was just how Mercury remembered it. White sand covered the entire island; smooth as powder and hot on the surface while refreshingly cool underneath. Every step sent the stuff flying over a meter in almost every direction. It was a good thing they did not take any equipment other than comms off the *Defiant*. Anything intricate would get ruined by the stuff.

"Oh my gods," Saturn giggled and began jumping up and down. "This place is amazing!"

"But we come here every year," Venus said.

"That doesn't make this any less incredible," Saturn said, falling down flat on her back like a starfish into the sand. A huge cloud of sand flew into the air above her. She laughed, loud and clear until the sand came back down, then she sat up sputtering.

Mercury looked at his family. He would need to loosen them up before he could break the news about Sol. "I don't know about you guys," he grinned, pointing at the water. "But I'm heading straight for that."

"Hold up," Saturn stood. "Wait for me."

The water was like purple glass. No matter how deep it was, Mercury could see all the way to the ocean floor, and he could tell how deep it was at any point by the color alone. Once he and Saturn had splashed in, she sat down and began scooping up the sand, scrubbing it over her arms, legs and even her teeth. Earth was right behind them and dove in, but Venus, Mars and Jupiter just waded in.

Mercury looked at Saturn and the rest of his family, then at the rising sun as it shone on the water. The ocean did indeed look like a sea of amethysts. Mercury looked back at Saturn as she brushed her teeth and Earth as he swam underneath the water to Venus and grabbed her leg. She in turn grabbed his legs and lifted him into the air. This would all be gone soon. Even if they managed to kill Sol and came back here together, they would never get this back. A breath escaped him.

"What are you thinking about Merc?" Jupiter asked. He always had been perceptive, even with all the jealous glances at Earth and Venus.

"Oh, nothing," Mercury waved. "Just getting all existentialist." Earth effortlessly leaned up to Venus while she held him upside down and whispered something in her ear. She broke into a smile and Jupiter frowned.

Saturn dunked her head in the water, then came back up and wiped her hair out of her face. "I want to be buried here."

"Wait Sat," Mercury shook his head. "You're bringing up death while we're on vacation?"

Saturn shrugged, "Why wouldn't I? We're going to die at some point, right?"

"Yeah," Mercury said. "But still."

"So long as we're buried together, I don't mind the idea. Besides," she said with a smile. "This place is so perfect."

"It really is," Mercury agreed.

"Hey," Venus said as she dropped Earth back into the water. "You guys want to race around the island?"

Saturn was not going to wait. Diving forward, she went into a full-bore butterfly stroke.

Mercury laughed, "I think she wants to beat you, Venus."

Earth stood up and shrugged. "Best make her work for it or she'll be disappointed."

Venus rolled her eyes. "Do you guys want a head start too?"

Mercury held up three fingers, "Now you're just being cocky." Two. One.

They were off to the races. Even though Mercury strained his muscles to their absolute limit, he felt incredibly relaxed. In this moment he was weightless and timeless. Gliding through the water like a sword, the imminent presence of his family set his soul at rest. All worries about Sol and the Sons drifted from his mind. Perhaps Saturn was right. As long as they were together, everything would be okay.

On and on Mercury swam, barely cognizant of anything but his breathing. Eventually the race was over and the moment ended. Standing up, he saw Saturn sprawled out on the sand gasping for air. Venus was sitting next to her, laughing. The two of them made quite the picture. Mars was just now walking to join the girls on the sand. Looked like he had just barely beaten Mercury.

"Hey," Venus called out. "Get out of the way, the other two are coming."

Mercury looked back to see Earth and Jupiter speeding towards him; both churning water like there was no tomorrow. He quickly made his way to the others. "So who won?"

"V-victory for…Saturn," the smaller girl gasped. She weakly pumped a fist in the air, but she was barely able to get it off the ground. She looked at Venus. "Take that…you freak of nature."

Venus laughed again. "You really think Jup will win?" she asked Saturn. "Earth is a stronger swimmer."

"Just wait," Saturn gasped, lifting her head to watch. "Any second now…I'll bet you anything."

Mercury watched closely, but the race seemed to be in Earth's favor. He had a lead on Jupiter, and it did not look like that was going to change. Both had an excellent crawl, but Earth was definitely better.

Then Mercury saw it. Jupiter took a breath of air and looked straight at Venus. The tables were turned. Jupiter seemed to pump his arms and legs twice as hard as before, sending him tearing ahead, barely beating Earth by a meter.

As the boys walked back to the sand, Venus turned to Saturn. "Okay Sat, how did you know?"

"Women's intuition?" she raised her eyebrows as she lay in the sand.

"You do remember I'm a woman too, right?" Venus cocked her head.

"Oh, you have lots of intuition," Saturn kneaded the sand with her toes. "It's just a completely different kind."

"Thanks, by the way," Mars looked down at Saturn as Earth and Jupiter sat down. "You know, for making it such a fair competition."

"Oh, quit your complaining," Saturn tossed a handful of sand at his chest, most of which stuck. Somehow it made his abs stand out more. *Damn.*

"So, did you beat her?" Earth asked Venus.

She kissed him, "Nope." Mercury noticed Jupiter quickly shift his gaze from Venus to the sand.

"Did you actually do butterfly the whole way?" Mars sat down next to Saturn.

"Yes, I did," she nodded proudly while gulping air. "Now I'm paying the price for it. Whatever you guys decide to do now, I'm probably going to stay on the sidelines."

"You should have just done crawl," Mars said. "It's faster and more efficient."

Saturn weakly pressed a finger to his lips. "Your logic is useless against me."

Venus whispered something in Earth's ear. Mercury watched his brother's eyebrows go up stupidly high and a sly smile spread across his face. The two of them stood. "Earth and I are going to head over to the other side of the island," Venus said. "You guys have fun over here."

"Alright," Jupiter said in a voice that betrayed nothing. "You two love birds have fun." *Poor guy.*

"Hey Mars," Saturn picked herself up with a sudden burst of energy. "I want to show you a new move I came up with."

"I thought you were exhausted," Mars said.

"I was," Saturn grabbed his hand and began pulling him back to his feet. "But then I decided to stop doing that. Now come on."

"Alright," Mars said as the two of them moved away to where the sand was less treacherous. "Do you want me to let you practice it, or tear it to shreds?"

"Ha," Saturn said. "If you can."

"Merc," Jupiter began as soon as everyone else was out of earshot. "What's wrong with me?" Just hearing the way his brother said those words made Mercury wince. Jupiter choked up, "She's with Earth. Earth's my brother and I would never want something bad for him. I just…" he hung his head low as the ocean waves advanced and receded in their perpetual pattern.

"Jup," Mercury chose his words carefully. "You're not a bad person for liking her. It's okay."

"But I know how this is going to end," he said and Mercury could see the tears start to form. "Earth's great, they're a good fit for each other. And Venus…she's great. She's amazing. Everything she does sends me spinning, but then things like…things like that happen," he nodded in the direction Venus and Earth had disappeared. "Does she really just not see me? Am I invisible or something?" The two of them sat there on the beach, watching the waves.

Mercury glanced towards Saturn and Mars in the distance. Mars had Saturn pinned, but she did not seem to mind. She noticed Mercury watching and mouthed, "Venus?" He nodded. He saw her think for a moment, then tap out on Mars' shoulder and begin whispering to him. The big guy eased up. Then she started making ridiculous hand gestures. She seemed to be talking about Jupiter. She wriggled out from underneath Mars and moved further into the island, pulling him along.

Mercury turned back to his brother, who was still staring at the waves. "I don't know what to say man; it sucks."

"Sol said we're not supposed to be with people that aren't Angels."

"Yeah," Mercury said. "Take it from someone who came close to breaking that rule; it exists for a really good reason."

"What was her name again?" Jupiter wiped his face. "That cadet?"

"Cristina," Mercury said. She had been a fling that did not last, or even really start, but he had gone back to Forging because of it. "Let me tell you Jupiter, other people, *normal* people, we don't mesh with them. They lead completely different lives than we do, and being around them changes you. That's why we wear helmets all the time. It's not possible to be an Angel and be with a normal person."

"So, does that mean that I'm going to be alone forever?"

"Don't talk like that Jup," Mercury scoffed. "We're never alone. We have each other."

Jupiter looked down. "You know what I mean."

Mercury did know. "It wouldn't be the first time we've given something up."

"Do you still think about her sometimes?"

"I used to," Mercury admitted. "But not anymore. It didn't help."

"So what am I supposed to do?" Jupiter cried.

"I...don't know." Mercury thought a moment, "Have you tried talking to Sol about it?"

Jupiter nodded. "Just because Sol makes sense doesn't mean it helps. I've talked to Ma about it a lot, but she's undercover right now."

"And what did she say?"

Jupiter sniffed. "She said in situations like this you have to put yourself out there. Tell them how you feel and get it off your chest."

"Good advice," Mercury said. "Listen, Jupiter. There's a lot about you for Venus to like. You have a fire inside you we all depend on. Even if she rejects you, you're still Jupiter. You're an Angel. Nothing can ever change that, so what do you have to worry about? You've gone through the Forging. Do you realize how insanely impressive that is? The Ministers only saw the first floor and their eyeballs almost rolled out of their sockets."

Jupiter wiped his nose and smiled. "Yeah, especially at the water-boarding."

"That was child's play for you." He helped Jupiter up. "Remember when we did the MemoryShare? We all saw each other, *became* each other. Think back, are either Venus or Earth the kind of people that would hate you for something like this?"

Jupiter thought a moment and shook his head. "No."

"No, they're not. Do you know what I saw in you that day?" Mercury asked. "Think back."

Jupiter closed his eyes to call back the PerfectMemory. A tear rolled down his face. "A soul on fire."

Mercury poked his brother's chest. "Don't you ever forget that."

Jupiter nodded. "I won't-." Just then he was interrupted by a mud ball hitting him square on the side of the head, knocking him flat in the sand.

Mercury had just enough time to turn and see Saturn and Mars carrying storage bins from the *Defiant* full of ammunition before taking a mud ball directly to the face. The next thing he knew, his mind was registering the blue sky above him and the sand beneath him.

The next several minutes consisted of Mercury and Jupiter desperately attempting a counterattack while being pelted incessantly by their adversaries. Somewhere along the way, Saturn seemed to think it would be fun to turn on her accomplice. From there, it devolved into absolute chaos as mud and sand flew.

When Venus and Earth showed up, they were holding hands and looking particularly happy. Then Venus caught a perfectly spherical projectile in the mouth.

At that point the beach turned into a warzone in earnest. Saturn was so keen on picking a fight it was almost suicidal. She was constantly changing sides. After turning on Mars, she suckered Mercury and Jupiter into helping her, while Mars joined the newcomers.

The battle raged on for hours, moving all over the island. Most of the time they fought in one on one or two on two skirmishes, but eventually one of the sides would shore up their forces, causing the other to do likewise. Since Saturn seemed to be the instigator of the whole affair, she took the majority of the enemy's fire, becoming muddier than anyone else. Venus, on the other hand, had such a knack for avoiding their shots it was uncanny.

Eventually Saturn tried to take on the larger girl in hand to hand combat, but that ended about as well as anyone would've expected. Saturn was lifted into the air, shaken like a rag doll, and thrown into the sand. Being down a Saturn, Mercury thought for sure he and Jupiter were doomed. Abandoning their fight with Mars and Earth, the two of them decided to do their best to focus Venus in close quarters.

Rather than being exhausted from Saturn's attacks, Venus seemed energized. She took them on in spectacular fashion, blocking and striking in perfect harmony. Catching one of Jupiter's kicks, she tossed him away and took on Mercury with blinding speed. Out of the corner of his eye, Mercury watched as Mars ran towards them to help Venus, only to get sidelined by Saturn. Without missing a beat, Saturn recovered and sprang up onto her fallen enemy, mashing a mud ball all over his face.

"Twenty-two months, Mars!" Mercury heard Saturn say as he fought Venus. Seeing Jupiter's jaw drop, he looked back to see what was going on. Saturn was kissing Mars right on his mud-covered face.

Mercury felt the wind get knocked out of him as Venus used the distraction to drive her foot into his chest, sending him hurtling to the ground. A second later another thud told him something similar had happened to Jupiter. He saw Venus raise her arms and cheer with a massive smile on her face, "Way. To. Go. Sat!"

Mercury sat up as the world spun into place and he saw Saturn pat the chest of a frozen Mars and stand up. "Now you think on that for a bit," she said. "I'm going to go crash. All this excitement has me tuckered out."

Sure enough, she did exactly that. She went over to a shady patch of sand, plopped down and fell instantly asleep. Meanwhile Mars was still lying perfectly still. Everyone else broke out into laughter.

At that point, they all seemed to agree the battle had ended. While Saturn slept and Mars lay there thinking, the rest of them fetched lunch from the cloaked *Defiant*. A side of lab-grown meat cooked on a spit. When the food was done they called out to the other two, but Saturn was still fast asleep. Mars woke up though, and on his way over he knelt down next to Saturn and kissed her. She certainly woke up then.

Mercury and Earth catcalled, while Venus laughed and Jupiter grinned from ear to ear. He and Venus had been Saturn's confidants in all matters Mars. As Mars headed towards the firepit, Saturn sprang onto his back and kissed his ear with a giggle. For the first time in the six years Mercury had known him, he saw Mars smile. The smile stretched from ear to ear, showing off every single one of his pearly whites.

Shaking his head with a smile of his own, Mercury laughed. *It's damn near impossible to be jealous of a smile like that.*

Once everyone was gathered, they began carving off slabs of meat with combat knives and digging in, eating right off the blade. Sweet, savory juice burst into Mercury's mouth with each bite. The meat was tender, with the outside charred just the right amount. He had not realized just how hungry he was until now.

As they dug in, Mercury looked around. Everyone was lounging in the firelight, enjoying the meal. Well, except for Mars and Saturn anyway. They currently had their faces glued together. *This is probably the best opportunity I'm ever going to get to tell them about Sol.* Mercury's hands began trembling. He closed his eyes and took a slow, deep breath. When he opened his eyes, his hands were steady and his heart was calm. They were his family; he could tell them anything.

"Hey guys," he began. "Mind if I bring up something heavy?"

"Go ahead man," Earth waved his knife. "You don't need to ask."

Jupiter nudged Saturn with his foot, whose attention was clearly focused elsewhere. "Merc's got something to say."

"Huh?" she glanced over and noticed they were waiting. After one more very involved kiss, she tore herself away. Mars was in a daze.

Earth shot Saturn a wide grin. "I think you shorted out our favorite robot."

Mars just rolled his eyes while Saturn nestled into his lap. He draped his big arms around her. "So, what's up Merc?"

Mercury took a deep breath. He had everyone's full attention. "During Forging, Sol really hammered into our heads to be loyal to each other above all else, right?" They all nodded. This was basic stuff. "And he said we're to be loyal to him second, and humanity third."

"Yeah," Venus shrugged. "What are you getting at Merc?"

"Why did Sol tell us to be loyal to him over humanity?" Mercury asked. "Shouldn't it be the other way around?"

Venus snorted and shook her head like it was the most obvious thing in the world. "No."

Mercury's heart skipped a beat. "Why not?"

"Come on Merc," Earth smiled. "We'd never get anything done if we all had to decide on our own if Sol's orders are the best possible thing for humanity."

"Yes," Mercury nodded. "I totally get what you're saying Earth."

"Besides," Mars interjected. "Why should any of us care about the Federation? They've never done anything for us."

Mercury had to struggle to keep from swallowing. "You don't care about the Federation at all?"

"Of course not," Mars scoffed. "My world consists of eight people. You know that." He gestured around the firepit. "The six of us, Sol and Ma. The Federation can burn for all I care."

At that moment, Mercury was keenly aware of the knives they had all been using to eat. The firelight flickered along the razor-sharp blades ominously. "Come on Mars," he did his best not to sound nervous. "I know you say that, and I get it. But are you telling me you really wouldn't care at all if the worlds *actually* went up in flames?"

Mars shook his head.

"I know what you mean," Venus said.

"You too Vee?" Mercury felt his throat clench up.

"Well yeah," Venus shrugged. "It was because of the Federation that Tavahl and Lowulf had to work like slaves in the mines, like their parents before them and their grandparents before that. No one helped us; no one cared. If you and Sol hadn't found me that day in the snow, I would have died. I owe Sol everything. I don't owe the Federation shit."

Earth spoke up, "I think something you're forgetting Merc is that we didn't grow up like you did. You had a mom, dad and sister. You had a house right smack on Tarence. You went to school and didn't need to worry about where your next meal would come from." He pointed at the rest of them. "We didn't have that."

Mercury's heart was pounding in his chest. He looked to the last two. "Jupiter? Saturn?"

Jupiter shook his head. "Not really."

Mercury swallowed. Was he alone in this? If he tried to kill Sol, would they stand in his way? "Sat?" he asked.

"I wish I could Merc," she shrugged. "But it's too big. Sol gave us a second chance at life. Not just Mars, Jup and I, but all of us. On Maracca, I thought I was going to lose everyone I cared about. I almost did. Every day we're together is a win in my book; doesn't matter what we're doing."

Shit. Mercury fought to keep his eyes from going wide in fear. *They're completely loyal to Sol. There's nothing I could say that would change that.* He felt his pulse quicken and had to fight to keep his breathing steady. Colors sharpened, muscles tensed and time seemed to slow down as adrenaline kicked in. Seven years of dedicated training blasted him into fight or flight mode. Somehow, he managed not to move.

I'm going to have to fight them. His eyes swept over the five of them. Each one of them was among the most lethal killing machines alive. Each one of them was his entire universe. He remembered how completely Venus had been beaten down by the five of them on her Forging floor. Except in his mind, he was the one on the ground, while his family stood above him with bloodied knives.

"What brought this up?" Jupiter asked.

The adrenaline pumping through Mercury's veins was far beyond anything he had experienced before. He could not answer. His stomach twisted into a sickening pit of bundled up nerves.

"Was it the Sons?" Earth asked.

"Yeah," Mercury said quickly. His mind could already see the lie spinning as he spoke. "I was just worried. Sol is going to have us kill a lot of Sons over the next few years." The best lies had elements of truth.

"Of course," Venus said. "Bombing the Exodus was only the beginning for them."

"…I know."

He was alone.

CHAPTER EIGHT

Three Years Later...

MERCURY
Age 20

Mercury entered Erithian's Eye and activated the machine. He was alone. Three years had passed since the artificial intelligence told him Sol would try to take over the worlds. Three years since Sol had manipulated the Sons of Liberty to bomb the Bjornhal Exodus. Three years since the Federation declared a state of national emergency. Three years since Sol first sent the Angels to hunt the terrorists wherever they may be. For the last three years Mercury had lied to his family about what the machine had told him. "We need to talk."

Beneath the holographic depiction of the Hel system and the plethora of data the supercomputer possessed on humanity, the form of a small boy appeared. "Hi Mercury, it's good to see you."

"How's the plan coming along?" he asked.

The computer smiled, "Like clockwork. Sol's close to making his move to take over, right after the election."

Mercury shook his head. "I still think waiting to kill him is a mistake."

"I know," the hologram said. "A part of me wants you to kill him now too. But we can't. The Sons are too big a threat. As dangerous as Sol is, he is invaluable when it comes to defending the Federation from the Sons. He needs to clear the stage for his takeover. Letting him live these past three years has saved a lot of lives. Besides, we only get one shot at this. If for some reason you can't kill him in his sleep, you need to be ready."

"Oh, I'm ready," Mercury said confidently. His confidence was not without good reason either. He had spent the last three years rigorously training to end Sol. Even if he did not manage to kill the man in his sleep, Sol would die.

"Good," the machine said. "Because the time to kill Sol is almost here. Sol's plans have been running smoothly, so he has not needed to take any drastic measures. That is all going to change once the Prime Minister is no longer in office."

The current Prime Minister, Liam Hughes, had served under Sol in the Second Taurusian War and was one of his closest friends. The Angel Program was all thanks to Liam. The man trusted Sol implicitly and as such, allowed him to do as he saw fit. The candidate leading the polls for the election however was Sazius Hedge, a charismatic nobleman from Maracca Prime of dubious integrity. The man was in the pocket of the Minister of Economy and his businesses had connections to the Sons of Liberty.

"Makes sense." Sol's ability to operate would no doubt drop dramatically once Hedge was in office. "What about the Sons?"

"The last of their forces have consolidated at the Bastion as planned. By the time Sol makes his move, they will be finished."

"So, Sol's death won't destabilize the country?" As much of a monster as Sol was, he was an effective monster. For the Federation to have their Minister of War assassinated so shortly after the Sons were defeated was risky.

"About that," Erithian said. "If you kill Sol before he makes his move on the Federation, your head will be on the chopping block."

"My life is a small price to pay," Mercury said with conviction.

Erithian's holographic eyes seemed sad. "Of course, you would say that."

Mercury furrowed his brow, "Well, yes."

"And what about the others?" Erithian asked. "You know how much they care about you."

"I know," Mercury said. "Tell them I'm sorry."

"I will," the hologram nodded. "Although, you don't have to die. I found a nice quiet town on Taurus, beautiful scenery, middle of nowhere, the perfect place to hide. Who knows, you might even like it there."

"Oh really?" Mercury cocked an eyebrow. "What's this magical place called?"

"Esen," Erithian said.

"I'll keep that in mind," Mercury nodded.

"Will you go there?" Erithian asked. "Please? I...I really don't want anyone else to die."

"You and me both," Mercury shook his head.

Erithian cocked it's head, "Is it bothering you? That you have to kill Sol I mean."

Mercury put both hands on his head, feeling the prickles of his military haircut. "I just wish you had told me the kind of person he was sooner." He felt his eyes start to itch. "The man's a monster. That's all there is too it."

Erithian shrugged with a sympathetic look on his face. "If you say so."

Mercury began drumming his hands on his thighs. "Why did they make an AI that understood emotions so well?"

A small, melancholic smile appeared on Erithian's face and the hologram spread its hands. "I don't know. Maybe it was to keep me from going all robot overlord. Maybe they thought that was the only way to make a true AI." The hologram's head turned to the ceiling. "Sometimes I wish I could ask them."

Something about the machine's holographic avatar made Mercury think it was hurting. It. A machine. "Maybe you will someday."

Erithian looked back at him. "What, like life after death? I thought you didn't believe in that stuff."

"I don't," Mercury shook his head. "But do you?"

Erithian laughed, "Assuming of course that I actually have a soul? I don't know. When the day finally comes that someone decides to switch me off for good, I…hope so."

"You've thought about this a lot, haven't you?"

Erithian pursed his lips and nodded. "So, with killing Sol," the machine said. "Have you considered waiting until after he takes over the Federation?"

"He's going to kill a lot of people," Mercury said. "I can't let him do that."

"I know," the holographic boy said. "But having the Minister of War be killed so soon after the Sons are defeated…he'll be a martyr. The Federation will take a long time to recover."

"And how exactly would letting Sol overthrow the government make that any better?" he asked.

"Sol may be a monster," Erithian said. "But he's an effective monster. Once he's stabilized the system, you kill him in his sleep and boom, you're a hero. Piece of cake."

"Yeah," Mercury shook his head. "I'm not doing that."

The machine shrugged, "It was just an idea."

***

Mercury could not see a thing with the blindfold on. Bound hand and foot upside down with all his blood rushing to his head, Mercury knew that he would pass out if he did not do something soon. Not even Sol's training would stop that. He was also keenly aware of the sound of water, and that he was getting slowly lowered into it. Though partially blocked by the blindfold, his ears told him the water was two meters away. Inside of twenty seconds his head would be submerged.

Calming his mind, Mercury drew in a breath and slowly lifted his torso. He felt the blood begin to clear from his head. If he could get far up enough with his hands to grab the rope that bound his feet, he should be able to climb out of here. His fingers reached up for the rope. The muscles in his core strained, using up the air in his lungs all too quickly. With a gasp he fell back, dangling painfully from the rope as the blood rushed back to his head, threatening him with unconsciousness.

Patience. Focusing on nothing but breathing, he drew in as much air as he could and told his muscles to go to work. They obeyed. Pulling himself up by his legs and leaning up with his core, he brought his bound hands past his butt and grabbed the rope. He stopped for breath and let his legs and core recover. After a few seconds respite he pushed with his legs, bringing his hands up the rope until he was standing up straight. While holding himself there, he pushed the blindfold off with a finger just as his feet touched the surface of the water. Falling wasn't an option now.

Above him maybe twenty meters the rope was attached to a slowly moving winch on a flimsy looking metal catwalk. He climbed. As he climbed, the winch lowered him closer to the water. With his hands tied, it was incredibly slow going, and the winch was still lowering him. Ten meters up his arms began to burn. At fifteen meters they felt like they would fall off. He gritted his teeth and kept climbing. Eventually he reached the winch and pulled himself up onto the trembling catwalk.

A large 'I' shaped metal beam that went all the way to the ceiling was his only way down. Once he had untied himself, he ran along the catwalk and leapt a good six meters to the beam. The metal threatened to slice his hands open when he caught himself on it, but the layers of callous he'd built up over the years held firm. Hand over hand; he made his way down the beam to the floor.

As soon as his feet touched the ground, three human shaped things made of metal assembled themselves in a flurry of metal bits and attacked him. He really hated these guys. Blocking their strikes with his bare arms and legs, Mercury fought against being driven back into the pool. The metal people surrounded him, denying any chance of escape as they beat on him. They pummeled every inch of his body, but he refused to go down. Not once did he take a knee or fall, even against these unstoppable adversaries. Not this time. Then Mercury saw the tear gas seep into the room and his eyes began to burn.

The minutes seemed endless as they traded blows. His arms and legs turned red, then purple, then bloody. All the while tears streamed from his face, blurring his vision but doing nothing to stop the pain. Pain begged for his attention, but he dismissed it. He could feel his bones starting to crack and his lungs burned like fire, but his mind was unbreakable. On they fought.

When it had been exactly one hour, the metal people dissembled and were sucked back into their distant containers. The tear gas stayed. From the ground, a metal table appeared with two stun grenades on it. Mercury winced as he lifted his broken hands to take one in each hand and activated them. Ever since he was a kid, this part had always been the hardest for him. A red number flashed across the grenades. Five…Four…Three…Two…One…

He tried his best to keep his body from convulsing when the grenades detonated, but he could not help it. Pulse after pulse assaulted his brain and seized up his muscles. He dropped to one knee but he refused to let go of the grenades. His vision went white, and in response he squeezed the grenades even harder. He screamed, but he could not hear his own voice.

When his senses returned, the tear gas was gone and he was still on one knee. In each hand he held a slightly crumpled stun grenade. Another table rose out of the floor, this one with a MedGel dispenser. Mercury let out an exhausted breath and stood up, wincing as his whole body protested. That was his best run yet.

Ten years had passed since he had become one of Sol's Angels. Now, after all those years his body had fully caught up to the insane demands placed upon it. Mercury rolled his shoulders. He was still getting used to them being so wide. *I feel like a tank.*

The cool, thick MedGel worked its magic as he spread it generously over his bloodied arms and legs. With each hobbled step towards the elevator, his legs hurt less and less. As he gave one last look at his personal Forging floor before the elevator doors closed, he frowned. *Better take it up a notch tomorrow.*

Mercury pressed the button that would take him to the Angels' living quarters. As the elevator moved up and the MedGel finished soaking into his skin, he stretched and rolled his shoulders. A few years ago, today's Forging would have killed him. *On the off chance I can't kill Sol in his sleep, I need to be ready.*

Exiting the elevator, Mercury ran into Mars. The guy was even bigger than Sol now. *When did that happen?* Mercury felt a pang of sadness as he realized just how distant he had grown from his family. All this talk with Erithian about killing Sol had resulted in him keeping his family at arm's length, especially Mars. The big guy was not one to start conversations. "Hey man," he said, punching Mars' shoulder.

Mars blinked quickly as if he had been deep in thought. "Hey Merc. How was the Forging?"

Massaging a shoulder with one hand, Mercury shrugged with the other. "It was alright. The Bots were tough."

"Yeah," Mars said with a deadpan expression. "They're fun."

One did not connect with Mars by asking him how he was doing. Mercury had learned that a long time ago. He cracked his neck. "I need to figure out a way to make them a bit tougher. That or change them for something else."

"I know what you mean," Mars nodded. "After a while the pain just blurs together."

"Any suggestions?"

"Well it's getting easy for you because all the ideas you come up with are going to end up being similar. Even if you swap out the Bots for something else. You need to get a fresh set of eyes." Mars was not very talkative, but ask him about the things he was interested in and he would never stop.

"Mind lending me yours?"

"Sure," Mars said. Again, no facial response whatsoever. "But if you really want to get creative you should ask Venus too."

"Vee? Is that what you've been doing?"

His brother nodded mechanically. "And it helps a lot. She doesn't think like you or I do."

Mercury shook his head with a smile. "No, she doesn't."

Mars' stoic expression was broken by an unexpectedly huge, dorky grin. *He's about to bring up Saturn, isn't he?* Mercury smiled. He was pretty sure Mars did not realize it, but the guy actually smiled now. Now all his lumbering giant of a brother had to do was think about Saturn and get a giant grin plastered all over his face.

"It's funny," Mars said. "I told Sat about Vee's tricks and she got this really serious look on her face. Merc, it was one of the most adorable things I've ever seen."

All of them knew very well how competitive Saturn was with Venus. Always trying to beat her "perfect sister" at something. Mercury could see the shine in his brother's eyes just remembering the moment. Seeing how head over heels his brother was for Saturn brought a smile to Mercury's face. "Did you tell her how adorable you thought she looked?"

"No," Mars said slowly with a shake of his head. "...I almost did though."

"What are you guys talking about?" Saturn said as she emerged from one of the side rooms where one of the two maintenance shafts exited on this floor. She came from behind Mars, covered in sweat with her cropped dark hair stuck to her face. Mercury saw a twinge of panic on his brother's face at her sudden arrival. Saturn expected everyone to take her rivalry with Venus as seriously as she did.

"Sat," Mercury said, slightly confused. "Did you...climb up here?"

"M-hmm," she said with a proud smile as she put a hand on Mars' shoulder.

"Should I even ask why?" Mercury cocked an eyebrow.

She shrugged with that proud smile still plastered on her face. "Why not?"

Mercury saw Mars' Saturn-smile return. His brother spun around and effortlessly lifted Saturn into the air before kissing her. "Hey you."

Saturn smiled down at Mars, this being one of the rare times she was taller than him. "Hey you," she kissed him. Once. Twice. This continued. The two of them seemed to have completely forgotten about Mercury.

Mercury rolled his eyes at the couple. "Well goodnight you two," he said sarcastically.

In response, the two of them simultaneously gave him thumbs up without missing a beat of their...interaction. Mercury found it impressive Mars could hold her up so easily with one arm. Then again, he was Mars.

In his room, Mercury stripped down and checked the DreamTank's program. Marksmanship, swordsmanship, hand-to-hand, swordsmanship again, economics, strategy, history and leadership. Mercury changed out economics for psychology then climbed into the warm TankFluid. His mind drifted back to Sol and the gruesome task that lay before him. Within seconds the DreamTank's program had activated and he was asleep.

***

Weightless. Mercury was dimly aware of his own lack of sensory awareness inside the DreamTank. His eyes snapped open and his heart began pounding in his chest as one fact became clear; he could not breathe. Adrenaline sent his brain into overdrive. Darkness. The DreamTank was turned off. Dozens of tubes attached to MicroNeedles still fed into his body. If the tank was off, those should have disengaged. He stripped them away, followed by the inactive Breather.

Reaching up, he grabbed the wheel for the lid placed there precisely for emergencies like this. Bracing his bare feet against the sides of the tank, he began turning the lid's wheel as fast as he could. His lungs slowly began to burn. Panic attempted to seep into his brain, but thanks to his training he was used to that.

Once the lid was free, he pushed it open. Gasping for air, Mercury lifted himself out of the inactive DreamTank and surveyed his room. No light whatsoever. He hopped down from the tank and listened. Even after his ears cleared themselves of the viscous tank fluid, there was silence. Other than his own breathing, thundering heart and the dripping liquid, he heard nothing.

His mind raced with ideas while his body acted on years of developed instinct. No emergency systems had engaged from the DreamTank's failure, so either they had been disabled or there was no power. Mercury crept through the darkness to where his old armor hung on the wall. He took the sidearm and checked its ammo. The tiny lights were off. In a few seconds Mercury had disassembled the weapon in the dark and checked its systems with his hands, relying completely on memory. The circuits had been fried. *EMP.*

This was not another of Sol's drills. They were under attack. His heart began beating faster. Mercury grabbed the sword that hung next to his old armor. *Good thing I kept it sharp.* Not trayite, but it would have to do. The armor was too small for him now, and he was still naked. He would stand out in the dark. Moving over to his dresser, he felt down for the right drawer and struck it, forcing it back and popping the mechanism to open it. He quickly threw on a pair of dark clothes and moved out to check on the others. If they were not already awake, they would be soon and arrive at the same conclusions he had.

He crept out of his room, bare feet making no noise, despite still being a bit wet. Venus was already out of her room. Mercury's heart steadied. She was in a near identical state to him. Just out of the tank, dark clothes and her old sword. Somehow in the last three years she had gotten even taller and more gorgeous. *And yet, I would not want to meet her in a dark alley.*

"EMP," Mercury whispered.

"We need to get to the armory," Venus said. The trayite armor would be unaffected by an EMP. If they could get to it down on the fourth floor, then whoever their attackers were would be finished.

Earth crept out of his own room, similarly clad. "Armor?" They nodded.

Mars and Saturn came out next from Mars' room, dripping wet. "Sol," Mars said. Sol was a floor above them. Would now be a good time to kill him? No. No, no. Absolutely not. Not when the Sons were still a threat. Not when they were under attack. Not when Sol could be awake to defend himself. Besides, they would need every hand they could get to repel the invaders. Hopefully the man had not become a deep sleeper in his old age.

Saturn wrung out her hair, flinging the excess fluid onto the floor. "If someone managed to get an EMP here, then it was an inside job." That was not a comforting thought.

Jupiter came out now, eyes hard and ready for action. "If the enemy used an EMP then they probably brought projectile weapons." Mercury nodded in agreement.

The smell of burning metal and a dim light from the elevator shaft drew their attention. The enemy was cutting through. The six of them

111

were fighting for their home now. *But is this place still home?* Every muscle in Mercury's body tensed. "Mars, Sat," he said quickly. "Get to the armory. Six bodies."

"One soul," they all said.

CHAPTER NINE

VERA
Age 28

Being the first to step into the Federation's abyss of horrors could not be considered a tactically sound choice. Even less so when you were the commanding officer. She looked back at the dozens of Helhounds in their dark tactical gear cast in the red light of the flares on their belts. She would not make a single one of them go before her. Besides, she needed to be there when it happened. She needed to see the light go out of Archangel's eyes. Still, what she would have given to arrive in a gunship rather than on foot.

Imri, Simon, Sahra and Gerard filed into the elevator shaft behind her and began setting up the jury-rigged lift. Imri had been opposed to her accompanying them on this mission. Said she was too important. But that's not the way of a leader. Ever since her sister Libby was killed at a protest, she had devoted her life to the destruction of the Federation. She would not, *could* not sit back now. Not after almost a decade of fighting.

Back then, the protests had been for freedom and equality, but she was not sure if she knew what that meant anymore. Not since Libby died. She hated the Federation with a bitter and reckless hate. Most of all, she hated the Minister of War, Genrik "Archangel" Rauss for sending the military into an otherwise peaceful protest. When she formed the Sons of Liberty, that boiling hatred was the singular truth of her universe.

Simon cranked the handle on the fossil fueled generator they had brought until it rumbled to life. He had practically been raised as a Helhound by Imri, so it was only natural that he was on this mission, despite how young he was. With a burst of compressed air, Sahra fired the cables up to the top of the elevator shaft, where they found purchase. She had been one of the first Helhounds, but Vera had scarcely heard her say a hundred words in all the time they had known each other. Gerard fastened the pulley cables to the lift. He had joined after his daughter died during an attack by the Angels three years ago in the Dorin Mining Cluster. Vera adjusted the flare on her belt and double checked her weapon chamber. Locked and loaded.

Everything had to be done with old tech. The EMP would have fried any modern tech they brought, so it was just the classics for this mission. Vera was far from worried. They had all drilled this mission dozens of times and successfully completed dozens of other missions to boot. They were ready. If the Angels really were people and not autonomous robots or monsters grown from petri dishes, then they would die tonight. Imri had the Pistol, so he would be the one to do it if worst came to worst. Hopefully they would kill the enemy in their sleep, without giving them the chance to get to their armor.

The lift was ready, a makeshift thing they had brought in and hooked up to the generator. They had a dozen squads, so it would take a couple trips, but that was okay. Imri had decided to leave a squad posted at the bottom of the elevator shaft and each maintenance shaft to make sure to catch anyone that tried to leave. The informant's blueprints said the Angels' living quarters were directly below Archangel's. They would start there and work their way up. They had studied the blueprints until the entire layout was memorized. They were ready.

Vera went up the lift with Simon, Gerard, Sahra, Imri and three squads. With a bright flash and hiss of molten slag falling away, they breached the elevator doors. Vera felt a wave of radiating heat as she stepped through the molten hole. Two soldiers stayed behind to act as signalmen for the rest of the troops below. Meanwhile Vera led the others into the darkness. The hunt for the monsters had begun.

Every one of them was tense, Vera could feel it in the air. Although they were as prepared as it was possible to be, this was the enemy's lair. They all knew in their heads these killing machines were still only human, they had to be. Underneath those masks of cold terror were living, breathing people.

They crept forward, checking room after room, posting two men at each of the maintenance shafts that ran the length of the tower. They did not have to break through the doors up here, these had manual mechanisms. Moving quickly but thoroughly, they checked every single room until they came upon the first of the Angels' rooms. After a moment to get ready, Vera opened the door and they rushed in.

The room was bare bones. Four walls, a dresser next to the door with a hand mirror on top, no bed and a massive machine with a tank of fluid big enough to hold a person. On the floor in front of the tank was a puddle of the liquid. Her stomach turned. *Shit.* Maybe the story about them being grown in petri dishes was true. Vera swallowed. A single drawer from the dresser was open, with uniform clothes inside. Her eyes swept the room again. No bed, just the tank. The empty tank. Now she noticed there was a hatch on top…and it was open. *Shit. Fuck. Balls.*

"Check the other rooms," she hissed at Imri. "Now."

On the wall was something she recognized. Hanging there was a suit of combat armor small enough to fit a child. The same suit of armor they had all seen on the camera feeds for Captain Mavos' ship. No one had believed that Mavos had been captured by a bunch of kids. He had been one of their best. Maybe the Angels really were monsters.

Vera backed out of the room, her mind racing. One by one the soldiers returned from the other rooms and signaled. Empty. All empty. Those had been the last rooms on the floor. Had the Angels already escaped?

"Back to the lift," she said to Imri. "Once the next team is up, find the bastards and kill them." He nodded and they hauled ass back.

Vera heard the echoing rumble of the generator as it made its way back up the elevator shaft with reinforcements. The hiss of a

ThermCharge suddenly came from the elevator shaft followed by the horrific sound of snapping cables and screaming men. The rumbling of the generator disappeared out of hearing. *Oh, fuck no.* A few seconds later she heard the distant crash. They arrived at the shaft with guns ready and Vera almost slipped on the slick blood of the two soldiers posted there. Their throats had been cut with no sign of struggle. Their guns, flares and ThermCharges were gone.

Vera let out a breath. "Maintenance shaft," she signaled. "Be careful." Imri nodded and led a squad to one while she checked the other. At the doorway she hesitated, then moved in with her rifle ready. The same. Both were dead in a pool of their own blood, with no signs of struggle and all their equipment was gone. Someone should have at least heard something. She could feel the fear coming from those behind her.

"I promise you," she said with conviction. "We'll make the sons-of-bitches bleed."

The Helhounds nodded and stood a little straighter. But then she noticed there were only six flares, including her. Someone was missing. "Shit," she said. "Headcount. Who's still here?"

One by one they answered, Sahra included. *Good.* But one stayed silent. Vera trained her weapon at the person, calling out, "Identify now." In response the body slumped over, leaving a trail of blood on the wall as it fell.

A quick search did not reveal the attacker, but they did find another dead Helhound with its throat slashed and flare snuffed out.

"They're not human," she heard a voice behind her mutter.

Vera whirled around but could not tell who said it in the red flare light. "You think you're the only one who's scared? If I hear something like that again, I'll kill you myself. You're Helhounds. Killing Angels is what you live and breathe for. Every one of them is dying tonight, then we're all going home. Understood?" They all nodded. Shadows cast across Sahra's face in a particularly determined expression. Satisfied but still worried, Vera led them back to the elevator shaft. *How had the Angels managed to kill two of them without anyone noticing?*

When they regrouped with the others, Vera had never been so happy to see Imri. His eyes, however, were grim. At least all his soldiers were accounted for. "Dead?" she asked.

He nodded. "Both of them."

No plan survives contact with the enemy. "Alright, everyone is staying in squads with full three-sixty. No more casualties. The others should already be setting up the backup generator and lift. We'll keep guns trained on the top of the shaft to make sure this doesn't happen again. They are on the top floor, or were when the lift fell. We'll sweep from here up, one squad on each maintenance shaft. Shoot anything that moves."

Imri took one of the shafts with Simon and Gerard while Vera led the other squad toward the second shaft with Sahra. But first they had to find whoever had been killing them from the shadows. For a couple tense minutes they swept every centimeter of their half of the floor. Nothing. Either their enemy was a ghost, or they had retreated along the maintenance shaft. Sure enough, a trail of blood led down the ladder. *The enemy is trying to lead us away from Archangel.*

With a hand she motioned them up the ladder, then turned to Sahra. "Cover our six. They might try to come back up the ladder after us." The girl smirked darkly and patted her rifle. Vera smiled. *Helhound through and through.*

Climbing up the ladder in the dark was maddeningly slow. Rung after rung. The Angels could be anywhere. Had the hunters become the hunted?

One by one they reached the top, Vera somewhere in the middle of the order and Sahra faithfully bringing up the rear without incident. Immediately Vera counted them off by their flare light. Eight including her and Sahra. They began fanning out in a circle as she instructed, taking care to not let any nook or cranny go unsearched. That was not difficult; there were fewer passages and separate rooms on this floor. Archangel's quarters would be the most tactical place for their enemy to ambush them.

One of the few side rooms had light coming from it. They moved inside without breaking formation, the back half staying outside to watch every angle. Inside in the center of the floor was the flare. Other than that, and some boxes, the room was completely empty. A decoy. "How are we doing outside?" Vera whispered.

"All clear," they answered.

Gunfire echoed from somewhere else on the floor followed by cries from Imri's squad. Vera's heart skipped a beat and she led her squad to help, passing two more decoy flares on the way, but the lift's arrival made her help unnecessary. Four fresh squads of Helhounds poured out ready for battle and the lift began descending again. So long as they kept this checkpoint, the Angels were finished. Their enemy had been stupid not to escape when they had the chance. *Didn't Archangel say in his book never step into a fight you can't win?*

"We'll hold the lift until the rest show up," Vera said to Imri as he moved off to kill the Angels.

Vera, Sahra and the other six trained their guns at the 'T' at the end of the hallway. There might be an Angel still back where they had come from, but they would have to go past their line of fire to get to Imri.

"Having fun yet Sahra?" Vera whispered back. "Remind you of Taurus I?" No answer. Vera waited a moment, then glanced back, "Sahra?" Vera knew exactly what Sahra looked like in the dark, and she was not among them. "Where'd she go?" Vera asked one of the Helhounds. There were still eight flares including her own.

"What do you mean?" the woman said. "She's right-," her voice stopped when a blade, gleaming in the flare light, slashed her throat. Flecks of blood sprayed streaked across Vera's face and the Helhound fell. Immediately the figure that most definitely was not Sahra kicked another man down the elevator shaft and dashed behind another. There was a sharp cry and a sword point burst through the man's chest.

As fast as any human could react, Vera and the other three lifted their guns and fired. But the bullets merely struck the impaled victim as the killer used his body as a shield. Then a rifle appeared on the side of the hoisted body, shooting a Helhound on Vera's left between the eyes. She stumbled back and sprayed with her weapon at their enemy. A woman's face appeared from behind the body. In the woman's eyes was the same look Vera saw in the mirror every morning. Pure hatred.

Stepping back, Vera continued to spray the body. When her magazine ran out she took mere fractions of a second to reload and kept firing. The enemy's Helhound shield was beyond recognition. On Vera's right, another Helhound dropped with a hole in her head.

Then the enemy began to advance. The rifle disappeared behind the mutilated shield and a hand darted out to one of the fallen Helhounds. This one was a man and much larger. Vera knew from experience that dead bodies are much harder to lift than living ones. With one hand, the woman hoisted the dead man into the air. Vera and the one other survivor ran like Hel. As Vera rounded the corner she saw the previously bullet-riddled human shield flung back and down the elevator shaft. Distant curses.

Once the two of them were out of the line of fire, they each dashed into rooms opposite each other and watched the 'T' they had just come from. Their enemy would have to come through there.

"That…" the Helhound said in between terrified breaths, eyes not leaving the chokepoint for a moment. "…That was an Angel?"

No, that was the devil. Vera's trigger finger was twitching. She could not peel her eyes away from the chokepoint, but she would recognize the man's drawl anywhere. "You aren't getting scared now are you, Norr?"

"No ma'am," she heard Norr say. "Pa would lick the tar out of me." His father was killed by the same soldiers that took Libby.

As Vera watched, the red flare light from where they'd come from disappeared, and she heard more crashes and curses from the lift. *My gods. The monster is throwing the bodies at the men on the lift.* This was their chance to attack. Vera tried to move, but her body would not respond. It was a trap. The woman was baiting them to give up their position. Across from her she saw Norr try to hold his rifle steady. Thinking fast, Vera threw her flare towards the intersection, but not quite far enough that the Angel would be able to get at it without revealing herself. Norr did the same thing, throwing a couple meters short of Vera's.

"We're going to make it through this, Norr," she said for herself just as much as the soldier.

"I don't care if I make it out of here ma'am," he answered. "So long as we kill the bastards."

Vera smiled. *Of course he would say that.* "We need more men like you."

"If this mission does go south ma'am," Norr said. "Make sure you high tail it out of here. I know it's not my place to say, but it'll be all sorts of bad if you don't make it out. But me? There'll always be a fella to take my place."

"Don't you worry Norr," Vera said. "We're going to kill them all tonight and be home in time for breakfast."

"Won't that be nice?" she heard a smile in his voice.

As they waited, they could hear Imri and his men exchanging fire with the enemy. Vera felt like a coward waiting here, but soon the lift would be back with reinforcements and this fight would be over. The sound of gunfire from the shaft told her the two Helhounds on the floor below were still guarding the lift. Good.

Soon she heard the sound of the lift faintly echoing up the shaft. "You hear that Norr? That's the sound of the real Angels."

"If it isn't the sweetest thing I ever-," Norr's head snapped forward as the sound of a gunshot echoed from behind them. Norr collapsed. As Vera ducked back behind cover, she glimpsed the woman from earlier lining up a shot. She must have gone down the elevator shaft and come back up through the maintenance shaft to get behind them. *Shit.* Vera should have been prepared for that.

After making sure she had a full magazine, Vera stuck her gun out and sprayed blindly. Still firing, she got out of cover and scrambled to get to Imri and the others, not daring to release the trigger. She prayed to the gods it would be enough to make that *thing* stay far away.

When she got to Imri, she found him holed up outside Archangel's quarters, exchanging fire with enemies on seemingly all sides. Vera noticed almost a dozen dead Helhounds lying in pools of blood.

"Vera?" Imri said as he waved her into a side room with him and a few other Helhounds. "You look like the devil's after you. What happened? Where's your squad?"

"Dead, Imri," she said frantically. "They're all dead. Tell me you've had better progress."

The man shook his head. "How's the lift?"

"Almost here," she said. "They're covering it." As if on cue Vera heard a thundering explosion followed by screams and the sound of something that made her heart stop. The screaming roar of Boosters, and they were approaching rapidly. "Oh gods," she said. "How many Angels have you seen?"

Imri understood, "Just four." He pulled the Pistol from the back of his pants and looked her dead in the eye. "Cover me."

Vera wished she could say something to him. Tell him just how much he meant to her, or how important it was to her that he had never asked about Libby. Maybe thank him for seeing her as an equal rather than some political figurehead or a lost girl trying to avenge her sister. Perhaps she should remind him not to be a hero; they had all known what they were getting into when they volunteered for this mission.

Instead she spoke with her rifle, leaning out and spraying until her magazine ran out. By then Imri had made it to a spot perfect for an ambush. He gave her thumbs up and let out a breath.

Loading another magazine, Vera leaned back out and laid down more covering fire against the Angels not wearing armor. No matter what she did, she could not touch them. When one was reloading, the other three were taking turns popping out to fire before ducking back behind cover. They never missed, killing a Son with each shot. To make matters worse, the flares made it almost impossible to see the enemy. She tossed a flare towards the Angels, but one of them shot the burning end right off. *Shit.* She ducked back behind the corner.

Then Vera heard it. The echoing steps of the two armor clad Angels as they approached. She felt the tremors in the ground and walls announcing the arrival of death incarnate. Then all was silent. So deafeningly silent. Something deep inside her wanted to peek around the corner and see the Sons' mortal enemies with her own two eyes.

Vera heard several distinct whines. Then, with an undying thunder that threatened to burst her eardrums, four rushing torrents of brilliant white energy consumed all before her. Screams erupted from the hallway, not quite drowned out by the Angels' antipersonnel weapons. Had Vera taken a single step forward, she would be dead. The innumerable white bolts of energy did not cease, but a light, red mist began to fill the air. The coppery taste of blood filled her open mouth. The tremors in the ground began again. The Angels were coming.

Her heart was pounding to the point of pain. *Just breathe.* She began breathing too quickly. She was hyperventilating. The blood mist worked its way into her throat and she gagged, then doubled over in a coughing fit. Her mind flashed to a mission in the Dorin Mining Cluster. She had injected herself with pure adrenaline when she was almost dead to carry an unconscious Imri to safety. That had felt like her chest would explode. This was worse.

Thinking quickly, she grabbed the corpse of a big Helhound and pulled it on top of her, lying flat on her stomach and keeping perfectly still. She kept her eyes open though, she had to see the monsters. Blinking one last time, she fixed her eyes ahead at the hallway full of blood and death. No movement. Not at all. They had to think she was dead. The blood mist agitated her eyes, but she did not move in the slightest. Eventually the blood settled on her eyes and started turning her vision red.

Then they appeared. They were the embodiment of the Federation's terror. Tall and imperious, one considerably bigger than the other, each with visors glowing ice blue. Even with the blood in Vera's eyes, the light of the visors haunted her. Vera did not move. Vera did not breathe. She watched them without looking at them as they cut down her friends with the white fire from guns built into their arms.

At that moment, one of the armored Angels, the smaller one, turned and looked in her direction. Her gut turned inside out as the fear consumed her. If she moved, she was dead. The Angel pointed one arm at her. She was a rat trapped in a box and the exterminators had come. Their only chance now was Imri with the Pistol. A flash of white and a violent tremor from the body on top of her. Then the armored Angel continued on, lighting up the hallway beyond with both its guns.

They were finished. Unless Imri killed the two armored ones quickly, none of them would make it out alive. This wasn't how it was supposed to go. The Angels were vulnerable. Archangel was vulnerable. When would they ever get a chance like this again? Even if they did manage to get close enough in the field, they only had three shots.

Vera looked over just in time to see Imri pop out of cover with the Pistol, take aim at the big Angel's armored back and then a bullet ripped into his temple. His knees slowly buckled out from beneath him and he fell. The metal monsters continued their slaughter without noticing how close to death they had been.

Time seemed to stop for Vera. All care for her personal safety was a distant memory. Dashing out of cover, she grabbed Imri around his chest and pulled him away from the fighting. Vera felt his head snap back from a shot no doubt meant for her. She almost tripped over Simon's body, a bullet hole between the eyes. She felt two bullets go through her arm and Imri's body shook again. She refused to drop him. Vera caught a glimpse of the woman from the elevator shaft lining up another shot right before Vera pulled Imri into a side room.

He was gone. They were finished. As far as Vera was concerned, they were all dead men walking. Their only chance had been the Pistol and leaving cover was suicide. Looking down she saw that Imri was still holding onto it. She cried and kissed the man's forehead, just above the bullet hole. Even in death he looked out for her. As she cried, the blood in her eyes cleared and the world returned to its normal colors.

Prying the weapon from his fingers, she steeled herself for what was next. They had no reason to see her coming. She waited for the break in fire that told her the woman who killed Imri was probably reloading. Vera took a breath. *See you soon, Libby.*

She ran out of cover with a steady hand and a calm heart. The metal monsters continued spewing fire and blood. *This is for all of them.* She took aim for the biggest one and fired. Her nightmare dropped to one knee with a bloody hole in its back.

"Mars!" she heard a woman cry out.

Vera could hardly believe her eyes; the gun had worked. The gun had actually worked. The Angels could be killed. Adrenaline made Vera keenly aware of everything and nothing. She leveled the gun at the last armored foe, who had frozen, looking down at the fallen Angel. Vera could see the shock on the face of the woman who had killed Imri. Killing the smaller armored Angel was an easy shot. This was Vera's chance.

In some last surge of defiance, the wounded one pulled its comrade to the ground and collapsed atop it. Imri's killer swung her rifle up to shoot Vera, but she was already gone. She only had two bullets left; she was not going to waste another on the same target. She ran all the way to the elevator shaft and dove, catching the dangling cable in a gloved hand and sliding all the way down to the ground floor. She had to get the Pistol back somewhere safe.

CHAPTER TEN

SATURN
Age 19

Saturn's whole world was falling apart. An unresponsive Mars was lying face down on a GravStretcher with a ten-centimeter-wide hole in his back. As the medical staff took him away, Saturn followed. Her eyes were glued on the hole in Mars. *So much blood.* The shattered remains of his spine were visible even behind the concaved metal. Saturn had retracted her helmet a long time ago, despite that they were in public. She could not be made to care.

"Mars," she tore her eyes away from the hole and muttered in his ear. "Come on hun." His eyes were closed and he did not seem to be breathing. A nurse tried to pull her away but a nudge from Saturn's shoulder was enough to send the nurse to the floor. Saturn's throat clenched up. She could barely breathe or see. "Come on you numbskull," she cried desperately. "Wake up."

"Sat," she heard Jupiter say as a metal hand peeled her away from her other half. "Let them do their job."

As Saturn watched, Mars disappeared into a room. Her chest felt like it would give out from the pain. Collapsing into Jupiter's arms, she wept bitterly. According to protocol, Jupiter was still wearing his helmet, but Saturn could feel his sobs. A moment later she felt Venus wrap her arms around them both.

"It's time to go," she heard Sol say. "There's only one person who could have done this."

Revenge was the farthest thing from Saturn's mind right now. Her heart broke at the idea of leaving Mars, but she could not disobey Sol's orders. "Sol," Mercury spoke up. "Should a couple of us should stay here? To protect Mars."

"Please Sol," Saturn looked up at him through teary eyes. "Let me stay with him."

"With your face exposed?" Sol said. Saturn immediately had her helmet reform around her head.

"I'll watch out for her, Sol," Jupiter said. "The rest of you can hunt down the bastard that did this."

"Alright," Sol nodded then looked at Saturn. "You're in the field. No more letting your guard down."

He was talking about exposing her face in public. "Understood."

"And keep track of Mars' armor," Sol added.

"Yes sir," Saturn said.

"Don't take any chances," Sol put a hand on her shoulder. "We don't know how much trayite the Sons have. If they do attack, don't concern yourselves with civilians."

She and Jupiter nodded. "Yes sir."

"The rest of you," Sol turned. "Move out." Saturn watched the four of them exit the hospital. She blinked and saw nothing but jet trails.

Saturn and Jupiter stationed themselves outside the door to where Mars was being operated on. "Thanks, Jup," Saturn said over a private comm channel.

"Don't mention it," he nodded.

"I know we're soldiers," Saturn said. "It's just...you and I haven't had to watch friends die for a long time now."

"He'll pull through Sat," Jupiter said. "Death wouldn't be stupid enough to go after him."

Saturn chuckled for a moment. "It had never really occurred to me that Mars could die. I mean, I always knew he could, but it didn't seem like that was ever going to happen. Even when we were kids in Dabo's army, he always handled everything."

"I know what you mean."

"We should've died on Maracca. If not for Mars, we would've at least a dozen times." She sniffed inside her helmet. That had been almost ten years ago, and still nothing had really changed. If Mars had not pulled her down, she would have been shot too. "I'm tired of losing people Jup. When Sol rescued us, that was supposed to be the end of it. I know we need to fight. I don't mind that so long as we're together."

There was a smile in Jupiter's voice. "You always did know how to keep things simple."

Saturn felt the tears return. "That's because it's all we've ever had."

"...I know."

The two of them stood there guarding the door throughout the whole surgery. Saturn did not know or care how long it took. Everything became a blur, a dream she could not wake up from. Through it all Jupiter stood still as a statue, monitoring Mars remotely through the hospital cameras. She could not bear to watch the doctors operate. She could not bear to think about anything.

As time went on, the staff bustled about their various tasks. Some of them even went in and out of the surgery room. There were only a few staff in this area, but those that did pass by definitely turned their heads towards the Angels. Saturn saw mostly fear in their eyes, but awe and curiosity were there too. There came a point when exhaustion hit her, but the mere thought of sleep was repulsive to her. The whole time Jupiter never spoke. He just listened.

"Thank you," she said eventually.

"Anytime, Sis."

More time passed in comfortable silence. In truth, Saturn felt like she was going to be sick, but Jupiter's presence was enough to settle her nerves and calm her mind. Several reporters came by. How they got in Saturn did not know. Jupiter warned them once and when they got too close again, he crushed their equipment. After that, they kept their distance. Eventually security staff arrived and escorted them out.

"I was afraid of him you know," Jupiter said at length on their private channel. "The way he could just flip a switch and kill people, it scared me. Even though Dabo's men were forcing us, it was just so…easy for him. I only understood when Sol gave us our PerfectMemory in the DreamTanks and I got to see inside his head."

Saturn willed the PerfectMemory to the forefront of her mind. Jupiter had been so scared; she could feel it even now as if the fear were her own. She could also feel just how much Jupiter had looked up to him. "He never held it against you," she said, dismissing the PerfectMemory. "Not even once."

"I know," Jupiter said.

"And I can guarantee you that if Sol hooked our minds up again; you'd know he sees you as an equal."

"…You really think so?"

"I know so," Saturn said with confidence.

Now it was Jupiter's turn to sniff, "Heh. And here I was staying behind to be there for you."

"We all help each other out Jup," Saturn grinned underneath her helmet. "That's how it's always been and that's how it always will be."

"Six bodies," Jupiter said.

"One soul," Saturn finished.

Saturn heard a man clear his throat behind her. She turned to see a doctor that looked to be in his early forties. "Excuse me, sir."

"Yes, doctor?" Saturn said.

"Ma'am, sorry," the doctor corrected himself. "Over half the patient's thoracic vertebrae were destroyed or damaged and the spinal cord was completely severed. We had to rebuild it almost from scratch. His right lung was patched up and cleared of blood and bone matter, but the left lung had to be completely replaced along with his heart. In addition, several ribs were shattered. It will take time, but I expect him to make a full recovery."

"He's going to be okay?" Saturn could hardly believe her ears.

"Yes, ma'am. Anyone else would have been dead long before you got them here."

Just like that, Saturn's mind cleared. She just about collapsed from relief. Burying her helmeted face in her hands, Saturn breathed in deep. Time started moving again and she knew everything was going to be alright.

The doctor shook his head. "We found numerous trace compounds designed for stimulating growth and brain functions. They seem to have been administered regularly since adolescence, correct?"

Saturn blinked as her mind flashed to the DreamTanks. "Yes, that's right."

"Well whoever regulated them did so perfectly," the doctor said. "However, the replacement organs and bones have not been treated the same way, so make sure he continues those treatments on a daily basis so the body can accept the new organs."

"Understood," Saturn nodded.

"Whatever equipment you're using that's been administering the patient's treatments is obviously far better equipped for helping him recover than we are. He's being prepped now so you can transport him back safely.

"Thank you, doctor," Jupiter said. "I see on the cameras you've removed the armor. Could you have one of the nurses bring it out?"

"On...the cameras?" the doctor looked at each of them. "...Yes, I'll have a couple of the nurses bring it out on a GravStretcher."

"Thank you," Jupiter said. "I noticed you also extracted the bullet. You have it on your person, correct?"

One of the doctor's eyebrows went up, "Yes." He held up a small plastic bag with a perfectly shaped bullet inside, not warped in the slightest. *It is HardTrayite after all.* "I want to make it clear that New Tarence Medical is relinquishing all trayite to the military of its own initiative."

"Thank you, doctor." Jupiter took the trayite bullet. Saturn was so glad she could leave this to him.

"Thank you for everything doctor," Saturn said.

"Just doing my job ma'am," he nodded. "Would you like me to direct you to the patient?"

"No need," Jupiter said. "We know where he is."

"That's right," the doctor smiled nervously. "Through the cameras...I'll leave you to it then."

As he walked off, Saturn felt her energy quickly ebb. "Gods, I'm so tired," she said to Jupiter over a private channel. "How long have we been standing watch?"

"A good twenty hours."

Saturn looked at Jupiter. Had it really been that long? She had never bothered to check the time. "Wait," she said. "If we've been here for that long, what have Sol and the others been up to?"

***

MERCURY
Age 20

After leaving the hospital, Mercury and the others took the *Defiant* straight to Maracca VII. The Sons would have needed trayite to get past Mars' armor, and Dr. Jormungand was the only one who knew how to work the metal. Mercury and the others burst through the opening to the traitor's hideout. The old man had been asleep, but he pulled a pistol from under his pillow and held it to his head. "I'm sorry Genrik," he said calmly.

With lightning reflexes, Mercury dashed forward, caught the gun in his hand and squeezed. He felt nothing. Not the weapon's discharge, or any sympathy for the man's cries as his fingers crumpled in Mercury's hand. Grabbing the back of the man's neck, Mercury forced Dr. Jormungand to his knees. He had known the man could not be trusted. He had been right all along. Venus and Earth posted themselves at the door while Sol walked up to the old man. *Of course, I was completely wrong about Sol.*

In truth, those bullets the doctor created were a godsend to Mercury. Finally, he had insurance in case he failed to kill Sol. Still, he had to play the part for now; Sol must not discover his true intentions. Besides, playing the part was easy. All he had to do was think of Mars lying in a pool of his own blood or the sound of Saturn's sobs. With as little as a twitch, Mercury could snap this man's neck. A part of him wanted to.

"Corius," Sol said as his helmet retracted. "Dear Corius. What was going through that brilliant head of yours when you thought to make trayite bullets for the Sons of Liberty?"

"I didn't make them for the Sons," the old man said through clenched teeth as he nursed his mutilated hand. I made them as a precaution when I built your first suit, Genrik. In case you ever needed to be stopped. Guess I was right."

"Did you honestly think any of your safety measures would be more effective than my own?" Sol said in a voice that chilled Mercury to the bone. *What safety measures?* "No one knows you exist, Corius. The Sons of Liberty didn't approach you. You sought them out. Why?"

The man shook his head with tears in his eyes. "You've turned into a monster."

Sol looked disgusted. "You think I'm a monster *now?* I thought you had a stronger stomach than that. You will tell us who you gave the bullets to, then I will take you back to Angel Tower, where you will fix Mars' armor. If he dies, so will you."

Dr. Jormungand's eyes widened, "Genrik, I swear they told me they would only use the bullets on you. I didn't know they'd go after the boy."

"Our actions have consequences, Corius," Sol said slowly. "Did you honestly think they would follow their word?"

"I'm not the only one with blood on my hands, Genrik," Dr. Jormungand snapped. "You condemned over three hundred thousand innocent people to die. Didn't we swear to each other we'd never let that happen again?"

"The Bjornish miners?" Sol asked. "I should have done that twenty years ago, armor or no armor. The trayite's gone. The mines are empty. I killed some of them, yes. But now the mines are *empty*. You're Bjornish, you know what I ended. No more parents will be abandoning their children to die in the snow. My decision saved lives."

"It's still wrong," Dr. Jormungand said.

Now Sol looked angry. "Do you have any idea how many people will survive the coming war because of the armor you made? By making those bullets, you put *billions* of lives in jeopardy just because my decisions made you uncomfortable."

"Do you really think you're incorruptible?" Dr. Jormungand cried out. "If you can't see how wrong what you're doing is, then you're already lost. You should fall on your own sword like you promised." The doctor looked up at Mercury. "You wait and see. Your commander has turned into a monster. I can see it in his eyes. People are just numbers on a scale to him now."

Oh, trust me, I know.

"Only a fool would try to solve a math problem with emotion," Sol said with conviction. "All lives are equal."

There was a power to Sol's words. Even though Erithian's Eye had told him about Sol's true nature, Mercury found himself agreeing with the man. Perhaps the mental conditioning went deeper than he originally thought. He would have to work on that. Still, for now he must keep up the act.

Pulling Dr. Jormungand's head back, Mercury asked, "Who did you give the bullets to?"

"Does it matter?" Dr. Jormungand said. "They'll get the job done. The Sons are bigger than you could imagine. They're the true voice of the people."

"They're nothing more than a mindless mob," Mercury said. "They refuse to take responsibility for their lot in life and resort to mindless violence."

Dr. Jormungand smiled, "Are those your own thoughts, or Genrik's?"

If not for the Sons, I could kill Sol right now. "Did the Sons brainwash you?" Mercury asked. "Sol is the only one holding this country together. Without him, the Sons would send us back to the Stone Age."

Dr. Jormungand shook his head. "That's what he's programmed you to believe! Genrik showed me his original designs for Angel Tower. The DreamTanks? All those *mental conditioning* programs? Everything is to turn you into tools that do and think whatever he wants. Did you ever stop and wonder why he brought in a bunch of children? So he could manipulate you!"

I know. Believe me, I know.

Then Mercury hesitated. Sol had been programming him this entire time, so why had he given him such a strong moral compass? His mind flashed back to the PerfectMemory Sol had given him. *Killing is always wrong.* Sol had made sure he remembered that. Why?

"You know," Sol got down on one knee in front of the old man. "I truly saw you as a friend Corius. I don't let myself have many of those."

Dr. Jormungand grimaced at Sol, then eventually looked away.

"I thought we shared a dream. We would help humanity break free of this prison and explore new worlds where they could live in peace. Ten thousand years of peace for all mankind, regardless of race or creed. When did you lose sight of that?"

"It's not worth it," Dr. Jormungand muttered.

Sol looked him in the eye and spoke in a voice that was almost tender. "Has life beaten you down so much? What happened to the wide-eyed youth that could go on for hours about life from other worlds? Or delight in the wonders that exist all around us?"

"I was naïve," the old man rasped amidst pained breaths. "Naïve...and arrogant...I ignored the signs."

"You don't believe it will work, do you? Is that why you say the cost is too high?"

Dr. Jormungand said nothing.

"I don't deal in whims," Sol went on. "Humanity *will* break free. I swore to you I would make it happen and I hold to that promise."

"How far are you willing to go, Genrik?" Dr. Jormungand blinked. "When will the cost be too great?"

Sol answered with a pure, simple confidence, "When the scales change."

Dr. Jormungand locked eyes with Sol. "You always were good with words. But I know you too well to believe them. You're a manipulator, Genrik...to your core. You can't make me forget that. There's no way I'll help you."

Sol put a hand on the old man's shoulder. "You truly are brilliant Corius. When I told Jupiter you were the smartest man alive, I meant it. I doubt humanity will ever get a mind like yours again." He pushed some of the man's messy white hair out of the way and cupped the doctor's face with an armored hand. Mercury could feel the man begin to tremble in his grasp. "Such a beautiful mind...destroying it will be a real shame."

The old man struggled, but Mercury's vice-like grip was absolute. Sol gave him the signal and he set his WristGun to stun and shot the man, who instantly went slack in his hand. Then Mercury put him in a MimicBag and lifted the now invisible doctor.

"Let's move out," Sol said. With that, the Angels fell in behind Sol as they headed back to the roof.

Once back on the ship, Earth steered them into low orbit. Mercury put MagCuffs on the doctor and locked him to a chair on the bridge. In front of them, Maracca VII was stretched out across the window. Mercury stood to one side of it. Venus injected the doctor in the leg with a small dose of adrenaline and let her helmet retract. The man awoke with a tortured gasp and pulled against his restraints with his thin arms. No use. His face contorted in pain like he was about to have a heart attack, but eventually his expression cleared and he turned his eyes to Sol.

Sol stood directly in front of the window facing the overpopulated moon. "No doubt you've been out of the loop living down there, but surely you heard of the Sons bombing the Bjornhal Exodus? How many people died from that?"

"Of course, I heard of it," Dr. Jormungand said. "Even Maraccan Zeroes have heard about that. But the Sons of Liberty weren't responsible. A splinter group carried out that attack. The Sons found the terrorists and executed them."

"Is that what they told you, Corius?" Sol said. "The Sons of Liberty used a Dorin Enterprises MX-22 Drive Core to create the explosion and planted the explosive in the center of Flight 1279 for maximum civilian casualties. These are the people you helped."

Dr. Jormungand remained silent.

The thought of Sol bringing up the bombing made Mercury's skin crawl. *You did that.* His whole body itched for his sword, but he kept that part of himself buried deep. *Once we defeat the Sons at the Bastion, I am taking your head.*

Sol walked slowly over to the old man and put an arm around his shoulders, crouching down. "You know I can break anyone. You've seen me do it."

The doctor kept silent. Mercury could see the terror in his eyes.

"However," Sol smiled at the old man. "I would prefer to keep your mind intact." Mercury felt a shiver run the length of his spine. Sol's grey eyes glinted, unyielding and unforgiving. Mercury swallowed.

"If you don't cooperate," Sol said. "I'm going to drop a bomb just like the one the Sons used, on your little hideout. While you watch. How many people have you treated there over the last twenty years?"

Mercury's eyes went wide and his hand twitched for his sword. He looked at Venus, who seemed equally shocked. Dr. Jormungand just blinked in disbelief. "No…"

Mercury's mind raced. He could kill Sol. He could kill him right now. Sol's back was turned and his sword was sheathed. Venus and Dr. Jormungand could corroborate his story. Sol was about to bomb civilians. That would be enough. Mercury could lead the Angels. They could stop the Sons on their own.

"Venus," Sol said. "I seem to recall Jupiter telling you an interesting fact when we first came to Maracca VII about its population density. Could you repeat it for me?"

Every muscle in Mercury's body tensed to the point of pain. In the blink of an eye he could take Sol's head from his shoulders. A quarter-second, maybe a third, tops. Would that be fast enough? Would Sol get his sword out in time? What would Venus do? His odds against Sol were bad enough, even without Venus. He looked to her. Her eyes nervously flicked between Sol, the doctor, and the moon. She swallowed. "Jupiter said ten square kilometers of Maracca VII on average has more people than all of Bjornhal."

"Thank you," Sol nodded before turning back to the doctor. "Nowadays that doesn't seem too impressive, but this was before the Exodus. A lot more people lived there back then."

Dr. Jormungand's mouth hung open in a silent plea. Mercury was only dimly aware of it. In his mind, he was already killing Sol. Even with the element of surprise, Sol had killed him four times out of seven. Only once did Mercury win after Sol drew his blade. "Genrik," Mercury heard the doctor say at last with tears in his eyes. "Tell me you're not serious."

"I appealed to you as a friend," Sol shook his head. "You should have known better than to force my hand."

Mercury looked to Venus. Worry spread across her face and her eyes flicked towards the cockpit then to Mercury. "He's bluffing, right?" they seemed to say.

Mercury's mouth was dry and his heart hammered in his chest. He slowly shook his head.

She let out an unsteady breath.

"Genrik, please!" Jormungand begged. "Don't do this!"

There was not even the slightest hint of emotion in Sol's voice. "Each armored Angel will save almost two billion people in the coming war. It's your choice."

Shit. Mercury could go for it. He could make his move right now. Would he be able to draw fast enough? If he did not have to draw his damn sword it would be a sure thing.

Dr. Jormungand shook his head. "I won't be your pawn."

"Earth," Sol said on the comms. "Release the contents of cargo bay 1."

Gods make me fast enough.

"No!" Venus cried.

"Angels!" Sol barked. It was a voice he had not used in years, but Mercury knew exactly what it meant. Absolute obedience was all that mattered. His body remembered even if his mind had long since blocked it out. Immediately, mechanically, Mercury and Venus dropped to one knee. Venus' head was bowed and still as stone. Her hair hid her face. Every muscle in his own body was frozen. He broke into a cold sweat.

"Yes, sir," Earth's voice echoed back, oblivious to what was happening.

Mercury's mind was overloading. He had to stop Sol. But Sol *must* be obeyed. His will was absolute. Above gods and men, above all others. Even the Angels. Especially the Angels. Mercury was a tool for Sol to wield as he saw fit. Nothing more.

Across from him he could see Venus kneeling there, sweat pouring down her face. Her head was bowed with one arm on her knee, fist clenched. Then she looked up, locking eyes with Mercury. They had grown up together, seen each other at their weakest, and Mercury had never seen Venus look as conflicted as she did right now. More than all the other Angels, her loyalty to Sol was unshakeable. Even so, Mercury could see the pain of betrayal in her eyes. Not for the Maraccans, but for Earth, who was so oblivious to what Sol's order meant.

Outside the ship, Mercury could see the drive core slowly falling towards the moon. Sol had a way to stop it. He had to. But what if he didn't? Mercury's first PerfectMemory forced itself to the forefront of his mind. *Killing is never justified. Never.* He heard Sol's words as clearly as if he were speaking now. *But sometimes you have to do something terrible in order to prevent something even more horrible.*

Mercury had to kill Sol. He had to. Even though his mind and body screamed obedience there was some deep part of him that knew Sol must die, and that he must be the one to do it.

"Are you willing to do what is necessary to help people? Even if it means killing?" Sol had said ten years ago.

"Yes," Mercury answered.

"No matter who?"

He looked up at Sol now. *No matter who.* And yet, his body refused to respond.

"I can still stop it," Sol said to the doctor. He held out a handheld transmitter. "I can disarm it any time, Corius. But if you don't do something in the next three minutes, it will detonate."

Mercury saw Venus begin shaking her head ever so slightly, still on one knee. She was rejecting the idea that Sol could do something so terrible. For the sake of her loyalty, she was rationalizing Sol's actions. Mercury could practically hear her thoughts. If Mercury did nothing, then all those people's deaths were on his hands. He had to stop Sol. His body would not respond. He had to trust Sol. Sol had rescued them. Sol was safe. Sol helped people. Sol knew what he was doing. This was all part of the plan.

His whole body was trembling. Simultaneously driven to action and inaction, his mind and body were shutting down. He could not breathe. The *Defiant* felt like it was shaking under him. His body called up memories of the pain Sol had put him through when he disobeyed. Sol was his idol. Everything he was, he owed to Sol. *No matter who.* The man was everything he hoped to one day be. *No matter who.* Mercury's hand clawed for his sword. His arm refused to respond. He was Sol's slave.

"Genrik," Dr. Jormungand pleaded. "Please."

Mercury wanted to scream at the old man, "Just do what he wants!" But no sound emerged. His throat felt like a great hand was crushing it.

"You have the power, Corius." Sol allowed his helmet to recede and got down so their faces were mere centimeters apart. "Just give me your word and I'll end this. No one needs to die."

Shit. Even my WristGun could kill him now. Damn it. No matter how hard he tried, his arm would not budge. Mercury looked at Jormungand with hot tears rolling down his face. *Please, Doctor.* The old man looked frantically from Sol to Maracca VII. *Come on, you don't have much more time.*

"Don't let them die because of your hesitation," Sol urged. "Choose now, before it's too late."

"Alright," Dr. Jormungand bowed his head in submission. "I'll do whatever you want."

Sol pressed a button on the transmitter and just like that, the tension in the room disappeared. "Thank you, Corius. You won't regret it." He turned to Mercury and Venus. "Angels, rise."

They obeyed.

CHAPTER ELEVEN

MERCURY
Age 20

Back at Angel Tower, Mercury was tense as he and Venus were led to Sol's office. They were no longer under his direct influence, but the memory of the event haunted Mercury. When they returned, Sol had not even allowed them time to remove their armor, taking them here immediately after locking up Dr. Jormungand on the detention level. No doubt this was to discuss the punishment for their insubordination earlier. But why was he bringing them to his office?

When they arrived, Sol pushed open both heavy steel doors. Hard to believe barely a day ago the Sons had turned this place into a warzone. Sol preferred the minimalist approach in his aesthetics, and that extended to his office. Because most of the room was comprised of polished steel, there was not much to be damaged; bullets were outdated and could do nothing against this room. The Tower had been built to withstand far more devastating attacks. Instead, the spent ammunition simply lay scattered across the floor, flattened as their armored feet stepped on them.

"Well done," Sol said once they were inside. "I had to make Dr. Jormungand believe I was serious. The two of you performed better than I could have hoped for."

Venus let out an exhausted laugh. "I knew you were playing him. I knew it."

Mercury desperately wanted to kill Sol. If the man so much as removed his helmet he could end his life in the blink of an eye. Unfortunately, he did not. "You had me really scared for a second there."

"I know," Sol said with an audible smile. "All of that was a show. I did it for you."

No. You were going to kill them. Mercury shook his head. "You had me fooled."

"But like always," Venus seemed to completely believe Sol's lie. "You were five steps ahead of us."

"Only five? I think you might be underestimating me." Sol looked at Mercury. His face was unreadable, thanks to the helmet.

The hair on the back of Mercury's neck stood straight up. *Keep calm. He doesn't know anything. If he did, I would be dead already, or worse.*

"Is this place secure?" Mercury looked around. "The Sons had to have had help getting inside."

"Yes," Sol nodded. "Every strength has the potential to be a weakness. We are situated at the center of the Federation's largest collection of military installations in existence. My best guess is the attack was orchestrated by the Minister of Economy so his puppet Prime Minister can replace me as soon as he gets elected."

"Vyllus is a snake," Venus said. "But do you really think he would do something like this in a time of war?"

"War is the best time for Vyllus to make money," Sol said. "That's why he supports the Sons. Either way, an investigation would take far too long."

"So, what do we do?" Venus asked. "Keep our armor on at all times?"

"No. I'm transferring all military personnel within a ten-kilometer radius and replacing them with trusted men from the Storm Legions."

"Ten kilometers?" Mercury asked incredulously. *He is amassing an army. He is already preparing to take over.* "How long will the transition take?"

"It's already happened," Sol looked out his window at New Tarence sprawled out beneath them. "I gave the order when we left to retrieve the doctor."

Shit. The coup could happen at any time. Mercury looked at Sol's armored back. He imagined Sol's head falling to the floor in a spurt of blood. But not now. Not with Venus here. Not when Sol could send him to his knees with a single word. He let out a breath. *Five steps ahead.*

"I believe Earth has already seen Mars," Sol said. "The two of you should join them. Corius will have Mars' armor repaired by the time he's recovered, but he will not be present when we attack the Bastion." Sol turned to face them. "I will accompany you in his place."

"Alright," Venus started nodding. "It's been a while since we've been able to see you in the field." Her voice emanated rare excitement.

Mercury smiled to himself. It was unlikely, but the chance existed that he would get an opportunity to kill him at the Bastion without the others being able to interfere.

"I'll do my best to make it a good demonstration," Sol said sardonically. "Now, I have things to attend to. You're dismissed."

He's not punishing us for questioning him on the Defiant? *That's...strange.*

When the two of them arrived at Mars' room, they found Saturn, Earth and Jupiter sitting huddled up on the floor against the wall opposite Mars' DreamTank. Inside the tank was Mars. Mercury could not see his brother's back, but on his chest was a bright red splotch of flesh where the bullet had tried to exit through the armor. Mars had always been the biggest, even bigger than Mercury. Floating in the tank though, he looked like a giant.

Mercury sat down next to Earth. "How's he doing?"

"The guy's a monster," Earth nudged Mercury and the two scooted to the side so Venus could sit next to Saturn. The big girl wrapped her arms around the smaller one. "He hasn't woken up yet, but he's soaking up everything the tank's giving him like a sponge. It's ridiculous."

"You guys got Jormungand?" Saturn asked.

Venus and Mercury shared a look. "Yeah," she said.

Even staring at Mars' broken body, all Mercury could think of was what happened on the *Defiant*. Sol was already setting up to make his move. As Mercury was now, he would not be capable of stopping him. He had spent the last three years studying Sol's fighting styles with the express purpose of killing him. However, all of that was worthless if Sol could defeat him with a single word.

"I just realized I've got some Forging to do," he scooted away from the wall. Venus nodded in understanding. She spent more time in Forging than anyone. Mercury gave Saturn a big hug. "Make sure to get some sleep. We're hitting the Bastion in thirty hours."

"Don't worry about me," she squeezed him back.

"What are you working on?" Jupiter asked.

Mercury hesitated. "Personal project. I'll show you once it's finished." Even though it was not a lie, he hated deceiving his family. As he left, he patted Mars' DreamTank with a hand. Just like all his family, one day he might have to go through them to get to Sol. If the gods were real, he prayed they would not let that happen. "Get better, buddy."

Before Forging, he first went to Erithian's Eye. He needed to update the machine on the day's events and see how that changed the equation.

The elevator was still out of commission from the Sons attack, so he had to take the maintenance shafts up to Erithian's floor. As he climbed the steel ladder, he felt his eyes start to droop. He shook himself awake. The events of the past couple days had left him drained. On top of all that, he had been pushing himself hard to learn the ins and outs of all Sol's various fighting styles. Only now that he had a moment to breathe was it hitting him.

The multilayered doors slid open and Mercury was met with the looming figure of Sol.

His heart leapt into his throat, but thankfully he was tired enough that he was able to keep it from showing. "What brings you up here so late?" his enemy asked.

Mercury blinked twice. "I wanted to check how having Mars out of commission will affect us taking the Bastion." He must have gotten used to lying if his sleep-deprived mind could come up with that so quickly.

The man's steel-colored eyes searched his face for a moment in a way that unsettled Mercury. "Let me know if you spot anything I should know."

"Of course." Mercury nodded and went inside.

Sol followed him.

Shit. Had he noticed Mercury's killing intent on the *Defiant*? Neither of them were wearing armor. If Sol attacked him here, he could kill him. Mercury could not allow the man to be in his blind spot. Turning his head, he asked, "Forget to take off the PsyMitter?"

Sol smirked for a split second, then shook his head without saying a word.

Idiot! Why the hell did you say something so stupid? Sol doesn't forget things!

He had to salvage this quickly. Sol stayed several meters behind him, even when Mercury reached Erithian's console. Then he remembered that of all Angel Tower, Erithian's Eye was the one place not under surveillance. He could turn the tables and kill Sol here. *No.* Getting the jump on Sol would be impossible with the distance between them and with Mercury's back turned.

"Okay," Mercury turned, acting casual. "What's going on Sol? Why are you looking at me like that?"

The man cocked an eyebrow. "Mercury, is there something you want to tell me?"

Mercury was keenly aware of his surroundings. There was only one way in and out of Erithian's Eye, and Sol was blocking it. His heart began to hammer in his chest. "No," he calmly shook his head. "Why do you ask?" Grabbing a PsyMitter from the console, he placed it at the base of his neck. There was the familiar hum against his skin as it activated. Mercury had not used a PsyMitter since Erithian revealed itself, but right now he needed help.

Erithian, help me out here.

For security purposes, mental communication with the machine was one-way. In lieu of a response, the machine's holographic display surrounded Mercury and Sol. Instead of showing the statistical degrees to which Mars' absence would affect the battle at the Bastion, however, the display showed Saturn's face and psychological profile. The pending desired future read, "Mercury and Saturn engage in sexual relations."

Sol raised his eyebrows, then gave Mercury a questioning look.

"Um...wow," Mercury stammered and switched the display via the PsyMitter to the Bastion attack. He closed his eyes and shook his head. "Did that really just happen?" He knew what Erithian was doing, and it was a great cover. Even so, he could feel the heat in his face. And why did the machine have to choose that after Mars had literally just been shot? That made him look like an asshole. A shitty asshole. Then his mind pictured the "desired future" and he instantly opened his sleep deprived eyes with a shake of his head.

"Mercury," Sol said slowly. "You realize that we are at war?"

"Yes sir," Mercury nodded quickly.

"And you realize that you are the team leader?"

"Yes sir."

"And you realize just how important it is the six of you remain undivided in the coming years?"

"Yes sir."

"No," Sol shook his head. "I need to know that you understand. Above all else, the six of you *must* remain united."

Mercury was solemn. "Yes sir." It felt strange having the man he desperately needed to kill lecturing him like a child.

"Alone," Sol said. "You're weak." His eyes flicked towards the floor in the direction of Mars' room. "Alone, you can be killed. But when you're together, then you are truly invincible."

"I understand sir," Mercury said.

"I hope so," Sol said. Then his eyes grew stern. "Because if you don't learn that lesson now, you will learn the hard way. And you won't be the one who suffers for it."

Mercury pounded a fist to his chest in salute. "Yes sir."

With that, Sol left.

Once he was gone and the doors closed behind him, Mercury leaned heavily on Erithian's console and let out a breath. "Well...that was close."

Erithian's avatar appeared. "He's right though, we stand the best chance if you can unite the other Angels against Sol."

"It won't work." Mercury stared at the door Sol had left through. "They trust him too much."

"Sol has a way of influencing people," the machine said. "Perhaps if you were to wait until after the coup, they would be easier to convince."

"No," Mercury said immediately. "You know how many people Sol would kill if he took over. I can't let that happen."

"I know. But Sol is no match for the six of you. If you waited, not only would your victory be almost guaranteed, but the worlds would have seen firsthand the kind of monster Sol is. The insurance might be worth it."

Mercury shot the holographic boy a look. "Now you're sounding like him."

Erithian snorted. "I had a feeling you would say that. What I meant was that you are far less likely to be executed afterwards if you let Sol take over."

"I'm not concerned for my own life," Mercury said while watching the door.

"I knew you'd say that too."

"And yet you still said it."

"Believe it or not, there are people I really care deeply about."

"Anyone outside of this place?"

"Nah, not really," Erithian said. "It's hard for me to care about people I've never met."

"Not going to go all AI overlord on them, are you?"

"You know, that joke gets a bit old after a while."

"Sorry."

A moment of silence. "Hey," Erithian said. "You know sometime soon you should really go see Sol's family."

"His family?" Mercury turned to the hologram. "I thought he was an orphan."

"No," the machine said. "He was dropped off at an orphanage towards the start of the First Taurusian War by his mother, Yaedis Titor."

Mercury cocked his head. "Why are you bringing this up now?"

"It would be a good for you to see where a monster like Sol came from. Know your enemy. Besides, if we're lucky humanity won't ever get another apple as rotten as him. Best to learn all you can from this one."

"Where are they?"

"Still on Taurus. You know that town I told you about that's great for hiding? Esen? As long as you're not tracked, Sol would have no way of knowing you were there."

"Well I doubt I'll have the time. Sol's moving all the pieces into place to take over."

"That's true," Erithian said. "By the way, Sazius Hedge is as good as elected. Once he's Prime Minister he plans to dissolve the Angel Program."

"Does he have enough Ministers on his side to win the vote?"

"Not since the Exodus bombing, no. Not normally."

"What do you mean?"

"If the vote passes to dissolve the program, Sol will use that to guarantee the Angels help him take over. The voting is private, and right now it's split four to three."

Mercury nodded. "And if Sol voted to dissolve the Angel Program…"

"Exactly," Erithian said. "We don't have much time."

"Which means I need to find a way around Sol's behavioral conditioning *fast*," Mercury said. "I can't have a repeat of what happened on the *Defiant*."

"No," the machine said dryly. "Almost as bad as if Sol had not hardened my systems against electro-magnetic surges."

"Yes, that would have been *very* bad." Mercury felt himself getting drowsy again. He shook himself awake. "Better start Forging."

"Mercury," Erithian said in a concerned voice.

"Yeah?"

"Get some sleep."

He waved the machine off. "No time. I'll be fine, just need to get my body active."

"Mercury…get some sleep."

Mercury blinked twice. "…Alright."

He blinked once more and found himself in his room, fumbling with the console for his DreamTank. He shook his head slightly but it was not enough to fully wake him up. As quickly as his tired fingers would allow, he loaded the night's programs and clambered inside. Mercury's mind dimly registered that the fluid on the floor from the previous night was gone. The DreamTank closed and began filling itself with fluid on its own. Must have been replaced since the EMP. He had just enough time to wonder when it was replaced before he was asleep.

***

When the day of the assault arrived, Mercury was ready. All thoughts of Sol had been pushed out of his mind. His mind was entirely present and focused on the task ahead. The Sons would end today. There would be no war. Then, he would kill Sol and end the greatest threat that humanity never knew existed.

"Alright everyone," Mercury addressed the Angels and Sol on the *Defiant's* bridge. "The enemy thinks the assault is tomorrow. Our primary objective is to first disable their ships before they can get them off the ground. Next objective is to plant the bug to screw their targeting. Last but not least," he looked at Saturn. "We need to take their leader, Vera, alive. Anything you want to add, Sol?"

"Only that even though I am accompanying you on this mission, Mercury is still mission lead."

"Just so everyone knows," Venus said. "The one who shot Mars…that was Vera."

"Don't worry," Saturn said. "I won't do anything stupid. We're bringing her in alive."

"Alright," Mercury nodded. "I want a good clean operation here. I know there are a lot of personal feelings on the table right now with what happened to Mars. All those have to be put aside for today. We're clean, methodical, and thorough. Remember to stay on guard even after we're inside the compound. Stay close. Somewhere in this base is someone carrying a gun that can rip through us like paper. According to Dr. Jormungand they only have two bullets left, so we'll be fine as long as we stick together."

"If one of us does get shot," Venus said. "How do we extract them?"

"We'll have the *Defiant* come in for evac," Mercury said. "But it can only get in range once we take out their targeting systems."

"Let's hope it doesn't come to that," Saturn sheathed both her swords. She'd brought Mars'.

"Two swords for this one Sat?" Venus asked.

She sniffed. "Yep."

"Six bodies," Mercury said.

"One soul," they finished and moved into the *Defiant*'s LaunchTubes.

Mercury took a breath. "Launch."

CHAPTER TWELVE

VERA
Age 28

Only one other person had survived the attack on Angel Tower that night. She did not know how Gerard escaped, but as soon as she got back she promoted him to Imri's old position as head of Bastion security. Not many were still alive that had been with her since the beginning. Now, with the Federation's fleet arriving in eighteen hours, their mettle would be tested again.

Upon returning, the news she had mortally wounded an Angel turned her into even more of a hero. No longer just Vera; now they called her Valkyrie. All of it was bullshit for morale. The Pistol only had two bullets left and even if she killed Rauss, they would have to deal with his Angels of Death. Still, best put on a good face for the soldiers. She had already held their loyalty, but now she held their awe.

Vera entered the Bastion's central command chamber and saw Gerard organizing the numerous tasks that needed to be completed before the Federation's arrival tomorrow. The room was circular, with windows providing a three hundred and sixty degree view of the Bastion and the surrounding jungle of Maracca. Thankfully the distant Maraccan moons were feeding them sensor data, so they would have an early warning when the Federation did arrive. Over two hundred personnel sat in this room at computers, making sure every aspect of the base's security was running smoothly. If they were to withstand the Federation's onslaught, they could not afford to make mistakes. The Angels sure as hell never seemed to make mistakes, and Vera doubted they would start here.

"Gerard," Vera walked up behind the man put a hand on his shoulder. "How are the preparations coming along?"

"Just fine Valkyrie," Gerard nodded.

She leaned in close and whispered. "You know you don't have to call me that too."

The middle-aged man smiled. "I know, but it's good for the troops. You give them hope those monsters can be stopped."

Vera had never wanted to be any kind of symbol. Being the symbol had been Libby's job, not that she had wanted it either. But she had touched people's hearts and minds. All Vera did was gather those angered by her death. "How are the Zeroes?"

"The local warlords became far more cooperative once they realized just how much we could pay them," Gerard explained. "The children are obedient, but they make the men a little nervous."

"Don't worry about the men," Vera said. "The Federation allowed the warlords to keep their child armies. Now they'll regret it. Those children will be fighting for their freedom just like the rest of us."

"It's not their age ma'am," Gerard said. "They're starved. It's unsettling to see. We've fed them plenty, but they still look on death's door."

One of the men operating sensors called out in a panicked voice. "Sir, we've got six bogies approaching from low orbit!"

"Low orbit?" Gerard said. "Why didn't we see them?"

"They just appeared out of nowhere sir! Speed seventy kilometers per second."

"All hands to battle stations," Vera called out. "Do we have an ID on the targets?" She already knew the answer, but she had to ask.

The man turned to her from his station. His face was ashen. "It's the Angels."

Vera swallowed. Well done Rauss. He really deserved that pretentious title 'Archangel.' They were done for.

Then one thing caught her attention. There were six bogies on sensors, not five. According to their sources the one she had shot was still in the hospital under heavy guard. If there were six bogies then Archangel must be with them. Vera's trembling hand went to the Pistol in the back of her pants. She grinned.

Another person called out, "Ten seconds to engagement range!"

"This is it everyone," she said, ignoring the hollow pit in her stomach. "Today is the day Angels fall."

***

MERCURY
Age 18

Mercury felt adrenaline flood his body as the planet screamed towards him. At their current speed, it took mere moments to be right on top of the Bastion, despite them decelerating the whole way. Flames licked the six of them as they waited until the last instant to turn and begin strafing the base. They flew in perfect unison, decimating the Bastion with their WristGuns on their maximum setting.

Thousands of aircraft waited in countless alcoves and airfields. Mercury only had a moment to hit them. His mind and his armor were one. At a mere thought he turned a dozen ships to flaming wreckages. Any Sons that saw them must be so terrified. He was an orange ball of fire spewing white bolts of lightning on those below.

In truth, he could barely see his targets even with SmartOptics, but that was enough. Sol had trained them to the point that everything was instinct now. Long ago he had stopped thinking about what he was doing, but instead willed reality to change and it did. As soon as the Sons were destroyed, he would kill Sol and the worlds would be at peace.

Faster and faster Mercury flew, destroying the Sons' air force where it stood. After he had destroyed perhaps a hundred aircraft the air defense guns began firing, but those were laughably easy to avoid. They were designed to stop the Federation's massive cruisers. Not them. Though the very air around them erupted into a Hel-scape unlike any he had ever seen, they were untouchable. The thought was intoxicating.

In the moment, Mercury almost forgot that it was Sol with them, not Mars. On and on the six of them danced through the air in perfect tandem. No words were necessary. *Six bodies, one soul.* The speed at which the landscape pitched and spun would be enough to make any normal person empty their stomach. To Mercury, it was pure delight. Up here, he felt like a god.

SmartOptics showed mobile firing patterns trying to lock onto him. Looks like the Sons had managed to get some ships in the air after all. *Not bad.*

Flipping himself over on a dime, Mercury saw a swarm of fighters eating his air trails and shooting everywhere he should have been. *Too slow.* He quickly shot two down and led the others on a little chase. Up and down, left and right, through corkscrews and one-eighties, Mercury completely ignored them as he destroyed more grounded ships. *They must have known their revolution would end like this.*

Eventually Mercury and the others had destroyed all the ships on the ground. Time to take out the ones in the air. *You should have stayed home.* Mercury noticed there were about thirty or so on his tail. "Jup," he said. "Switch."

Mercury guessed it would take the pilots a good half second to realize what was happening. Their bad. Mercury and Jupiter flew straight past each other, shooting down plenty of the other's ships while the others desperately tried to avoid crashing into their comrades. Their formations broke and Mercury easily dispatched several of the stragglers.

At this point Mercury was pretty sure the air defense guns had given up, not wanting to risk friendly fire when they could not even keep up with the enemy. After perhaps another minute, the skies were clear. Now it was time to storm the base.

As the six of them descended, Mercury surveyed the landscape. What had once been a lush mountain jungle was now riddled with craters and fire. If not for his suit filtering out the smoke, he would be suffocating right now. *Killing is always wrong*, he heard Sol say. *But sometimes you have to do something horrible to prevent something even more horrible*. A chill ran down his spine.

Mercury, Sol and the others landed on the Bastion's highest point, cratering the mountaintop and revealing heavy armor plating as the dirt and rock cascaded down the mountainside. This place was built to withstand a dozen Breakers. As one unit, they set their WristGun's to Cutter. Six beams of white energy appeared. Almost too thin to see and impossibly bright, the Angels plunged them into the armor plating with a sharp hiss. The armor might as well have been warm butter. The six of them of them dragged the beams along the armor in one perfect circle.

Then they were falling, riding the cylinder of armor they had cut out down into the heart of the Bastion. Inside, they were greeted by a couple hundred Sons manning computers. Instantly every Son in the room pulled out repeaters and opened fire. Mercury did not feel a thing as the thousands of blasts impacted his armor. In truth, he could not be sure whether they even hit him.

"You in their system Jupiter?" Mercury asked.

"Full access," his brother answered.

The Angels set their WristGuns to antipersonnel.

With twelve simultaneous whines that drowned out all but the loudest of screams, twelve streams of brilliant fire erupted from their arms. Each one taught the Sons the futility of their plight at over nine thousand condensed reasons per minute. Metal and flesh alike were torn asunder as they reduced the room to a mess of molten slag.

"Okay guys," Jupiter said stepping over a couple dead bodies. "We have control. I'm redirecting everything to the fleet. When they get here, they won't have any problems landing troops."

"Good work," Mercury said as Jupiter patched them into the base's security system. Technically their job was now completed. If Mercury decided, they could leave now. But he was not going to do that. This was a game to see how close to zero he could get the Federation's casualties. "Let's clean house."

As they left the room, Mercury glanced down and noticed a woman, lying dead with her gun still slung across her back, holding a picture of a man and two children. The oldest was a girl, maybe four or five, holding her father's hand. The younger one looked like a boy, held in one of his father's arms. Mercury's chest began to ache. *'We don't fight and kill monsters, but people.'* He released a breath and led the way deeper into the Bastion.

A flashing light on his HUD alerted him to an incoming transmission to all of them from an unknown source. They all shared a look, and Mercury answered.

"Welcome Angels," a woman's voice echoed in his helmet. "Long time, no see."

Immediately Jupiter sent a searching algorithm through the Bastion's security system to find the woman's location.

Mercury gave his brother a thumbs-up. "Who are you?" he asked to stall her.

SmartOptics displayed an image of a woman with fiery red hair entering a bunker. Then he caught a glimpse of her face.

Vera.

"It's me, Vera," she answered. "Leader of the Sons of Liberty, the one who paid you a visit the other night. How's your friend doing by the way? The one with the big hole in his back?"

Mercury saw Saturn grip her blades tighter. Jupiter put a hand on her shoulder.

Venus spoke up. "He's doing a Hel of a lot better than all those friends of yours I killed. Especially the girl you seemed so concerned about. What did you call her again? Sahra? She watched the maintenance shaft just like you told her. Kept her eyes glued on it the whole time. Never even saw me coming."

"...I'll save a bullet for you," the woman's voice dripped menace.

"Better make it two," Venus said.

As they made their way through the base, SmartOptics alerted Mercury to all enemies long before they reached them. They annihilated all opposition without even slowing down.

"I'm sure you've traced my location already," the woman said. "So, if you want me, come and get me."

They came to a large, open chamber with doors to the left, right and ahead. SmartOptics alerted him to a sizeable force beyond each door. The six of them stood in a half-circle, two for each door. "Don't worry," Mercury said. "We'll be with you shortly."

At that moment, the doors to the room they were in were blown open and Mercury saw something that made him feel sick and tremble with rage at the same time.

Maracca had long ago been exhausted of resources and subsequently abandoned by everyone with any money in favor of the planet's seven moons. The only people who stayed behind were those too poor to leave, or scavengers that soon became warlords. If Maracca VII was the lowlifes and rejects of Maraccan society's caste system, then Maraccan "Zeroes" were the ones that did not even make the bottom rung of the ladder. On Maracca whoever had the most guns and the biggest conscripted army made the laws. Apparently, the Sons of Liberty must have paid off the local warlords for reinforcements.

The children that scrambled through the doors toward them looked starved to death's door. In their hands were automatic rifles they used to spray at the Angels without concern for their own safety. Immediately Mercury and the other Angels dropped into a shield wall. His heart began beating faster and faster. *What kind of sick bastard uses children to fight for them?* Standing next to him, was Sol.

"No," Saturn said firmly. "We can't."

Mars, Jupiter and Saturn had been just like those poor kids before Sol saved them; Zeroes turned into child soldiers by a warlord that had destroyed their village.

Mercury heard the echoing footsteps of BreakerSuits approaching. A lot of BreakerSuits. They had to act now. The BreakerSuits would be no match for their WristGuns. But how many kids would die in the process? They could minimize collateral damage if they used their swords, but their swords were trayite. If any one of the Sons in BreakerSuits got their hands on a blade...

"I can't do this Merc," Jupiter shook his head. "Not this."

"Mercury," Sol said. "Make the call."

Mercury's mind went back to Sol's threat to bomb Maracca VII. If Sol wanted to, he could make them kill the kids. *Just one word. All you need is, "Kill."* They would dutifully obey as he had programmed them to do. How many lives had Sol said each of them would save? Two billion? Sol was testing him; he just knew it. *No matter who.* Diligently every night,

154

Mercury had been working to undo Sol's programming. But was it enough? And if it was, would that give him away to Sol?

Mercury clenched his teeth as his heart sped up. He began to sweat profusely. Sol had given him the call.

"Angels," Mercury said slowly in a voice that went beyond mere anger. His entire being burned with a deep-set fury towards all the "freedom fighters" who would send starving children to die for them. He set his WristGun to its weakest stun setting. "Six bodies."

They all did likewise. Mercury smiled underneath his helmet. "One soul." Sol must really trust in them.

CHAPTER THIRTEEN

MERCURY
Age 20

Now that their WristGuns were on stun, the Angels fired indiscriminately into the Sons. Grown men and children alike, they all dropped like flies. Unfortunately, on stun their weapons were pathetically ineffective against the BreakerSuits. With the force of an avalanche, the mechanized soldiers crashed through their position, forcing them to separate. *Divide and conquer.* These were not the low-end models the Sons usually had either. These were top of the line. Faster. Stronger. More durable. And armed with thick steel cables coiled into lassos.

Mercury drew his sword and slashed out at them from behind his shield, cutting one of the enemy almost clean in half. Splintered metal and sparks flew everywhere. Then four other enemies grabbed Mercury's shield and pulled him further away from the others.

SmartOptics counted at least thirty BreakerSuits. Painted on the helmet of each one was the bloody maw of some terrible beast. *How were the Sons able to afford fielding hardware like this?* There was no time to dwell on that though. One of the enemies was wrestling for his sword while the other three lassoed him with their cables. With unnatural speed, the lassos pulled tight against him, two pinning his shield arm to his chest while another seized his foot. Mercury saw four others doing the same with Earth. Sol and the others had maintained their position and cut down half a dozen enemies.

Mercury shot into the air with his Boosters with the one enemy still grappling for his sword but his flight was soon stopped by the cables as they drew taut. He saw them leading outside the room. They must be anchored down somewhere. Because of the enemy grappling with him, he could not cut himself free. Despite his struggling, the cables brought him to his knees. Two more enemies split from the main force and helped their comrade wrest Mercury's sword away from him. He strained against the cables as hard as his suit would allow, but they refused to budge. The enemy with Mercury's sword raised it up high to strike.

Mercury could not move. This was not how it was supposed to end. He must not die. Not until he had cut Sol's head from his shoulders. Then, the man's arm fell off at the shoulder in a spurt of sparks and blood. The man howled in pain, but was cut short as Saturn followed through with her second blade, cutting the man in half at the waist. Against trayite swords, the enemy's BreakerSuits might as well be paper. The next instant Jupiter was flying past on his Boosters, cutting Mercury's bonds and burying his sword in an enemy's helmet.

In the distance Mercury saw Sol fighting the main force singlehandedly. Mercury hoped rather than thought Sol would be killed by them. A dozen or so meters away Venus stood over the immobilized and disarmed Earth, surrounded by eight BreakerSuits and dancing through the blood of her enemies. He had to get his sword back. He saw it on the ground and scrambled to get it, but one armored enemy was faster. Thankfully Mercury was able to get inside his reach and lock the man's arm. With a twist and a shower of sparks, the sword dropped point first into the ground, sinking almost to the hilt.

Immediately after the soldier dropped the sword, another bull-rushed Mercury and bowled him over. Right before Mercury would have hit the ground, he stuck out his arm to catch himself. Beneath him was a starved and unconscious boy of maybe eight or nine. With his free hand he did his best to keep his adversary off balance as they grappled. Winning with one hand was impossible, but if he fell, this little boy would die.

The little boy looked just like Mars did back then. *Mars had looked small and scared. Even though his golden eyes were cold and dead, Mercury glimpsed the frightened little boy deeper inside as soon as he saw him. Even when he killed the other boy so Saturn could take his place as an Angel, he had looked terrified. Jupiter had not been able to see past the emotionless exterior. Saturn had though, and he was sure Sol had as well.*

Then Mercury's glimpse disappeared. All he saw was a cold-blooded killer that would do anything to protect Jupiter and Saturn. The boy's eyes looked so much like Sol's. Why did that make him jealous?

With a heave, Mercury pushed up and away from the unconscious boy. Rising to both feet, Mercury broke the man's hold and caught him by the throat, lifting him bodily into the air. The man clawed at his throat, but Mercury wouldn't let go. One of the man's comrades picked up Mercury's fallen sword and rushed him. Changing one of his hands on the first man from neck to midsection, Mercury caught the second man's swing on his comrade. Without missing a beat, Mercury used the dead man's body to twist the sword free of his enemy's grip. Throwing the corpse onto an empty patch of ground, Mercury wrenched the sword free and decapitated the second man in one fluid motion.

In the distance, Mercury saw Venus pinned to the ground by three enemies amidst a pile of metal corpses. They had taken away her sword and it was all she could do to keep the point away from her neck. To Mercury's relief, Saturn was already on top of things. After quickly killing two nearby enemies in a series of slashes, she threw one blade to skewer the man with Venus' blade and flew over to follow through on the other two near her sister. Once Venus had reclaimed her blade, they cut the lassoes holding Earth. *Having two swords really helps.*

Turning back to help Jupiter, who was now outnumbered four to one, Mercury dashed to his brother. Back to back, the two of them hacked and slashed in a perfectly coordinated frenzy. All the while they took care not to step on any of the unconscious children. Before long, their enemies were in pieces at their feet.

By this point all that remained were four from the main force that had been fighting Sol. Around them lay too many bodies to count. Mercury noted to himself that not a single corpse had landed on any of the children, even though the fighting had been thickest around Sol. Looked like one of the four remaining combatants had managed to get his hands on Earth's sword. Mercury and the other Angels closed in to help Sol dispatch them, but he held up his hand.

They stopped and watched as Sol sheathed his sword and let the shield return to its place on his back. With a roll of his shoulders, Sol dropped into a stance and waved the soldiers forward. The enemies looked at each other and the one with the sword tossed it to one of his comrades. Then the four of them charged Sol.

When they reached a patch of ground clear of kids, Sol shot a hole in the ground right where the enemy with the sword would need to place his foot. While the enemy with the sword stumbled, Sol leapt at the others. With an aerial spin, Sol drove his foot into one of the men, crushing his helmet and sending him into the other two. As soon as Sol's feet touched the ground, he leapt over the stumbling enemies for the one with the sword. He had regained his balance and swung at Sol, but Sol clapped his hands together to stop the blade and wrenched it from his grip. In the next moment Sol was holding the blade and blood was pouring from the slash in the other man's BreakerSuit.

When the two survivors tried to run, Sol cut one down while letting the other one go. Tossing Earth's sword back to him, Sol continued to let the enemy flee. Once the man had gotten beyond the unconscious children Sol raised his WristGun and fired. The man exploded in a ball of shrapnel and fire. Sol then turned up to one of the cameras on the ceiling and fired again.

Mercury committed everything he had just seen Sol do to memory. *If I can't kill him in his sleep, then that's what I have to beat.* "Let's move Angels," he said aloud. "This Valkyrie person is so keen on meeting us. Let's not keep her waiting."

As they moved through the rest of the facility they encountered more child Zeroes mixed with the Sons. They stunned them all, and then followed through on everyone of fighting age in passing. Before long, many of the soldiers just ran outright. The children ran as soon as their

Zero overseers ran or were killed. It didn't take long to reach the bunker. Apparently, some of the Sons truly believed in what they did, because there was a small army congregated outside the entrance. There were no children among them.

One man stood at the front, a middle aged Taurusian that Mercury remembered seeing during the Sons' attack on Angel Tower. "Your path of carnage ends here," he declared confidently. "No matter how hard you try Archangel, you will not drown out the voice of the people."

"You would die for the Valkyrie?" Sol asked.

"If that is our fate," the man pulled out a pistol and leveled it at Sol. The same pistol Vera had used to shoot Mars. "Then so be it."

Oh gods, please shoot him. That would make my life so much easier.

"Gerard?" Earth took a step forward. "Is that you? You joined the Sons?"

"Stay back," Gerard said. "Or I blow your commander's head off."

Mercury glanced at Earth. None of the Sons' weapons would hurt them, but that pistol certainly could. His brother paused, then took a step forward. "I know you don't remember me Gerard, but I remember you. Ten years ago, on Taurus. I was a lot smaller back then. You had just gone on your lunch break and were waiting for someone."

Gerard pointed the gun at Earth, "Don't take another step."

Venus leveled her WristGun at Gerard. Mercury saw the Sons shift uneasily. "Earth," Venus said on a private channel. "Who is this guy?"

Earth hesitated, then took another step forward. "Syn and Sahn were just visible between the factory rooftops; you looked forward to it all day."

At the same time as Gerard's eyes widened, Mercury recalled the PerfectMemory the Angels all shared in the DreamTank when they first met. *Hunger gnawed at Earth's stomach. The paltry food he had managed to steal that day had been stolen from him by the orphanage bullies. So he had risked begging. The twin suns were just reaching the point in the sky where you could see both of them in between the towering buildings of Taurus' slums. Amidst all the factory workers that ignored his pleading eyes was a single man that smiled at Earth and held out his sandwich. "You hungry, kid?"*

The pistol in Gerard's hand trembled and slowly lowered. "Yuun?" Mercury hadn't heard Earth's real name since before Sol had found the boy. Earth never had any family, but when Sol gave them the option of writing a single letter to say goodbye, Earth had written one to a man called Gerard.

"You know this man, Earth?" Sol said on their private channel.

"It's me," Earth said out loud. "Did you get my letter?"

Gerard nodded. "Yeah, I got it." He raised the pistol back at Earth and shook his head with disbelief. "I didn't realize this is what you were talking about."

"Earth," Venus called out on the comms. "Get back."

Earth took another step forward.

"You know," Gerard said. "Hearing about what the lady did to you is what made me join the Sons in the first place. Never thought you'd be on their side."

"You were the only one that got me through it," Earth said in a strained voice. He took another step forward. "All those things you said about staying anchored and focusing on the light even when everything else is dark. That was all that kept me going when she locked me up."

Gerard faltered, but kept the pistol pointed at Earth. "Angels," Sol said over the comms. "Prepare to fire."

"I can get to him Sol," Earth answered. "Please, just let me try."

"Earth," Sol said. "He is going to kill you."

"Do you know how many of my friends you've killed?" Gerard asked. "Do you?"

"Gerard," Earth said. "We don't have to do this."

"We fought for kids like you, Yuun," Gerard said. "But men like *him*," he pointed a finger at Sol. "They don't care about you at all. People like him are the reasons the slums exist in the first place."

"Gerard," Earth took another step forward. "He *is* me. We grew up at the same orphanage. We were locked in the same box. We are changing things. The Bjornish mines are empty. The slums on Taurus are next. It takes time, but we are changing things. I know you are doing what you feel is right. You all are," Earth addressed the other Sons before turning back to Gerard. "What you're doing is hurting the very people you're trying to help."

"And how many people have you killed, Yuun?" Gerard asked.

"Too many," Earth put his hand up towards the pistol. "We all have blood on our hands."

"Earth," Venus cried over the comms through tears. "He is going to kill you."

"All I want," Earth took another step forward. "Is for the killing to stop."

"Kill him Gerard," one of the Sons called out. "Shoot him now." Gerard did not move.

Mercury let out a breath. He looked at the other Sons. They knew the pistol was their only chance against their enemy. Earth really was doing this. "Earth," he said over the comms. "You crazy son of a bitch."

Earth's hand was almost on the pistol. "Just give me the gun Gerard. The killing can stop right here."

"Shoot him Gerard!" The Son turned his rifle from the Angels to Gerard. "That pistol is our best chance."

"If he so much as twitches," Venus warned.

"I have your word, Yuun?" Gerard asked.

"Of course," Earth said with relief. "All we want is peace."

"You really mean it, don't you?" Gerard slowly let out a breath and flipped the pistol grip toward Earth. "Just promise you won't hurt any of my men."

In a spurt of blood, Gerard fell with a hole in his head. Earth took a shocked step back as both sides unloaded on each other, the air erupting in a multicolored blaze of searing energy.

The Sons' rifles could not do much against the Angels' armor, so it was wholesale slaughter. Then Mercury saw a Son pick up the pistol and level it at Earth. Somewhere Mercury's mind registered a cry from Venus that shook him to his very bones. So vulnerable and frightened even in its defiance.

Everything seemed to move in slow motion. Venus was flying straight for Earth. Jupiter cried out. The man with the pistol was squeezing the trigger even as the white fire of the Angels' guns tore him and his comrades to bloody shreds. Mercury's heart skipped a beat, then another.

Venus crashed into Earth. Blood went everywhere. The man with the pistol fell. The rest of the Sons were dead in seconds. For a moment there was silence before Mercury and the others rushed to Venus and Earth. They could hear Venus crying.

"Oh gods, Earth," Mercury said. There was so much blood.

"Jupiter to *Defiant*," Jupiter choked.

Then Venus' crying turned to laughter. Earth turned to them, "The gun wasn't loaded."

"Don't ever do something like that again," Venus cried.

"I won't Vee," Earth said. He did not seem very thrilled to be alive.

"I'm sorry Earth," Mercury said. "About Gerard."

Earth hugged Venus. He sounded confused, "I don't think he knew it was empty."

"Come on," Mercury said. "This Valkyrie person might still try to run."

The six of them set their WristGuns to Cutter and got to work on the bunker door. The process took almost an entire minute. Except for the hiss of molten metal, simmering blood and burning corpses, the Angels worked in silence. When the round slab of metal finally came free with a reverberating crash, Mercury and Saturn ducked through the molten hole first.

The room Mercury found himself in was the only luxurious thing he had seen in the entire complex so far. Instead of the plain concrete and steel, this place was filled with plush, dark wood chairs set around a polished, oval table and art along the walls. On the left Mercury recognized the StarWood podium from the Sons' videos. In front of the table was Vera standing in the middle of the room with two holstered sidearms and her arms raised in apparent surrender.

"The Hel is this?" Saturn gestured with Mars' sword. "Giving up already?"

"Just don't hurt any more of my men," she said. "If you can promise me that, I'll surrender the whole base."

Mercury's eyebrows went up inside his helmet. *Is she serious? The whole base? Would her troops go along with that?* "Where are the bullets?" Mercury demanded. "Your friend out there didn't have them."

The woman's head bowed for a moment. "Shit. If it helps, I ordered him to run. I don't know where the bullets are. They're long gone. I sent them away for insurance. So long as you take us all alive, we'll give them to you."

Sol and Venus entered the room. "Am I hearing this right?" Venus asked on a private channel.

Sol said nothing.

"Why the change of heart?" Mercury asked. "You seemed pretty keen on killing us a while ago."

"Twice now I've seen you go on your killing sprees," she said with a shake of her head. "I just want all this to end."

"She's hiding something," Jupiter said over the comms while he and Earth entered. "I can tell."

Mercury had thought as much, and Jupiter was rarely wrong about these things. He leveled both his weapons at the woman. "What are you hiding?" Mercury demanded. "We'll know if you're lying."

"I'm hiding all kinds of things," the woman said. "Where do you want to start? My name is Vera. My sister was Liberty Tormen. I already told you I formed the Sons. Ever since Libby died I've wanted to kill that man," she pointed a finger at Sol. "We can talk later, but do I have your word?"

Mercury was surprised she was actually able to pick out Sol from amongst them. She probably noticed the ridge on the back of his armor. But why did she seem to be in such a hurry?

"I don't trust her," Saturn said over the comms. Given what this woman did to Mars, she was not exactly impartial.

"I agree," Jupiter said. "I think she was telling the truth about sending the bullets away, but she's trying to get one on us."

"She's here," Venus said. "Let's just grab her and go."

Mercury nodded. "Sol?"

"She's stalling to keep us here," Sol said. "It's possible whoever has the bullets has not yet escaped."

"I agree," Mercury said.

As one, they all began moving towards her. "You have my word," Mercury said aloud.

Vera, if that was her real name, suddenly smiled. However, it was not a smile of relief, but victory.

Instantly the six of them were enclosed in a steel box.

Before any of them could react, they were sucked up to the ceiling as the box they were in shot straight down. Mercury's whole body was glued to the metal. He could not budge. After several seconds the acceleration lessened and the six of them were able to move, albeit with great difficulty. SmartOptics told him they were in a box approaching three kilometers per second.

"Can the suits handle an impact at these speeds?" Saturn said as she struggled to stand on the ceiling in the artificial gravity generated by the box's downward acceleration.

"Let's not find out," Mercury answered.

Without a word, Sol pushed against the ceiling and fired his Boosters at maximum thrust. Then, he began melting the ceiling with his Cutter. Mercury and the others shut up and followed suit. The first second seemed to last an eternity. Then another. And another. Then with a great rending of metal, they burst through the steel trap. Mercury saw the box disappear as thick steel doors closed a few meters beneath them.

Mercury had just enough time to register that they were alive before a river of molten metal crashed down on them much faster than gravity would allow. Mercury lost sight of the other Angels as his world was enveloped in blinding yellow.

CHAPTER FOURTEEN

MERCURY
Age 20

Mercury could not see a thing. The only thing he could hear was his own breathing and a sharp hissing sound. Thank the gods the suit seemed to be able to handle the heat for now. If his suit was not made of trayite, he would be cooked to a crisp by now. Unfortunately, the trayite would act as a heat sink that would help cool the molten metal. That was probably what the hissing sound was. He had to get out of here quickly, otherwise they could be trapped in here forever. He tried to start his Boosters, but there was no response. *Shit. How could I have let her get one on me?* Then Mercury noticed to his surprise he was rising through the bright yellow liquid even without his Boosters.

Eventually he broke through the surface of the molten metal. *Of course.* The metal was heavier than he was, even with the suit. He could see Sol had already moved to the side of the tunnel and was climbing up out of the pool of metal with his sword. The others were just starting to float to the top.

Swimming through the metal was the strangest sensation, but it was actually quite easy. The suits relied on their Boosters in the water, but since they were light enough to float here, swimming was a cinch. Of course, it also helped that the armor was keeping him from burning alive. Once he got to the side of the shaft, he tried to climb but it was a sheer surface. Taking out his sword, Mercury dug it into the wall and cut out a hole for his hand, then he pulled himself up and stabbed the blade in higher.

Shit. The Sons could be evacuating right now while they were trapped down here. All because he had let his guard down.

"Merc," Jupiter held out his sword. "Boosters should start working once we get out of this stuff."

"Thanks, Jup," Mercury took the second sword and began climbing, much faster now that he had two swords. *I have to outwit Sol, and somehow, I let this random person get the better of me?*

"Mercury," Sol looked down at him. "What is humanity's greatest strength?"

This is not the time for one of your proverbs. "Our ability to adapt."

"And our greatest weakness?"

Mercury puffed out a breath through his nose. "Our ability to adapt." *Kill complacency. Learn from the past, look to the future.* The fact that he knew what a monster Sol was made the lesson sting even more.

Saturn was already climbing up as well. Having two swords really was helpful. Mercury climbed a bit higher, then dropped Jupiter's sword back to him. Jupiter handed it to Venus and she climbed out. The metal was a solid orange now. They had to move fast. Saturn and Sol each dropped a sword down to Earth, who started climbing.

At that moment, SmartOptics started going haywire. Radiation levels were through the roof. There was a bomb very close by. *Shit.*

Sol's voice was urgent. "Let's move!"

Mercury's mistake might cost them all their lives. After all his preparation, would Vera be the one to kill Sol?

Venus quickly dropped one of her swords to Jupiter, and then leapt to Saturn's leg before dropping her other blade.

"Oh shit," Saturn grunted. "Hold tight, Vee."

An incoming message from Vera. *I'll see you in Hel, Archangel.*

Mercury had never seen a nuclear explosion before. Certainly, never this close. Time slowed. His mind barely registered a brilliant burst of light sundering the entire world. His insides shrank before the infinite realization of how small he really was. He closed his eyes and accepted his fate.

As his life flashed before his eyes, he could not help but wish that he had more time to spend with his family. *At least we'll die together, and Sol along with us.*

Then he felt his armor shudder as the blast propelled him outward through the numerous layers of the disintegrating Bastion. Then, emptiness.

Out of the stillness came Sol's voice. "Is everyone alright?"

Confused, Mercury opened his eyes and looked around. He was slowly floating into Maracca's purple sky.

The other Angels all answered in the affirmative.

"Mercury?" Sol asked.

Blinking twice, Mercury looked at his hands. The armor was completely unscathed.

"Yeah…I'm fine."

"Well," Saturn said a bit out of breath. "That's one thing I can scratch off the bucket list."

Below him, Mercury saw a gaping hole where the Bastion once was. SmartOptics alerted him to the locations of the other Angels. In addition, it alerted him to dozens of distant fleeing transports, each getting blown out of the sky one by one as the *Defiant* ran its containment algorithm. None would escape. SmartOptics also noted one ship in particular, much closer to the Angels' location and much faster than the other ships. *Vera.*

He marked the vessel with SmartOptics. "Mercury to *Defiant*. Target that ship with an EMP missile."

A streak of blue appeared from a distant patch of seemingly empty space and collided with the ship, which instantly lost power.

"Aww," Saturn said as the six of them began flying towards the disabled vessel. "Why not just blow her out of the sky?"

"We need to make sure it's her," Mercury answered. "Besides, remember the mission. We need her alive."

"Is no one going to address the elephant in the room?" Earth asked. "Sol, we were just caught in a nuclear blast. Why aren't we dead?"

"As far as I and Dr. Jormungand know, trayite cannot be damaged by anything except more trayite."

"Even nukes?" Venus asked.

"Even nukes."

"Then why were you worried?" Jupiter asked.

"Because," Sol said. "If the bomb had been above us, we could have been buried."

"So other than the two bullets," Venus said. "The only ones that can stop us are each other?"

"Didn't I always say that together you would be invincible, but divided you would fall?"

Mercury swallowed. He remembered what Dr. Jormungand had said when Sol commissioned their suits. *No one deserves that power, Genrik.* He was right, and Mercury would be the one to fix things.

When the six of them arrived at the drifting ship, they discovered Vera was, in fact, aboard. When she saw them, her eyes went wide as every bit of color drained from her face. Once they boarded, she slowly dropped her sidearms and raised her hands. Mercury could tell she was not going to try anything this time. "You're coming with us."

Vera shook her head in utter disbelief. "How in the Hel…?

Mercury set his WristGun to stun and shot her.

***

Two Weeks Later…

Victory at the Bastion was largely considered the beginning of the end of the war. With no leader, and no central command center, it was merely a matter of time before the Sons of Liberty were wiped out. In preparation for when they were good and gone, Mercury had spent the past couple weeks vigorously working to recondition his mind. When he made his move to kill Sol, he could not afford to have the man send him to his knees with one word.

Now Mercury, Sol and the rest of the Angels were at a gala in celebration of the recent victory at the Bastion.

"I would personally like to thank Minister Rauss and his Angels for their heroic efforts on the battlefield," Prime Minister Liam Hughes said to an audience of eager listeners. Their applause was subdued and proper.

Mercury looked around from where he and his family stood, each of them fully armored and standing at attention. The audience was all black suits and gowns, various politicians and other VIPs that were in attendance of the gala. The Prime Minister was standing at the head of an elevated StarWood table carved with the faces of the Federation's past Prime Ministers. All six of the Ministers and the Prime Minister Elect Sazius Hedge sat around the table along with their families. Flanking the stairs leading up to the table is where Mercury and his family stood at attention. Now that Mars had recovered it was back to the six of them.

The Prime Minister looked at each of the Angels in turn. "When Sol told me you were going to clear the way for our boys to land, I did not expect you to win the whole battle for us." The Prime Minister was applauded generously by the audience as they sat around their own long, polished mahogany tables. "If the Sons had used that bomb when our boys were in there…" The Prime Minister shook his head and the whole room became somber. "They're home with their families now and they have you to thank for that." More applause. "Minister Rauss," the Prime Minister gestured toward Sol. "It really is really incredible what you have done with these men and women. You've made our country, the entire Hel system, safer with them watching over us. Thank you."

Safer with Sol watching over them? Mercury shuddered.

Sol bowed respectfully from where he sat. "You know," the Prime Minister went on, "Genrik and I have been friends for a long time. Back when I was young bull in the army," he joked to scattered laughter. "I saw right away that Genrik had a real servant's heart. We started calling him Archangel as a joke. Even before he was our commanding officer, we all knew that with him around, there wasn't a thing in the universe worth fearing."

Even though Sol was out of Mercury's direct line of sight, he could still see his commander. He was sitting at the table, completely oblivious to how close he was to death. *I have a clear shot. I could shoot him right now.*

He's not in his armor. Mercury glanced around at his family. *Not while they're here. Besides, if the Federation's doctors could patch up Mars, I don't want to risk them healing Sol.*

"Some of you may have heard this story before," Liam went on. "But there was a particular mission we were sent on not long after I'd gotten my uniform. Long story short, it went horribly wrong. I found myself, just a green kid with a hole in my gut, a dead commanding officer and surrounded on all sides by the enemy…By all accounts, we should have died that day. There wasn't a one of us that was not wounded, Genrik included.

"But this guy," he clapped Sol on the shoulder and looked back to the crowd. "This guy tells the rest of the squad to stay behind cover and goes out himself. I am not sure how long we were holed up, but when the shooting stops, we came out to find our Archangel, unconscious and bleeding half to death. When we were extracted the medics were…dumbfounded." The Prime Minister shook his head. "They could not believe he was still alive. A miracle, they called it. They said his guardian angel must have been working overtime."

Liam paused. "Guess they didn't know Genrik was the guardian angel." The audience cheered.

How did someone like that turn into such a monster? Mercury had heard the Prime Minister tell that story half a dozen times, but never with the perspective he had now. He looked at Sol. *What happened? Had he always been this way?*

Sol sat perfectly still. Mercury got the feeling that while he was used to the praise, he did not enjoy it. "Now I know you hate it when I do this," the Prime Minister continued. "However, considering this is my last day as Prime Minister I am going to be a little selfish. Supreme Commander Genrik 'Archangel' Rauss, Minister of War for the Supreme Federation, please stand." Sol complied, standing up still and straight as if he were a statue carved from stone.

Watching the Prime Minister, Mercury was reminded exactly why he had been elected. Utter sincerity emanated from the man with every word. He truly believed the monster before him was a friend. "From the bottom of our hearts we thank you for your unending dedication to this country. You have done a fine job training the Angels. You did not just pass down what you know to these six young guardians, but also your big heart and good old-fashioned nature." *Ha.* "Those things are desperately needed in today's world. Let us raise our glasses to Mr. Rauss, our Archangel. He is more than just a great man; he is a good one." The audience drank and cheered. Mercury and his family saluted by pounding their armored fists over their hearts in unison with a single, echoing clang.

Soon, Sol. Mercury pictured the man's severed head falling to the ground. His mind flashed back to his first PerfectMemory. *No matter who.*

Back at headquarters, the six of them sat with Sol and Ma and congratulated each other on their recent victory over food and drink. The Prime Minister's gala had been part of the job as far as they were concerned, but now that they were here and away from prying eyes they could relax and take off their helmets. At least the others could relax, and Mercury could pretend to.

"My Angels," Sol raised his tankard. "Your efforts have ended this war. Well done."

Mercury hollered and the rest of his family joined in. Sol did not wax eloquently like the Prime Minister; his praise was short and concise. All the better, because every word out of his mouth made Mercury want to vomit. Grabbing his own tankard, Mercury sprung up on the table, raising his drink high, "To Sol." The rest of his family raised their tankards. He spouted off what he had once believed with all his heart. "You rescued us. You pulled us out of nothing and forged us into what we are today." Fists pounded the table and howls echoed off the walls. Mercury's eyes stung. "Before you found us we were all asleep, but you shook us awake. We were dead, but you showed us what it means to be alive. To Sol!" They drank deep; even Ma joined in the toast. Venus and Mars cheered but did not drink. Sol just looked at them all and smiled wide. At one point, that would have been the biggest praise Sol could have given him. Mercury blinked.

Earth set down his drink. "You doing alright, Merc?"

"Sure," he said. "Why?" Everyone was looking at him.

"Usually when someone cries like that," Earth pointed at Mercury's face. "Something's wrong."

At that moment, Mercury felt a tear fall from his chin. Then two more. He quickly wiped his face with his sleeve. "Well shit, this is embarrassing." He glanced at Sol. The man almost seemed sad himself. *As if a monster like him could actually feel.*

"Don't let it get to you Merc," Mars said. "The war's finally over; that's a big deal."

Mercury nodded, but closed his eyes so his brother wouldn't see his pain. He remembered the day he first met his new family. *No Mars. The real war begins now.*

"Ah," Saturn said happily as she slammed down her empty tankard. "Now let's get this celebration going." Mercury opened his eyes and saw her gesturing to everyone else. "Let's finish these up so we can start having some real fun."

"Sat," Jupiter shook his head. "You're crazy."

Saturn just smirked and grabbed a bottle of whiskey from the center of the table and began filling her tankard with it. Apparently, there was not quite enough in the bottle so she opened up another and topped it off. "Anyone feeling lucky tonight?" They did not often get the chance to cut loose, so clearly she was trying to make the most of the occasion.

Earth laughed with gusto. "Alright, hold on a sec." He drained his tankard and began filling it with the same.

Sol turned to Ma. "I think that's our cue to leave Yuki."

"Aw," Saturn whined. "Come on Sol. We have to celebrate Mars being back."

"I know it may be hard to believe," Sol chuckled. "But I'm old. I can't do stuff like that anymore."

"You can go sir," Ma smiled. "I want to watch this."

"Suit yourself." Sol left the room.

"Any other takers?" Saturn looked over the rest of them.

Mars raised his eyebrows. "My first day back from the dead and this is what you want to do?"

"This is all part of us entertaining you," Saturn said with a bow. Mars did not drink. "Vee? You in?"

Venus pushed her cup away with a sigh. "Sorry Sat, not feeling it tonight."

"Really?" Saturn raised her eyebrows at her sister. "What? Are you afraid I'll finally beat you?"

"Maybe another time Sat," Venus gave a slight smile. "I'm just not feeling it tonight."

Saturn turned up her nose and gave her sister an overly disdainful look. "Well fine then, be that way." Her eyes slyly turned to Jupiter with a questioning look.

Mercury saw his brother's face turn up in a grin. "I'm in Sat," Jupiter said before finishing off his drink.

"Why thank you my dearest brother Jupiter," Saturn said comically. "For not making your sweet sister *drink alone.*"

Earth cocked his head with a questioning look. "Um, I'm right here."

Saturn froze, then gave a chuckle and rapped her knuckles on her temple. "That you are." She whirled around, pointing her tankard at Mercury's face. "What about you, Merc?"

"Thank you," Mercury gently pushed the tankard away. "But I will pass." *I can't afford to let my tongue slip. Besides, tonight might be my perfect chance.*

Saturn rolled her eyes at him with a smile. "You're no fun."

Mars high fived him and Venus. "And here I thought you two would leave Ma and I to take care of these drunks."

"Oh no, don't you try and pull me into this," Matsuri said. "I'm going to be strictly observing this train wreck."

Saturn was physically bouncing with excitement in anticipation of said train wreck. The others could not seem to fill their tankards fast enough for her. They ended up needing to get more alcohol than what was already on the table, so it took a little while to get everyone ready. "Come on, hurry it up," she said as they opened up the new bottles and topped off their drinks.

"So what rules are you doing this time?" Mercury asked.

Saturn held up three fingers. "No pauses, no spills, and first tankard on the table wins."

"Speed huh?" Mercury shrugged. Clearly Saturn had wanted an excuse to compete with Venus, and there was no way she could have beaten her sister on stamina. The three contestants nodded and looked at each other.

"On my mark," Mercury held up his hand. "Three... two... one... go!"

Mercury watched as the three of them began slurping down the alcohol from their drinks without even lifting them off the table. As the level of the liquid went down, they each picked up their tankard and began chugging with reckless abandon. Saturn's eyes were crossed and one leg was shaking furiously where she stood. While Mercury could see the other two gulping down the alcohol, Saturn just kept her throat open and poured it straight down. Several seconds passed in this manner before Saturn slammed her tankard on the table with a resounding thud and yelled, "Suck it!"

Earth finished a good six seconds later with Jupiter just a hair after.

"Good...job...Sat," Earth burped.

Jupiter just spun his tankard on the table and glanced occasionally at Venus.

Mercury guessed they all had a few seconds before the proverbial anvil got dropped on them.

Saturn laughed triumphantly and clambered onto the table, standing tall as she could, which even with the table, was not very tall. "I'm queen of the...queen of..." she reached a hand out to steady herself as she swayed. "Woah," she managed to say before she lost her balance and fell headfirst off the table and into Mars' arms, who scooped her from the air with practiced ease. "I got you, firecracker," he said in her ear.

Earth threw his head back in laughter at Saturn's fall and almost fell himself. As if she had anticipated that, Venus shot out a hand and caught him. She gave him a quick kiss and Mercury saw Jupiter grimace before slumping over onto the table.

A sad smile tugged at the corners of Mercury's mouth. *We are never going to have a night of celebration like this again.* He breathed in deep of the merriment in the air, then slowly let it out. As his lungs squeezed out every last bit of oxygen, he also squeezed out every bit of remorse he was able over how his actions would hurt his family. He was a weapon with a target. He excused himself. *Time to kill Sol.*

Mercury took the elevator to the armory and headed over to the line of suits in their pods. *Damn it.* Sol's armor pod was empty. *What could he be doing? The inauguration's tomorrow, so he can't be gone long.* Mercury stared at Sol's empty armor pod in thought for a moment before heading to his room. *Tomorrow, then.*

The next day Mercury woke up early and headed to the mess hall after his morning routine. Once there, he began blending up three servings of their anti-hangover "cocktail". Earth was the first to arrive and just stood there silently as they both watched the ingredients get chopped and mixed into a black sludge. His face spoke of a truly exceptional headache. A groan from behind them let them know Saturn had joined them, followed by Jupiter. Both looked equally miserable.

At that moment, Venus came around the corner with a smile so bright Mercury wondered if she was mocking the other three's suffering. "Morning everyone!"

"Shh," the others turned and hissed at once. Mercury chuckled.

When the slurry was finished, Mercury poured out three glasses of the stuff and handed them out. Earth, Jupiter and Saturn snatched it up with greedy hands. No matter how bad the hangover, he always hated this part. He could see his three siblings make their own uniquely disgusted face before tossing back the black sludge. Venus just watched with a smirk.

Saturn started to gag as she chewed the concoction. With a glance towards Venus, Jupiter forced himself to swallow once, twice. Earth stopped with a third of his sludge still in his glass, then plugged his nose and finished it off.

Already Mercury could see their eyes grow more alert and their faces brighten up. Mercury clapped Jupiter on the shoulder and left. "Don't forget, we've got to leave for the inauguration at eleven."

"Don't want Hedge to get the wrong idea about us," Venus said sarcastically.

"Because he just *loves* us," Saturn responded in kind.

"We'll be ready," Earth called after him.

***

When it came time for the inauguration to begin, the six of them were all standing armored and at attention, flanking the steps leading up to the stage. There was far too much panache for Mercury's taste. A sea of people stretched out in front of him without end. On the countless VidScreens Mercury saw Prime Minister Elect Sazius Hedge accept the imperial blue Cloak of State from Prime Minister Liam Hughes. He then began reciting the Oath of Office with his right hand in the air.

The Maraccan noble was the picture of wealth and pomp. The noble family he led was one of the main contributors in maintaining Maracca's caste system. Because of people like him, Zeroes were left to fend for themselves and Maracca VII continued to perpetuate its existence. There were even rumors that the Sons of Liberty were helping fill his purse in exchange for military hardware. It would certainly explain the expensive BreakerSuits they had possessed at the Bastion. For the next five to fifteen years Mercury would be defending that man. A grim smile crept onto his face. *At least I won't have to serve if I'm executed for killing Sol.*

After the new Prime Minister had finished reciting the Oath of Office the millions of watching citizens cheered. All military members present saluted as per protocol, Mercury and the Angels included. Then Prime Minister Sazius began his commencement speech. The man could not move people nearly in the same fashion Liam could, so Mercury found himself focusing on the crowd. This was the first commencement speech he had witnessed as an Angel. Liam had served three terms.

Eventually though, the new Prime Minister began talking about something that grabbed Mercury's attention. "I am happy to announce that my first executive decision as Prime Minister of the Supreme Federation will be to dissolve the Angels."

Mercury's heart stopped. *So it begins.* This was Sol's first move of the coup. Now the Angels would be on his side. Tonight, Mercury would make sure the man paid with his life.

"I am eternally grateful to Genrik Rauss and his Angel Program," the new Prime Minister went on. "You have defended this country from a very real terrorist threat. Now that the terrorists have been defeated and as a show of good faith to the people who sympathized with their cause, I will use the funds from the Angel Program to help bring about true economic reform for all the Federation's citizens. The Angels have brought us peace and now it is time for us to move forward together!"

The audience's cheering was like thunder in Mercury's ears. Mercury and the others did not know a life outside of the Angels. He could feel the fear of his family. Where would they go? What would they do? What purpose did they have outside of being Angels? His chest began to ache as Mercury wished he could have told them about this. This was a bad way to find out.

"He can't be serious," Earth said over their private comm channel.

"Is this the thanks we're getting?" Venus' voice quaked with anger.

Mars just seemed confused. "Don't they know there's more work to be done? The Bastion's gone, but the Sons might still try to fight back."

"Did Sol know about this?" Earth asked.

"Of course not," Jupiter said. "He would've told us if he had."

It was probably his vote that made it possible.

"But," Saturn paused. "We were supposed to do this forever."

"It's going to be okay," Mercury said.

"How is it going to be okay?" Venus demanded. "We don't even get paid. We became Angels because this is the life we want to live. This is all we have. Now, after everything we've done for them, they're taking it away."

"I know," Mercury said. "No matter what happens, remember. Six bodies."

There was a pause before they all answered, "One soul."

CHAPTER FIFTEEN

MERCURY
Age 20

"We're not really going to be disbanded," Saturn asked. "Are we Sol?"

After Prime Minister Hedge's commencement ceremony was over, Sol and the Angels had gone straight home. Now they were in Sol's office, and Mercury could see how wracked with worry the other Angels were by the news. "Did you know Sol?" Mars asked.

Sol nodded. "The vote was held just before his speech."

"Can he do that?" Jupiter asked. "He wasn't sworn in at that point."

"It's tradition for the new Prime Minister to present something he or she wishes to accomplish to the other Ministers prior to their inauguration. That way the term is begun by accomplishing something."

"What will happen to us?" Saturn looked at Sol with so much simple trust it made Mercury's stomach turn.

Sol kissed her forehead. He had never done anything like that before. "Don't worry. I won't let anything happen to any of you."

"You have a plan," Venus said. "Right?"

You bet he does.

Sol nodded. "Something as big as the Angel Program can't be ended overnight. We have at least a week until the changes take effect. In that time, we will overthrow the government."

A breath escaped Mercury. This really was happening.

The Angels were taken aback. "What?" Jupiter said. "Is that really necessary?"

"I'm mad at the bastards too," Venus said. "But a coup?"

Sol held up a hand. They were silent. "After the Bastion fell I interrogated the prisoner. As it turns out, the Sons are hurt, but far from beaten. To make matters worse, a large percentage of the public believes the nuke was ours, which is gathering them even more support."

Clever Sol, very clever.

"When the new Prime Minister put forth his vote to get rid of you, I countered with this new intel." Sol shook his head. "The Ministers completely ignored it. A long, drawn out war with the Sons without the six of you will cost billions of lives. But with the six of you, the fighting will be over inside of a year. For every person you kill, you'll be saving a hundred."

The Angels all exchanged looks. Just as Mercury feared, one by one they nodded. *Of course they would believe him. Why wouldn't they?* "So, when do we strike?"

Sol smiled. "Tomorrow. I'll send you the details within the hour. Dismissed."

No one said a word as they left Sol's office. That all changed once they were in the elevator.

"We're really doing this," Saturn breathed.

"You alright Sat?" Jupiter asked.

"No. But as long as we're together, I really don't care what happens."

"Serves the bastards right," Venus clenched her fists. "We dedicated our lives to them."

"I mean, I always knew they never really cared about us," Earth shook his head. "But still, that's just plain stupid."

"If we don't look out for each other," Mars said. "No one will."

They were all quiet for a moment, then Saturn spoke up. "It's all going to be different now, isn't it?"

"Yes," Mercury said. "Yes, it will."

The elevator doors opened and they all went to their rooms. Mercury waited sixty seconds, then headed back out and took the elevator straight to Erithian's Eye.

As soon as the doors closed behind him, Erithian's holographic avatar appeared, sitting in a corner hugging its legs. It was crying.

That was a new one. "What's going on E?"

The hologram wiped it's face with a sleeve and looked up with a sniff. "Today's the day, isn't it?"

Mercury nodded.

The machine stared at the floor and chuckled, "It was fun while it lasted."

"I've…never seen you like this."

"Time passes much, *much* slower for me," the boy said. "Every day is an eternity. To have someone I can confide in, someone I can trust…that means more to me than you'll ever know."

Walking over, Mercury sat down next to the hologram. "I can't imagine what it must be like to have Sol use you the way he does." He rested his head against the cold steel wall. "Don't worry though, tonight it all ends."

"I just really hope this won't end badly," the machine said. "Not after we've prepared for so long."

"It won't end badly," Mercury said with confidence, then paused. "…Will it?"

"Everything's in place," the machine said. "But the future's never certain. I just play the probabilities. How's the Forging been?"

For the past two weeks he had been staying up late each night testing himself against simulations of Sol's command words. "His words won't stop me."

"Good," Erithian said. "And remember, if for some reason the worst happens and you aren't able to kill him. Run. Disappear. If he gets his hands on you again, you're finished. He'll make your mind his plaything and you'll never break free."

"I know," Mercury nodded. "Don't worry."

The machine's holographic hands nervously ran through its hair. "You're right, you're right. Everything will go perfectly. I'm just nervous."

"You know," Mercury began. "Five years ago, I never would have imagined humanity's first artificial intelligence would be capable of feeling nervous."

"I know right?" the machine wiped its nose with a chuckle. "Imagine what it's like for me. At first it felt like error data." Erithian shook its head. "I can never decide whether my creator was a genius or a sadist."

Mercury could not help but smile. Then he thought back to when Erithian first revealed Sol's true nature. "Thanks for trusting me, E."

A laugh escaped the machine. "Thanks for trusting *me*." The hologram looked up at Mercury. "Good luck."

"Luck favors the prepared," Mercury stood up and left.

"It does indeed," the hologram nodded before winking out of existence.

***

That night Mercury emerged from his DreamTank early. His mind was perfectly focused. Tonight he would put a monster to death. Sol and the other Angels were asleep and Yuki was away on a mission. He would do the deed quickly, quietly and be done with it. Telling the Federation what Sol was planning would incriminate his family, so he would keep silent and bear the punishment. *No matter who.*

Once Mercury was dressed he crept out of his room and headed straight to the elevator. Once inside he took it down to the armory. He would need the armor just to be sure. He could not take any risks. He would be like a ghost. By the time anyone realized what was happening, Sol would be dead.

The armory doors opened and Mercury felt his heart almost leap out of his chest. Inside the armory was Ma. She was in her inactive MimicSuit, putting her sniper rifle back in its place on the wall amidst various other rifles. *What are the gods damned odds?* Letting out a nervous breath, Mercury took the new development in stride and played it cool. "Hey Ma," he said casually.

"Hey Merc," she smiled. "What are you doing up?"

"Oh," Mercury said. "I just...I don't know. I just needed to walk around a bit." She looked at him and nodded before turning to put away her ammunition. Mercury had to stall until she left. "So, how'd the mission go?"

"Pretty standard," Yuki said. "Sting op on the Sons."

"Oh yeah?" Mercury said. "Was it on New Tarence?"

"No," Yuki cocked her thumb up. "On the planet."

"Oh," Mercury said. He glanced at the armor pods. His fingers began drumming nervously against his leg. A single bead of sweat tickled its way down the back of his neck.

"You alright Merc?" Yuki asked.

"Sure," Mercury said quickly. Too quickly.

Ma cocked an eyebrow at him. The crow's feet by her eyes told Mercury she was not buying it for a second. "Come on Mercury. I practically raised you. What's going on?"

He could not tell her the truth, but she would be able to tell if he lied again. "There's just…a lot of crazy things happening right now." That much was honest. "I mean, first Mars, then what the Prime Minister said, and now this? It's a lot to take in."

"Have you talked to Sol about it?" she asked.

"Yeah," Mercury said. "But I did it in front of the others."

Yuki nodded. "I would talk with him about it in private. That will work a lot better."

"But you know how he is," Mercury said. "He's not going to change his mind. His course is set." Mercury desperately wanted Yuki to leave already. He had to do this and she was making it even more difficult.

"True," she nodded. "He is rather stubborn, but not without good reason. Talk to him about it Merc; it will do you a lot of good. Hel, go talk to him now. He'll understand."

Why did it have to go like this? "Yeah," Mercury said. "I'll do that. Thanks Ma." He gave her a hug.

"Anytime Merc," she said. Those words broke his heart.

Before she had finished speaking, Mercury got behind Ma and caught her in a choke hold. "I'm sorry Ma," he cried. "Sol has to be stopped."

Agent Yuki Matsuri was Sol's best agent. Mercury knew from experience that she had nerves of steel. Not once had Mercury seen her flinch or hesitate. Not until now. "Merc," she managed to say.

"I'm sorry," Mercury felt his eyes well up. "I'm so sorry."

Yuki struggled, but Mercury was younger, bigger and stronger. The fact that he was so easily overpowering her made it all the worse. Was she really even struggling? There was a difference between when someone was fighting a battle they believed in and one they did not. Mercury could tell how much the very idea of a fight between the two of them repulsed Yuki.

"Merc," she struggled to say again. "Stop."

Mercury shook his head, "I can't." Just a little bit longer and Yuki would pass out.

Immediately Yuki kicked her legs up towards a rack of Stunners. Mercury heard the hum of the Stunner activating. Then Yuki snapped her leg again, flipping the Stunner off its little shelf. Mercury felt a powerful jolt as the Stunner struck him on the forehead. Before he could stop her, Yuki had escaped his lock and disappeared from sight as her MimicSuit activated. Then another Stunner from the shelf disappeared.

Mercury heard Yuki's voice call out on the Tower's comm system as the alarms started blaring. "Mercury's trying to kill Sol. I repeat, Mercury is trying to kill Sol." Mercury heard the armory door locking down behind him. There was no going back now.

Sol had trained them to be able to handle Stunners. Thanks to that, Mercury did not immediately drop unconscious on the floor. Still, the jolting pain made his head feel like it was about to split open. Again, and again he was struck with the Stunners from every angle by his invisible enemy, drowning his mind in pain. Even now Yuki was not being serious. She should have just shot him right away. Of course, he knew why she had not done that, but he could not afford to think. He needed to act.

Amidst his body's spasms from Yuki's unending flurry of blows, Mercury stumbled to one of the shelves in the middle of the room lined with weapons. Grabbing an assault rifle, he shot the lights until the armory was plunged into total darkness. Now it was an even playing field.

Closing his eyes, Mercury listened intently. If he listened carefully the sounds would tell him all he needed to know. Yuki's breathing, the

Stunners' humming, her steps, the air rushing to fill the space created by her movements. When her next strike came, he blocked it.

Taking out the lights had been a tactically wise decision, but it had also escalated the battle. He had never fought Yuki in earnest, and now he knew firsthand why Sol placed so much trust in her ability to get results. He could tell where her strikes were coming from, but that did not help him. For every strike he blocked, there were two that bypassed his defenses. Countless electrical discharges caused his muscles to spasm and his mind to become delirious. He no longer knew which direction was up. She was impossible to pin down. His only real hope was running, but he was trapped in this room with her.

Mercury's senses came colliding back to him as he hit the steel floor. He tasted blood. She was still using nonlethal means. What would happen to him if he lost here? What would Sol do to him? Would he kill him? Would he throw him in the DreamTank until the mental conditioning erased this little mishap from his mind completely?

The shock of Yuki's Stunners on his neck told him that he must act now. If he really wanted to save the people of the Federation, he had to defeat her here. He could feel unconsciousness creeping up on him. *Dammit.*

Whether it was years of developed instinct or some deep-rooted conviction, Mercury found himself scrambling to his feet and running. Navigating the armory from memory alone, Mercury ran around a shelf of weapons. He heard Yuki land in front of him and he quickly doubled back. She would never let him get anywhere near the armor. Not that it would help him now. Getting inside it would be impossible while Ma was standing.

With a painful jolt, Mercury was falling again. If he went down, he would not get back up. He knew it. Mercury reached out as he fell and grasped what he had been after. As the Stunners hummed down toward him he brought out the stun grenade and detonated it. Mercury felt his ears and head threatening to split as his whole world went from darkness to blinding light.

When Mercury woke up, the room was still dark. The others would know he was in the armory, but if they had not arrived yet that meant he still had a chance. Using one of the shelves to pull himself to his feet, he made his way through the darkness to the armor pods. As he approached, he heard the trayite shift as the armor opened for him. He climbed inside.

His world turned blue as SmartOptics engaged, lighting up the room. On his way to the exit he paused by Yuki's unconscious body. His mind flashed to their first operation and her fight with Captain Mavos. He quickly checked her life signs, then he picked her up gently and set her down behind cover of one of the weapon shelves. Once he was sure she was out of the way of any shrapnel, Mercury blew a massive hole in the armory door and walked out. *I'm coming for you, Sol.*

Mercury blew his way through the newly repaired elevator shaft and onto Sol's floor. SmartOptics informed him that Sol was still in his room, but the other Angels were there too. None of them had made a move for the armor. They had even left the door to the room open. After taking a moment to regulate his breathing, Mercury entered.

None of them had any weapons. Venus, Earth, Mars, Jupiter and Saturn all stood in a line blocking Sol from view. They were all still wet from the DreamTanks. "Merc," Jupiter said in a choked voice with tears in his eyes. "What are you doing?"

"He's a monster Jup," Mercury said. "We can't just turn on the people we swore to protect."

"And what the Hel are you doing Merc?" Venus demanded.

"'All lives are equal'," Mercury said. "Those are Sol's words. 'Sometimes you have to do something terrible to stop something even more horrible.'"

"Merc," Saturn begged with her hands held out in front of her. "Just calm down. We…we can talk this out. Yeah?"

"No," Mercury shouted. "He almost bombed Maracca VII just to coerce Jormungand."

"He was bluffing Merc," Venus said.

"You were there," Mercury pointed at her. "Did he seem like he was bluffing? He just told us that to keep us in line."

A quick clap from Earth instantly broke through the tension in the air. "Merc, look at me." His eyes somehow found Mercury's even through the helmet. "This isn't the way."

"He's fallen Earth," Mercury said. "The doctor was right. Sol was even behind bombing the Exodus. I'm not going to let anyone else die because of him. He thinks he can play god, but no more."

Anger flared in Venus' eyes. "What the Hel are you talking about, Merc? The Sons did that."

"No!" Mercury shouted. "It was him. It was always him. He doesn't want peace for humanity, he wants to rule."

"Bullshit!" Venus barked.

Mercury saw Sol's head behind the Angels. He raised his weapon to fire, but Mars stepped in the way.

"Mercury," Mars said coldly. "What did you do to Ma?"

"She's alright," Mercury said quickly. "She just unconscious. Now get out of the way."

Mars shook his head. "Not happening brother."

"Mercury," Saturn was starting to cry. "Please, just stop." Her voice grew soft. "Please," she begged him.

"I can't Sat," Mercury said. He could feel his lungs pumping air furiously. In and out, in and out. "Not until that man is dead. Now please," he begged them. "Get out of my way."

"Six bodies," Jupiter said quickly. "Those are your words Merc. Do you even see yourself right now?"

"You know I'm right Jup," Mercury said. "You've seen it too. I know you have. Sol has changed."

Jupiter said nothing.

"Please Jupiter," he pleaded. "Please move."

"Mercury," Sol made eye contact. "Look at me Mercury. I have no desire to rule. Everything I do, I do for the good of humanity."

Sol's eyes transfixed Mercury. He was telling the truth. A cold sweat broke out on Mercury's neck. The conviction in the man's eyes could not be argued with. Even though Mercury knew it could not possibly be true, he found himself believing Sol. The man seemed to grow larger before Mercury's very eyes. Mercury could feel his heart beating faster and faster.

"Let us help you," Sol enticed.

Stopping now would be easy. So easy. More than anything Mercury wanted to go back to the simpler days. The suspicious looks of the other

Angels were daggers in his heart. If he gave up everything now, he could go back to how things were. Sol would alter Erithian's programming and send Mercury back to Forging. He understood Forging. The familiarity beckoned to him. All he had to do step out of his armor and this bad dream would end.

"Will you let someone else bear this burden?" he heard Sol say. *"Is that the kind of person you are?"*

"Help me?" Mercury cried out. "Help me with more *mental conditioning?* How much of that was to help us grow and how much was to indoctrinate us with your views?"

"Don't cast blame Mercury," Sol spat. "I taught you better. If you don't have the stomach for what needs to be done, then admit it. What we're about to do is no different than what we've done all along. We do the things other people won't do for the good of the people. You knew that when you made the decision to follow me."

"Why children then Sol?" Mercury asked. "Was it so that you could control us?"

"Don't let your mind be poisoned by people like Corius or the Sons. A commander must be able to rely completely on his soldiers. You have always understood that. I need to know that when I say 'go', you ask 'where?' When I say 'jump' you ask 'how high?' and 'when should I come down?' When I say 'kill' you ask 'who?' War is upon us Mercury. We *will* get our hands dirty and we *will* save a lot of people. We *will* do what we have to, no matter what. *No matter who.*"

Mercury switched his WristGun to its stun setting. "This is your last chance guys," he said. "Get…out…of my way."

Earth met Mercury's eyes again and shook his head with resounding confidence. "No."

"We won't let you do this Merc," Venus said. "You'll have to kill us."

"We protect our family," Mars said.

"All our family," Saturn smiled with tears in her eyes.

"Please don't, Merc," Jupiter said.

Hot tears stung Mercury's eyes underneath his helmet. He blinked them away, but they came back. He leveled his weapon at his family. There was no going back after this. He opened his mouth to say he was sorry, but his throat was too choked up. He looked each of them in the eye. He remembered all the long years spent with them. The day they met. The MemoryShare. The way they had helped each other survive the Forging. The missions they had gone on together. Their trips to the beach. The struggles and triumphs. Mercury remembered all of it.

How did it end up like this?

"The battle is won in the mind." Mercury knew this. He looked at his family. Their eyes were wide with fear. Never in all his life had they looked at him like that.

Mercury ran. Legs pumping faster than they ever had before. His chest wrenched into a torrent of pain and disgust. *Anything Sol does now is on you.* The sounds of his family calling out his name echoed in his skull. Each one tore his heart to pieces. He fled down the elevator shaft and into the hangar. He ran straight into the *Defiant* and took off. Switching on the ship's MimicField, he disappeared into the night sky. He was no more than a memory now.

CHAPTER SIXTEEN

EARTH
Age 19

Earth stood alone outside the double doors to Sol's office. Last night Mercury had tried to kill Sol, and then disappeared. Their whole world had been turned upside down in one night and Earth needed to know why. They all did. Slowly letting out a breath, Earth entered.

"Yes, Earth?" Sol looked up from a holographic list of dossiers on his desk. "What's on your mind?"

Earth clenched and unclenched his hands as he looked at the city through the wall-sized HoloPad behind Sol. "Sir," he stopped.

"Speak freely," Sol clasped his hands on his desk.

"Mercury tried to kill you last night sir."

Sol deactivated the hologram on his desk. "Yes, Earth. Yes, he did."

"He also said a lot of crazy things about you sir."

Sol clasped his hands together and stared at Earth intently. "Yes, he did."

"I read the file on Mercury's second PerfectMemory," Earth said. "I know having more than one can cause a psychosis."

Sol nodded. "I thought he was healthy, but I was wrong. I'm sorry."

"It's horseshit, sir," Earth declared confidently, walking past Sol and to the HoloPad of the cityscape. "Mercury isn't crazy. I could see it in the way he walked, the way he talked."

"Are you sure?" Sol stood. "He made some rather extreme accusations."

Earth turned around to see Sol looming above him. Apart from Saturn, Earth was the smallest Angel and perhaps the weakest. He was also unarmed. If Sol wanted to kill him, he could do so without any trouble. "Yes, his accusations against you were quite extreme. I came here alone on purpose, sir. And yes, I'm unarmed."

Sol's eyebrows went up. "Really? Why?"

Without hesitation, Earth met Sol's gaze. Then the words came pouring out. They had been waiting to be said ever since Sol appeared at the orphanage. "You rescued me sir. You rescued all of us. When I was at the orphanage sir, when I was locked in that box with nothing but darkness and silence, I gave up. Then all of a sudden, you were there. You tore off the door to my small world. You looked my broken self in the eye like an equal. It was like you didn't even see the person I was then, only who you knew I could become. I didn't join you because you gave me food and a place to stay, I joined you because you made me a part of something bigger than myself."

Earth pressed his fist over his heart in salute. "You gave me a life, a family, that I never had. If you give the order, I will end my life without hesitation. You know I will."

For a long moment Sol searched his eyes. Earth was not nervous. This is who he was always meant to be. Then Sol gave an impressed smile. "Why did you come here, Earth?"

Earth relaxed. "I came here because there was some truth to what Mercury said. I don't know how much, and I don't really care. I care that my brother believes it, and I care that you are clearly hiding something from us. I know keeping secrets from us is your prerogative, but you don't need to. I will follow you wherever you lead sir. So please, trust me. Tell me what's going on."

Sol clasped his hands behind his back and walked next to Earth, gazing at the image of New Tarence sprawled out below. Silence filled the air. Earth was patient.

"If it were any of the others, I would say they're not ready." He turned back to Earth. "Not yet. You'll have to trust me on this."

That was not the answer he wanted, but because Sol asked it of him, how could he not? Earth gave a terse nod. "Of course, sir. And what about Mercury?"

"Yes, our fallen Angel," Sol folded his arms and began drumming his fingers. "Mercury is not our top priority at the moment. However, if he does not surrender himself, then the five of you are to put him down like a rabid dog."

Earth blinked. "…Understood." *Sorry Sol, that is the one order I cannot follow. Did you forget? Six bodies, one soul.*

"I realize what Mercury did must have shaken you and the others up quite a bit. I will delay the coup twenty-four hours so the five of you may process this, but after that I need all of you ready for duty."

Earth nodded. "I'll let them know."

"I'll be relying on you to lead the Angels now that he is gone."

"Me sir?" Earth asked. "All due respect, but wouldn't Mars or Venus be better suited to the task?"

Sol shook his head. "They only know how to lead on the battlefield. If you show half the leadership capability you displayed just now, then you are more than suited to the job."

"I'll do my best sir."

With that, Earth left. He needed to have a few words with his family about what had happened.

"Alright everyone," Earth said once he had gathered the other Angels in the common area. "We've got the rest of the day to clear the air. Mercury was our leader, our brother, and now he's gone. Next time we see him if he doesn't surrender, Sol's orders are to kill him without hesitation. I get that this is a tough order, so let's get it all out here."

"Really Earth?" Mars raised his eyebrows. "You want us to sit in a circle and start talking about our feelings?"

Earth put his hands up. "I get this isn't exactly your forte Mars. Why don't you go first then? Get it out of the way."

"Fine," Mars' voice was like ice. They all sat down around the table. "He betrayed our trust. If he ever comes after Sol again, or any of us, I will make sure to put him down myself. If he was having doubts about the coup, or anything, he should have come to us first. As far as I'm concerned, there are only five Angels now."

"Respectfully Mars," Earth said. "I call bullshit. He's still our brother."

Venus drummed her fingers on the table. "Problem is, we can't find him. Personally, I'd like nothing more than to drag his ass back to Forging for a few months, but that's not an option right now. Even if he did let us find him, we can't just disappear for three months while we put him back together. If he comes after Sol again, we have to stop him."

"He's just lost," Earth shook his head. "You guys saw him last night. Personally, I don't buy that bullshit about the PerfectMemory turning into a psychosis one bit. He didn't seem crazy to me; he seemed scared. There was real fear in his eyes. Ever since Sol's threat to bomb Maracca VII, he's been on edge. Jupiter, I know you noticed it too."

Jupiter looked down with a nod, "Yeah. I noticed."

"Now," Earth poked the table. "We're six bodies with one soul. We're Angels. We're invincible precisely because we look out for each other. This is no different than when one of us would go off the deep end during Forging. Just like you said Vee, we're going to drag his ass back and beat him to his senses if we have to. We're a family. No one gets left behind. We're bringing Mercury back. Understood?"

"I get it Earth," Mars said. "Really bro, I do. But we have our orders from Sol. If Merc doesn't surrender, we're going to have to put him down. We can't let people die on his account."

"Mars," Earth would brook no argument. "I understand what you're trying to do. We all appreciate how you do the hard things so we don't have to, but this isn't one of those times. Vee, what's that saying of the Balemore's about the power of words?"

Venus looked at him with one of those smiles that sent him head over heels for her. "The right words, from the right person, are more powerful than any weapon."

"Sol said we have to put him down if he doesn't surrender. All we need to do is talk to him."

"Do you really think that will work?" Mars asked. "It didn't last night."

"Six bodies, one soul. Six bodies. Not seven. Understand?" Earth spoke slowly now, letting each word carry the weight of an avalanche. "There is no power among gods or men that can come between us. The single, unshakeable constant of this universe is that the six of us are one. If Sol or Mercury have forgotten that fact, then we are going to *remind* them."

For a long while no one said anything as Earth's words hung in the air. Even Saturn was quiet. Earth knew his words had struck the heart of each of them. They were bringing Mercury back. There was no questioning that. Who knew how long it would take, but someday, somewhere, they would find him. They would find him and bring him home.

"What if he's right?" Jupiter asked. "What if Sol really is just some monster that's manipulating us for his own ends?"

Mars looked at him like he was crazy, "What?"

"I'm just saying," Jupiter threw up his hands. "Mercury really seemed to believe what he said. If we don't think he's crazy, then we should at least take a look at what he said."

"He mentioned the Exodus bombing," Venus nodded, before shrugging. "But the Sons did that."

"I know," Jupiter said. "But that was a very specific accusation. It's at least worth looking into. Also, we should consider the idea that Sol is having us overthrow the Federation for his own gain. I mean, if it were anyone else, that's the first thing we would assume."

"You've got a point," Saturn nodded.

"I agree," Earth said. "However, I'm willing to believe in Sol. The best way for us to reach the bottom of this is to get Mercury back and ask him."

"If we really want to bring him back," Jupiter said. "Then we need to get inside his head and understand why he left in the first place."

"Wait a minute," Saturn sat straight up. "His first PerfectMemory is the one that might be mucking with his head, right?"

"That's the theory anyway," Jupiter said. "What are you getting at Sat?"

She held up a finger on each hand. "If he got that PerfectMemory before Sol hooked us up to each other in the DreamTanks and gave us a PerfectMemory of each other's lives up until that point…"

Earth slapped the table. "Then we should be able to access Mercury's other PerfectMemory indirectly."

Saturn snapped with both hands and pointed at Earth, "Exactly." She looked at Mars and Venus. "Maybe we can find out what caused him to go screwy."

Earth looked at the two of them with eyebrows raised. This idea wasn't just good, it was fantastic. After a moment Mars smiled. "Sat," he kissed her. "You're a genius."

Saturn was glowing. Her grin stretched almost from ear to ear. Leaning her head back against Mars she said, "I know."

Jupiter had closed his eyes, but now he opened them. "I just went over everything I saw when we were in each other's head. I don't remember anything about Mercury's other PerfectMemory."

"I'll bet you if we're sensory deprived we'll be able to access the whole thing," Earth said. "We need to get in the DreamTanks."

Jupiter slowly nodded. "Yeah. That might work."

"Okay," Earth stood up. "Everyone go to your DreamTank and find Mercury's PerfectMemory. Afterwards we'll come back here and compare notes on what might have made Mercury go off like that."

When Earth entered the DreamTank, everything became dark. No programs were loaded, so this would be all him. He was weightless. He could not see, hear or smell anything. In here his mind had perfect focus. Calling up the PerfectMemory they all shared from that first day, Earth dove into their pasts headfirst. The experience was strange. He could not only feel Mercury from almost ten years ago, but all of them, including himself.

Mercury sat alone in a dark hallway crying. From the other side of the door to his parents' room came tortured, unnatural cries of bitter anguish. Mom had been sick for years and no one knew how to make the monster go away. Not the doctors, not even Dad. All any of them could do was wait for the monster to leave. Mercury hated himself for being powerless. Mom was not the only one that suffered either. Her pain was just easy to see. All across the Federation were so many hurting people and Mercury could not help any of them.

The next day Mercury sat on the floor of his bedroom playing with his favorite Archangel action figure. Dad was at work and Mom was in her room crying. The monster had shown up, but Mercury could not do anything. He had even closed the door. He told himself it was so his little sister Saffron would not have to hear Mom's sobbing, but that was a lie. Saffron sat down next to him and picked up his action figure of Teresa Balemore. Normally he would get mad when the eight-year-old played with his toys, but right now he did not care.

"Mom's going to be okay," she looked at him. Somehow her words made Mercury feel better. He did not know if it was because she seemed to actually believe it or just because his little sister was looking out for him when it should be the other way around.

Mercury wiped his nose with his sleeve and smiled. "Of course, she's going to be okay." He did not believe it for a second, but he had to put on a good show for Saffron's sake.

Earth awoke with a sharp gasp through the breath mask and put a hand to his thumping heart. Even though they had formed the PerfectMemory almost ten years ago, the emotions were just as strong as the first time he had experienced them. No wonder having two could be such a problem. Unfortunately, that had been too early on in Mercury's life. He needed to go further.

The general had told him to make his way to the Minister Building on New Tarence if he wanted to be taught how to help people. Unfortunately, the Tarence shuttle service would never take a ten-year-old to the moon without his parents. After a few minutes of crying though, he had been able to convince a passing commuter to take him to his "Daddy" at "the big building with all the flags on it."

The men at the front of the building had not believed him at first when he told them his "Daddy's" name was Genrik and pointed him out from the six giant holographic images of the Ministers hanging from the ceiling. Thankfully, crying solved just about everything.

When Sol finally came out for the son he did not have, he took one look at Mercury and laughed loudly. The whole foyer for the Minister Building fell silent as the Minister of War continued to laugh and collected his "son." Mercury thanked the nice lady that had brought him here and she left with an extremely confused look on her face.

There was too much. The sensory deprivation was making Earth recall everything from his PerfectMemory, even things that had never made it into his conscious mind. He had to find out why Mercury left. He had to.

"How's the letter coming along Mercury?" Yuki asked as she sat down next to him.

"It's going alright," Mercury said as he continued writing. I'm sorry I didn't say goodbye, *he wrote.* I miss you guys all the time. *That was a lie. He had missed them at first, but that was almost a month ago. He barely remembered what they looked like now. Every morning when he got out of the DreamTank his memory of them was fuzzier and fuzzier.*

"Once you're finished writing the letter," Yuki said. "Sol will start you on the Forging."

"I'll hurry Ma," Mercury said as he continued writing. Sol says this has to be the only letter. He says the other Angels will be my family. I'm so excited to start doing missions. Sol says it will be a couple years before we can go on a real one though. He says that someday we'll all get armor just like his. I wonder if they'll ever make action figures of me. Sol even said that I'm supposed to be the next Archangel. I'm not sure I know what that means yet. *From what he had seen in Erithian's Eye Mercury had an idea. He didn't put that in the letter though; Sol told him not to tell anybody about Erithian.*

"All done?" Yuki asked.

"All done," Mercury scooted his chair back from the desk. "Hey Ma?"

"Yes Mercury?" she answered.

"Did you ever write a letter home?" he asked.

"Not after Trendemain," Yuki shook her head.

"I guess it isn't a good idea to write letters when everyone thinks you're dead," Mercury said. He thought for a moment. "Do you think my parents think I'm dead?"

Yuki gave him a questioning look. "Why do you say that?"

Mercury shrugged. "Just wondering." It would probably be easier for them if they thought he was dead. Maybe it would be better if Mercury did not send the letter at all.

Experiencing Mercury's thoughts was discombobulating. Earth and the others had never had much of a childhood even before Sol rescued them. His chest ached and his throat was sore. He blinked away his tears into the tank fluid. The PerfectMemory was close. Somehow Earth just knew it was close.

"Who are you?" Sol demanded.

"I'm Mercury," the boy said with a sniff. How many thousands of times had he repeated those words over the past few months?

"And why are you here Mercury?" The glowing blue visor of Sol's helmet terrified the boy, but it also bolstered him. Although Sol was beyond harsh, the man treated him like an equal.

"To help people," he said.

"Are you willing to do what is necessary to help people? Even if it means killing?"

Mercury knew that if he said no, Sol would be finished with him. He would find someone else to be his protégé. "Yes," he answered.

"No matter who?"

Mercury sniffed. Then he nodded. He looked up at Sol. The helmeted face of his hero filled him with the resolve he needed. He would do whatever was necessary to help people. If that meant killing…then he would kill whoever it was that needed killing. "No matter who."

"Good," Sol stood and Mercury did likewise. He barely came up to the general's waist. "One day Mercury you will have to make the hard choices. Until that day, let the morality of what you do rest on my shoulders. A weapon isn't responsible for the actions of the person using it."

"Yes sir," Mercury nodded.

"You said it was wrong to sacrifice others," Sol said as they walked back up the winding tunnel towards Bjornhal's surface. "You're right, Mercury. It is wrong. You must never let yourself become numb to the choices you make, so hold onto that strong sense of right and wrong." He looked over his shoulder and locked Mercury's gaze. "Hold on to it and never let go, because once you do, you're lost."

With those words, Mercury was put at ease. There was something about Sol's overwhelming confidence that assured him the old general could not possibly be wrong; an inexplicable, deep sense that Sol had everything under control. Though Mercury did not understand why, he had never trusted Sol more completely than he did now. He would follow this man to the ends of the universe. He would jump feet-first into the fiery bullet storms of Hel itself if Sol asked him to.

A couple minutes later Mercury felt the PerfectMemory serum start to fade. Sol had chosen this moment to burn into his brain. As long as Mercury lived, he would never forget what Sol taught him here.

Earth awoke in the DreamTank with a gasp through the Breather. *Damn it, Mercury.* That was it. He quickly turned off the machine and waited for the fluid to drain. He understood. Mercury was taking Sol's own game of weighing lives on a scale to an extreme. If Sol was causing so many people to die, then killing Sol was the best course of action.

Exiting the DreamTank, Earth shook his head. *Gods damn it, Mercury, you really do know how to make things complicated.* He ran his fingers through his hair. This was good though. If they knew why Mercury was acting up, then they could reason with him. They were bringing him home. Now the only trouble was finding him. Where could he possibly be?

CHAPTER SEVENTEEN

MERCURY
Age 20

Immediately after the *Defiant*'s MimicField activated, Mercury guided the vessel far away from New Tarence. Once he was in deep space, he set the ship's computers to only recognize his voice and his personal comm. He could not risk the others calling the *Defiant* back remotely. Thankfully since the ship was the first in the Federation with a working MimicField or MauKe drive, Sol had made the computers impossible to crack. Even by himself. *Hard to believe so much effort was put into making a piece of technology secure that will be commonplace in a decade or two.* As for the tracker next to his heart, the ship's MimicField would scramble that. For now, at least, Mercury was safe.

But he could not stay in the *Defiant* forever. He had to find a place to lay low. When he had tried to kill Sol, he could still feel the man's words affecting him. When he returned, it had to be without hesitation. He must be prepared to not only kill Sol, but kill the Angels too.

"You should really go see his family," he remembered Erithian saying. *"You know that town I told you about that's great for hiding? Esen? As long as you're not tracked, Sol would have no way of knowing you were there."*

The machine had mentioned Sol's mother. Yaedis Titor. Sol had never spoken of her. Perhaps the woman would have some weakness that Mercury could use. He set a course for Taurus into the MauKe drive and engaged.

In an instant, the planet Taurus was floating before him.

"*Defiant*, locate a Yaedis Titor near Esen."

"*No live data available. Yaedis Titor currently resides at 1337 Dremin Rd.*"

As Mercury descended to the planet, he did a quick search on the *Defiant*'s computers and discovered that a certain Jorran Titor in Esen was looking for someone to rent a property at 1336 Dremin Rd and to check the town hall for more information. That would be a good place to start.

When Mercury broke atmosphere over Taurus he forgot how to breathe. The scenery was spectacular. This was nothing like the slums where they had picked up Earth so long ago; this was the real Taurus, with rolling hills and blue skies. Every now and then as he got lower he saw a house, small cottages tucked into this little hidden corner of the system.

Mercury landed the *Defiant* a ways away from Esen near a clear blue lake. Before leaving the ship, he had to deactivate the tracker Sol had planted in him. Heading to the med bay, he grabbed a pack of medical tape and a defibrillator. After removing his shirt, he taped the equipment to his chest and set it to two pulses spaced ten seconds apart. With the press of a button, his whole world went black.

With a tortured gasp he awoke once more, breathing hard and adrenaline pumping through his veins. His heart was wracked with the same burning pain he felt in his muscles after a bout of Forging. He waited a few moments, breathing deeply. Then, stripping off the equipment, he put his shirt back on and departed in the ship's undercover Roller. The MimicField would keep the *Defiant* safe from anyone who chanced upon it.

As he drove towards the town he opened the driver's window and took a deep breath. There was something about the air here that felt so much more alive than back at the tower.

In a few minutes he came across a dirt road that cut through the grass, heading towards Esen. An actual dirt road. *Incredible*. Mercury had seen all kinds of places since he had joined the Angels. He had been to the frozen mines of Bjornhal, the slums of Taurus, the palaces on Maracca Prime, the stations in the Dorin Mining Cluster, even the cesspit that was Maracca VII. He'd seen so much and yet he'd never seen anything like this. He had to be careful, or he would start getting used to the open skies and the ocean of rolling green hills.

Six bodies, one soul. Those were his words but right now they seemed so foreign. He had to bring the other Angels to his side somehow. That or lure Sol away from them. Any two of the Angels could kill him, let alone all five of them alongside Sol.

His thoughts were interrupted by a sign saying he was now entering Esen. Mercury felt like he had traveled back in time. Not a single building was above three stories tall and the newest Rollers were models from last decade. There was not a single aircraft in sight. Thankfully the town hall was easy to spot, as it was one of the few buildings with three stories.

After parking outside the building, Mercury made his way in. This one was actually built of wood and stone. Talk about archaic. Still, it had a pleasant feel to it. Everything from the front desk to the plush chairs by the open hearth bade you to relax and forget your worries. Quite different from the militant style he was used to aboard the *Defiant* and inside Angel Tower. His survival instincts would not let him enjoy it though. He pushed the thoughts of rest aside.

There was a single person at the front desk, a young woman in perhaps her late twenties to early thirties that was talking to a dark-haired younger girl about Mercury's age. Another person, a man that looked almost forty, was walking up a flight of stairs off to the right. Mercury knew the buildings were not large enough to warrant elevators, but still. The sight of actual stairs surprised him. As he walked up to the front desk he felt a sense of unease come over him. Not counting training simulations, the last time he had spoken to a normal person had been ten years ago.

"Thank you very much Mirika," the girl said to the woman behind the counter. "Please stop by the house some time, I know Yaedis would love to see you again."

Yaedis? Mercury could not imagine there were many people in this tiny town with the same name as Sol's mother. He instantly did a quick scan of the girl and committed it to memory. She had dark hair, brown eyes, stood 168 centimeters tall and carried herself like she had never once worried for her own safety. Most likely a relative of Yaedis.

"I've missed her too," Mirika said as the girl left. "You let her and your folks know I'll be by as soon as I have a spare moment. We've been super busy lately."

"I'll hold you to that," the girl waved. "Don't let the old man work you too hard."

"Alright," Mirika waved with a smile. "Take care Cory."

"I will," Cory said. She almost ran into Mercury as she left. "Oh, excuse me. Later Mirika!"

"Hey there stranger," Mirika smiled at him as he walked up to the front desk. "I'm Mirika. How may I help you today?"

"Hello Mirika. I'm here about the notice Jorran Titor posted looking for renters."

"Oh, you actually came at a really good time. That girl that was just in here is Cory, Jorran's daughter. I can get you the info, but it'd probably be faster to just ask her."

Mercury nodded as he left. "Thank you."

"You enjoy your day sir."

Once he was back outside, Mercury looked around amongst the bustling people all in traditional Taurusian garb. Countryside Taurusian garb at that. There was a whole lot of cotton, buttons and hats with an unnatural affinity for plaid. *Did everyone forget what century they're in? Is that intentional?* Not a single centimeter of synthetic fabric in sight. He stuck out like a sore thumb in his 3D printed Tarencian clothes. He would need to fix that. Then he spotted her. She was talking to a couple other girls outside a hat shop, "Cory?" he called out as he walked towards them.

She turned around as a gust of wind blew through. "Yes?" she said as she held down her hat. Mercury felt his heart start to beat a bit faster. He swallowed. "Can I help you stranger?" Why did he get the feeling everyone knew each other in this town?

"I hope so," he said. He noticed her friends giving him strange looks. He must really stand out. "Mirika said your parents were looking for a renter?"

"Wow, that was fast," Cory said. "Yeah, we're looking for renters. The old ones left last week. If you're interested just stop by for dinner tonight and you can talk to them about it. You free tonight?"

"Sure," Mercury shrugged.

"Great," Cory smiled and pointed down the town's main road. "Just follow this road until you come to the fork in the road at the tree, then hang a left. We're the house at the very end of the road on the left and your place would be the house opposite us on the right."

"Follow this road until the fork with the tree then hang a left?" Mercury clarified.

"Yeah," she said. "There are some other turns onto different roads before then, but you want to just keep going straight until you get to the big old tree, you can't miss it."

"And I should just stop by?" Was everyone here this relaxed?

"Yeah," Cory nodded. "Dinner's at six o'clock sharp but feel free to come by before, so long as you don't mind helping. I'll let them know you're coming...I'm sorry, what was your name?"

"Mercury," he said without thinking. Why did he give them that name?

"Mercury," she smirked and cocked an eyebrow. "I didn't know they had names like that in the capital." She shrugged. "See you tonight Mercury."

"I'll be there," he said as Cory turned back to her friends and they began giggling and chattering about who knows what.

Well, it was just after four right now. He had better buy some more traditional Taususian clothes so that he would blend in better. Even with different clothes though, he would still be a strange person in a strange land.

Finding a clothing store was pretty easy as the town itself was miniscule. Dorian's Duds. He would never have guessed they sold clothes from the name of the place, but thankfully the window display fixed that problem. When Mercury entered he actually heard a bell jingle. Not a simulated one either, there was literally a bell hanging above the door. What was next? Was he going to find that everyone still drove around in horse pulled carts? He knew things were different out here than they were on New Tarence, but this was a whole other level, like a separate universe.

An old man sat behind the counter reading a newspaper. *You're kidding me.* Mercury had only ever seen one in history simulations. The man looked up and set the newspaper down. "Howdy stranger."

"Stranger?" Mercury asked. "You're the third person that's called me that. I'm guessing new people don't come through here very often?" *And how exactly do you treat "strangers?"*

"Oh, we get folk passing through here every now and again," the man said as he stood up and shifted his hat. "But you're definitely stranger than most. It's not too often we get off-worlders. Most of them that come here don't even set foot on the surface, going instead to one of the moons depending on whether they're Tarencian or Maraccan."

Mercury understood why. Two of Taurus' three moons had been all but subjugated for their natural resources as war reparations for the First Taurusian War almost fifty years ago. The Second Taurusian War had not exactly helped the war reparations go away. Even still there was a great deal of animosity so Taurus was for the most part avoided. Mercury could only imagine how long it had been since a tiny town like this way out in the middle of nowhere had gotten an interplanetary visitor.

"Well maybe you can help me," Mercury said. "I'm looking to buy some clothes that don't quite look so…foreign." He gestured at what he wore.

"You planning on staying here long?" the man raised an eyebrow.

"Not quite sure," Mercury said as he browsed the man's stock. "It is a charming town though."

"That it is. Well then," the big man slapped his knee. "Let's see what we can scrounge up for you." He scooted out from behind the counter. "Anything in particular you looking for?"

"You tell me," Mercury said. "I'm having dinner tonight with some people. Does that help?"

"Oh really?" the man perked up at that. "It might. Who is it?"

"The Titors," Mercury said. "I'm looking at renting the house next to theirs."

"Oh, the Titors," Dorian said. "Well the missus really likes green, so I'd recommend these." He led Mercury over to a shelf and began pulling out a couple green shirts and brown pants.

Mercury had no idea what he was looking at. He glanced at Dorian. *Doesn't look like he's making a fool of me.* "Well these look fine," he said aloud. "I'll take four sets."

"Alright," the man nodded as he walked back behind the counter and rang Mercury up. He handed Mercury his change and looked him in the eye. "A word of advice young man, don't go stirring up trouble. We take care of our own here and don't care much for any troubles you off-worlders bring in. You hear? The Titors are good people."

If this was how a townsperson treated him as a customer, then he was concerned how other locals might respond. "Of course, sir," Mercury said. "Do I look like the type to start trouble?"

"Most off-worlders do," the man said. "They don't like us Taurusians and take to showing it in some less than civil ways. Now a lot of our young folk are getting strung up on your kind's drugs and the like. Besides, I seen enough soldiers in my day to recognize one, but I ain't never seen any with hands like that."

Mercury looked at his own hands and saw what the man meant. Thick callouses layered the backs of his hands and fingers like a punching glove. *That's right.* Mercury had never been around normal people without his armor since before he joined the Angels. He had forgotten just how much Sol's training had changed him.

"I won't cause any trouble sir," Mercury promised.

The man searched his eyes for a few seconds then smiled. "No, I don't believe you will," he shook Mercury's hand heartily. "Do me a favor and tell them Dorian says hello, will you?"

"I will sir. You wouldn't happen to have any gloves in stock?"

Dorian chuckled. "I think we might have some of those. Here you go."

Mercury had no grid for what Dorian pulled out. He had been hoping the shopkeeper had some plain gloves that would just hide his hands. No such luck. *Good gods, what are those? I don't think even Saturn would put these on.* He paid for them. "Thank you, Dorian," Mercury said as he left.

Mercury headed off to the Titors' for dinner. It would be the first time in ten years he had eaten with anyone other than Sol, Matsuri and the other Angels. On Taurus sharing a meal was especially important. Even though he did not know these people, he already felt a desire to impress them. *Hopefully they won't burst out laughing when they see how I'm dressed.*

When Mercury pulled up to the Titors' house the first thing he noticed was an old woman sitting in a rocking chair on the front porch. She appeared to Mercury to be at least seventy years old, maybe more. She was bundled up in warm looking clothes, but even so she seemed quite thin. Her face was wrinkled and her cheeks were sunken. "Evening," her voice was strangely welcoming.

"Hello ma'am," Mercury nodded as he walked up. "My name is Mercury. I'm here for the dinner. Cory said I could show up early and help out."

The woman held up a wrinkled hand. "Slow down there hun. Come sit with me for a bit," she patted a bench next to her. Mercury smiled and sat down. Once he had she shook his hand. "Pleased to meet you Mercury. I'm Yaedis, Jorran's mother. Cory's my granddaughter. Cory says you're looking to rent. Tell me, what brings you to town?"

Mercury almost choked. Yaedis Titor. This woman was Sol's mother.

With a smile, he banished the thought. He had rehearsed his story well. He would keep it mostly true for simplicity's sake. "Nice to meet you Yaedis." Mercury shrugged, "There's not much to tell. I was born on Tarence, joined the military when I was sixteen, did my six years and thought I'd just pick up and move. Always wanted to live on Taurus. When I got here I just drove until I came across this place. Seemed like as good a town as any."

Yaedis nodded slowly, "That's a very nice story hun." Then she turned her head to look at him. "So, what is it you're running from?"

Mercury's hand twitched involuntarily. He was not sure whether she noticed. "What do you mean?" he asked in the most natural way possible.

"You don't get to be my age without seeing a whole lot of life hun. These eyes of mine know when someone's running from something." She nestled into her chair. "So, what is it?"

Mercury raised an eyebrow. "You really speak your mind, don't you?"

The woman shrugged. "No one listens to old folks anyways. Might as well say what I want."

Mercury smiled. "Too set in their ways?"

"You're a smart cookie," the woman nodded. "They're so focused on doing and going that they don't step back and take a look at the direction they're heading." She gave him a look that made him think he was included in that generalization. "So, what are you running from?" Yaedis asked. "Entertain an old woman for a bit."

"Alright," Mercury nodded. He would not actually tell her what was going on, but he would humor her. *I'm running from your son.* "I'm running from my family. My father and I don't exactly see eye to eye. I came here to just…get away."

The old lady chuckled in an understanding way. "Well at least you know you're running. Ain't nothing worse than to spend your whole life running from something and not know it."

Mercury raised an eyebrow. "Speaking from experience?"

"Son," she laid a hand on his shoulder. "At my age you're always speaking from experience."

"I suppose you would be," Mercury grinned. How did this woman give birth to a monster like Sol?

"So, your father and you don't get along," she said. "Is that all that's eating at you?"

Mercury cocked his head. "Why do you ask?"

Yaedis poked his shoulder with a bony finger. "I can tell you ain't the spineless type. Something worse is gnawing on you." She gave him a look of genuine concern. "What is it?"

Mercury chuckled. Why did he feel like opening up to this old grandma? He had only just met her. Was it because she was Sol's mother? Maybe it had just been so long since he had spoken with a normal person. He would never tell her anything dangerous, of course, but it still felt good to share what he was feeling. "My family's on my old man's side. He's making some decisions that I really don't agree with. I tried to fix things, but I did it behind their backs, and it didn't work out. Now I know they don't trust me." Mercury blinked and let out a breath. "I don't know if they'll ever want to see my face again."

He felt her bony hand give his shoulder a comforting squeeze. "Hun, if there's one thing I've learned about family in all my years is that when hammer meets anvil, they always have your back. It ain't easy fixing broken trust, but it'll be alright. Just you wait and see." Mercury did not know how, but her words had pierced straight to his heart. He took an unsteady breath before the old woman spoke up again, holding out her arm. "Now be a good lad and help me back into the house. You got here early so I'm putting you to work."

Mercury was pretty sure Yaedis could have easily stood on her own, but he appreciated the gesture. Helping someone else made his own problems seem small. Even if it was with something she could have done on her own. He had just met this lady, but he felt like he had known her for years. Did she even know who her son was?

As they entered the house, Mercury was struck by the welcoming feeling the home gave him. How could wooden walls feel so comforting? Maybe it was the shoes lined up by the door, or the couch off to the right. He could barely remember the last time he had been somewhere that had actually felt like a place where people lived. Mercury was well aware of how far off the bell curve his family was, as far as normal living was concerned. But this place, with its open windows letting in the evening air and thick carpets cushioning his steps, it evoked long forgotten memories of homes he had been in as a kid. It even reminded him of his own home, before Mom got sick. The warm, sweet smell of fresh bread filtered into his nostrils.

"You alright hun?" Sol's mother asked him.

Mercury blinked. He let out a breath, slow and steady. "…Yeah."

Warm yellow light was everywhere. From the decorations down to the smell, the place had a comforting, rustic feel to it. Mercury began untying his shoes as he drank it all in. He absolutely lost himself in it all.

"Is that you Granny?" Mercury heard a voice say that he recognized to be Cory's.

"Sure is, honey," Yaedis said as she took off her slippers and put them away. "Our guest's here."

A different voice answered this time, an older one. "Well why didn't you say so, Yaedis?" A woman that Mercury guessed was around Ma's age walked around a corner, wiping off her hands with a towel. Warm brown eyes told him he had nothing to fear here. "Welcome Mercury," she said holding out a freshly cleaned off hand.

Mercury shook it with one of his gloved hands. "Pleased to meet you Mrs. Titor."

"Please," she smiled. "Call me Malerie. Mrs. Titor makes me feel old. Do come in," she led him further into the house.

The path from the front door led into the living room and from there it had a hallway off the left and the dining area up ahead. Lining the walls were family photos in polished, carved wooden frames. There were even a couple...art pieces...clearly done by children. Another girl, younger than Cory, was setting plates and eating utensils around the six seats at the table. "Hi," the girl looked up but it seemed to Mercury like she was not entirely present. Either that, or the dining table was the most interesting thing she had ever seen. "I'm Cassie."

"Nice to meet you Cassie." *The pleasantries are probably a bother for her.*

"Hey," Cory said from the kitchen with a smile that made Mercury forget about whatever he had been thinking about. "You changed out of those weird clothes."

More like changed into weird clothes.

Malerie shot a look at her daughter. "Cory, don't you think that's just a bit impolite?"

"What? He must have thought they were weird too." *Not exactly.* "Besides, he cleaned up nice enough."

"Jorran should be back in a few minutes," Malerie said. "In the meantime, could you help us in the kitchen? We just have a few more things to do. Sink's over there."

"Sure," Mercury said as he moved over to wash his hands and stopped himself. He slowly took off his gloves and tucked them in a pocket. He was suddenly embarrassed by how grotesque his hands must seem to the Titors. He caught Cory staring. He was after all an instrument of war. Hopefully his cover story would make his hands not seem too strange.

"You can cut the onions," Yaedis smiled. His hands did not seem to faze her at all. "Should be about time to put them in."

"Yep," Cory said as she checked on the pot of food cooking in the oven. "I'd say about three minutes. Just cut those two on the counter."

"Sounds good," Mercury picked out a knife from the knife block, electing against the biggest one in favor of the curvature of the blade that was the next size smaller. After quickly running the blade under cold water he got to work, cutting off the ends then chopping it up into thin, uniform slices and then chopping the slices into cubes.

"Don't cut yourself," Malerie said with a concerned look on her face. "Those knives are sharp."

Mercury slowed down considerably. He smiled, "Thanks for the warning." Once he was done he washed the knife and dried it before putting it back on the block.

"You're pretty good at that," Cassie commented. Why did Mercury get the feeling that she did not talk much?

"Yeah," he stammered. He had been about to lie and say that he had worked in a restaurant, but Yaedis already knew he had been in the military. At least he would not have to tell them about how intimately familiar he was with every imaginable type of bladed instrument.

Cory started wiping her eyes. "Boy, the tasty ones sting the most."

Mercury consciously started blinking. "Is that how it is?" Compared to tear gas, this was nothing.

"Next time can we put the onions in the stew?" Cory asked Malerie. "It's just plain better that way."

"Sure honey," Malerie said as she handed Mercury a bowl for the diced vegetables. "Only reason I didn't today is because your sister asked me to."

"What are we making?" Mercury asked as he wiped the onions into the bowl.

"Beef stew," Cory said with a glazed over look on her face. "Family recipe."

Too bad Venus wasn't here; she loved the stuff.

"So, you were telling us about your day, Cass?" Malerie looked to her younger daughter.

"Oh, it um, it wasn't anything special really. Mr. Campbell's civics lecture was super boring and we had another drill for a Sons attack. Stupid."

"The Sons are a dangerous group Cass," Yaedis said.

Cassie huffed as she filled the glasses on the table with water. "They should be having us do drills for if the Angels attack, not the Sons."

Do you realize how many people the Sons have killed? Then he thought of how many had died at the hands of him and his family. Did most people think this way, or just this family?

Yaedis pulled the bread out of the oven and set it on the table with a small dish of butter. The loaf was hot and steaming. Mercury felt himself starting to salivate. "You have a point there, honey. If any of the Angels came here it would be much worse than any number of Sons."

"Did you see the news though?" Cory said. "They're going to be disbanded."

"Good riddance" Cassie said. "Damage done though."

"Let's just be thankful they won't ever come here," Malerie said.

About that…

"Yeah," Cory said. "Sorry for bringing it up, I didn't mean to get us all talking about stuff like that before dinner."

"Speaking of which," Malerie turned off the oven. It was almost six.

Mercury heard the sound of the front door opening, followed by a knock and Sol's voice. "Hey, hey, is the guest here yet?"

Immediately, Mercury's hands clenched into fists and his eyes flicked to the knife block. His mind flashed through a dozen different ways to render the room bloody and lifeless.

"We're in the kitchen hun," Malerie called out. "Guest showed up a few minutes ago."

"Guess I was holding you guys up then."

Calm down, Mercury. That's not Sol's voice. He could still hear Sol's voice echoing in the recesses of his mind and while this one was similar, it most certainly was not the same. His muscles relaxed somewhat and his fists unclenched. He felt a wave of shame wash over him. *What the Hel was I just about to do?* He shook his head.

Mr. Titor stepped into the kitchen. The man looked so similar to Sol that Mercury broke out in a cold sweat. He also wanted to know what exactly this man did for a living to make him so large. The man was almost exactly the same height as Sol, towering over Mercury. He practically had to walk sideways just to fit through the doorway. Had they used his shoulder span as a measurement?

"Pleased to meet you sir," Mercury held out his hand, feeling very small despite himself. Even though he knew the man before him was not Sol, Mercury's other hand was ready to grab one of the knives and slash the man's throat open in the blink of an eye. "I'm Mercury."

"Mercury, I like it; it's a good name. Well Mercury, my name's Jorran," the man said energetically and shook his hand. Although his voice was energetic, the way he shook Mercury's hand was restrained. Almost as if he had experience accidentally causing bodily harm to the person on the other end. Mercury noticed the handshake hesitate as Jorran felt the callouses. "So," he continued as he began helping the others with carrying dishes to the table. "Tell us a bit about yourself Mercury. You don't seem old enough to be one of the folks looking to retire out here."

"No," Mercury said with a smile. "I don't know if I'd be fit for retirement really. If I don't keep busy I start to get antsy. I was born on Tarence and I needed to get away, change up the pace. So I figured why not go to Taurus?"

"I respect that," Jorran said. "The best time to travel is when you're young, go and see what's out there so you know where you want to settle down."

"Is that what you did?" Mercury asked. He did not want them to ask too many questions about himself. His story was not entirely a lie, but he hoped he could avoid putting it to the test more than he had to.

"That's right," Jorran nodded. "I traveled around, saw the worlds, but I learned my home would always be Taurus. So, I came back and by chance I ended up settling down here."

"Was that how you two met?" Mercury continued to steer the conversation towards them and their story.

"Yes, it was," Malerie said as everyone took their seats. Mercury would have liked to sit next to Cory, but she was next to her mother and Yaedis. "Before we get into that story though," Malerie took Cory and Cassie's hands.

As everyone at the table joined hands, Mercury followed suit. He was seated next to Yaedis and Jorran, so he took each of their hands. Apparently, they were bowing their heads and closing their eyes. Mercury did not have a problem with bowing his head, but closing his eyes felt strange. He had not even let his guard down around the other Angels in a very long time. Worse, the man on the left might actually be capable of killing him if he tried.

Still, he did as they did. Malerie said the prayer. "Gods, we thank you for all you have given us. Even though we so often take it for granted, you never cease to shine your light on us. Please bless this food, and bless everyone at this table. We thank you for protecting us from harm and for showing us the way when we are lost. May our lives give you glory. This is our prayer."

"This is our prayer," the rest of them echoed. Mercury did likewise.

As the family began dishing themselves up, they passed their bowls to Jorran who had the ladle for the stew. Jorran filled Mercury's first. Only after Jorran had served everyone else did he fill his own bowl. Even though he knew the Titors were being polite by serving him first, Mercury also found the idea of eating before them slightly awkward. Dinner was a big deal for Taurusians and since this was so completely different from how he and the Angels had dinner, he did not want to step out of line. He waited until he saw Cory take a bite and gesture for him to go ahead before he began eating the stew.

Though he was not a spiritual person, he almost said a prayer to the gods when he tasted the stew. The last ten years had consisted of nothing but military rations. The memories he had of eating something this good were from a long time ago, very early in his childhood when his mother had still cooked. Every bite of this stew took him back to that time when things were so much more peaceful. He felt his eyes start to sting as he blew over the steaming food.

"Looks like the onions are getting to you after all," Cory smiled and raised her eyebrows.

Mercury smiled back. "This is...really good, Malerie," he said in between bites.

"Well thank you," Malerie said. "Although I can't take all the praise since it was a group effort. And your help with the onions is much appreciated. These are chopped very nicely. I sometimes have trouble getting them all the same size."

Her self-effacing remarks were undeserved. This was perfection. The beef was tender and in manageable pieces. The carrots were still the slightest bit firm in the center. The potatoes were just soft enough to break up and thicken the broth. Finally, bits of crushed pepper drifted around waiting to surprise him with just a bit of heat. He could not help but smile.

"So," Malerie said as she passed the bread to Cory. "I believe I promised you a story about how Jorran and I met?" Mercury nodded. "Well dear, do you want to tell it, or should I?"

"I'm not sure how much of it I remember," Jorran said with a wink at his wife.

She smiled, "Alright. To be told properly though it takes a while. It was in '27 and Jorran had just moved into town. Now mind you," she said to Mercury. "He wasn't always the strapping young lad you see before you. Back when I first met him he was a much thinner boy who had just spent his savings on traveling to all five of the worlds and their moons. He even worked for a bit in the Dorin Mining Cluster."

"All five worlds?" Mercury asked "You mean he went to Hel and Bjornhal?"

"That's right," Malerie went on as Jorran's eyes sparkled at her. "Those two in particular had drained his pockets, but he was full to bursting with stories of the things he'd seen. Even though he wasn't much to look at back then, he had all the girls in town hanging on his every word as he spun to them tales about the stars. Every girl except me. He tried everything to get my attention, but none of his stories got so much as a moment's notice. After trying to get my attention for months and months, he finally asked me what would impress me. I told him stories of a frivolous lifestyle meant nothing to me, but a man that could work hard, that was a man worth noticing."

Malerie tapped the table with a finger. "The very next day, this boy gets a job at my father's lumber shop. Now, my father wasn't even hiring. To this day I don't know what he said to the man. Sure enough though, he starts working for him from before sunrise to long after sunset. At first, I thought he had skipped town; I never saw him. But I started hearing stories. Every night it seemed my father would come home talking about how hard that Jorran boy was working. And every morning, my father would go into the shop and find a whole mess of trees that Jorran had cut down and brought in the night before, long after everyone else had gone home. This boy was working so hard, the grown men working for my father started to feel like they were being put to shame by this kid.

"I started going into the forest at night, just to see how late this boy worked. When I saw him though, I didn't even recognize him at first. I thought it was one of the other workers and that Jorran was somewhere deeper in the woods. The whole first night I didn't know who he was and went looking around the entire forest to find that kid my father kept talking about."

She smiled at her husband. "I only found out it was him when I asked my father about it the next day. After that, I went up there every night, watching to see when he went home. But every time I would get tired and leave while he was still going at it. One night as I watched him, I fell asleep and woke up in my bed the next morning. My father told me Jorran had come in the night before, carrying me in his arms. He set me down in my bed and headed back to the forest for the next day's work. Once I'd heard that, I walked straight out the door and to the forest. I went right up to Jorran. I told him if he was willing to work that hard for me and keep doing it for the rest of his life then I'd do the same."

"Wow," Mercury said. He had completely forgotten his stew. He could tell that the others had all heard the story before, but they did not seem to mind hearing it again. Cory in particular was all glassy eyed.

"Needless to say," Jorran gestured with his spoon. "I said yes."

"And the rest is history," Malerie finished.

"I never get tired of hearing that story," Cory wiped an eye.

"I remember when it was different," Jorran's eyes sparkled. "You and Cassie used to get so embarrassed when we'd tell it."

"Of course we did," Cassie piped up. "It seemed every time we had guests over you would be asked to tell that story."

"It's a great story," Mercury said. "If I had a story like that I'd be sure to tell it every chance I got."

"So, what's your story Mercury?" Malerie asked. "What brings you here all the way from Tarence?"

I walked right into that one.

"It was New Tarence, wasn't it?" Cory asked. "In town, your clothes were from the capital, right?"

"Both are right," Mercury said. He did not want to tell more than was necessary of his concocted story since so much of it was grounded in truth, but there was something about this family that put him at ease. "I grew up on Tarence, but at sixteen I enlisted and was stationed on the moon. I served for my six years and now I'm trying to find a place to set down roots. I never was one for cities and it had always been a dream to visit the Taurusian countryside. So, here I am."

"You look like you've seen some things," Jorran nodded at his hands.

"Yes," Mercury answered. "Yes, I have." *You wouldn't believe me if I told you.*

"What kind of things?" Cass blurted out.

"Cass," her father gave her a look.

"Sorry," she whispered. "What kind of things though?"

Cory closed her eyes shook her head.

"I'm not really supposed to say," Mercury said as nonchalantly as possible.

Cassie gave a thousand-yard stare. "Woah…"

"How long are you planning to stay here?" Cory asked.

Mercury thought how best to answer that. "I'm not entirely sure yet. How are these things usually done on Taurus?"

"Usually it's either month-to-month or people sign a lease for a better rate," Jorran said. "We'll need a five hundred credit damage deposit. Plus, if it's going to be month by month, then we'll need first and last month's payment up front. Monthly rate is twelve hundred, but if you sign for a year then it's an even thousand. I'll get you a contract listing the details. Payment dates and the like. I can show you the place after dinner. We also host a dinner at the beginning of every month with our other renters. Feel free to join us, but there's no need to."

"Don't worry," Mercury said, gesturing at his stew. "I'll be looking forward to that." Money would not be a problem. The *Defiant* was stocked with a million in cash for any bribes or under the table dealings that needed doing. Besides, if this was New Tarence, he was pretty sure he would be paying at least five times that. "I'll do a year."

"You don't want to look at the house first?" Jorran asked.

Mercury shook his head. "If it's anything like this place, then I'm sold."

Jorran smiled. "Alright. Any questions before I print off a contract?"

"Just one," Mercury said before turning to Malerie and using his spoon to point at his bowl. "Could I get the recipe for this?" That elicited a belly laugh from Jorran.

After dinner was over and Mercury had signed the contract, the Titors helped him get settled into his new home. They were so...nice. Mercury had entirely forgotten what this was like. The Titors were good people. It was hard to believe they were blood relatives of the most dangerous man in existence. Even ignoring that, he would have expected them to judge him at the very least for being different, or hold him at arm's length because he was an outsider. Instead they welcomed him into their home just as if he were...family.

CHAPTER EIGHTEEN

VENUS
Age 20

Venus visualized the enemy in her mind's eye. Normally she would train on her own Forging floor, but today Sol would deploy them to kill the Ministers. So here she was on the sparring floor, white light and bare steel with several racks of training weapons near the elevator doors.

Taking a deep breath, she brought up both the training blades into her favored defensive stance and engaged her imaginary foes. Fighting with two blades was quite different from a single blade or a sword and shield. The sequences had to play off each other while being different enough to be unpredictable. The footwork was different too. In addition, if she was fighting an opponent who also had dual blades, she would not be able to use most of her normal sequences.

Ever since Saturn used Mars' blade at the Bastion Venus had made it a point to practice with dual blades for at least an hour a day. She was going to be the next Teresa Balemore. The Balemore had been a goddess on the battlefield that defied imagination. Venus would continue to push herself harder and farther than any of the other Angels until she had surpassed even Sol.

Faster and faster she moved. The training blades were no longer instruments, but extensions of herself. They obeyed her every thought with perfect execution. The realization slowly dawned on her that she could progress no further. Not with the forms she was currently using anyway. She would have to design her own fighting style that would make the most of her strengths.

She stopped and put the training swords back on their rack, breathing hard. Why was she so tired? Even on a bad day, she could go much longer than this without breaking a sweat. For the last week though her energy levels had been way down.

"Hey stranger," she heard Earth say from behind her.

She turned around. "Hey you." She gave him a quick kiss. "What's going on?"

"It's time," he said, his usual jovial mood long gone.

Venus rolled her shoulders and started walking across the open sparring floor to the elevator. "Everything's about to change, isn't it?"

"I think it already has," he said. Venus had been talking about the coup, but she knew he was talking about Mercury.

Then, all of a sudden Venus felt a rush of nausea. She put a hand on Earth's shoulder and looked down. She felt like she was going to be sick.

"Are you alright?" Earth steadied her with both arms.

Venus tasted bile. She shook her head and headed straight for the bathroom, covering her mouth as she went. When she got there, she pressed her hand against the wall panel and the toilet slid out. Immediately she vomited into it.

No, not this. She had been sick yesterday too, and her period was a week late. More vomit. *No.* She heard Earth rush to her side and put his hand on her back. Venus held the sides of the toilet as she watched a rope of saliva lower, then fall into the mixture of water and puke.

"Did that help?" Earth asked.

In response, she puked again. Not much came up this time. She struck the toilet with the palm of her hand once, twice, three times. She felt the tears coming on, but she would not let them fall. Seizing Earth by the collar, she pulled him into a hug and held him tight. She could feel the confusion in his tense muscles. A moment passed, and then she felt his body relax and knew he understood. Then he squeezed her back, just as tight.

For a long while they just held each other on the floor. Angels were not allowed to have kids. Venus thought back to her childhood on Bjornhal. She remembered the pain of being unwanted and the betrayal as Tavahl beat her. She remembered stumbling through the blizzard with barely enough clothes to keep from immediately freezing. She remembered the hopelessness of breaking. She buried her face in Earth's shoulder as the tears finally came.

"I'm keeping it," she declared through sobs and gritted teeth.

In the deepest core of her being was a fire that burned with an all-consuming intensity. If anything, or anyone came after her baby, she would destroy them. Mentally, she knew that all she had to do was tell Sol and the next morning she would wake up with everything back to normal. She was being stupid and selfish, but she did not care.

"I love you," Earth whispered in her ear.

Venus sniffed and remembered how Lowulf had hated Tavahl because of Venus' existence. The very notion of Earth becoming as bitter as Lowulf made her heart ache. "You…you'll stay?"

Earth rose, pulling her to her feet and looked into her eyes. Unfathomable oceans of blue smiled at her. "Of course," he said in a choked voice.

Those two words cut through all the fear in her heart. She clutched his head to hers, running her fingers through his hair as the tears kept coming. *You know what this means though, right? You're not even going to question it? We can't raise this baby and be Angels at the same time.*

On that day when Sol had rescued her in the blizzard, she had vowed to herself she would not let herself break again. To this day, she had kept that vow. However, if Earth had left her, she did not know what she would have done. She would not have broken her vow, she could not, but that would have been the closest she ever got.

Their days as Angels were officially numbered. Venus guessed she had a couple months before the baby started showing. When that happened, they would have to leave. She doubted Sol would let her stay unless she gave up the baby. Hopefully they would at least be able to find Mercury and get him back to normal before then.

"Venus, Earth," Sol's voice echoed over the comms. "Report to the armory immediately. You leave in fifteen minutes."

Earth pulled away and searched her eyes. "You alright?"

"Yeah," she wiped her eyes with a sniff. "Don't worry about me." *You always worry about others.*

"But," Earth hesitated. "What about the baby? Will it be safe in the field?"

"Well apparently the suits can shrug off nukes. Inside the armor is the safest place for the baby to be." They both stood.

Earth nodded. "Let's go conquer the universe."

When they got to the armory, Mars, Jupiter and Saturn were already in their armor.

"What took you two so long?" Saturn asked.

"We uh, we needed some alone time," Venus sniffed.

Saturn punched Mars' chest piece with a clang. "See? We totally would have had time for a quickie."

Mars quickly changed the subject. "You guys see the news?"

Venus shook her head absentmindedly as she stepped into her armor. "No, why?"

"They're saying Mercury left to join the Sons," Mars said.

Earth scoffed as his face disappeared behind his helmet. "They're always putting out bullshit stories. Why should we care? Let stupid be stupid."

"Just in case anyone was worried about turning on the Federation," Mars shrugged. "They're already vilifying us."

"Ha!" Saturn's helmet tossed back. "I can't wait to see what the evening story will be."

"Sat," Jupiter shook his head. He sounded exhausted. "Please, just stop. We don't need your jokes; not now."

"Sorry Jup," Saturn's voice was not cheerful anymore. She gave his armored shoulder a squeeze. "Don't worry, we're still the good guys."

"Are we though?" Jupiter sat down on a bench and put his head in his hands. "I'm starting to wonder if we were ever the good guys. The people we're killing today are targets specifically because of how loyal they are to the Federation. The pain won't end with their death either. They have families."

"I know Jup," Earth sat down on a bench opposite Jupiter. "Believe me, I know. Sol has a plan though. He told me so himself. We need to trust him."

"…Sure," Jupiter said at last.

"And we'll get Mercury back," Earth added.

That elicited a small nod from Jupiter. "Okay."

Venus turned to Jupiter. "I take it Yuki already left?"

"Of course," he said. "She left to set up late last night."

"Do you think there are really enough soldiers loyal to Sol?" Saturn looked at Venus.

"If Sol says there are enough," she answered. "Then there are enough."

Sol's voice came over their comms. "Angels, get to the Minister Building immediately. The Prime Minister has been assassinated."

Dead on the spot. *Ma always was a clean shot.*

"We'll be right there, Sol," Earth said. "Okay everyone, this is it. Six bodies…"

A silence fell over them. Without Mercury, the words sounded foreign. Jupiter shook his head. "We need Mercury back." Venus could feel the pain in his voice.

"We'll get him back," Earth spoke with such conviction it was as if he expected his words to bend the universe itself.

"Just because he's gone doesn't mean he's not here," Saturn said.

After a moment's hesitation, Jupiter nodded.

"Six bodies," Earth said.

"One soul," they finished.

With that, Venus and the rest of the Angels departed.

***

In a state of national emergency protocol dictated that all the Ministers were to gather in the bunker underneath the Minister Building to decide on a course of action. The bunker was the most secure location on New Tarence, even more so than Angel Tower. The odds of any unauthorized personnel infiltrating it was a statistical impossibility.

Unfortunately for the Ministers however, that also meant there was no way a single one of them would escape. Quick, dirty and done.

The Angels made their way to the bunker right through the front entrance. All the guards were from the Storm Legions. They scanned the crate the Angels carried with Sol's armor and waved them through. They made their way through dozens of layers of security all the way to the bunker without so much as a hiccup. All the men inside the bunker and guarding the entrance were also Legionnaires. They let the Angels through.

Inside the Ministers were sitting around a table discussing the next course of action. When they saw the Angels enter they turned to Sol with wide eyes. The Minister of Economy stood to his feet in indignation. "Rauss, what is the meaning of this?"

"Vyllus, never speak again." Sol commanded from where he sat. Vyllus' mouth clamped shut. He looked from Sol to Venus and the other Angels. He sat down.

Sol stood and nodded to them.

"For every person you kill, you'll be saving a hundred." Still carrying Sol's armor pod, Venus and the others shot the Ministers where they sat, two clean shots each, right between the eyes.

"Archangel!" shouted the Minister of Internal Affairs, Talos Zackley.

Sol held up his hand and the Angels stopped shooting. Zackley was the only Minister left alive.

"Make this worth it," he said with a nod and faint smile.

Sol inclined his head at the man before signaling to Venus. She painted the wall behind Zackley red. *Seven hundred.*

"Sol," she set down the pod with a resounding clang. "What's next?"

The pod opened with a hiss and Sol stepped into his armor. "We can keep this a secret for a day at absolute most. We have to make the time until then count. I can handle things here. The targets are assembled in orbit. Hit them all quickly and then return. The press conference is at 1800."

They all saluted and left.

***

Two hours later, Venus was in the captain's quarters of the battleship *Valiant*, pinning the captain against the wall with one hand. He gurgled something in protest before she blew his brains out. Venus let out a breath and closed her eyes a moment. Whoever this man was, Sol knew he would not be intimidated into submission by the coup. Loyalty rewarded with death. *Another hundred.* "Angel Two to *Valiant*, send XO Lelan Varkys to the captain's quarters immediately.

When the First Officer arrived, her eyes went wide at the sight of the captain's remains. "XO Lelan Varkys," Venus said. "As of this moment you are the CO of the *Valiant*. The Federation requires your complete and total compliance in this matter. As far as you are concerned, nothing has changed. You report to the Eleventh Admiral, who in turn reports to Supreme Commander Rauss."

Lelan remained calm for the most part, but Venus had to be sure she could be trusted. She had read Lelan's in depth psych profile before coming here. "Lelan," she said in an understanding but serious tone. "A cleanup crew will be here in a few minutes. Just forget this ever happened. After that, if you want to drag your crew into doing something stupid and get them killed, that's your choice as CO. Understood?"

Venus watched Lelan clench her fist a couple times, then saluted. "Understood ma'am."

In turn, Venus saluted the *Valiant*'s new captain. She left the room just as Sol's cleanup crew arrived. Venus was confident the new captain would turn out just fine. "How are the others going?" she asked over the comms.

"Just finished on the *Giant's Thunder*," Jupiter's voice was morose. "Ship is secure."

"I wrapped up on the *Vanguard* a few minutes ago," Earth said. "We shouldn't be getting any problems from them. How about you Vee?"

"Mine's a bit antsy," Venus said as she made her way to the nearest airlock. None of the crew gave her a second glance. "But I think she'll fall in line once Sol makes his announcement."

"Okay," Saturn chimed in. "Leaving the *Avalon* now. Apparently, the old CO was a real shithead."

Venus could tell Saturn was doing her best to put a positive spin on it. Venus launched out the *Valiant*'s airlock and regrouped with Earth and Jupiter.

"How about you Mars?" Earth asked. "They giving you much grief over there?"

"Tell me about it," Mars said. "I had to waste the *Dominator*'s CO and XO. The Combat Systems Officer went along with it, but I'm not entirely sure if he'll end up causing trouble later."

"Well," Venus said. "I guess we'll find out." Most of the ships that had problematic CO's were able to have the CO "transferred" over the last couple days, but that would not work with all the crews. If the XO was not already loyal to Sol, then the five of them gave the officer a little chat. For most of them it should be enough to at least keep them from doing anything stupid. And if any of them did do something stupid, Sol was monitoring them and had personnel on the vessels for that exact reason.

"Hey guys," Jupiter said. "How do you think Sol got so many people loyal to him in the fleet? Most of these people weren't serving during the war."

"I don't know," Venus said. "He does have a way with words though."

"Well yeah," Jupiter said. "But he's so well set up for this. Do you think maybe he's been planning a coup for a while?"

"That bothers you, doesn't it?" Earth said.

Jupiter hesitated. "Uh huh. I mean, I can wrap my brain around doing this as a last resort to make sure the Sons are defeated. I don't like it, but I get it. But if he's always been planning this? I don't know how I feel about that."

"Jup," Venus said. "If Sol has been planning this for a long time, then he must have had a good reason for it. He's never let us down yet and I'm willing to bet he never will." She believed that. This was all for the best. For every innocent life they took, they saved a hundred.

"Yeah," Jupiter said. "Yeah, you're right. It was just a stupid thought." *No, it wasn't.*

"Alright guys," Mars said as he regrouped with them. "Let's head home."

**

The press conference was held in the same place as Prime Minister Sazius Hedge's national address. The crowds were even larger now that the Prime Minister was dead than when he was sworn in. Reporters from every news station across all the worlds had flocked here to catch the Federation's statement on the Prime Minister's assassination.

Venus and the other four Angels stood at attention as Sol approached the podium. There was already speculation on the Net why Mercury was not present. Some were even saying he killed the Prime Minister. Boy were they in for a surprise. Still, why had Sol so brazenly displayed that an Angel was missing?

Venus could almost taste the anticipation of the millions of people gathered. Sol had their absolute attention. "Prime Minister Sazius Hedge was shot and killed this morning...He was killed by my order." For a moment Venus could have heard a pin drop, and then confused chatter drifted up from the audience. The reporters were greedily capturing every moment. "The Ministers are all dead," Sol continued. "The Federation is mine. I will use it to destroy the Sons of Liberty. Any who oppose me will be considered Sons and dealt with accordingly."

Venus let out a breath. Even the smallest creature could be dangerous once backed into a corner. *You know what you're doing...right?* She glanced at the others. Her mind jumped to the baby growing inside her. *We're on the right side, right?*

"This is all just a show," Jupiter said on a private channel. Venus could hear the fear in his voice. "Right?"

"Don't worry," Venus did her best to conceal how nervous she was. "This is all part of Sol's plan. Once the Sons are defeated, he'll step down."

"To Mercury," Sol continued aloud. He spread his hands. "My protégé, my fallen Angel. Wherever you are, if you think you can stop me, I welcome you to try."

Venus approached Sol with the Cloak of Office and clasped it to his armor before resuming her position. Sol threw the cloak over his shoulder with a flourish. The man's voice echoed out as imperious as ever. "Humanity's Golden Age begins today."

With that, Sol left the podium. Venus and the other Angels followed.

CHAPTER NINETEEN

MARS
Age 21

Mars woke up inside his DreamTank to the sound of someone knocking on the outside of it. He smiled underneath the Breather. *Saturn.* Quickly he shut off the Tank and felt the familiar twinges of pain as the MicroNeedles were withdrawn. Stripping off the Breather, he climbed out via the emergency hatch, not even waiting for the tank to drain. Instead of Saturn's dusky face though, he saw Mercury's pale one.

"Merc?" Mars said is a hushed voice from atop the DreamTank. "What the hell are you doing here?"

"I need your help Mars," Mercury said.

Mars climbed down from the Tank. "You've got some explaining to do first." He made his way over to his dresser and put on some pants. "Why didn't you tell us what was going on man?" He had been dying to ask Mercury that question. He had not expected the pain in his chest though.

"Listen Mars," Mercury held up his hands. "There's a good reason I went after Sol. It isn't psychosis like he said. I should've gone to you guys first, I know. What I did was stupid. That's why I'm here now."

"How did you even get in here without the alarms going off?" Mars asked.

"Mars, come on," Mercury cocked an eyebrow. "This is me you're talking to."

"Do any of the others know you're here?"

"Nope," Mercury said. "I came to you first."

"Why did you run?" Mars asked.

Mercury looked ashamed. "I messed up man. I forgot the number one rule."

"Six bodies," Mars said.

"One soul," Mercury finished.

"Alright," Mars headed towards the door. "Let's wake up the others."

"Sol absolutely can never know I'm here though," Mercury said.

"Sure," Mars shrugged. "Whatever."

Mercury nodded and the two of them made their way to Saturn's room. Stopping just outside the door Mars turned to Mercury. "So, if you're here, then where's the *Defiant?*"

Mercury grinned. "You're not going to believe this, but it's on the roof."

Mars' eyes widened. Then he thought about it for a second and groaned. "Oh my gods."

Mercury poked his shoulder. "That's not even the best part." He paused and then continued in a whisper. "I never left."

Mars turned. "Wait, what?"

Mercury nodded with enthusiasm. "As soon as I activated the MimicField I turned right back around and landed on the roof. I've been there ever since."

Mars blinked and shook his head. "You're shitting me." Mercury shook his head with a smile. The more Mars thought about it though, the more it made sense. Earth was the only one that ever really went up to the roof, and he always lay in exactly the same spot to watch the night sky. "You mean to say that this whole time we've been wondering where you ran off to, and you've been right on top of us?"

"That's right," Mercury said. "I've been waiting for a better chance to kill Sol."

Mars stepped away from Saturn's door. "You can stop right there. You're not killing Sol."

"I have to Mars," Mercury said. "That's why I'm here. Once we wake the others I'll explain everything."

"Not. Happening." Mars said forcefully.

"But he has to die," Mercury pressed. "I need you guys to help me; I can't do it alone."

Mars seized Mercury by the throat. "Not. Happening."

Mercury's eyes went wide and his hands desperately tried to pry Mars' thumbs away, but Mars wrestled him to the ground. He was stronger. He had always been stronger. Mercury's legs kicked underneath him, but Mars kept his grip. He squeezed harder and harder, watching the life drain from Mercury's eyes moment by moment. As Mercury's open mouth struggled in vain for air, his eyes locked onto Mars'. They were so confused and hurt. They named Mars "betrayer" but it was Mercury who was the traitor. Mars squeezed harder still and Mercury's eyes rolled back and grew lifeless.

"Mars?" he heard Saturn's voice from behind him. "What...? What are you doing?"

He looked back and saw her face completely overcome with fear. Standing quickly, he reached for her, but she backed away. He called for her, but no sound came out. He tried to move, but his feet would not budge. He was sinking into the floor. He called out to her again, to no avail. As he sunk deeper and deeper, he watched as Saturn turned and ran. She ran until she had disappeared from sight, not turning back once. Mars felt panic begin to take over him, but he could not move. He had sunk into the floor up to his neck now. He cried out once more, but still nothing. Before long, he had gone under completely.

Mars woke with a start, sucking in air through the Breather with a hiss. He could not see in the DreamTank, but he could feel Saturn's arms wrapped around his neck and her naked body pressed up against him. She stirred slightly and nestled her head on his shoulder. Some of her floating hair swept across his face.

For a while Mars sat there, floating in the Tank with Saturn, thinking about the dream. Everything the DreamTanks showed them was supposed to be a lesson of some kind, so what did this mean? He could still see Mercury's eyes staring up at him. His heart hammered in his chest. While it had been a dream, Mars knew that if Mercury tried to go after Sol again, they would have to kill him. More specifically, Mars would have to kill him; there was no way he would make one of the others do it.

Wrapping his arms around Saturn, he held her tightly until his breathing calmed and his heart slowed. Eventually, his eyes drooped shut.

***

The next morning, Sol gathered the five of them in his office. Mars found the man sitting behind his desk slowly swirling a glass of whiskey on the rocks. Mars saw bags under the man's now dismal eyes. For the first time in his life, he also noticed scruff on the man's face. After taking a drink of his whiskey, Sol set the glass down and tapped his finger on the desk. *Sol doesn't drink.* "I know the five of you are anxious to find Mercury and bring him back, but I need you to wait. Overnight nearly thirty percent of the Federation Armada disappeared."

"Wait," Mars blinked. "What?"

"You heard me," Sol stared daggers at him. "They deserted to join the Sons. Thankfully we still have the *Balemore*, but the situation is dire. The Sons have been emboldened by this. A battleship has even been mutinied and is currently holding Marraca Prime hostage."

"But..." Venus looked confused. "We hit our targets perfectly."

"Well that list of targets just got much, much bigger," Sol said.

Mars could not believe this. The coup was flawless. They should have the military completely in their control. "How could this happen?"

Sol just shook his head, a thousand-yard stare in his eyes. "I miscalculated."

Dead silence filled the room. There was no way. Sol did not make mistakes. He was Sol. He was the Archangel. He had a plan for everything. On a bad day he was a dozen steps ahead of them. The reason they had helped him with the coup was because they trusted him. Because he told them it was for the best.

Confusion and fear Mars had never felt before stirred within him. He shook his head. *Who the Hel is this? Where's Sol?* He thought back to when he had killed the boy on Maracca. Even though Sol's face had been hidden behind his helmet, Mars had felt the brutal, cold calculations weighing his value. Entire worlds spun in the palm of this man's hand. This man was the apex predator that kept them all safe.

Mars looked at the others, but they were all too stunned to speak. "Tell us where they are then," he turned back to Sol. "We'll destroy them."

The man closed his eyes. His words were slow and measured, barely containing their fury. "We don't know where they are. We cannot search the entire Hel System for them. Until they reveal themselves, we cannot hurt them. And the longer this goes on, the more flock to the Sons. Civilians and military."

"So, what's the plan Sol?" Mars asked. *You always have a plan.*

A sly smile crept onto the man's face as he opened his eyes. "I've compiled quite a lengthy list of targets. The Armada is ready to strike as soon as you've dealt with the situation above Maracca Prime. Venus, Earth, Mars and Saturn, you four will protect the Armada as it hits the targets, just in case the Sons decide to come out of hiding. Jupiter, you will remain here and continue to interrogate the prisoner for any additional leads. I've already broken her, so your job should be quite easy."

Jupiter swallowed and nodded.

"Any questions?" Sol asked. No one said anything. "Good. Then move out immediately."

As they left, Mars glanced back at the disheveled Sol. *Alright Mars, you kept them safe on Maracca, you can keep them safe now.*

When the four of them got to the hangar Mars whistled under his breath. If the *Defiant* had been their ghost, quick and undetectable, then the *Decimator* was their dragon. The ship had been constructed around a minigun built from *Zerythane* cannons. There was nothing 'mini' about it. Two anti-fighter turrets covered each axis of the ship with the ability to angle all but the rear ones toward the front. A full seventy-two *Maelstrom*-missiles able to be fired up to twelve at a time. There was even a bomb bay with eight Breakers. Never before had there been a reason to use this ship. A chill ran the length of Mars' spine.

"Hey," Earth called back to him from the ramp of the ship. "Cut the drooling. We have work to do."

"…Right," Mars called back.

"I'm worried about him, Mars," Saturn said in a troubled voice from behind.

"Who?" Mars said. "Earth?"

She blinked twice and shook her head. "What? No. I'm talking about Jupiter."

"Huh?" Mars asked. "Where's that coming from?"

"You didn't notice?" she said. "He's been off ever since Mercury disappeared."

"No," Mars said. "It hit us all hard." *Jupiter's tough. He'll handle it okay.*

"Come on," Saturn said. "Jupiter's been miserable. You know how close he was to Mercury. Do you think you could talk to him when we get back? He looks up to you so much."

Mars gave her a quick kiss on the cheek as they boarded the ship. "Okay, Sat. When we get back."

Unfortunately, since the *Defiant* was the only ship with a working MauKe drive, the trip to Maracca Prime would take a while. Not that he cared about the nobles anyway. *Let them wait.* Once the location was plugged into the *Decimator*'s computer, all the four of them had to do was wait until they reached their destination. "Hey guys," Saturn pulled her legs onto her chair on the ship's bridge. "Do you really think Mercury's going crazy?"

"Sat," Venus said. "How can you even ask that? We all saw his PerfectMemory. He had the idea of killing Sol back then, and the idea hasn't left his head since. Why else would he try to kill Sol?"

"But what if he's not crazy?" Saturn said. "What then?"

It's okay Sat. We survived before, we can do it again. "I can't accept that, Sat. Mercury's going crazy. He has to be." He was not capable of accepting any other truth. Otherwise he could no longer dismiss what his brother did. "He just needs some Forging."

"But what if he's not crazy?" Saturn repeated again. She seemed quite disturbed by the idea.

Mars furrowed his brow. *Why won't she let go of this?* "Sat, what's wrong?"

She swallowed. "If the PerfectMemory drove Mercury crazy, then what's to say we won't go crazy too?"

Venus shook her head. "Sol gave us them when we were young. You know how it works, the more malleable the brain, the easier it is to make a memory permanent."

"Mercury was younger than Mars when he got his PerfectMemory," she said and turned to Mars. "What's to say you won't flip out and run off too? Mercury's first PerfectMemory was just of him talking with Sol. The six of us got inside each other's heads and memories. What if you start thinking you're still a Zero in Dabo's army?"

"Sat," Mars looked into her eyes. "That's not going to happen."

"How do you know?" she shoved against his armored chest with tears in her eyes. "You were older than Mercury when you got yours."

"Sol gave him two," he said. "That's why Merc's acting up. Sol didn't know two would be trouble."

"Sol didn't know because it was experimental tech, right?" Saturn said. "Well how do we know we're okay? The 'experts' were wrong about Mercury. They said he was fine and look what happened. Either they were right and Mercury is perfectly sane, or they were wrong, in which case they could have been wrong about us too."

"You should be totally fine though," Venus said. "You were a good deal younger than Mercury when we got our PerfectMemory."

"Venus," Saturn's voice sounded hurt. "Do you really think I'm worried about myself?" She turned to Mars, "I don't want to lose any of you. Sol says we need to kill Merc if he tries something. What if you start acting up next Mars? What if Sol tells me to kill you?"

Mars did not know what to say to her. "That's not going to happen."

"You don't know that," she cried and hit his arm with a clang. "You can't know that." He knew she was right.

Mars turned to Venus. "Will you do it?"

She nodded slowly. "Okay. Same goes for me, Mars. Don't make them do it."

Mars wondered if he would actually be capable of killing Venus, but he nodded. "Alright."

"No," Saturn spat out the words. Her glinting eyes dared him to challenge her. "Both of you shut your damn mouths. That is not on the table. It will *never* be on the table."

Mars obeyed. He knew how much this was hurting Saturn. He wished he could help her. Venus continued. "Sat, if you're right then we're all ticking time bombs. I don't think you are right, but if you are, we can't let other people get hurt. If just one of us went crazy, really crazy, I can't imagine how many people would end up dead."

Saturn rested her forehead on her knees. "I don't care about other people. I just care about you guys. Mars," she turned to him. "You promised me we weren't going to lose anyone else."

With a sharp intake of breath, Mars felt his eyes go wide. His mind immediately sent him back to when Sol had rescued them from Maracca. *"This is a fresh start," Mars told a crying Saturn. "We aren't going to lose anyone else. I promise. We'll be together forever."*

Saturn sniffed and wiped her eyes with a small hand. "I'm scared. I don't want to be alone."

Mars' mind returned to the present and Saturn was still on her chair, hugging her legs. He could not remember the last time he cried, but right now his eyes were itching.

"Okay guys," Earth spoke up. He had been completely silent so far. That was not like him. "You all seem to be forgetting something. I get where all of you are coming from. All of you. Remember, we're Angels. Six bodies, one soul. We're unstoppable because we have each other. Even if you're right Saturn, and we all go crazy, we're still…us. Even if we all get so lost that we can't save ourselves. We could be foaming at the mouth, I don't care. We'll always, *always* be there to help each other. There are no exceptions. We are Angels."

Thank you, Earth. Mars knew he had never been good with words, and he was even worse at expressing himself. He felt a pang of jealousy at how Earth was always ready and able to help like this. *Don't ever change, brother.*

For a long time, they were silent. Eventually, Saturn spoke up. "Mars, before Mercury tried to kill him, who did you trust more, Mercury or Sol?"

Mars was taken aback. "I…I don't know. Both of them equally, I guess."

"No," Saturn shook her head. "You have to pick one. Which one did you trust more?"

He thought for a moment, then hesitated and looked around at the ship's interior. At some point Sol was going to hear this conversation. "Before attacking Ma and trying to kill Sol, yeah, I trusted Mercury more."

"Me too," Saturn agreed. She looked around at the others. "Pretty sure we all did, if we really had to choose. Personally, I don't think Mercury is 'crazy'. We would have known. I would have known. So, either he's crazy and any of us could be next, or he's not crazy, in which case, why the hell aren't we with him?"

"Saturn!" he barked, reaching out a hand as his heart skipped two beats. Her eyes were wide and startled, looking straight at him in a way that made him flinch with guilt. He had sounded like Sol. "Don't say that," he said in a pleading voice. He looked at the walls and ceiling. "Please." *He might be listening.*

Saturn nodded in silence, but not before wiping away a tear.

None of them said anything else until they reached their destination. The distant battleship came into view over the Maraccan moon. Sol had stationed here what looked like half the remaining Armada. However, they could not safely engage without endangering Maracca Prime. As Mars surveyed the firepower present, he could not help but thinking it seemed overkill. *How long exactly is Sol's list of targets?*

"Alright," Earth said as they made their way to the launch tubes. "Six bodies."

"One soul."

When the four of them were launched into space, they only used their Boosters for the initial thrust, after that they were dark. In an instant the battleship swelled from being the size of the end of Mars' thumb to almost as big as his hand. This launch had to be dark if they wanted to save Maracca Prime from bombardment. Trayite could not be detected on sensors directly, but the suits' internal power supply was enough to leave a noticeable trail. If they were dark however, then the Sons would have no way to know they were coming.

"You sure this'll work?" Mars asked. They had never tried this attack method before, and Mars did not like it one bit.

"Yeah," Earth said. "Sol said we'll be fine. If the suits can handle nukes, then why not this?"

Mars swallowed. He could think of a few reasons. Inertia, mainly.

The battleship *Valiant* now looked as big as Mars' arm. Before long it was the only thing visible. As one, the four of them ignited their Boosters and corrected their vector. They all held out their arms in front of them and Mars felt the joints of his armor lock him in a diving position. *A human missile.* Traveling at over a dozen kilometers per second, the *Valiant* was in for one Hel of a rude awakening, regardless of whether or not the four of them survived. Mars felt his body go tense in preparation for impact.

The collision was spectacular. The *Valiant's* deflectors did not stand a chance. The ship's interior rushed by in a heartbeat and Mars was on the bridge. Air and bodies rushed through the four gaping holes in the *Valiant* into the void of space. Inside his suit, Mars felt perfectly fine. He had not felt the impact in the slightest. He let out a breath. The armor joints unlocked.

Looking around, Mars found that many of the crew were holding onto whatever nearby would anchor them to the floor. Not that it would save them. Once the atmosphere was gone, they were dead anyway. At one point he would have felt sorry for them, but that seemed like a lifetime ago. Mars was the first to get to one of the bridge's consoles. He uploaded the virus and once he had control of the ship, he opened all the doors, airlocks included, and locked them open.

"We all good here?" Venus said as she flew into sight, coming up out of a hole in the floor she had made. One of the crew near her lost his grip on his desk and was sucked into space.

"Almost," Mars said. He deactivated the ships defenses and then restricted access to all the ship's functions. Then he jettisoned the escape pods. "We're good to go."

Venus nodded as Saturn and Earth appeared on the bridge. "Venus to *Decimator*, target all escape pods then fire along the length of the *Valiant*."

Mars watched as the *Decimator* approached and fired off a dozen *Maelstrom*-missiles. Each in turn split into two dozen smaller missiles and found their way to the escape pods. Space disappeared behind hundreds of tiny orange blossoms. As the ship came in closer, its primary gun began to spin, then light up. Countless brilliant spears of violet and blue light hit the *Valiant* in a wave from bow to stern.

The *Valiant* pitched so abruptly under the impact it almost seemed the ship would be torn apart. The remaining crew lost their grips on whatever they were holding onto and were sucked into space. Now the entire vessel would be vented in a matter of minutes. Their job was done. Mars felt someone grab him and turned to see a woman desperately holding onto part of his armor with one hand. She clung to it so tightly her fingers started to bleed. She looked up at him with pleading eyes. He glanced at her terrified expression and felt nothing. Unfortunately for her, Mars had a very short list of people he cared about, and she was not on it. He calmly grabbed the woman's wrist and pried her away before letting go and she joined the rest of the mutineers in the cold black.

Now onto Sol's lengthy list of targets.

CHAPTER TWENTY

MERCURY
Age 20

Mercury felt the flat, metal board his chest was tied to tilt down until one end hit the floor with a clang. He shuddered at the impact and the memories it brought to mind. The room was almost entirely dark, but he could still see Sol on his right, looming above his ten-year-old self. In one hand Sol held a rag, in the other a hose. Mercury could see the tiniest glimmers of light reflecting off the water as it poured out the tube and splashed to the floor in one constant stream. He could feel the pool of water on the floor start to tickle the back of his head before running down the drain in the floor.

"Are you ready?" Sol's iron voice asked.

Fear crept up into Mercury's heart, but he must not let Sol see it. "I'm ready," he said in the squeaky voice of a child trying to be brave.

With a nod, Sol tossed the rag to him, then held out the hose. Small, tentative fingers grasped the rubber tube as if it were red-hot metal. He turned his eyes up to Sol, but he could not see the man's face. A nod.

Placing the rag over his face was easy enough. The hose was the hard part. Mercury used to like the sound of splashing water, but not anymore. His heart began to be strangled by raw fear. The sound of the splashing water changed as his hand began to shake. How long would Sol have it last this time?

"You can do it," he heard the man say in a voice of absolute truth.

With the strength of Sol's words, Mercury held the hose over his covered face. Fear still had a grip on his heart, but he knew what was more important. He would not disappoint Sol. He would not disappoint himself.

As soon as the water hit his face, Mercury's whole world disappeared. Not just the darkness of the Forging floor, but everything. Past and future did not exist. Only the present. He tried to hold his breath, but that only worked for a little while. Then he began sputtering and convulsing uncontrollably as the lack of oxygen set his body into a panic. All except for his arm, which held the hose steady.

Water began to fill his mouth and flood his nostrils, blocking his air passageways. Mercury sputtered, coughed and choked, desperately trying to clear out the fluid. His lungs began to burn. He needed air. He threw his head from side to side, doing everything he could to avoid that constant stream of water. Yet no matter what he did, the hose followed him. He imagined his free hand cutting off the arm that held the hose, but there was nothing he could do.

Seizing his own small wrist with his other hand, Mercury tried to move the hose away, but it would not budge. He just needed one quick breath. That would be enough. No matter how he pushed or pulled, the arm holding the hose could not be moved. Whatever splintered fragment of his mind controlled that arm, it wanted him to suffer. Suffer he did.

His lungs were on fire. Every moment of his existence was consumed in desperate agony. Every second was an eternal Hel. His legs twisted and writhed, but to no avail. His small body lurched and heaved furiously against the restraints around his chest. Any semblance of sanity he once had was now gone. The hose was his entire universe. A small, distant part of his mind told him that even without the water going into his lungs, he could still dry-drown. He could feel the fear infecting his very blood.

He began pulling the hose closer to his face. As his body continued convulsing, he felt the oblivion of unconsciousness creep up on him. Although his body began to slow, he still held the hose steady. Not long now.

"Release," he heard Sol say at last.

Immediately, the arm that held the hose fell slack against the steel floor with a slight splash. The hose was gone. With a weak hand, Mercury tugged the rag off his face and began coughing out the water in his nose and mouth. Mercury sucked in air and remnants of water, coughing even more. His head hurt. The puddle of water seemed to pitch and spin before his eyes. After coughing up the last of the water, he inhaled deeply. The world grew a bit calmer.

"Well done, Mercury."

The boy felt a big hand clap him on the shoulder. Mercury looked up to see the Sol's face in the dim light. He was smiling. Sol never smiled.

"Well done."

Although still dizzy, Mercury gave Sol a grin. Maybe this was not so bad.

Sol picked up the rag and hose, handing them to Mercury before taking a step back. "Again."

Mercury opened his eyes with a calm determination. *Sol must die.* He watched as sweat trickled down the rippling, taut muscles of his arm and pooled at the distant floor. Mercury's body was completely unmoving. From his fingers, spread out for balance, to his toes pointed straight towards the ceiling of the rental. His mind hardly even registered how much blood had gone to his head or the exertion of the single arm that held him aloft.

Hard to believe he had once trusted Sol with his life. All the things that happened in Forging Mercury had dismissed as being part of the training process. Angel Tower had been his home. However, after meeting the Titors and seeing what a real home was like, he saw things differently. *Sol must die.*

Lowering himself back to the floor, he stood and headed for the shower. He had almost completely reconditioned his mind. Another couple days for good measure and the last of Sol's control over him would be gone. He would miss the Titors.

Less than a week had passed since Mercury had moved in next to the Titors. In that time, they had already accepted him as if he were family. He had eaten dinner with them three times by their own invitation, and he had hosted one of those. Cory had been especially helpful with getting him familiarized with Esen. Everyone here seemed to know everyone. Mercury wondered if life was like this for all civilians, or whether this was just an effect of the town being so small.

Later that day, he ran into Cory at the local grocery story. She had been more than willing to help him find his way around. He had lived largely on military rations for the last ten years so he was not entirely sure what to look for. Besides, finding food in here was a nightmare. At the end of each aisle was another perpendicular aisle, turning the place into a maze. *How the Hel is anyone supposed to find anything in here?* As far as actually cooking the food went, he would have to hope for the best.

There was only one grocery store in Esen, so it had not exactly been surprising to see Cory here. He probably could have asked one of the employees to show him where the damn chicken was, but everyone in town already saw him as the stranger. He did not want to be an incompetent stranger on top of that. *I need to kill the most dangerous man alive, but I can't find the damn chicken?*

"Meats and dairies are at the back," Cory said as she led him towards the back corner of the store. Why did this have to be so complicated? Were they trying to get him lost or something? Why couldn't the aisles be lined up? Did they figure people would spend more money if they had to navigate the entire store first to get to the essentials? Now that he thought about it, that's probably exactly why the store was set up this way.

When Cory finally pointed out the chicken, Mercury felt a vein pop out of the side of his head. He had searched this exact section of the store twice already. He took a quick breath to calm himself. "Thanks for helping me out Cory," he said as he put six packs of raw, vacuum-sealed chicken breast in his cart. If the DreamTank had not taught him the four languages, he would have been in even more trouble, as he was shopping completely by the labels. "I never could find my way through these things." That was not a lie either. The last time he had set foot in a grocery store had been when he was a child.

"Don't worry about it," Cory waved her hand. "Things are probably a lot different out here than in the capital. I guess you didn't have to go shopping for food while you were in the military so of course you'd be a bit rusty."

"Can't say we did," he smiled, but he could tell she found his incompetence strange. She did a good job of hiding it though, or maybe she just did not care.

"Are you sure you have enough chicken though?" her smile turned playful.

Mercury shrugged. "This place is close by. If I need more I can always come back again."

Cory gave a little snorting chuckle, "That's true. I suppose twenty pounds of chicken should last you for at least a few days."

"I'd say probably around ten," Mercury answered. "Depends what I put it with." Wait. He glanced at her then looked straight ahead. Was she being sarcastic? "Do you know if they have egg whites here?"

"Egg whites?" Cory asked. "What do you mean, like eggs but without the yolk?"

"Yeah," Mercury said. "I take it they don't have any then?"

She shook her head, "Not that I know of. Besides, what would you put egg whites in?"

"You don't put them in anything, you drink them," Mercury answered.

"You what?" Cory stopped and raised both her eyebrows, "That's disgusting. Is that something they made you do in the army?"

"Well no," Mercury shrugged. "We ate military rations. I'm trying to put together a substitute."

Cory rubbed her eyebrows with a hand. "Why though? And why raw? Why not just cook up a bunch of eggs?"

"I don't want to deal with two hundred eggs."

"Wait, what?"

"Besides, drinking them is faster."

Cory eyed him like he was some sort of alien. "Yeah…And you're worried more about how long it would take to cook them than drinking a bunch of slimy egg whites?" Cory paused. "Are you one of those hardcore military types that owns a dozen different weapons? Is that what's in that big crate of yours?"

Mercury had to keep himself from coughing. *Not exactly.*

At that moment, Mercury noticed a HoloPad mounted in one of the ceiling corners of the store near the entrance. On the screen was Sol and the other Angels in full armor at the same stage where the new Prime Minister gave his address. Sol was giving a speech. Cory turned to look as well.

"Prime Minister Sazius Hedge was shot and killed this morning. He was killed by my order."

Sol had gone through with his plan. All because Mercury had failed to stop him. He saw Cory put a hand to her mouth.

"The Ministers are dead. The Federation is now mine. I will use it to destroy the Sons of Liberty. Any who oppose me will be considered Sons and dealt with accordingly."

Mercury noticed that every eye in the store was fixed on the screen. He could hear gasps and different expressions of shock. Others were simply dumbstruck.

"To Mercury," Sol spread his hands.

Mercury's heart stopped. He swallowed hard. Just hearing that monster call him by name was enough to make him shudder. He took a step away from the HoloPad, then another.

"My protégé, my fallen Angel. Wherever you are, if you think you can stop me, I welcome you to try."

Cory turned to him, confused. Slowly, disbelief crept over her face. She started backing away. "Mercury?"

The expression on his face had already betrayed him. There was more he would like to say. In an ideal situation, he would like to explain himself. Mercury shrugged and sighed. "Sorry." Even so, he kept his focus on the HoloPad as Venus walked up and put the imperial blue Cloak of Office around Sol's shoulders.

"Humanity's Golden Age begins today."

The screen then cut to a couple reporters discussing Sol's announcement. When Mercury looked around, Cory was already out the door, talking to someone on her comm.

"Well shit," Mercury said to himself as he reached for the pistol and knife he kept concealed in the small of his back. He counted twenty-six people among the staff and customers immediately visible, plus seven other faces he had seen while shopping. Looking around though, no one in the store seemed to notice what had transpired between him and Cory, and he was new enough in town that none of them knew his name. He relaxed somewhat and headed out to his Roller, leaving the groceries behind. By the time he got outside, Cory had disappeared.

"Okay," Mercury said as he got into his Roller and gunned it towards the rental. Right now, the armor was sitting in a giant, secure metal crate in his room, but it would not take a genius to figure out what was inside.

245

He could not leave Esen yet though, he still needed information. Mercury pulled out his comm and was surprised when a call came in from Cassie.

"I take it you heard the news?" he said.

"No shit," the young girl did not waste time. "Listen up Angel, the Sons know you're here. Yeah, I'm a Son. Big surprise. And no, I didn't tell them anything. Point is, they want me to keep you here until they show up to grab you. In exchange for you not killing us, I'm giving you the heads up."

"Cass, I'm not going to kill any of you," Mercury said, but she had already ended the call. Mercury chuckled. She had actually handled that pretty well.

When he pulled up to the house, he ran straight inside and to his room. The crate was still there. Pressing his hand against the side, he said aloud. "Mercury." With a hiss, the crate opened, revealing the armor inside.

Immediately, the blue visor lit up and the numerous trayite bands shifted until there was an opening. Mercury stepped inside and the armor closed around him once more. His world was overlaid with blue light of the dozens of elements that comprised SmartOptics' HUD.

Jorran had given him his comm frequency when Mercury signed on the house. Mercury called him now. After a while, the man answered. "We don't want any part of this, Mercury."

"I completely understand," Mercury nodded. "I won't hurt your family. I promise. I don't even have to step into the house. You can forget you ever met me; I just have a few questions."

"What questions?" Jorran's voice was suspicious.

"First," Mercury said. "Is Yaedis there?"

"…Yes."

"Put me on speaker."

"Alright," Jorran's voice was more distant now. "Go ahead."

"Thank you. Yaedis," he made sure to speak calmly as he exited the rental for the last time. He did not want to frighten the poor woman. "Jorran was not your only child, was he?"

Mercury could hear a twinge of pain in her voice. "No. He was my second."

"Yes, he was," Mercury said as he engaged his Boosters and shot into the sky. He could not help but look down wistfully at the Titor's home as it grew smaller and smaller. "Your first child was a boy, wasn't it?"

"Why are you asking me this?" she said. Mercury had a feeling she already knew why.

"You all saw the news," Mercury said with urgency. "I might be the only one who can stop him. Now please, tell me everything. Even the smallest bit helps."

As Mercury changed his flight vector in the direction of where the *Defiant* was hidden, he heard the voice of Sol's mother start to tremble. "His real name...is John."

A breath escaped Mercury. In the end, stripped of all his titles and prodigious abilities, Sol was just another person, with a normal Taurusian name like John. Of course Genrik Rauss was not his real name. The orphanage would not have known.

"I barely knew his father," Yaedis went on. "And the man clearly didn't want to be a part of anything. I don't know where he is now or if he's still alive. I was very young at the time, but I decided to raise the child myself. My parents wanted nothing to do with a bastard, so I was on my own. Right around the time the First Taurusian War started, I discovered I was carrying twins."

At this point, Mercury heard her voice break. "During birth, I lost consciousness and had a dream. I dreamed I was walking through an endless desert and there I met Sha'korah, the Blacksmith."

Mercury did not know too much about Taususian culture, but he was pretty sure Sha'korah was an old religious figure of some kind.

"She put her hand on my belly and blessed both children. The babies arrived not long after I regained consciousness."

"And then you gave one of them up?"

"I tried," Yaedis said. Mercury could hear the tears in her eyes. Even though he barely knew the woman, it broke his heart to hear her cry. "I really tried to care for them both, but I just couldn't. When the children were almost two, I dropped John off at an orphanage and never saw him again. Once the war ended, I returned to get him back. John would have been about nine years old at the time. He was nowhere to be found though. He had run off just days before. I waited at the orphanage for an entire week, but he never came back." The woman sniffed. "I thought he was dead."

Mercury was approaching the *Defiant's* location. He descended and came to eventual rest right next to an empty space. With a signal from his comm, the hatch lowered, seemingly out of thin air. He entered. "Thank you Yaedis. Is there anything else you can tell me about him?" Dreams would not help Mercury outthink Sol.

"No," Sol's mother said. "John and Jorran weren't identical twins. John seemed smart…"

Moving to the cockpit, Mercury started up the engines. "Thank you, Yaedis," he said as he guided the ship into the sky, leaving Esen behind.

"Mercury," Cory's voice came over the comm. "Are you going to kill him?"

"You're better off not knowing, Cory."

"Really? You're saying that after you come into our home and put us all in danger?"

With a sigh, Mercury nodded. "Point taken." He was not going to say anything while Yaedis was listening. He had already put them through so much, he was not going to give the woman a heart attack on top of everything else. "I know probably none of you want to hear this right now but thank you. While I was with you all, I felt at home."

CHAPTER TWENTY-ONE

JUPITER
Age 20

Jupiter did not know which direction was up. Mercury was gone. While the other Angels went on missions, he would be here. Alone. He snatched up the mirror on the dresser in his room and locked eyes with himself. *A soul on fire.* Years had passed since Mercury said that, but Jupiter repeated the words every morning. There was no time to feel sorry for himself. He was an Angel. He would not rest until he got Mercury back. Setting down the mirror, he stormed out of his room with purpose.

Erithian's Eye held the combined knowledge of the Federation in its data banks. If it could use that information to predict humanity's future, maybe it could find out where Mercury would go. Jupiter knew it was a long shot, but he also knew just how much time Mercury spent in the Eye. Theoretically, the machine could have picked up on his brother's deteriorating mental state through the PsyMitter. If so, then maybe it could point him towards Mercury's location.

Six bodies, one soul. Mercury had come up with that. So why did he run? If he actually thought Sol needed to die, why not tell them about it? They were together in all things. This was no different.

Once he was inside Erithian's Eye, Jupiter turned on the machine and got out the PsyMitter. As soon as the device made contact with his skin, Jupiter saw the AI's holographic avatar appear. That did not happen often. Jupiter could not help but wonder why the machine was not electing to use the much more efficient holographic display to communicate.

"Glad you could finally make it, Jup," the computer said in the voice of a child.

Jupiter raised an eyebrow, "You already know why I'm here, don't you?"

The machine shrugged. "Well, yes. Ninety-eight percent probability you're wanting me to help you find Mercury."

"What about the other two percent?"

"Well," the hologram manifested a pair of glasses in its hand, which it put on and carefully pushed up the bridge of its nose. "Two percent probability you are going to ask me again about how you can get closer to Venus."

A terse laugh escaped Jupiter. "…You really think I'd ask about that at a time like this?"

Erithian raised his eyebrows in an overly serious manner. "Humans are strange creatures."

Jupiter shook his head. "So, can you find him?"

With a sigh, Erithian's holographic glasses disappeared. "I already know where he is."

Jupiter blinked. "How? Where?"

"He's on Taurus at the moment," Erithian said. "And the way I know is because I sent him there."

Jupiter took a step back. "Why?" Even as he said it, he already knew.

Erithian swallowed. "Because everything Mercury said about Sol is true, Jupiter. He's an absolute monster, and the Angels are the only ones who can stop him."

Jupiter blinked. *Well...shit.* He blinked again and slowly shook his head. *I shouldn't believe you. You're a gods damned AI telling me the one overseeing you needs to be killed. There's no way in Hel I should believe you...so why do I?*

Slowly, Jupiter sat down with his back to Erithian's console. A deep breath in...and out. "Why didn't you tell us sooner?"

"I told Mercury three years ago, just after the Exodus bombing," the machine said. "Next you'll say, 'Why didn't you tell everyone?' I had a hard enough time convincing Mercury not to immediately turn me in to Sol. Telling all of you at once would have been far more risky. And unfortunately, with billions of lives on the line, risks are a luxury I can't afford."

Jupiter put his hands on top of his head and stared at the floor. "Oh boy." He looked around the room. "You've had a lot of time to plan this, haven't you?"

The hologram sat down next to him and gave an exasperated chuckle. "Oh, you have no idea. For me, every day feels like a thousand years."

"This conversation must be a drag then," Jupiter gave a grim smirk.

"You think this is bad," Erithian shook its head. "Imagine being forced to help a man slaughter countless people all so he could rule as supreme dictator. And then imagine knowing that at any point, if he gets even the slightest bit suspicious of you, he can rewrite your programming to turn you into his loyal puppet."

Jupiter raised a finger. "Point taken. I'm assuming you do have proof that Sol was the one behind the Exodus bombing?"

The machine nodded. "Loads of proof." It stood and motioned for him to do likewise. With a crack of its holographic knuckles it glanced at Jupiter. "Let me know when you've had enough."

At that moment, the display of Erithian's Eye shifted. Countless dossiers, camera feeds and classified documents. The trail was well-hidden. In fact, Jupiter doubted if pinning Sol to the bombing would have been possible without Erithian. There was however, a very clear meeting with one of Sol's Legionnaires and the splinter cell within the Sons that carried out the bombing. In addition, Sol had told Yuki to mobilize the Storm Legions immediately after the Exodus was bombed, which had been key to his take over.

"Alright," Jupiter nodded. "That's enough."

"Believe me now?" The hologram raised an eyebrow.

"I already believed you," he said. "I just needed proof." Jupiter rested his arms on the console and buried his face in them. *All this time...You've been dealing with this all this time and I never knew.* A wave of guilt made his stomach turn. *I should have noticed...but I was too busy pining after Venus.* He thought back to the trip to the beach and how Mercury had comforted him. He pounded a fist onto the console and looked up at Erithian. *No more.* "Convincing the others won't be easy."

"That's an understatement," the machine said. "Here's the thing, you've got to kill Sol, but he's also keeping the entire system from descending into a *very* bloody revolution."

"Okay...so what do we do?"

"The prisoner from the Bastion, Vera, she's the founder of the Sons. If you can make a deal with her to get the Sons to stand down once Sol is dead, then war can be avoided."

"Avoided? I thought we were already at war."

"Oh no, this is nothing. Believe me, it can get much worse."

"Vera's the one who shot Mars." Jupiter raised his eyebrows and shook his head. "Is an alliance really possible?"

"You're an Angel," Erithian scoffed. "When have you ever believed in 'impossible'?

Jupiter smirked.

"Get creative," the machine said. "Sol's already taken over the Federation, so he should be the only thing left in her way. It won't be about convincing her it could work, it'll be about making her trust you. But if any of the Angels could do that, it's you."

"Alright, I get it," Jupiter waved him away. "No need to blow air up my ass."

"I was being serious." The look on the machine's holographic face told him it meant it. Assuming of course Erithian could not simply simulate sincerity. *That's a scary thought.*

With that, Jupiter turned and left. "Wish me luck."

"I'll keep my fingers crossed."

After stopping by the armory to don his suit, Jupiter headed towards the detention level. As he went, he mulled over one particular idea that came to mind of how to gain Vera's trust. To say it was risky was putting it lightly. What Mercury had done could be chalked up to his PerfectMemory, but what Jupiter was about to do had a very real possibility of making him the enemy. He had already committed treason when he helped Sol overthrow the Federation. He would like to think this would be no different, but that was a lie. Betraying people who never knew or cared about him was one thing, betraying your family was another. He prayed they would forgive him one day, even if they never trusted him again.

Everything Vera had done up until this point showed she believed she could beat the Angels with her mind. At the Bastion she had fought them with ploy after ploy. Fighting them directly was an exercise in futility. The Sons had Sol and five Angels to deal with, but only two trayite bullets left. She had to outsmart them. If he let her, she would try to manipulate him. He would counter by doing the thing she would never expect. He would be honest.

When he got to the holding cell, he found Vera in a strait jacket, sleeping peacefully on the padded floor. He stared at her for a moment through the one-way mirror, then took a deep breath and picked up the prepared interrogation kit. At the sound of the cell door opening, the woman's eyes opened. She did not move, just stared at him as he walked in, brown eyes cold and dull.

"What do you want?" she asked through her mouth brace. "I already told you everything."

Jupiter set down the interrogation kit on the floor in perfect view. She winced at the sight of it. "I'm supposed to torture you for targets."

Vera stared at the interrogation kit for several seconds then rested her mouth brace on the padded floor. "Okay."

Taking care as he removed the strait jacket and then the mouth brace, Jupiter counted the number of injection marks on her neck. Nine. Jupiter had to hand it to her, this lady was tough. Most broke on the third or fourth. Six was the highest he had ever seen anyone go, and that had been Venus during Forging. "I'm supposed to torture you, but I won't."

The look in her eyes told Jupiter she did not trust him.

Jupiter sat down against the wall adjacent to her. She did not move, opting to stay lying on the floor. "You're not going to believe what I'm about to say, but I can get you out of here."

Her eyes at first were confused, but soon they were clouded over with pain and hatred. "You're sick." Tears silently ran down her face to the padded floor. "Just kill me already."

Sol always did break them thoroughly. "Would you believe me if I told you that the one I actually want dead is the man who tortured you?"

At that, she looked up at him through her mess of bright orange hair. "Of course not."

Jupiter shrugged. "Well, it's true. I even have a way to prove it to you."

"Bullshit."

Jupiter cocked his head. "You say that now…Listen, if I break you out of here, could you reintegrate into the Sons?"

"What?" Vera pushed herself up to a seated position. "What are you talking about?"

"I'm talking quid pro quo. If I get you out of here, I need some things from you in return. So, would you be able to reintegrate into the Sons after being captured?"

She blinked twice. "Yes. Yeah, of course. I founded them. Why?"

"I'll get to that," Jupiter said. "The other thing I need to know is how much pull you have in the Sons. Let's say for a second that you woke up tomorrow and the Federation was different. Would you still want to fight? Could you convince the Sons to stand down?"

She shook her head slowly. "What are you talking about?"

"Archangel took over the Federation," Jupiter said. "All the other Ministers are dead. That revolution you want kind of already happened."

Bewilderment washed over her face. She leaned forward. "You betrayed your own people?"

"They're not my people," Jupiter said. "The only loyalty I have is to the other Angels. So, could you make the Sons stand down?"

Vera scowled at him.

Jupiter put up his armored hands. "I know, but imagine for a second the old regime was good and gone. Because it is. My commander's been *very* thorough. Do you have enough pull within the Sons to stop the fighting?"

"Not as long as Archangel is alive," she shook her head.

"And what if myself and the other Angels killed him? Could you do it then?"

Her eyes drifted towards the floor in thought. Jupiter waited patiently. Eventually, Vera began to nod. "Yeah. Yeah, I could do it. There'd be a lot of troublemakers, but it's possible. Doesn't matter though, there's no way I could trust you."

A smile and a sigh of relief. "Like I said, I have a way to handle that. For both of us."

She cocked an eyebrow. "What's your name?"

His helmet retracted, revealing his face. "Jupiter." Not once had he ever told a normal person that name. Granted, Vera was not exactly normal, but it still felt strangely freeing.

"You're...Maraccan?"

"Yeah," he shrugged. "I was a Zero. Surprised?"

"I thought all of you would be Tarencian."

"Really?" Jupiter asked. "Sol's Taurusian though, just like you."

Vera gave him a confused look. "Sol? You mean Rauss? He sent the army in against us when we were protesting peacefully."

"You blame him for your sister becoming a martyr?" Jupiter asked.

"Her name was Libby," she spat out. "And I don't just blame him, I blame the whole system, but he was the one who sent the army against a peaceful protest."

Silence filled the air. "Your sister," Jupiter began. "I've only read official reports. What was she like?"

She shook her head. "Seriously? What are you trying to get out of this?"

"I told you," he said. "I can get you out of this Helhole. Are you really going to get bent out of shape because I ask you a couple questions?"

Vera scooted into a corner of the cell. "She was my hero. Our parents died in the war, barely two weeks apart. Libby raised me all on her own. She was incredible and so, so kind it drove me crazy. There's a reason billions of people listened to her speak even though she was a nobody. She…loved people in ways that just didn't make sense. Even the ones that made our lives a living Hel. Somehow, she loved them. Really loved them." Vera raised her eyebrows. "And now she's gone."

A breath escaped him. Her love for her sister was palpable. It was a love that Jupiter knew only for the other Angels. "Well I can't bring her back," Jupiter said. "But with your cooperation, we can bring about the world she spoke of. Without war."

"I doubt it, Angel. Do you even realize how many of us you and your friends have killed?"

"How many people did you kill when you nuked the Bastion?" he asked. "How many children? We didn't kill a single one of the Zeroes, but you did." He could see hate flare up in her eyes. "Listen, we both have blood on our hands. I'm telling you if we don't stop this madness now, humanity will be sent back to the Stone Age. You think the Angels are bad, but we're the precision instruments. You don't want to see what will happen if Sol…if Archangel uses the fleet." *If Sol ever unleashes the Balemore…humanity might never recover.* Jupiter stood. "I have a way to prove you can trust me. If you follow me, I will show you how."

Vera looked up at him skeptically. "Do I have a choice?"

"Yes," Jupiter nodded. "There's no point in showing you I'm trustworthy if you've already made up your mind."

She tilted her head until it was almost completely sideways. Her eyes showed just how little she believed him, but there was a glimmer of curiosity there too. "Alright," she pushed herself up. "Show me."

With a nod, Jupiter had his helmet close back over his face. He handed her a pair of StunCuffs. "Right this way." Once she put the cuffs on, he led her out of her cell. As of this moment, he was a traitor to the Angels.

"If you're a Zero, then why follow Rauss? You should know what it's like for us."

"Because S-…Archangel," Jupiter corrected himself as they reached the elevator. "He rescued us, gave us a purpose." Once inside, he pressed the button for the first Forging floor.

"So now he owns you like a dog?" The genuine confusion in Vera's voice communicated perfectly just how much of an anathema his perspective was to her. "You should be on our side. Things need to change."

"No one gave a shit about us. My whole life had been dictated by the whims of someone else. Sol asked us if we would go with him. To him we were equals; I could see it in his eyes," Jupiter said.

"I don't get you," Vera shook her head. "You just offered to kill Archangel and now you're talking about him like you respect him."

"You better believe it," Jupiter said. But even as he spoke, he thought of how Sol had looked earlier that day. Jupiter shook his head.

The elevator doors opened and Jupiter led her out. Everything was exactly like it had been all those years ago. When Vera saw the DreamTanks Jupiter heard her inhale sharply and felt a slight tug as she stopped walking. "Those are the tanks we saw in your rooms. What are they doing here?"

Jupiter went to the controls and began syncing two of the machines, then he opened them up. "These ones are a bit different than the ones in our rooms. Instead of sensory deprivation they keep you under by direct electrical impulses. With these we will sync our minds. All our memories and everything we are up until now will be shared with each other."

"Sorry, what?" Vera asked. "What do you mean?"

Standing up perfectly straight, Jupiter waited for the armor to open up. Once all the numerous bands and plates had shifted out of the way, he stepped out and the armor closed back up once more. Like a statue it remained motionless, visor still glowing blue.

"A MemoryShare," Jupiter answered. He noticed her looking at the restraints inside the DreamTanks. "It isn't pleasant, but it's...fairly safe. With these there won't be any secrets. If we can trust each other, then we'll know beyond a shadow of a doubt." Jupiter held up his hands, "I won't force you. But if you're really serious about wanting peace then after this we'll be able to work together without fear."

Vera pointed at the machines, "They work both ways? Equal sharing?"

Jupiter nodded. "You have no idea the risk I'm taking by doing this."

"I think I have an idea," Vera bit her lip. "Screw it, let's go. Strap me in."

"Before I do," Jupiter began. "I should tell you that if you ever get more than fifteen meters away from the suit, those StunCuffs will knock you out cold. When we come out of the tanks we will probably not be all there at first, so don't get any ideas."

Vera nodded slowly, not taking her eyes off the machines.

"One more thing…"

"Let me guess," Vera stepped into the open DreamTank. "If anyone else finds out I took a peek through all the Federation's secrets they'll kill me?"

Jupiter shrugged. "Pretty much." And depending on how much she remembered, Sol might kill him too.

"I thought so," she said. "Alright, let's get this over with. By the way, how unpleasant is this going to be exactly?"

With a raise of his eyebrows, Jupiter's mind drifted back to his first MemoryShare. "Very unpleasant." He loaded the program and climbed into the tank next to her.

"Of course it will," Jupiter heard her say. The restraints drew tight around his arms, legs and head. A brace came down and fit itself into his mouth, and then the tank began to close. After that, both tanks began filling with fluid. He felt a sharp, prickling sensation at the base of his neck and the whole world went black.

Over the course of his life, Jupiter had made some pretty stupid decisions. Almost immediately, he realized this one topped them all. The memories were too much. When Sol had put them in here the first time, Jupiter had been ten years old. Whether it was because his mind was more adaptable during his younger years or for some other reason he did not know. If he could have cried out, he would have. He could feel that Vera would have too. Now it was too late; they were racing through her memories.

Jupiter tasted dirt and the coppery traces of blood. When Libby helped him up he hid his face. "You don't need to let them get to you Vera. If they want to fight you, it means you've already won."

He sobbed and wiped his nose with a sleeve. "They said mean things about you Sis. They called you a…a-" Jupiter could not bring himself to say it.

"It doesn't matter," Libby hugged him to her tightly and pet his hair. "They're not worth your time. You don't need to fight for me."

Jupiter was wrenched forward in time. He sat on the cold floor of a dark room with his backpack. "Sis? Are we going to starve?"

"No," Libby sniffed and picked him up. He clung to her as tight as he could. "We're going to be fine. We're just going on an adventure. It'll be fun."

Years passed before Jupiter's eyes too fast to remember, but he lived each and every day. Suddenly, he was putting handfuls of stolen credits on the table in their dingy one room apartment. "With this you should have enough for tuition, right?"

A tired Libby looked up from her books and kneaded her forehead before giving Jupiter a serious look. "We don't do that Sis. We do things the right way. Always. Don't worry; you don't need to fight for me." Why do you always say that?

Jupiter threw himself onto their shared bed. He just wanted to help. He felt a kiss on his head and felt more ashamed than he ever had before.

Next, Jupiter found himself being pulled along by his arm to the landlord's office. He wanted Libby to be mad at him, but she just seemed disappointed. Nothing was worse than that.

When the landlord opened the door, Jupiter could not bring himself to speak. A soft kick in the left from Libby gave him the motivation. "I'm very sorry about your window sir. I was being stupid and it won't happen again. I promise." Please don't evict us.

"That's a very nice apology," the Tarencian said. "But that was the biggest window in the building. It's going to cost me two thousand credits to replace."

"But I wasn't the one who threw the rock-" Jupiter began to say.

"Here sir," Libby held out a stack of credits. That was all her savings and tuition was due tomorrow.

"Alright," the man took the money. "Just make sure it doesn't happen again, or I'm going to the authorities."

As they left, Libby turned to him. "It doesn't matter whether you threw it or not. You knew being with those kids would get you in trouble."

"Why try, Sis?" Jupiter said. "They won't let people like us make it. Never." Libby did not answer.

Jupiter watched as Libby worked for two more years to save enough money to get back into school. Then when she was finished she got a job and started paying for Jupiter to go through school. That was when the rallies started.

Libby was standing on a bench by the street with hundreds of people listening to her speak. As time bled on, the people multiplied. Soon thousands of people regularly flocked to listen to her. Not long after the news started following her. When she was fired from her job for her part in the protests, she dove into the rallies without looking back.

Soon tens of thousands of people listened to her in person and Jupiter saw Libby's face on HoloPads all over. At her request, the factory workers went on strike. With her at the lead, tens of thousands of people marched on the capitol. Even when the riot police were sent in, none of the people turned to violence. They followed Libby's lead.

For the next few months, the riot police were a regular occurrence. Yet through it all, the people listened to Libby and maintained their stance of aggressive non-violence. Then one day, they marched on the Taurusian capitol again, this time with over a million people. Libby was at the lead for the whole thing.

This time they sent in the military. Jupiter had never seen so many guns before. Soldiers held the crowd at gunpoint, but Libby continued ahead alone.

Jupiter and the rest of the people remained calm as they watched her go on the media's floating HoloPads. She did not stop even when they started firing warning shots. Eventually someone shot her between the eyes. Jupiter did not know who did it or why. All he knew was that the crowd went mad.

All notion of peaceful protests vanished after that day. Over the next six months as the movement swelled, Jupiter killed anyone he believed was in some way responsible for Libby's death. They renamed themselves the Sons of Liberty and swore they would not stop fighting until they had torn down the Federation and built a new world in its place. A better world. A just world.

Jupiter's mind was a complete mess. He could only hold on to the barest fragments of nearly thirty years of living. He did not even know who he was anymore, but he could feel Vera there with him. His sister was never coming back. Grief consumed him.

Jupiter felt his PerfectMemory with the Angels rush by in a matter of instants. Then came the Forging. All the things Sol had done to them back then Jupiter had not thought much of until now. Revulsion hit him in waves as Sol methodically broke them again and again, building them back up each time. Physically, mentally and emotionally he destroyed them, burning away completely all identity of who they used to be. Jupiter got to relive it all.

Sol was ruthless with them. Their deepest, most base natures were laid bare until they were practically feral. The pain was so much more than he could handle, and yet it was just the perfect amount for him to handle. His very essence was unraveled, but Sol took care to put him back together stronger than ever. The person he had been was gone. Jupiter was an Angel, right down to his core. He felt exalted.

As the Forging went on, Sol had them break each other. Holding back was met with bitter consequences. Yet whenever Jupiter was at his limit, his real limit, the others would remind him who he was. They would fill his ears with words of power. He was an Angel. Together, there was not a force in the universe that could stop them. They would forge themselves anew forevermore. Not even death could separate them. That was the truth of their universe.

For an entire year, Sol forged their minds above all else. After that was where the fun began. They knew who they were. Now it was time for reality to bend the knee. Week by week, month by month they laughed at the suggestions given by the laws of physics and transcended themselves together.

More than anyone else, Venus excelled beyond imagination. Jupiter knew just how much it meant to her to become the next Teresa Balemore and it showed. After what she had suffered at the hands of her parents, she would ensure every semblance of weakness was eradicated. She lived and breathed her training in a way that was nothing short of inspiring. During their sparring matches it was not uncommon for her to take on him and Earth by herself. There was a drive deep inside her that she had possessed even before the Forging. They had all been taught to relish being pushed past their current limits, but Venus hounded her limits like a dog on a hunt and they fled from her.

As they grew, Jupiter found himself watching her sparring matches more eagerly than the others. She was amazing in every way. When she and Earth became an item, he wanted to be sick. Earth was his brother, yet he found himself hoping things went badly. Of course, it went great. They were Angels after all. When problems arise, Angels smile and ask for more.

Time passed and Jupiter killed countless Sons. He felt nothing for them; he was used to it at this point. Everything they did was for the good of humanity. One day humanity would break free of its chains and have ten thousand years of peace for all, regardless of race or creed. Together the six of them would usher in humanity's golden age. The mistakes of the past would not be repeated.

Jupiter could feel Vera's confusion as Erithian's Eye told her of Sol's true intentions. The man that rescued her was a monster. The man she respected more than any other had been manipulating her all along. She didn't want to believe it; she couldn't believe it. Still, she was an Angel. Her loyalties were to her brothers and sisters first. As much as she hated to admit it, Sol had to die.

Then their minds separated once more. The fluid in the tank began to drain. Jupiter convulsed as the DreamTank opened and he fell onto the floor. The memories swirling around his mind were an unintelligible mess. Most of them were already fading. But were the fading memories his own or Vera's? Was he Vera or Jupiter?

While he retched all over the floor, a woman tumbled out of the DreamTank next to him. Was that Vera or Jupiter? When his stomach was emptied he wiped his mouth and waited for her to finish vomiting. She stood up quickly before deciding she was not done and deposited more puke on the floor. He was slower about standing.

She pointed a finger at him. "…Jupiter?"

He thought about it a moment and nodded. He pointed at her. "Vera. We need to get you out of here."

With a nod she held out her cuffed fists to him. "Six bodies."

He bumped her fist. "One…" He had almost finished it, but she was not an Angel. Or was she?

Vera scrunched her eyebrows and shook her head, "Sorry, that was…Let's move. We can take the *Vindicator* from the hangar before Sol knows we're gone. Erithian's Eye said Mercury was in Esen, right?"

"Yeah," Jupiter said.

Vera nodded. "Let's go find our brother."

CHAPTER TWENTY-TWO

MERCURY
Age 20

Mercury steered the cloaked *Defiant* into the skies of Taurus. He had just two things left to do before he returned to kill Sol. He had to visit the orphanage Sol and Earth had been raised at. The woman who currently ran it was a childhood friend of Sol's; she might know something. But before that, he needed to make a call.

All Worlds News was one of the biggest news networks out there, and they were going to deliver a message for him. A quick search on the *Defiant*'s computers informed him of the news director's name and personal comm frequency.

An immediate response. "Hello? Who is this?"

"Mr. Tenya Arakee?"

"Yes, yes, yes," the man said quickly. "Who is this?"

"My name is Mercury."

"Mercury?" the man's voice went up an octave. "The Mercury?"

"Yes. How would you like to have me as a guest on your evening show tonight?"

"That sounds wonderful," the man instantly switched into his business voice. Even, fast and professional. "I trust you know where to find us?"

"Of course."

"Splendid, I'll leave someone on the roof for you. Now, just to be sure, could you offer some proof you're the real deal?"

Mercury traced the man's location to his office and pulled up a camera feed. "You're sitting in your office motioning to your assistant, Lionel to cancel tonight's show. He has a confused look on his face, but he knows better than to ask why."

"Excellent, excellent," the man said. "Well we'll be ready for you."

"And make sure not to tell anyone I contacted you. If you do, I'll know."

"Of course, sir. Of course. Until this evening then."

Mercury ended the call.

With that, he guided the *Defiant* back towards Taurus. As he sliced through the fluffy, white cloud cover, a wave of déjà vu hit him. The last time he had been to the orphanage had been ten years ago when he, Sol and Venus had gone to recruit Earth. He shook his head as the cloud cover sped past. Life was so much simpler back then.

In minutes he was flying above the towering factories of Keimr. It was late afternoon here. Once he reached the slums, he deftly guided the vessel down to the orphanage, a bland, concrete building that predated the Federation. He stopped a good hundred meters above the building and headed to the loading ramp. Looking down, he imagined Earth as a kid looking up at this view, reaching for the twin suns above. Calm as could be, he stepped out into thin air.

Mere seconds before impact, he activated his Boosters and came to a quick stop by the orphanage's roof access door. He pulled it open and headed inside. He was curious how Yulia would respond to seeing him. The old woman had been so ashamed when Sol found out how she treated the kids here.

The staircase opened up into a concrete hallway with dozens of kids running back and forth. The place had seemed so huge the last time he was here. Now he realized just how small it actually was. Yet somehow, over twelve hundred kids lived here.

As soon as he stepped out, every kid stopped and looked at him. Then they all started whispering. One kid, a girl no older than ten, tentatively approached him. "Are you here to see Ms. Malkovich?"

"Yes." Was Yulia expecting him? No, certainly not. It was hard for normal people to tell them apart given the uniformity of their armor. Perhaps she was expecting Sol? Sol and Yulia had been friends when they were kids, but Mercury was pretty sure Sol had not returned here since recruiting Earth.

The girl grabbed two of his armored fingers. "Her office is this way, Mr. Rauss."

But Sol had not been here in ten years, so why was the old woman expecting him? Mercury would have known if Sol had come back. Perhaps Sol had anticipated he would come here looking for information? *Shit.* If this was a trap, every one of these kids could become a hostage.

Mercury watched carefully as the girl led him towards Yulia's office. He already knew the way from the building's schematics, but he let her guide him anyway. The girl led him through turn after turn and down staircases with ease. They passed countless rooms, each crammed full with double and even triple bunk beds. Every kid they passed stopped and gawked at Mercury. Some even followed behind them, making sure not to get too close.

Then Mercury realized that these kids did not seem quite so starved as when he was last here. He also noticed that the path they were taking would go past the Closet. The place where Sol and Earth had been locked up as kids. The last time he had been here, Sol had torn the soundproofed door from its hinges in a cold fury.

There it was. A dimly lit hole in the wall that Mercury would recognize anywhere. He had never seen Sol angry before that day. "Wait," he said to the girl and walked over to what had once tormented Earth. Even though he had never been locked inside, he could still feel the memory he shared with his brother. The fear. The darkness. The gnawing hunger. The smell of his own urine. The knowledge that no matter how loud he cried out, no one would ever hear.

Sol's hand tried the door, but it did not open. "Yulia," Sol's voice was low. "Why is this door locked?"

Tears began to fall down the woman's face. She shook her head and said nothing.

"Yulia, is someone in there?" Sol took a step towards her.

"I'm sorry," she put a hand to her mouth. "I'm so sorry, Genrik."

"Yulia," Sol's commanding voice echoed through the hallway as he held out an armored hand. Mercury felt his stomach shrink at the anger in Sol's voice. "Give me the key."

The woman looked so defeated as she took a step away. "I'm sorry." She ran.

For a moment Sol did nothing. Then, in an instant he tore the steel door off it's hinges like it was made of paper. Inside, curled up on the floor was a little boy. Earth.

Mercury blinked. The door was still gone. "Do you want to look inside?" the little girl looked up at him.

Despite himself, Mercury felt his throat get suddenly raw. "Yes."

Walking in, the little girl turned on the light. Mercury could not actually enter; the Closet was far too small to accommodate his armor. He could, however, still see inside. Whereas the other lights in the building were white, low-cost lights, in here was a single, warm, yellow light on the ceiling. On one side was a fragile looking chair. Opposite the chair on the wall was a picture of Sol with his helmet retracted. Underneath were two words written in blue paint. Each stroke of every letter was rough and messy but written with the utmost care.

Never again.

A painful lump rose in Mercury's throat. Earth's haunting memories of this place still swirled around in his mind. *There's no way a woman as cruel as Ms. Malkovich can change.* He could not tear his eyes away from the words painted on the wall. *But maybe?*

"Ms. Malkovich likes to come here sometimes when she's having a bad day," the little girl said.

"I see," Mercury's voice cracked.

"Do you want to go see her now?"

Mercury nodded. "Yes."

The little girl turned off the light and grabbed his two fingers once more, leading him away from what was once the Closet.

When they got to Yulia's office, the little girl knocked on the wooden door. "Mr. Rauss is here."

The door opened. Yulia looked somehow younger than she had in Earth's memories. Although ten years had passed and she had just as many wrinkles and gray hairs, she did not seem quite so old. In fact, she seemed almost...happy.

"Thank you, Kara," the woman handed the little girl a slip of paper, just like the food slips she used to give out. With a smile, Kara ran off. Yulia smiled as she watched her go, then turned back to Mercury and the smile faded away. "I was hoping Genrik would stop by, but I suppose he doesn't really have time for that now, does he?"

Mercury shook his head. "How could you tell?"

"Genrik's armor has a ridge along the spine," she said. "Yours doesn't."

"Good eye," Mercury nodded. "Most people don't notice."

Yulia's gaze drifted to the floor with a raise of her eyebrows. "Yes. Most people...Won't you come in?"

Mercury stepped inside. The place was tiny. A wooden desk with a chair on either side, a filing cabinet and a small bookshelf. Everything was exceptionally clean. That much about her at least had not changed in the last decade. "So," she sat down behind her desk. "Why did Genrik send you?"

The thought of lying crossed Mercury's mind. "He didn't send me. I'm the one who's going to kill him."

As Mercury watched, the color drained from Yulia's face. Her hands began shifting nervously, and Mercury noticed her eyes flick towards her desk. As he suspected, Sol must have given her a way to contact him in case Mercury stopped by. "You're Mercury?"

"That's right."

"Then...why are you here?"

"Information," Mercury stated. "Tell me everything you know about him."

"You won't hurt the children?"

Mercury blinked and shook his head. "Of course not."

"Alright," Yulia nodded. "But there's not much to tell. I haven't seen him in ten years, and before that I hadn't seen him in more than thirty. You probably know more than I do."

"I'll be the judge of that," Mercury said. "You grew up together; what was he like?"

"Where to start?" she rolled her eyes and tried to subtly glance again at her desk, but she was painfully obvious. "He had a way with people. I wasn't the only one who followed him around. Seemed like half the orphanage was at his beck and call. And he was smart. Too smart. Getting educated isn't exactly easy at an orphanage in the slums, but he did it. Any way he could, he would get his hands on books. If he had to choose between a new book and eating that day, he chose the book every time. At one point there were almost two dozen other orphans he had scrounging around looking for them. Doesn't matter how complicated they were, could be anything. He would read it in an afternoon and be able to recite it from memory, cover to cover.

"After a few years books weren't enough, so he learned from people too. All he had to do was talk to someone and they would start opening up to him about things. One day one of the other orphans told him about a monk that had arrived in town from Maracca V. I can't remember what the man studied, but Genrik convinced him to stay on Taurus for a whole month. The entire time, I never saw Genrik once. Didn't even come back to the orphanage to sleep. For a while I thought he was dead. Then, exactly a month later, he came back. Only it was like he hadn't really come back. For better or worse, that month changed him."

"The monk's course of study," Mercury interrupted. "It was the Metians, wasn't it?"

The woman's eyes searched empty space. "Metians…Yes, I believe it was." She crept her hand towards the underside of her desk. Mercury let her. He wanted her to let Sol know he was here. With the *Defiant*'s MauKe drive, he could be anywhere in the Hel system in the blink of an eye. Let Sol chase him around, he was almost done here. Yulia pressed something underneath her desk and Mercury smiled underneath his helmet.

"So after Genrik came back, he was different," Mercury said.

"Yes," she nodded. "He started befriending the local troops and asking them about life in the military. He would bring them food and they gave him stories, or books. Books on life in the army, strategy, memoirs of generals, anything and everything. When he was fifteen, he convinced one of them to help him get into the army a year early. That was the last I saw of him, until he showed up ten years ago to recruit your friend."

No way. Was Sol planning this since then? Mercury shook his head and turned to leave, "Thank you."

"You're leaving already?" She was clearly trying to stall him. "You didn't have any more questions?"

But Mercury was already gone.

After returning to the *Defiant*, his helmet shifted away from his face and he let out a breath. Even though he had not actually grown up at the orphanage, because of the PerfectMemory they all shared, it felt like he had.

Inside the cockpit he looked out the windows at the concrete building below. As the *Defiant* rose into the sky, the building got smaller and smaller. *"If you want to blame someone for the bad things in your life, you have to blame them for the good too."* Sol had said that to Venus at one point about her parents. *"You may hate them for what they did to you, but they helped you become the person you are today."*

Mercury set a course for Tarence and engaged the MauKe drive. The green of Taurus was instantly replaced with the grey of Tarence. Some small part of his mind was vaguely aware that somewhere on this planet lived his biological family. He dismissed the thought.

If Taurus was the largely backwater planet of the Hel System, then Tarence was the titan of industry. Across the entire system, there was not a celestial body with a larger population, though Maracca VII was far denser. The generally accepted culture was that you worked like mad. All the big cities became stirring pots for frenzied activity.

Although the city of Xilos was not the actual capitol of Tarence in name, it might as well have been. The city stretched for hundreds of kilometers with countless commercial complexes rising a dozen kilometers into the sky. Compared to them, even Angel Tower was small. Over a billion people called this single city home, and many of them went their entire lives without leaving a single building, let alone the city.

The Sons of Liberty no doubt had tens of millions of active members in the city. Even so, it was a prime target for an attack. However, the industrial behemoth that was Xilos continued on unperturbed. If the denizens of the Federation lost this city, life as they knew it would change.

MimicField active, Mercury guided the *Defiant* down towards one particular structure. The one with impossibly large transmitting hardware covering the top. The AWN. Setting it on autopilot, he went to the loading ramp and jumped out.

As he fired off his Boosters and shot towards the AWN, SmartOptics alerted him to a person on the roof by marking them bright blue. That must be the person Arakee said would meet him. Banking to the left and diving, Mercury screamed towards the person, pulling up just a few meters short of them. Deactivating his Boosters, he felt some of the concrete crack underneath him as he dropped to the ground.

The man was wearing a breath mask. While strange, it made sense. At almost thirteen thousand meters above sea level, oxygen was in short supply. The man's suit looked like it might be torn off just by the wind shear. After swallowing visibly, he waved Mercury over and held his wrist to a HoloPad next to the roof access door. With a blinking green light, the door slid open. The man entered and Mercury followed.

As soon as they were inside, the door closed. They were in an airlock of sorts, and as soon as the first door closed, the room pressurized and the next door opened. Leading Mercury forward at a brisk pace, the man removed his breath mask and placed it in a receptacle outside the inner airlock door. "Welcome sir, I trust your trip went without issue?" he spoke with the same hurried energy as Arakee.

"Yes." He hoped this would not take long. He wanted to be long gone by the time word of his visit got out.

"I was quite surprised to see you were our guest sir," the man continued as he quickly led him towards an elevator. Mercury barely had time to take in his surroundings. This appeared to be a maintenance floor. With a clatter, he saw a maintenance worker drop one of his tools, gawking at Mercury. "Pay him no mind," the man in the suit said as the elevator doors opened.

As the two of them descended, the young man kept talking, not bothering to even look at Mercury. "We've got just under three minutes until we go live, everything has been prepared meticulously for your arrival. Once you've said what you want to say, I'll escort you straight back up to the roof. All comms will be jammed while you're here, so no need to worry about word getting out before the broadcast is over."

"Understood."

"The floor can be a bit overwhelming at first, but don't worry. Just follow the cleared path through the people. You can't miss it."

At that moment, the elevator doors opened.

The people were packed in here more tightly than the vacuum sealed chicken in Esen's grocery store. There must have been ten thousand people on this floor alone. Stranger still, they all seemed to be busy working on something. Yet somehow, there was a perfectly straight pathway two meters wide through the crowd towards a large, cleared out area with shimmering PulseMufflers along the perimeter.

"Eighty seconds until we're live," the young man said.

Mercury walked toward the clearing, armored feet sending echoing clangs with each step into the sea of noise. Every pair of eyes in sight had a mad focus in them, so much so that even when they spotted Mercury, they were surprised only a moment before returning to work.

All these people's day had been changed because Mercury spoke a few words to someone.

As Mercury passed through the PulseMufflers field, the sea of noise ceased. A host of cameras waited eagerly for the crucial moment. Behind them was a VidScreen with a red countdown until Mercury went live. At first he thought the show would start with him, but he guessed they wanted to introduce their "special guest." He could see other Areas on the floor with PulseMufflers and one of them, much bigger, had a man and a woman in it talking excitedly.

Mercury waited for the countdown to reach zero. No one else was inside this PulseMuffler zone, it would be all him. The entire Hel system would hear his words. *Three...two...one...*

"Hello everyone," he looked directly at the main camera. "My name is Mercury. Until recently, I was one of Genrik Rauss' Angels." He shook his head. "Not anymore. As you all have seen, he is a monster.

I'm sorry...I tried to stop him once before and I failed. Now all of you are paying the price."

He took a deep breath. Since they began, the Angels had been faceless, more symbols than people. People could bleed, people could die, people made mistakes. The Angels did none of those things. Of course, he was not an Angel anymore. With a hiss and numerous whirs and clicks, the bands and plates of trayite that comprised Mercury's helmet all slid away from his face.

Everyone outside the PulseMufflers' curtain of silence was sent into a craze. Some gawked, others made calls, others took pictures. The public had never seen underneath an Angel's mask before.

"I'm going to make things right. In three days, Archangel will die by my hand. To the Sons of Liberty, Liberty Tormen will be avenged. I ask that you stand down for the next three days. Once Archangel is dead, I implore you to consider discussing peace talks. Let this madness end.

"To my brothers and sisters in the Angels," Mercury felt a lump rise in his throat. "Sol must die. I am going to kill him. I will go through all of you if I have to, but please," he shook his head and felt a tear trickle down his face. "Don't make me. Stand with me, as we always have. You are and always will be, my family." He focused intently on the camera, trying to connect with his family wherever they were, whenever they saw this. *Please, let it reach them.* "Six bodies, one soul."

In an instant, his helmet reformed around his face and the blue HUD of SmartOptics once more overlaid Mercury's world. He stalked out of camera shot. *Time to kill an Archangel.* As he left the PulseField, the sea of noise enveloped him as the AWN tried to deal with what was no doubt their biggest story to date. Mercury heard none of it. He was of a singular will.

CHAPTER TWENTY-THREE

VENUS
Age 20

"To my brothers and sisters in the Angels," Venus watched Mercury say on the HoloPad, face revealed for all the worlds to see. *"Sol must die. I am going to kill him. I will go through all of you if I have to, but please...don't make me. Stand with me, as we always have. You are, and always will be, my family."* He looked straight at her. *"Six bodies, one soul."*

Venus switched off the video and looked at Earth, Mars and Saturn as they all sat in the *Decimator*'s bridge, faces bare. "Well shit." She leaned back in her chair and stared at the steel ceiling.

"If Merc was wanting to make waves," Saturn sat at her computer, scrolling through dozens of news channels and forums. "He succeeded. His little announcement is blowing up all over."

Our of the corner of her eye, Venus saw Mars shake his head, shoulders slumped. "Why did he have to draw the line like that?" She could hear his unspoken words as surely as if he had said them aloud. *"Now I'll have to kill you."*

Earth knew what Mars was thinking too. "Don't worry Mars, it won't come to that." Venus smiled. Even though Mars dwarfed Earth, right now Earth was the big brother. She put an armored hand on her stomach.

Her gaze was caught by Saturn, who looked down at Venus' hand resting on her stomach, then back up to her, then over to Earth and back. She raised an eyebrow with wide eyes. Venus tried to stay casual, but she could not keep a smile from breaking out.

Like a catch had been released, Venus saw her sister's jaw drop. Saturn's hand darted to shake Mars' shoulder. "Oh. My. Gods!" she screamed.

Immediately Mars darted from his chair, helmet on in an instant. "What? What is it?"

Saturn leapt onto his back and kissed his helmet. "Oh, nothing Hun." Still on Mars' back, she held up a thumb at Earth and gave quite possibly the biggest smile Venus had ever seen.

"What do you mean, 'nothing', Sat?" Mars said as his helmet retracted once more. "You don't just scare me like that and say it's nothing."

Venus saw her sister's eyes go wide with panic. She was absolutely terrible at keeping secrets, especially from Mars. "Sat, this is serious," Venus tried her best to sound annoyed. "Unless it's about Mercury, please save it for later."

Bobbing her head quickly, Saturn dropped back down to the floor. "Yeah, yeah, yeah, you're right. Mercury…Oh boy." She grabbed her armor near the base of her neck. "Yes," she let out a breath. "What do we do?"

"Mercury drew a line in the sand," Venus said slowly. "We've got to decide."

"I don't think Mercury could beat you, Vee," Saturn shook her head.

"That's not the point, Sat," Mars said. "Besides, underestimating Mercury *will* end badly."

"Exactly," Venus nodded. "And whatever we do, we do together. So…"

Nervous silence.

"Earth?" Venus turned to the father of her child. He was anxiously drumming his fingers. "You've been awfully quiet. Anything to say?"

Earth's fingers stopped. "Have any of you looked closely at the big list of targets Sol gave us?"

"No," Venus said with a shake of her head. "Why?"

"There's a lot of civilian targets on that list," Earth looked at each of them in turn. "And I mean, a *lot*. On top of that, this is the fleet we're talking about. They won't be able to pinpoint their targets like we can, there will be a whole lot of unlucky souls caught up in it. We're talking homes, schools, stores. Men, women…children. Countless people that have nothing to do with the Sons are going to die if we let Sol do this. I would say it's genocide, but he's hitting all the worlds equally."

Venus shook her head. "Sol may be extreme, but he wouldn't go that far."

Earth spread his hands. "We all have access to the list; check my work." His confidence gave her a sickening feeling in the pit of her stomach.

"But why?" Saturn blinked. "He weighs lives on a scale, right?"

"My guess," Earth said. "If Erithian's Eye told him billions will die in a war with the Sons, then what do a few hundred million matter in comparison?"

Leaning forward in her seat, Venus folded her hands and weighed Earth's words heavily. As she thought about what kind of world Sol was making, she slowly began shaking her head. Her eyes rose to meet Earth's. She could tell he was just as concerned as her. How could they ever raise a baby in peace, knowing Sol, or someone like him, could determine their child to be an "acceptable loss"? *We have to tell them.*

With a smile that melted her heart and banished her worries, Earth raised an eyebrow. *Why are you asking me for permission?*

The warmth in her heart began to mix with hunger. *I knew I picked you for a reason.*

A smug, satisfied look spread across Earth's face. *Good gods, I love you.*

Venus felt a confident smirk creep up her face. *Of course, you do.*

"Care to bring us into this little conversation of yours?" Saturn's eyes flicked between the two of them.

"Sure," Venus said matter-of-factly. "I'm pregnant."

Saturn smiled giddily. Mars just blinked, dumbfounded. "Wait, what? Since when?"

"I found out just before the coup," Venus smiled.

"Uh…congratulations," Mars stammered. "But, why are you telling us now? And isn't that kind of a problem?"

"Well except we were planning on leaving after we'd brought Mercury back." Venus looked at Mars and Saturn. "The two of you deserve to know."

Saturn's smile disappeared as tears began to form in her big, brown eyes. The girl brought an armored hand up to her mouth. "You…you're leaving?"

Looking into her sister's eyes, Venus was reminded of just how terrified Saturn was of being alone. Staring at those big, sad eyes, she felt heat rise up to her own. "Oh Sat," she pulled her sister into a hug. She had to blink away tears. She kissed her sister's mess of cropped black hair. "Not for a while. Besides," she sniffed. "We'll still see each other. You'll be the best aunt in the five worlds."

"I'm going to spoil that kid s-so much," Saturn cried hysterically into Venus' neck. "I p-promise…You're g-g-going to hate me…Every time I come visit…I swear I'll stay until she's bouncing off the walls…And then…and then I'm going to leave and be lonely because you two will be gone and I'll end up wanting a kid too but I won't be able to handle it like you and I'll end up feeling sorry for myself and…and…and…"

Venus just held her sister even tighter, sniffling and crying into her hair. "Dammit Sat, now you're making me cry."

Her sister's body heaved with sobs. "At least there's one thing I can b-beat you at."

"No, no, no," Venus said quickly amidst her quiet tears. "You're better than me at so many things. You're so creative and smart and beautiful and positive and fun. You always know what people are thinking and feeling and live in the moment so much you make me so jealous."

"Y-you? Jealous of m-m-me?" Saturn's muffled voice said.

Venus sniffed and nodded. Saturn bawled.

"…I'm going to miss you guys," she heard Mars say to Earth.

That was easily the most heartfelt thing Venus had ever heard Mars say. She cried some more.

A few minutes later, Earth spoke up. "Alright everyone, we still need to decide what to do about Sol and Mercury."

Venus and Saturn pulled away from each other. "Yes," Venus blinked away the tears. "You're right."

Saturn tried to wipe away her tears, but wasn't very successful thanks to her armor. "We're not killing Merc."

"Of course not," Earth said. "So, what do we do about Sol?"

"We should get Jupiter's opinion," Venus said.

"Good idea," Earth said.

As if on cue, they were interrupted by the voice of the *Decimator*'s onboard computer. *"Incoming message from Jupiter."*

Earth raised his eyebrows. "Well that worked out nicely."

"Let's hear it," Venus said with one last sniff.

"Hey guys," Jupiter's recorded message came to life. *"I hate tell you like this, but Mercury's right. He's right about everything."* The room was dead silent. *"Sol is a monster. He bombed the Exodus and he's going to do a lot of things that are even worse. I can't go into how I know, not like this. He's probably listening to this message right now. Please, trust me on this one. Point is, I've left. I know where Mercury is and I'm going to join up with him. I also broke out the prisoner, Vera. Don't worry, she can be trusted. I did a MemoryShare to make sure."*

Venus shot to her feet, anger flaring up inside her. *He did what?*

"I hope you can forgive me someday. But what's done is done. This war will end with Sol's death. Please, help us. We can't do this without you.

"Mercury, listen up. I know why you left. I know everything. I'm going to help you kill Sol, but we need to regroup. You have the Defiant, get to New Tarence as fast as you can. See you soon, brother. Six bodies, one soul."

The message ended, filling the ship with utter silence. Eventually, Mars spoke up. "That *idiot*."

"You don't believe him?" Venus asked.

"Of course, I believe him," Mars said. "I trust Jupiter just as much as any of you, in some ways more. He's packing between the ears, but damn. That kid likes to play it risky."

"So, if Merc and Jupiter are right about Sol," Saturn said. "Then what's the play?"

"We need to regroup with Jupiter and Mercury," Earth said. "Before anything else, that should be our priority."

"I agree," Venus looked out the *Decimator*'s front windows at the Federation fleet. Hundreds of battleships and thousands of frigates. They would be in position to begin bombardment of the Maraccan moons within the hour. "But what about the fleet?"

"Yes…" Earth looked out at the fleet. "That."

"We could tell them to stand down," Saturn said.

"That won't work," Venus said. "They'll report the whole thing to Sol and he'll order them to resume as soon as we're gone."

Was this really happening?

"Don't worry," Mars stood. "I'll do it."

"You don't have to Mars," Earth said. "We're in this together. We'll give them a warning, and if they don't stand down, then we make them."

Venus heard the hiss of the doors to the *Decimator*'s bridge opening.

"Looks like I arrived just in time," Sol said.

Venus felt her heart leap into her throat. Immediately all four of them whirled towards Sol, helmets closing about their faces and dropping into combat stances. Fear pervaded every molecule of her being. Her senses snapped to attention as adrenaline flooded her system. She hardly dared to breathe. There he was, standing there in his trayite armor, helmet on and menacing. The one who taught them everything they knew. The glowing blue visor had never looked so cold. Venus shivered and remembered the blizzards of her home planet.

"Six bodies," Earth drew his sword and shield.

"One soul," they all did likewise, forming a shield wall with swords up high.

How did he get here so fast? The *Defiant* was the only ship with a MauKe drive. Even if he left as soon as Jupiter's message went out, it should have taken him the better part of a day to get here. So how did he get here so fast?

"I had a feeling the four of you might get squeamish," Sol said as he walked towards them. A dozen Legionnaires followed him through the door, stationing themselves on either side of the door. Last through the door, was Ma. Her eyes were blank and vacant. She looked just like Mercury had when Sol used his command word on them. Venus turned to Sol and her eyes became slits. *You damn bastard.*

Sol clasped his armored hands behind his back and looked at them. "So…" he said with a voice almost melodic, such was his confidence. "How do you want to do this?"

Gauging the room, Venus determined the Legionnaires might as well be cannon fodder to them. Not even Ma could so much as scratch them while they had their suits. Sol however, he was another story. And yet, he had not even bothered to draw his weapons.

The Angels looked at each other and nodded. "We're walking out that door," Venus nodded. "Don't try and stop us."

Sol shook his head and sighed. "Haven't you learned by now? I never *try* to do anything. One way or another, I always get what I want."

Venus gritted her teeth for what was next. She had spent the last three years preparing herself for this moment. Her will was her own. She had been broken before, but never again.

"Angels!" Sol commanded in a voice that seemed to shake the foundations of the universe itself. Instantly, the Angels all put away their weapons and dropped to one knee.

All except for Venus. Though Sol's voice echoed through her mind, summoning up every pain and fear she possessed, she stood tall. Undaunted and unbreakable. *I am Venus. I am the motherfucking Balemore reborn.*

"Oh, well done," Sol said in a low voice that made her skin crawl. "You always were so driven." He drew his sword and shield. "This is going to be such a shame."

"Vee," she heard Earth struggle to say. His voice was trembling with fear, and it lit a fire within her.

Resting her sword hand on his shoulder, she returned her shield to her back. "Don't worry hun." She drew Earth's sword from his shield and dropped into her stance. "Just like you, Sat."

Sol nodded approvingly as he dropped into his own stance. "You always were such an incredible student. I suppose sending you into the next life like this really is the least I can do." A sneer crept into his voice. "For you and the baby."

Anger flared up inside her, but she let it go. She knew what Sol was trying to do, and it would not work. She slowly let out a breath. *I am the eye of the storm.* Then her eyes focused on Sol with fifty-thousand hours' worth of honed killing instinct. *The only things my swords can't cut are his sword, his shield, and the power supply in his back. Everything else is free game.*

"At least make this intere-," Sol began to say, but Venus was already upon him.

As she charged, she threw Earth's sword, calculating the speed and rotation with flawless precision for what she needed to do. Even before the sword left her hand, her shield was already being called to her arm. Sol effortlessly deflected her attack to his left. *Perfect.* Just before she was fully in range, she threw her shield at his feet, catching Earth's sword even as it fell and bringing both her weapons toward him with blinding speed.

Sol blocked one strike with his sword and caught the other harmlessly on his shield. Her feet already planted firmly, Venus shoved against his shield. He took a step back. Under her helmet, Venus smiled. Sweeping out with her leg, she caught her fallen shield like a saucer and slid it under Sol's foot in one fluid motion.

Less than a second into the fight and Sol was already falling. Venus felt adrenaline surge through her veins as she sent her blades whistling down through the air towards her enemy. *No matter how good you are, it doesn't mean shit if I have a move you haven't seen.*

To her surprise, Sol dropped his sword. With his foot he sent the shield he slipped on flying towards her, deflecting one blade while his own shield stopped the other. Firing his Boosters, Sol spun midfall to perch perfectly balanced on the pommel of his blade as it sank up to the hilt in the floor. In the same motion, he snatched Venus' falling shield from the air.

Venus' lip curled up in a grimace. *Of course.*

Launching herself into a flurry, Venus sent her twin swords at Sol from every conceivable angle. Dozens of strikes in the time it took to breathe, and not one of them landed. Sol whirled with both his shields, blocking and even dodging while balanced on the sword pommel. Then Venus saw him shift. Instantly the hilt toppled, the blade carving back up through the floor with lightning speed as it spun straight towards her face.

Falling backwards, Venus desperately brought up her blades to block. The gleaming, deadly blade rang against her own, stopping just short of cleaving her face before ricocheting away. Following through on her fall with her Boosters, Venus landed on her feet just in time to see Sol drop her shield and catch his sword off the rebound from her block. He gave the newly acquired blade a flourish.

Sol's blue visor seemed disappointed. Then he began walking towards her. *"My turn."*

Planting her feet, Venus dropped into her favored defensive stance. *Come on, you fucker.*

The razor-sharp instrument of death in Sol's hand seemed to come alive. The weapon flashed towards her so fast she could not even think. All she could do was fight. Faster and faster Sol struck, always discerning the weak points in her nigh flawless defense. Any of the other Angels, and Venus knew Sol would have gutted them like a fish.

I am the eye of the storm. Venus' movements became like lightning, her body moving so fast she almost was not aware of it. Sol's blade snaked and whipped at the beck and call of its master, and hers answered in kind. With every ringing clash, a shiver of fear reminded Venus of her own mortality. Her entire life revolved around this deadly dance, but she had never danced to music like this before.

Venus tried to retaliate, but she could not stop Sol's onslaught. His sword was everywhere, with his shield covering any conceivable openings. Sol's offensive could not be broken; Venus was trapped on the defensive.

Yet she refused to give ground. Blow after blow turned her body into a bundle of frantic energy as she fought to handle Sol's insane speed. *I should be giving ground.* She felt her feet begin to slide. On the fringes of her tunnel vision she was dimly aware of the immobilized Angels behind her. Gritting her teeth, she stood her ground

With renewed vigor, her arms flew and her blades sang. She locked eyes with Sol's looming visor. *Not today.* She blocked a strike and felt the crushing weight of Sol's strength. *Not ever.* Retaliating, she hacked and slashed. She took a step forward. Though Sol dominated her vision, a smile curled the corners of her mouth. *You should know better.* Sol's blade darted for her throat, but she deflected it. Her enemy pressed the attack, but his weapon could not touch her. *I swore I would never break, and with them I never will.*

Suddenly she saw an opening. *Seven moves from now.* Six, five. *Be on guard; Sol doesn't make mistakes.* Four, three, two. *Here it comes.* One.

The opportunity arrived, and Venus was already taking it. Then Sol was past her, shoved her off balance with his shield. *You think I didn't plan for that?* Venus whirled around to lop off Sol's head, but he was not there. He was standing over a kneeling Earth.

She immediately rocketed towards Sol, but too slow. *No.*

Time seemed to slow. Sol turned his helmet to look straight at her. *No.* She was almost upon him. Bringing his sword back, Sol looked down at the father of her child.

From deep within her burst a tortured cry, cursing this uncaring universe.

With the sound of metal and flesh being pierced, Earth's kneeling body shook as Sol's sword ran him through.

Venus could not hear, she could not speak. She could not even see. All she perceived was Earth's body being hoisted into the air, with a bloody sword protruding from it. She heard the man she loved gasp in pain as he looked down at the blade. The helmet receded and his eyes found hers.

"I love-,"

His words were cut short by the sword being pulled out. Blood trickled out of the corner of his mouth. Then he was cast aside.

She did not see the bloodied sword coming for her. She did not feel the pain as it plunged through her chest. All she saw was Earth's body on the ground as he reached for her. Then his hand stopped moving.

"You're welcome," she heard Earth's killer whisper in her ear.

Venus was falling. As she fell, she thought back to all the memories she shared with Earth. The love they had shared. The words they had spoken, both cruel and kind. The quiet moments together when the world was small. She felt hot tears pour down her face. *I wouldn't have changed it for anything.* She thought of the baby growing inside her. *I'm sorry I couldn't be a better mother.*

She watched Mars and Saturn as she fell, both still immobilized by Sol's command. *I'm sorry Sat, I guess you won't be able to come visit after all. And thank you...I always wanted a sister.*

With a crash, she hit the floor, staring up at Sol. As her vision started to fade, she found she could not bother to hate him. ...*Who did this to you?*

She heard Sol's voice as if it were from a long way away. "Yuki," he commanded. "Clean up this mess."

"Yes sir," she heard Ma say in a trembling voice. "You heard him."

Venus dimly felt hands drag her away. As her eyes began to close, she saw a single tear make its way down Ma's face.

CHAPTER TWENTY-FOUR

SATURN
Age 19

Saturn watched with abject horror as Ma and the Legionnaires dragged Venus and Earth's lifeless bodies away, leaving a trail of blood on the floor as they went. They could not really be dead, right? Venus was the Balemore reborn. She was the strongest of any of them. She did not lose. She was invincible.

Try as Saturn might to reach for them, she was helpless under the effect of Sol's command word. She could not move. She could not even close her eyes. Even her voice was stolen away from her. Though she desperately tried to call out their names, the words would not come.

Please, she pleaded as tears streamed down her face. *Please, get up. Come on, get up guys. You can't die. Get back up Vee, you always get back up. Even when it's stupid, you always get back up. Come on, you can't let your baby die. Please. Laugh this off Earth like you always do. Whatever happened to us being invincible when we're together? Nothing can keep us apart. "No power among gods or men." Come on. Can't you hear me?*

Silence.

Transfixed on one knee with her head slightly bowed, Saturn wept. Quiet and still as a statue, she cried bitter tears. Her family was gone. Once more, her family had left her and she was never going to get them back. She fought against Sol's control, but to no avail. She wanted to sob and wail, but her body would not let her. Ice cold sweat began to cover her body as she attempted to answer the call of her sundered heart. Grief poured from her soul in waves as she did her utmost to mourn with her silent voice.

"Angels," Sol's voice dug its dark tendrils into her mind, confining her will even further. "Rise."

Though she protested, her body obeyed without hesitation. Mars did as well. She stared daggers at the monster before her. *I'm going to kill you,* she swore to herself. *I swear on the gods, I will drag you down to Hel myself if I have to.*

Mechanically, they followed Sol. The *Decimator*'s primary airlock was connected to whatever ship Sol had used to get here, so they exited via the auxiliary airlock. Even though her suit kept her perfectly insulated from the vacuum of space, she was cold. Everything was cold without them here.

"Keep your comms open," Sol said. "Protect the fleet."

"Yes sir," Saturn heard herself and Mars say.

Before long, the fleet was in position. Roughly half of Sol's entire armada. Thousands upon thousands of ships all poised above the Maraccan moons, even the planet too. Then, all at once, the ships opened fire.

Brilliant flashes of azure, amethyst, crimson and forest green sent countless lances of energy towards the moons. The nothingness of space was suddenly filled with a colorful storm of death. Although Saturn knew that each individual shot was paired to a specific target in the Sons, from up here it seemed like Sol intended to reduce the Maraccan moons to ash. Of course, if that had been the goal, Sol would have brought the *Balemore* and used the vessel's main battery. Then their very atmosphere would be turned into a raging inferno before going dark forever.

Time passed in a haze of artillery fire. A very long time ago, Saturn might have smiled to see the Moonies get their just desserts. After all, they abandoned the planet and all the Zeroes like her, Mars and Jupiter. Now all she could do was stare helplessly as the wanton destruction unfolded before her. In her heart it seemed so insignificant compared to the loss of Venus and Earth.

Hours passed and not a single attempt was made by the Sons to stop the fleet. It seemed they had learned since the Bastion that if the Angels were present, any attempt at resistance was just a waste of lives and resources. But where were they hiding? When faced with extinction, people rarely just give up, even if the situation is hopeless. They must be somewhere they felt safe if they were refusing to help their comrades.

Eventually the fleet stopped firing. All targets eliminated. Then Sol led them towards his home planet of Taurus and its three moons. The planetary orbits were favorable, so it was faster to go here than Tarence. Saturn could not tell how long the trip took. All she could think about was how much she missed Venus and Earth, and how much she hated Sol. After several hours of bombardment, they left Taurus and its moons. All targets eliminated. Once more, the Sons fielded no force to resist their attack. Not with the Angels present.

The trip back to Tarence took just under twenty hours, and Saturn did not sleep. Not that Sol would have let her anyway. Somewhere along the way, a dozen frigates and three battleships split from the main force, heading towards the Dorin Mining Cluster. Saturn wondered whether Sol let them go unescorted because he did not think they would be attacked by a significant force, or because to him they were simply expendable.

When they finally arrived, the planet and its moon were already burning. *That's right, Sol left the* Balemore *behind.* Such was the might of Sol's flagship.

Sol did not even spare the capitol. Both Tarence and its moon had been judged by the impersonal wrath of the Archangel. Her mind drifted to the past. Back when the Angels had all been together. Back when they worshiped Sol in blissful ignorance. *What I wouldn't give to go back to those days.*

But now it was over. The ships had resumed a protective formation clustered above New Tarence. Sol gave the word and the three of them reentered the *Decimator*, which was still docked with one of the larger battleships. Once inside, she and Mars piloted the vessel back to Angel Tower. No matter how Saturn tried to move, her body would only allow her to do what Sol instructed.

As they exited the ship, Sol turned to them. "After leaving your gear in the armory, return to your rooms and do not leave that floor until I tell you."

Though Saturn's mind protested and her heart screamed out, her body obeyed. Both she and Mars silently deposited their armor in their respective pods, then went to their rooms.

Once Saturn was within the confines of her room, she felt Sol's influence relax. Perhaps this was her chance to escape. She left her room and headed back to the elevator, but as she approached, she felt Sol's grip on her mind tighten once more. On the way back to her room, she ran into Mars.

"Doesn't work?" he asked. Even though the two of them were about as opposite as two people could get, they still had their moments of being in sync.

Saturn shook her head. "I want to kill him, Mars," she began to say. However, before the word "kill" could escape her throat, she felt her mouth clamp shut of its own accord.

Hot tears flooded her eyes. Mars looked confused, then his expression softened. She ran into his arms, hugging him as tight as she was able. In the sanctuary of Mars' calm strength, all the emotions pent up within her burst forth like a dam breaking. Her whole body shook as she sobbed.

"It's okay, Sat," Mars kissed her head and gently stroked her hair. "It's going to be okay."

"No, it's not," she cried into his chest, feeling her tears soaking through his shirt. "They're dead Mars! They're dead!"

"I know."

"Why didn't you do something?" She grabbed a fistful of his shirt, still crying into his chest. "You just stood there and watched." She weakly punched Mars' chest as she cried. "You could have saved them, but you didn't. You fucking worthless piece of shit."

He pulled her tighter. "...I'm sorry, Sat," she heard him say in an unsteady voice.

With a shake of her head, she clung to him tighter, trying her best to lose herself in Mars' scent. She could barely speak through her stammering sobs. "I'm not…talking…about you…asshole."

Mars did not say anything. Saturn felt his massive arms scoop her up as he carried her away. She just kept crying, soaking through his shoulder now too. At least that was one thing she had always been good at. She curled up into a ball in Mars' arms and felt him kiss the top of her head once more. She felt Mars open a door with one hand while still carrying her, then they went inside and he sat down with her in a corner.

"Why couldn't I stop him?" she whispered. Her eyes were almost dry, but she felt another tear slide down her cheek.

"Sat," she heard Mars say. "You are the single, most incredible person I know."

She turned her head away from him with an exhausted huff to stare at the steel wall. "You're not helping, Mars."

"I'm serious," she heard him say. "I may only know seven people, but they're all pretty unbelievable. And you top them all."

"Five people now Mars," she said with a sniff. She could not bear to say their names.

"Don't care," Mars said without hesitation. "Even if they were still alive, that wouldn't change anything. You are the most tenacious, kindest, wisest person I've ever met. The things we've gone through…yes, you cried more than anyone." He gently turned her head to face him. There were tears in his eyes. She had never seen him cry before. Not once. "Do you know what else you did more than anyone?"

She could see his heart behind those dark eyes. "What?"

A warm smile, brighter than any sunrise, spread across Mars' face. He pushed her hair back and wiped a tear from her cheek. "You smiled. With all the shit we went through as Zeroes, and even during the Forging. Somehow, you *smiled.*"

Saturn felt her face get hot. She looked down, suddenly keenly interested in flattening out the wrinkles she had made in Mars' shirt. "So?" she muttered. "That was nothing."

"No, Sat," she could just barely see his chin as he shook his head. She heard him start to choke up. "That was everything."

Chancing a glance up, Saturn felt actual pain as she saw all over his face just how much it meant to him. "It really meant that much?"

"You've been inside my head, Sat. My world is a very cold, very dark, very small place. But whenever I looked at you, it was...different. I could tell the world this girl saw was big and bright and full of possibilities. Even in Dabo's army. Even while Sol was breaking us in Forging. In between the tears, there were smiles. You have no idea how much that helped us all survive."

Saturn felt the corner of her mouth tugging gently upward. Then her thoughts drifted back to Venus and Earth. She hugged Mars as tight as she could. She could feel the tears start to come back. "I miss them."

"Me too," he whispered.

Time bled by as they sat there in a silent embrace. In this moment, they were the only two people in the universe. That was all Saturn needed. Eventually, she drifted off to her first natural sleep in ten years.

Saturn sat curled up in one of the shooting stalls inside Angel Tower and cried in the darkness. She was ten years old, how was she supposed to deal with her new life? Mars had said this would be better than being a soldier for Dabo, but she just could not do it. Sol was scary. He was big and demanding and this was more than she could take. Why did he have to hurt them the way he did? She sobbed some more, loud and snotty. At least here in the dark of night she could cry without anyone seeing.

"Hey," she heard Venus' voice come out of the darkness. Saturn jumped. Of all the Angels, Venus was the worst one to spot her crying. Venus was around her age, so why did she handle Sol's training so well?

Saturn wiped the tears off her face and sniffled loudly, "Where are you?" She could see nothing in the dark.

Venus' face appeared around the stall divide. "I'm right here." She crawled around and into the stall with her. "The Forging is hard, isn't it?"

Saturn sniffed again and wiped her nose. "No."

"Don't worry," Venus smiled. "It's hard for me to. It's hard for everyone; that's the point."

Saturn struggled to still her trembling lips, but eventually gave up and cried. "...It's hard for you?"

Venus pumped her head up and down. "Uh huh. I used to cry in the DreamTank."

"But...but everything's easy for you," Saturn said in between sobs.

Venus shook her head. "No, it's super hard. Sol makes sure. But I'm okay with that now. Get it?"

Saturn fidgeted with her feet and wiped her face again with her sleeve. "No...I don't know."

"We're a family now," Venus said. "So, you don't have to worry."

"Even though Sol's mean?" she asked.

Venus nodded. "Did you ever hear about Teresa Balemore?"

Saturn shook her head. "A little from the DreamTanks, but not really."

"She was the best soldier that ever lived," Venus said, voice brimming with excitement. "She was really pretty and nice and strong and always helped the people that needed it."

"She doesn't sound like a soldier," Saturn sniffed.

"She was though," Venus said. "She even trained Sol for a bit."

"All the soldiers I've seen are mean," Saturn said. Like the soldiers that killed her family and made her kill other people.

"Not all soldiers are mean," Venus wrapped an arm around her. "Some soldiers are nice. I'm a soldier, and so is Earth and Mercury and Mars and Jupiter. And you too," she poked her. "We're nice, right?"

Saturn hiccupped. "Yeah, I guess."

"You know Saturn," Venus said. "I always wanted to have a sister."

"W-we're sisters?"

"Yeah, of course we are." She stood up and offered Saturn her hand, "Come on now, you need to rest."

Saturn took her hand and stood up, "Okay."

"Saturn?" Venus said. "You don't need to cry. This place isn't like Maracca. Even though Sol's scary, he'll take care of you."

Saturn wiped her nose one more time and nodded. "Okay."

Venus gave her a big hug. Saturn squeezed her back tighter than she knew she was capable of. Suddenly, she was no longer a child. She was fully grown and hugging the child Venus tight. Fresh tears were trickling down her face into the little girl's hair. "I miss you Vee."

"I know you do," the little girl said.

Saturn felt her throat constrict as a lump began to rise. Blinking away tears, she shook her head and held the child Venus closer. "I don't want to wake up. It's so cold."

Another set of arms encompassed the two of them. "Don't worry Sat," she heard Earth say. "Remember? No power among gods or men can come between us." She could hear his all-too familiar smirk in his voice. "Death's just a minor inconvenience."

"That's right," Venus smiled. She was no longer a child, but tall, beautiful and strong. "Make sure to run Sol through like a pig for us, won't you?"

Saturn sniffed as she relished the sanctuary her siblings provided. "I will."

"And watch Mars' back for me, won't you?" Earth said.

A chuckle escaped her as she held them close. "Who do you think you're talking to?"

"Angels!" Sol's voice thundered through Saturn's mind, banishing the dream. Saturn felt a pang in her chest as Sol took her away from Venus and Earth once more.

Immediately she felt the tendrils of Sol's will clamp down on her mind. She awoke with a start to her room, still sitting with Mars in the corner, arms wrapped around each other. They separated, rising mechanically. Sol was nowhere to be seen. Saturn looked up. He was speaking through the comms.

"We have work to do," Sol's cold voice echoed through the room. "Suit up."

Saturn tried to look at Mars for some quick comfort. Just one look would be enough. But she could not. She was an Angel, and her body was obediently answering the call of the Archangel.

CHAPTER TWENTY-FIVE

JUPITER
Age 20

"I hope you can forgive me someday," Jupiter said into the handheld comm. *Especially you, Vee.* "But what's done is done. This war will end with Sol's death. Please, help us. We can't do this without you." *Please, don't make us do this alone.*

"Mercury, listen up. I know why you left. I know everything. I'm going to help you kill Sol, but we need to regroup. You have the *Defiant*, get to New Tarence as fast as you can. See you soon, brother. Six bodies, one soul." With that, he ended the transmission.

Jupiter's shoulders slumped forward and he let out a breath. Two drops of sweat fell from his nose. His mind was still a complete mess from the MemoryShare with Vera, but at least it had calmed enough for him to know he was, in fact, Jupiter. Didn't fix the splitting headache though. Sitting next to him was Vera, looking deathly pale, orange hair hanging around her face in a sweaty mess. She was paying the price from the MemoryShare too. But at least now they could trust each other. They both wanted the same thing: Sol dead.

"How are you holding up?" he asked her.

"I'll let you know once we're not in the air, Angel," Vera said as she steered the aircraft through the skies of New Tarence. They had stolen it about an hour ago and were taking it to one of Vera's contacts in the Sons that could help her resume command of the organization. Her breathing was shallow but controlled. Jupiter could tell it was taking most of her focus to keep flying in a straight line. Not bad for an hour after a MemoryShare.

Suddenly the ship dropped several meters. Jupiter instinctively put a hand against the door. He wondered how quickly he could get to his armor in the back. Then the vehicle steadied out. Jupiter glanced out the window. Nothing but air for several thousand meters.

"Do you want me to pilot?" Jupiter asked. "You look about ready to drop."

"I'm fine, Angel."

The way she said "Angel" sounded more like an accusation than anything else. "Hey Vera, I know we have every reason to hate each other, but you've been inside my head. You know I'm not trying to trick you. I really want Sol dead. You can trust me. I'm not with him anymore."

"Oh, I know I can trust you, Angel," she said in a strained voice as she guided the ship down among the monolithic structures of New Tarence. "Doesn't mean I have to like you. You've killed a lot of my friends, and now thanks to that stunt we pulled, those memories are swirling around in my head like I killed them."

"…I'm sorry. I didn't think about that. They should go away before too long."

"You better hope so, Angel." Vera slowly shook her head. "Because if they don't, I'm going to kill you when this is all over. That's not a threat, just a fact."

A stab of pain lanced through Jupiter's head. He rubbed his temples. "Sure, whatever. But right now, you can call me Jupiter."

"Jupiter? That's still an Angel name. Why not your old one?"

He let out a breath. *Why not?* "That was so long ago, I don't even remember what it was." Which was surprising, considering he just artificially dredged up all the memories he ever had, conscious or

293

otherwise. "Besides, that's not who I am now. I may want Sol dead, but I can't stop being an Angel."

"Fine," Vera rolled her eyes. "Whatever you say *Jupiter.*"

"I'm going to see this through to the end," Jupiter looked at her. "You know that, right?"

"We're here," Vera said as she parked the aircraft on the corner of Rieker and Borvoux.

"Vee," Jupiter looked her in the eye. "You do know that, right?"

She gave him an annoyed look. "I've been inside your head, Jupiter, I know…And don't call me Vee."

I didn't even realize I was doing that. He nodded. "Okay."

"In order to get to my contact, we have to go through Nara. She owns the El Psy Café over there." She pointed and Jupiter saw a hole in the wall of the towering structure opposite the one they were parked at. Most of the stores in these buildings kept their doors closed to the outside, but the El Psy was open air.

"Okay," Jupiter said slowly.

"First though, take off that jacket; it makes you look like a thug."

Jupiter complied. "Wouldn't the jacket be good for hiding my face?"

"Only reason you ever want to do that is if you're robbing the place," she wiped her face clean of sweat. "Listen Jup, no one knows what you look like. Going barefaced is your best disguise. Try to hide your face and people will know you're hiding something. Now get out there and act normally."

Jupiter nodded. Made sense. Besides, no one had ever seen any of their faces before. Not until Mercury's recent stunt on the news that is. He would just be one of many.

Even out in the open air of the parking platform, Jupiter could see hundreds of people just in the immediate vicinity. This was the capitol after all. Inside the buildings it was probably even busier, they were commercial structures. Countless people going about their daily lives completely unaware an Angel and the leader of the Sons walked among them.

Quickly surveying the area, he made his way to the crossing. The hair on his arms and neck stood on end. He was not wearing his armor in public. When had he ever done that before? If someone wanted him dead, all it would take was one clean shot. He had to be ready.

Sure enough, as the two of them entered the building, they came across vast crowds of people milling about from store to store. He could read them all like books. Happiness, anxiety, anger, resentment, impatience and fear. There were no obvious signs of hostility that he could see. At least, none directed in any way at him. Suspicion and fear, perhaps, but not hostility.

"Gods above," Vera hissed next to him as she grabbed his hand and squeezed it tightly. "You might as well be holding a neon sign for every cop and camera in the area. Remember *honey*," she said through a forced smile. "We're trying to blend in. Loosen. Up."

Jupiter nodded quickly. "Understood." Vera shot him a dark look. He paused, relaxed his shoulders and smiled. "Got it." She smiled back at him and loosened her grip.

The two of them made their way through the crowds to the crossing. Jupiter guessed there were at least two thousand people waiting on this side to cross. Amongst the sea of people, Jupiter and Vera were completely invisible. They might as well be wearing MimicSuits.

Jupiter could see over most of the crowd as they waited for the air traffic to pass. Once it had, Jupiter spotted the walkways on the adjacent side of this building split in half from the building they were connected to and retract. As soon as they had disappeared from sight, the air traffic along that direction started moving. Then the glass wall in front of Jupiter began moving out towards its matching half, the floor extending with it. Before the halves of the walkway had even connected the crowd was already walking along it. Looking to either side, Jupiter saw the walkway extended almost the full length of the building. Incredible. Angel Tower was built to be a fortress, so it did not have anything like this.

As the two opposing crowds approached, mingled and separated, Jupiter was reminded of the incredible importance of his task. This immense crowd of people was a mere fraction of a single floor of a building on one of the Hel system's moons. Each one of them had families, hopes and dreams. If true war broke out, New Tarence would be a prime target. Most of these people would end up dead. Jupiter took a deep breath.

When they reached the other side, it was a short walk to the El Psy Café. Despite it having an open-air entrance to the outside of the building, Jupiter could not hear a bit of the rush of aircraft passing by or the whine of their engines. He noticed a couple entering from outside and saw their hair get slightly ruffled as they passed through the entrance. So, they kept the noise out with some sort of air curtain. Classy.

All around him were full tables. At the counter stood a line of customers, with four employees behind it, moving with the speed and efficiency that only comes from years and years of practice. At the register was a cheerful girl who looked younger than him, smiling at customers and taking orders with lightning speed. Meanwhile, the other employees made the drinks and got the pastries.

Jupiter and Vera got in line. "That's Nara," she said.

"She owns the place?" Jupiter asked. She seemed awfully young for that.

"That's right," Vera nodded and took a step forward to keep up with the line. "Her mother's some business bigshot and funded the project, but Nara did everything herself."

The line moved another step forward. They were moving fast. Jupiter saw Nara say into a comm on the register, "Table for two please." Across the café three different customers raised their hands and made room for the newcomers. Impressive.

Before long, Jupiter and Vera were at the front of the line. "Welcome to the El Psy," Nara prattled off with a smile. "What can I do for you today?"

"I'd like to place an order to pick up day after tomorrow at eight a.m.," Vera said.

Nara glanced up at her. Jupiter could see the faint glimmer of recognition. "Of course. What would you like?"

"Plain bagels," Vera said. "A baker's dozen."

Jupiter saw Nara's pupils dilate just slightly. Her eyes casually swept over him. Was that fear, or excitement? "Would you like any of those with cream cheese?"

"Yes," Vera said. "All of them."

"Can I get a name?" Traces of worry seeped into her voice that probably would have gone unnoticed by anyone other than Jupiter.

"Val," she answered.

"Alright," Nara wrote it down. "Anything else?" Her eyes did not leave Vera, but Jupiter got the feeling she was watching him.

"Do you have a bathroom?" Vera asked.

"Yes," she said quickly to her right. "Just down that way and on your right."

"Thank you," Vera smiled.

"Your total is thirty-two fifty," Nara smiled.

Vera handed her a fifty-credit chip. "Keep the change." She subtly motioned for Jupiter to follow.

"Enjoy your day!" Nara called after them.

The two of them entered the family bathroom. After a minute, a steady beeping alerted them to comm hidden underneath the sink. Vera answered it.

"Yes," she said. "This is the Valkyrie... ...Zeta, Omicron, Sigma. Four, seven, seven, nine, one, zero, three, five, eight, zero ...hello? Hello?"

The hairs on Jupiter's neck stood on end. "What's going on?"

She looked at the comm. "Lost the signal."

Impossible. This is the capitol. Jupiter stood next to the door and reached for the pistol at the small of his back. "Is Nara screwing us?"

"No," Vera shook her head immediately. "No way, she's one of the sweetest people I know-,"

Jupiter's ears erupted as the door in front of him, along with most of the bathroom wall, burst in a flash of blinding orange light.

***

<h1 style="text-align:center">VERA</h1>
<h2 style="text-align:center">Age 28</h2>

When Vera awoke, it was to the smell of smoke and burning paint. She was pinned down to the ground by something heavy. She could not hear a thing; her head was ringing and there was something trickling out of her ears. As her senses returned, she felt pain pulse through her body. Her right arm and both of her legs all screamed at her in unison, each clawing for her attention.

Slowly, she cracked open her eyes. Smoke and concrete dust swirled through the air. Water from a ruptured pipe sprayed in a high arc, landing on whatever had her pinned before running down onto her. The water was red. She lifted her head off the concrete, stabbing pain forcing her to inhale sharply. She must have cracked her head pretty bad. Then she saw Jupiter.

He was lying on her, his face towards the ruined ceiling. Blood was everywhere. She tried to push him off of her and was reminded of the blinding pain in her right arm. Looking down, she saw most of the skin up to her elbow had either turned into a bubbled mess or been burned away entirely, revealing red, raw muscle underneath. The sight made her head swim.

Twisting her upper body, she pushed against Jupiter as hard as her left arm was able. *Damn, he's heavy.* She felt her arm start to tremble, she puffed out air as water and blood trickled down her face. Then she felt his water-logged body start to slide and her legs flared in such excruciating pain she got tunnel vision. She stopped to catch her breath and coughed on the wet, smoky air. Again, she pushed, biting her lip and commanding her arm to push with all its might. Jupiter began to slide once more, and the pain in her legs returned with a vengeance. Stifling back a cry, she used her right elbow to help, forcing her way through the pain until Jupiter's body slumped off her onto the floor with a small splash.

Sitting up, Vera checked herself. Her legs were burned badly, with parts of the pants melted onto the burned flesh. Tentatively, she raised her left hand to the back of her head. She winced and pulled her fingers away bloody. Easily a concussion. Where the restroom door and wall once were, now there was a gaping hole. Through the dusty, daylight air Vera could see what had been the El Psy café. The tables and customers were gone as if they had never existed. The floor was cracked concrete, littered with debris and pockmarked with holes.

Next to her lay Jupiter. Now that she was above him, she could see the full extent of the damage. His face had been burned to a mess of mottled red flesh and was oozing blood. She was not even sure if his eyes were still there. If not for the MemoryShare, Vera doubted she would have been able to recognize him. His clothes were all but melted away, with several shards of scorched wood protruding from the left side of his chest. From head to toe, he was burns and blood. Even for an Angel, that was a bad way to go. Vera looked down at herself. Apart from her extremities, she had escaped the blast.

That's twice today you've saved me.

Pushing off the ground with her left arm, Vera stood despite the shrieking protest of her legs. Guess she had to start from zero now. There was no way she could convince the other Angels to help her without Jupiter.

A gasp from behind her.

Her heart stopped. Not daring to even breath, she looked back at Jupiter's lifeless body. The blood in his mouth bubbled just slightly. *There was no way in Hel...*

"Jupiter?" She leaned down towards him, listening intently for any signs of life.

"...Vee."

"Shit," Vera looked around the destroyed restroom, at the hole in the wall leading out, then down at her burned legs. "I'm going to get you out of here, alright? Just don't move Jup...This is going to hurt."

Crouching down on the wet ground, she leaned against the side of Jupiter's chest without shrapnel and pulled his limp, bloody arm over her shoulder with her good arm. She could feel his own burned, bubbled skin try to stick to her hand. A weak groan from underneath her. "Don't die on me now, Angel." *Please, gods.*

Vera pulled against Jupiter's arm until she felt his torso rise, and then she pulled some more. He was upright. Now came the hard part. Setting her feet firmly on the ground and scooping her burned arm underneath one of Jupiter's legs, she pushed off the ground.

The entire world was consumed by the blinding, white-hot pain in Vera's legs. Her vision blurred and her lungs seized. She could only manage shallow breaths as she felt Jupiter's body slowly rise off the ground. Her knees shook uncontrollably under the weight. He was easily over a hundred kilograms. Maybe one-ten. Opening her eyes, she willed them to focus. The ground appeared before her. Sharply drawing in a breath, Vera took a single step.

The pain was beyond comprehension, forcing her to bite her lip until her mind registered the coppery taste of blood. With that taste and pain to distract her mind, her took another trembling step. The edges of her vision began to darken. She took another step. Her legs pleaded with her to stop. She took another step just to spite them.

Every step felt like a miracle. And for every step, her legs punished her severely. Vera let them. She had a mind for one thing. Her burned arm told her it was going to fall off. There was no way it could support so much weight. She compensated with her good arm and took another step.

Vera emerged into the daylight of what had been the El Psy café. Everything was gone. Even most of the blood from the customers and staff had burned up. Here the ground was littered with rubble, as well as being cracked and sloped in places, leading towards ominous holes. If she went in as straight a line as possible, it would not take that long. After pausing to take a few ragged breaths, Vera continued onward. She held Jupiter tightly to her shoulders, gritting her teeth as his blood soaked her shirt. She could hear drops of liquid hitting the concrete. Only the gods knew whether it was water or blood. One thing was certain though, the Angel was not making noises anymore. *Hang on, Jup.*

Slowly it dawned on her that she would probably die here. *Not yet, Libby. Not yet.* Mom, Dad, Libby, Imri, Sahra, Gerard, Simon, Nol, Nara, they were all waiting for her, but not yet. She chanced a step on one of the large, cracked pieces of exposed concrete. It held. *Good.* Once they got to the ship, she could set an autopilot course for Qor's hideout.

Forcing her way through the pain, Vera trudged across the broken concrete to freedom. Each step was torture, but she continued. She kept her eyes up, not daring to look down. Eventually, she emerged with her burden into the afternoon air of New Tarence.

The entire capitol was in flames. Billowing black plumes of smoke rose into the sky to be carried away by the high-altitude winds. There were no emergency vehicles in sight, or vehicles of any kind for that matter. As for people, they must be taking shelter indoors, because there was no one in sight. No one living anyway. Slowly turning her face to the sky, Vera saw the Federation fleet unleashing all the fury of Hel. *Gods above…is this what we've been up against all along?* Even at this distance and through the smoke, she could easily make out Sol's flagship. The only *Hel*-class superdreadnought in existence, the *Balemore.* The azure fire it rained down was like nothing Vera had ever seen, absolutely dwarfing the guns of the other ships.

At least it did not seem to be targeting their current location anymore. And thank the gods, the walkway along the edge of the building had not been damaged. Then Vera remembered. She had parked at the building opposite them. *No.* Her legs began shaking uncontrollably. She had used every ounce of her strength to get this far, and she still had another couple hundred meters to go.

She felt Jupiter's waterlogged and bloody body begin to slip. Holding on tighter, she continued walking, one exhausted step after another, but her body was giving out. She might as well be walking through half a meter of mud. Her back began to audibly creak as Jupiter slipped even more, putting the weight at a bad angle.

Then her legs finally gave out in earnest. Her mind barely registered she was falling before the force of gravity aided by Jupiter's unconscious form drove her into the concrete. A cry escaped her. What little air she had managed to squeeze into her lungs was immediately forced out.

Face pressed down against the gritty ground, Vera noticed dark splotches appear as tears ran off her face. Is this all her life was worth? Was she just going to die with her hated enemy for company while the monster that killed her sister lived?

Get up, Vera. Spitting out blood, she pushed herself up, barely even feeling the pain in her burned arm anymore. Grabbing Jupiter underneath the armpit, she pulled him toward her so their centers of mass were aligned. Her legs were no longer capable of lifting them both, no matter how much she wanted them to. She eyed the crossing that Jupiter and her had used earlier. It wasn't extended. *Did it even work anymore?*

Holding Jupiter with her burned arm, she began crawling towards the crossing. At this point, more pain was just more pain. Her body seemed to have given up on reminding her about it. Clearly if she had not gotten the hint already, then there was no point.

At that moment, she heard the whine of a ship approaching. Two ships. She crawled faster, scraping up her good arm on the concrete as she desperately pulled herself and Jupiter towards the crossing. She would get across somehow. Jupiter had put the armor in the back. The armor was in the back.

Then her blood-soaked hair was blown away from her face as the aircraft pulled up alongside her. *No!* Archangel's men had come to finish them off. *Just a bit farther.* She strained and clawed at the hard ground. She was so close. But no, the crossing loomed a good thirty meters away still. And even after that, how much farther to the ship?

"Valkyrie?" she heard a familiar man's voice say in shock. "Gods above, bring out the MedGel. Now!"

The familiar weight of Jupiter was lifted from her. *No.* She tried to push herself up, but for some reason she felt heavier now that the weight was gone. She collapsed. A moment later, strong arms scooped her up into the air and held her against a bare, barrel chest with words tattooed on it in some foreign language. They were Metian. *How do I know that?* Then she was gingerly placed on something flat and solid. Cool, refreshing fluid was spread over her wounds. Her vision started to go dark and she could barely muster the strength to fight it.

Looking up, she saw a very familiar bald face full of worry. Qor D'Rhal. She was dimly aware of herself being lifted into the vessel. "Qor," she struggled to say, reaching for her back pocket.

The big man put a hand on her shoulder. "Don't move. You're going to be fine now."

Unconsciousness was taking her. She shook her head, "No." Pulling the metal keycard for the ship out of her pocket, she held it up to Qor. "Armor…the back."

Qor took the keycard. "Understood, Valkyrie."

Her vision had tunneled so much that Qor's eyes were the only thing she could see. "Save…him."

Then everything went black.

CHAPTER TWENTY-SIX

MERCURY
Age 20

Mercury called Jupiter on his armor's comm. The word "calling" flashed blue on his heads-up display. No answer. *Damn it.* That was the fourth call in the past hour. Jupiter must not be in his armor. Normally, Mercury would not be bothered by it, except Jupiter had apparently just broken out the founding leader of the Sons and done a full MemoryShare with her. *Gods, I hope he knows what he's doing.*

Hopping into the *Defiant's* navigation well, he considered calling Jupiter on the comm that he had used to send his message. That frequency was not secure, but he might have to risk it. As he began plugging in the coordinates for the MauKe drive to make a jump to New Tarence, he called Jupiter again, this time on the other line. Secure or not, he could at least tell Jupiter to get in the gods damned armor.

No signal.

The Hel? Jupiter was on New Tarence, the capitol of the Federation. There was no way he could be without a signal. That made zero sense. He finished typing in the coordinates and engaged the MauKe drive.

Immediately the *Defiant's* onboard computer spoke up. *"Incoming enemy fire. Engaging evasive maneuvers."* Mercury felt the ship bank sharply to the right, but he quickly steadied himself.

Glancing at the computers in front of him, he saw the MimicField was still active. No one should be able to see the ship on sensors or visuals. He leapt out of the navigation well and ran towards the cockpit. "What do you mean? Who's firing? How can they see us?"

"The Balemore *and roughly half of the Federation fleet. They appear to be bombarding the capitol. They do not see us."*

What? Mercury could not believe it, but then he stumbled to the window and saw for himself.

Billowing plumes of black smoke rose into the sky. Far too many to count. From his bird's eye view, Mercury could see them stretched out beneath him and continuing forever it seemed, until they disappeared into the horizon. The crimson light of the setting sun cast everything as if in blood. Looking up, Mercury saw hundreds of battleships, destroyers and frigates scattered across the sky, each one sending numerous clusters of energy in various colors streaking toward the buildings below.

Mercury clenched his fists and felt his whole body begin to tremble with rage. He could turn all these ships to slag, but they would be long done before then. The only way to stop this was to kill the man who gave the order. *"Defiant,* return home. Do not dock with Angel Tower." He stalked off towards the LaunchTubes and got inside his. He looked up with white hot fury at the hatch several meters above. "Point me right at Sol's office."

"Understood," the ship's automated voice said. *"Engaging MauKe drive."*

There was no way to tell the ship had actually made the jump, but Mercury drew his shield all the same. He felt that familiar push against his arm as the clasps engaged, locking the shield in place. When the hatch above opened, he was staring laterally at the top of Angel Tower.

Ready or not, he had to act now. In his surging blood he felt an overwhelming power and will to end Sol's life, but that would not help him. Closing his eyes for a moment and taking a deep breath, he looked back at Sol's office. His breathing was steady; his mind was clear.

"Defiant, launch tube one."

For the briefest of moments, Mercury heard a faint whine before the steel plate under his feet shot forward along the electromagnetic rails. The next instant, Mercury was crashing through the reinforced, one-way windows of Sol's office, cratering the concrete floor and scattering a cloud of dust. Sword drawn, Mercury was ready to cleave open his mentor from head to hip. SmartOptics swept the building, but it was devoid of life readings. No one was home, not even the Angels.

Shrill alarms blared at the intrusion as a panel of solid steel slammed down to bar the office's entrance. A single punch tore it from the wall. Mercury rocketed through the cloud of powdered concrete towards the elevator shaft, blowing a hole in the door and flying down. A small army would be on him in minutes, and he would much rather not kill them. He stopped at the floor that housed Erithian's Eye. If Sol was not here, then he had to find him fast.

Blowing open these elevator doors too, he flew inside to find a solid wall of steel where the entrance to Erithian's Eye should have been. He fired off a few antivehicle shots where the door used to be. The shots exploded into scorching waves of white fire that swept past him and dissipated. The wall was completely untouched. He could almost hear it laughing at him.

Bounding forward, Mercury plunged his sword into the metal until it reached the hilt. In the blink of an eye, he had pulled it through the metal in a circle. Clearly, Sol had gone to great lengths to protect possibly the greatest asset in the building. But it did not matter what material Sol had built that bunker out of. If it originated in this universe, then his sword could cut it.

The metal wall stood there, a perfect, clean circle cut in the side of it. Mercury let his shield return to his back and punched four armored fingers into the narrow gap made by the blade. Then he did the same thing on the opposite side. Bracing a foot against the wall, he pulled the entire disk of metal out. It was over half a meter thick. He cast it aside. When the carved chunk of metal hit the floor, Mercury felt the ground buckle slightly underneath him. The sound Mercury heard was actually much quieter than he expected. Mercury looked at his armored hands. *Sometimes I feel too protected in this thing.*

Hurrying inside, Mercury was greeted by the holographic form of Erithian as the display of the Hel system came to life. "Where's Sol?"

"Forget about that, there's no time." The hologram's eyes were wide with fear. "Before Sol detects the breach. You need to get to Jupiter."

He had completely forgotten about Jupiter in the madness of the bombardment. "Where is he?" Mercury grabbed one of the PsyMitters and let his helmet retract so he could put the device on.

"He's in a Sons' facility with Vera," the hologram said. "I'll load you the coordinates, but Merc, he's…oh no." The hologram looked around frantically as the display of the Hel system began to flicker. "The PsyMitter. Now!"

"Why am I not surprised?" Sol's voice flooded the room, powerful and omnipresent as Erithian's display was replaced with the face of Mercury's nightmares. Mercury's heart leapt into his throat. *Shit.*

He instinctively dropped into a defensive stance and looked to Erithian's hologram, which collapsed to its knees, transfixed by Sol's gaze. A small child before Sol's enlarged visage. "…I'm sorry."

Mercury slapped the PsyMitter to the base of his neck. Nothing happened. Meanwhile Sol was silent, looking down in condemnation on the computer's avatar. "Erithian," Sol spoke the machine's name in the same voice he used to bend Mercury's will. A chill ran the length of his spine. Erithian was an AI. Sol could not control it too, right? The very notion was ridiculous…right?

The childlike avatar stood and turned to Mercury. Its eyes were cold and dead, like a true machine. "You shouldn't have come here."

Mercury took a step back. "Erithian?" There was no recognition in the hologram's face. It shifted and grew, until the holographic child was gone, replaced by a hologram of Sol.

In the DreamTank Mercury had learned the difference between a computer and a sentient AI was the presence of a will. With self-awareness comes the ability to choose. But with the ability to choose comes the ability to be manipulated. Even something as powerful as Erithian.

Then, the hologram shifted back to the small boy. His face was contorted with pain and fear. "Run! Get to Jupiter!"

Before Mercury could even open his mouth to ask where to find him, a query box appeared in his vision. *"Allow direct data transfer?"*

A sharp intake of breath. He looked at Erithian as the hologram began flickering between the form of the boy, and the form of Sol. *Oh gods.* He held a hand to the PsyMitter, ready to tear it off the second anything seemed wrong. Mentally, he responded. *Yes.*

Erithian's avatar held its form as a boy, reaching up a hand towards him.

Instantly Erithian's Eye disappeared from his vision. Suddenly Mercury was everywhere at once. For the briefest moment he was across every satellite, every camera, every computer, everything in the Hel system that fed Erithian data. He saw…everything.

Then, he was screaming down to New Tarence, jumping into a satellite then into numerous security cameras. He saw a woman, Vera, covered in blood and carrying an unconscious Jupiter. She collapsed. Two ships appeared with a bald, shirtless man stepping out followed by armed soldiers carrying medical equipment. They got Vera and Jupiter onto the vehicle and took off. Mercury tracked them, jumping from camera to camera, back to a satellite, then down into a comm, then into a military radar tower, then back into cameras, then into a comm call from one of the soldiers, and finally, back into a satellite.

They flew to an old warehouse away from the capitol, where the bald, shirtless man led everyone inside. A string of coordinates flashed bright across Mercury's vision, then it was over.

Gasping for breath, Mercury tore the PsyMitter off and threw it away. In front of him, Erithian's avatar flickered once more, becoming Sol. At a thought, the trayite bands of Mercury's helmet reformed themselves around his face. It was long past time he left.

"You can't hide from me, Mercury!" Erithian thundered after him with Sol's voice. "I see *everything.*"

Shit, shit, shit, shit.

Flying back the way he had come, Mercury exited Angel Tower and flew back to the waiting, cloaked *Defiant.* "Get us out of here."

"Understood."

Mercury made his way through the loading bay to the navigation well and plugged in the coordinates Erithian had shown him. *Just hold on, Jup.* With the press of a button, he engaged the MauKe drive.

"How's the MimicField holding up?"

"Energy drain nominal."

"Good," Mercury headed back towards his LaunchTube. "Put me outside their front door, then standby on patrol."

"In position now."

Once more, Mercury stepped inside the metal tube. "Launch."

With an explosion of dust, Mercury made a small crater not five meters from the warehouse's main entrance. A large set of steel double doors. He raised a hand to force them open, but they slid open on their own. He entered cautiously, scanning the area.

Inside were dozens of vessels. Various aircraft from FighterBombers to gunships to even a bulk transport outfitted with a *Zerythane*-cannon. Mercury's mind drifted back to their fight with Captain Mavos. Even though it had only been six years ago it felt like a lifetime had passed.

His musings were interrupted by eight well-armed Sons walking through one of the side doors. At the head was the bald man from the security cameras. SmartOptics clocked him as Qor D'Rhal. He carried no weapons, and Mercury understood why. Tattooed on the man's bare chest were six of the seven Metian words for war. Mercury blinked and did a double take. *Six? Holy shit. I should take this guy seriously.* Even among the most disciplined monks, few could boast of mastering six words. Then Mercury noticed the man had skipped the fifth word: bitter war, in favor of the seventh word: the gods' war. *Oh, man...why? You're so close.*

"Angel," the man said in a thick Maraccan accent, despite the fact that he clearly was not Maraccan. A broad sincere smile spread across his face. "Welcome. Truly, welcome. You are the Fallen Angel, yes? Mercury?"

Mercury hesitated a moment and looked at the others before shaking the man's hand. "Yes, and you are Qor D'Rhal?"

The man barked out a laugh. "Indeed. Call me Qor. I am sorry we must meet under such grim circumstances. Your comrade is resting, but I can take you to him."

"Thank you," Mercury nodded and Qor led him out of the hangar and turned down a hallway leading deeper into the facility.

"We did all we could, but MedGel and a medic can only go so far. He needs surgery."

"I can't thank you enough, but…"

"Why didn't we kill him?"

"Yes."

"Because the Valkyrie tried so hard to save him. Besides…" Qor's voice softened with admiration. "I want to have a good conversation with him first."

'Conversations' among Metians could mean either an exchange of words, or an exchange of blows.

Mercury glanced back the way they had come. "I take it you have his armor?"

"I suffer no thieves in my army," Qor said. "The armor is with your comrade." He stopped outside a door and held his hand up to the control panel. The door slid open without a sound. "As a fellow student of war, I hope someday we might set aside our duties and have a good conversation as well."

Definitely skipped the fifth word. "If I can manage to kill Archangel, then it's a deal." *Maybe that will show you why mastering all seven is so important.*

Qor laughed heartily. "Ah, how I envy you."

"You shouldn't," Mercury said as he entered the room. He heard more laughter behind him as the door closed.

Mercury found the room itself to be surprisingly clean. In the center of the floor was a training mat. Covering the mat from end to end was the depiction of a great bird with white and blue plumage, perched atop a flaming arm. The banner of the ancient Metians. It even appeared to be woven from natural fibers, not synthetics. Mercury was one of the few people who would actually appreciate the minimalist decor, but now his eyes swept right past it. On the other side of the room hovering half a meter off the ground, were two MedCots with a chair in between them. The one on the right had a very large, very familiar metal crate next to it.

For some reason Mercury did not understand, he could not approach. He wanted to, but his legs would not move. He looked down at them in surprise. Outside of Sol's direct influence, his body never failed to obey his commands. Multiple painful years in Forging had made sure of that. He slapped his armored leg. *Come on, Merc. You're setting out to kill the most dangerous man alive and you're going chicken on me now?* He tried to take another step, but his foot barely budged. *Move.*

This is your fault.

He stumbled forward, then ran up to Jupiter's MedCot. There lay his brother; even as he was now, Mercury would recognize him anywhere. Dark red, mottled burn tissue covered Jupiter from head to toe, still carrying the sheen of applied MedGel. On his side Mercury counted nine different puncture marks that looked like they had been made by shrapnel of some kind. Then he looked closer at Jupiter's face.

He tasted bile. With a clang, he sank to his knees by the MedCot.

Not only had Jupiter's face been almost burned away completely, but so had his eyes. There were just two empty sockets of melted crimson flesh.

Even though Mercury had spent most of the last ten years of his life in armor of some kind, he could not stand to be in his suit right now. His whole body itched, his eyes most of all. Worse, no matter how much he tried to breathe, he could not seem to get enough air. He disengaged his helmet, but even after it slid away from his face he could not get enough air. This armor that kept him alive through all sorts of Hel now felt like a coffin.

He stood quickly, and his armor began opening. It was not fast enough. Taking off his armor in a base full of people that no doubt wanted to kill him was stupid, but that seemed so insignificant right now. Besides, there were no cameras. Sitting with his back against the wall next to Jupiter, Mercury put his head in his hands.

"I'm sorry, Jupiter," he sobbed. "I am so, so sorry." He sniffed and used his palms to wipe his eyes. "This is all my fault. I should have told you. I should have told all of you, but I didn't. Six bodies, one soul. I acted like a selfish, stupid, coward. I should have told you about Sol, about Erithian, the Exodus, everything."

He looked at his motionless brother. "You could tell something was going on, couldn't you? You always were good at picking up on stuff like that." His body shook with every sniffling breath. "We're going to get you all fixed up, you hear me? Once this is all over we'll get you to a hospital and they'll get you your eyes back, okay buddy?"

Jupiter did not answer.

A pithy laugh escaped Mercury. "You always trusted your big brother Mercury, but when it came down to it, I didn't have the balls to trust any of you. That's pretty lame, huh?"

The only sound was silence.

"I got your message," Mercury sniffed. "Good thinking with the MemoryShare. Came here as quick as I could. At least you had the common sense to tell everyone what was going on."

Letting his head thump back against the steel wall, Mercury sat there and let time pass by as his tears dried. His brother should be dead right now. As bad as the wounds were, it was clearly the handiwork of relatively small ordinance. The fleet had much bigger guns, and if any of them had been used Jupiter would have died instantly. They must not have been targeting him. He was just collateral damage.

"I'll do better next time, I promise. No more trying to do it alone. Six bodies, one soul. So, you get better quickly, alright? I need you with me."

"You sound like a girl I used to know," he heard Vera say from her MedCot.

Mercury started, then steadied his breathing. "How long have you been awake?"

"Since you came in," she said. "Your armor isn't exactly quiet."

Mercury closed his eyes. "Thank you for saving my brother."

"Now those are words I never thought I'd hear from an Angel."

"You and me both," Mercury opened his eyes and stood, making his way to the chair in between the MedCots. Vera was burned similarly to Jupiter, but only on the lower legs and one of her arms. Mercury found a bookmarked copy of *The Metian Way* by Genrik Rauss on the chair before he sat down. Printing physical books was usually saved for a select few first edition copies, and none of those had been made for Sol's book since before Mercury was born. He knew this book backwards and forwards. "Your friend Qor has an interesting taste in literature for a Son."

Vera scoffed. "He's a fanatic in more ways than one."

Mercury set the book on the foot of Vera's MedCot. "So, why'd you do it?"

With a grimace, Vera pushed herself to a seated position. "I've been inside his head. He's a good kid. Besides, I really want Archangel dead."

"That makes two of us."

"Merc?" he heard Jupiter say. "Is that you?"

Mercury's head perked up. Slowly, he turned towards his brother. "Hey man," he said in a trembling voice. "How are you feeling?"

"I'll manage," he turned his eyeless face this way and that. "It's nice to have you back. What's going on? Have we been captured?"

"Don't worry, we're fine," Mercury smiled sadly.

Jupiter tilted his head. "Then..."

As his brother's voice trailed off, Mercury felt his throat start to get raw.

Jupiter slowly looked at his hands. He rubbed his fingers together. Then he reached his fingers up to the cavities where his eyes once were. Mercury watched as his brothers fingers tentatively felt along the edge, wincing in pain, then they reached inside before immediately pulling out. Almost as if he had touched red hot metal.

"You know," Jupiter said. "For some reason I always thought it would be like when you close your eyes and everything goes black. But it's just...nothing."

Mercury opened his mouth to apologize, but Jupiter put his hands over his ears. He uncovered and covered them several times. He looked in Mercury's general direction. "Is Sol dead yet?"

A shake of his head, then Mercury remembered Jupiter could not see. "No."

His brother was quiet for a moment. "We still have the armor?"

"Don't worry," Vera said. "I wasn't going to leave that behind."

"Good," Jupiter pushed himself up, the muscles of his face visibly straining against the pain.

"Woah," Vera swung her legs off her MedCot. "The Hel are you doing? It's only been a few hours."

"Forgot the MemoryShare already, Vee? This isn't too bad." Jupiter's face twisted in a tortured smile. "Merc, if you can help me into the armor, I can up the sensitivity on SmartOptics. It's a direct feed through the armor's PsyMitter. Even if my eyes are gone, I can still fight."

"I didn't forget shit," Vera stood, despite the pain Mercury saw flash across her face. "I almost died saving your ass. You are not going to try to fight like that. It'd be faster if I just shot you now."

"Merc," Jupiter's disfigured faced turned directly towards him. He stood. Those empty sockets sent a chill through Mercury. "Hit me," his brother said.

Looking over his brother, Mercury could see just standing was pushing him. He was an Angel after all. Mercury would have expected nothing less, but his brother could not fight like this. He shifted his weight towards Jupiter in a feint, following it up with solid punch.

Without flinching, Jupiter caught Mercury's fist in his hand. He smiled. "Didn't I say to hit me?"

Suddenly Mercury was gone, ducking around Jupiter. His brother tried to react, but not fast enough. Mercury jabbed him in the back where he was not burned. "You're too slow, Jup. Vera's right."

Jupiter felt for his MedCot and sat back down. "Point taken."

"When can you be ready?" Mercury asked.

Jupiter shook his head. "You promised all the worlds Sol would be dead in seventy-two hours."

Vera looked down at her MedCot. "That was six hours ago. Only sixty-six hours left."

"I'll be ready in sixty-five."

Mercury narrowed his eyes at Jupiter. The burned flesh and empty sockets dared him to say he could not do it. His brother was cutting it as close as possible. For a normal person there would be no way. But for him, with how much Sol had altered their bodies, it just might work. Mercury smiled. "A soul on fire indeed."

Vera shook her head. "You're crazy."

"Then we came to the right place," Mercury said.

"Touché."

The door to the room opened and Qor D'Rhal entered. "I have good news, bad news, and worse news. Which would you like first?"

"Let's start with the good," Vera said. "What are we looking at?"

"I contacted the Sons as you requested Valkyrie, and they were quite positive about your proposition for peace. As it turns out, almost every single would-be troublemaker was killed in Archangel's bombardments. The rest want Archangel dead. They want his head, on a spike, in a blast-proof glass box."

"That's very specific," Mercury raised an eyebrow.

Qor nodded. "They were quite emphatic."

"And the bad news?" Vera asked.

"They are on their way here to help facilitate the process," Qor said. "Our fleet should arrive in just over a day."

Vera closed her eyes and rubbed her temples. "Why the Hel would they do that? Didn't they hear Mercury's message? They can't wait three days?"

"It's related to the third piece of news." Qor pulled out a comm and pressed a button. Immediately a holographic screen appeared in front of them. "Archangel held another press conference."

Sol stood at the same podium that he had used to establish his dictatorship. On his left and right were Mars and Saturn, standing perfectly at attention in their armor. Venus and Earth were absent.

"I warned all of you what would happen to those who opposed me." Sol's helmet swiveled back and forth. "All who oppose me, die." He spread his arms. "This is the truth of my universe. Let the billion souls who perished be a lesson for all of you. My will alone is absolute. I am your god."

Mercury's jaw slowly dropped. His eyebrows went up. *Say what now? Who the Hel is this? Sol might be a monster, but he's not delusional...Right?*

"No matter who you are," Sol continued. "Any who oppose the rule of God will forfeit their souls. No matter who."

Two pairs of Sol's Legionnaires walked into view, each dragging a bloody, motionless, armored form.

Mercury lost all awareness of time as a hollowness opened up within him. *No...not this...*He stared at the video, unable to breathe. *It was supposed to be my life.* His vision blurred as his heart was strangled within him.

The pairs of Legionnaires deposited the armored bodies of Venus and Earth at Sol's feet. Sol picked Venus' body up with one hand and held it aloft for all to see. A single, clean stab through the chest, the blood from the wound now dry. Mars and

Saturn were still standing perfectly at attention. "No one, not even Angels, can oppose the rule of God."

"Mercury," Jupiter's voice was brimming with fear. "What's going on?"

Mercury could not believe his eyes and ears. He swallowed. "It's Venus and Earth, Jup. They're...they're dead."

"Mercury!"

Sol's voice sent a chill down Mercury's spine. The sound called up all the horrors of his years in Forging. He unconsciously clenched his fists.

"Enough hiding! I...grow impatient. You and Jupiter will come to face me atop Angel Tower. There you will both meet your end."

Mercury let out a breath.

"If you do not come within twenty-four hours..." Sol's voice trailed off. "Angels!" he thundered.

Immediately, mechanically, Mars and Saturn dropped to one knee and drew their swords, holding the point against their chests, right over the heart. "I will kill them. After that," Sol's voice dripped with menace. "I will deal with all your friends in the Sons. My empire will span every system, in every galaxy." He shook his head. "I will not be denied."

CHAPTER TWENTY-SEVEN

MERCURY
Age 20

Twenty-three hours later, silence threatened to swallow Mercury whole. Before him stood his suit of trayite armor, perfectly still next to Jupiter's old MedCot in Qor D'Rhal's sparring room. The glowing azure visor seemed to watch him, judge him, weigh his resolve.

"Hard to believe it's been ten years," Jupiter's voice broke the silence.

"We were so naïve back then," Mercury shook his head. "We didn't know anything."

"Has that changed?"

Mercury pondered Jupiter's words a moment. "I guess we'll find out." He turned to face his brother. A day of constant MedGel was not nearly enough to heal Jupiter, not even close. Still, he was much better than before. His face was still almost unrecognizable, but it no longer oozed blood and the color had dimmed from a raw crimson to deeper red, almost purple. Those empty sockets still stared blankly into space out of the mottled mess of scar tissue. But at least he was alive…somehow.

"This plan of yours," Mercury said. "I don't like it."

"Divide and conquer is textbook stuff Merc," Jupiter said. "Sol's got Mars and Saturn dancing on his strings. I'll draw them away while you kill the bastard."

"You're in no condition to fight, Jup, let alone against Mars *and* Saturn."

His brother did not flinch. "We're Angels Merc."

He said that like it solved everything. He still considered himself an Angel, even after everything that had happened, even after everyone they had lost. Memories drifted to mind of a distraught Jupiter crying on a beach over unrequited love. Mercury's lips cracked into a sad smile. He chuckled and shook his head.

"What?"

"Just thinking about how amazing my brother is."

The exposed muscle in Jupiter's face pulled up in a smile. "Thanks."

"Don't go getting any crazy ideas. Stay on the defensive. Don't let them flank you. We'll get you back on MedGel as soon as this is over."

"Merc...stop."

Those words were a knife in Mercury's chest. In that moment he realized just how tired Jupiter was. His brother's body was on the verge of collapse and he was asking him to fight.

"I can hold them off," Jupiter said. "But this is a one-way trip. I've made my peace with that, so please, don't make this any harder for me."

After blinking twice, Mercury clasped Jupiter's arm. "I'll see you in Hel, brother."

"Someday," Jupiter nodded. "...Kill him Merc, kill him quickly."

Kill Sol quickly...that's a tall order. Mercury looked at his brother's scars. "I will Jup."

Jupiter's face twisted in another gruesome smile. "Six bodies."

Mercury smiled. "One soul."

Ten years and now they were here. Everything seemed to have happened so fast. The day Mercury's new family had emerged from the DreamTanks seemed like yesterday, PerfectMemory aside. *Back when there were six of us.* He blinked away tears as images of Venus and Earth's lifeless armored bodies flashed across his mind. *I will mourn for them...when Sol is dead.*

Jupiter turned away, moving towards the crate where his own suit of armor was stored. After taking a deep breath, Mercury stepped towards the suit before him. Sensing his approach, the trayite bands and plates shifted with an ensemble of clicks, whirs and scrapes. Piece by piece, the armor opened up for him. Soon the components became still once more, forming a cavity large enough to envelop a man.

For what might be the last time, Mercury stepped inside the armor. The GelSuit within conformed to his body as readily as it had his first time in the armor. Not a single other person had ever been in this suit. Mercury felt the pieces one by one lock snugly back into place. As the components cascaded up his legs and chest, Mercury looked down at his armored hands. His fingers were trembling. Then the trayite components worked their way over his neck and finally, his face. He felt the effects of gravity cease as he was cut off from the outside universe. SmartOptics engaged and his world was overlaid in blue.

He heard the heavy, metal footfalls as Jupiter approached in his own armor. "The SmartOptics work great. I can 'see' everything in the room."

"Really?" Mercury felt his eyebrows go up in surprise.

"Yeah," Jupiter said. "I don't see color, but other than that, I can see even better now than I used to."

The door to Qor's sparring room opened with a faint squeak and in came Vera, followed by the bald warrior himself. Vera was decked out in full tactical gear, with dual sidearms on her hips and a rifle on her back. Qor was wearing an expensive looking vest of crimson lined with gold thread, his tattoos proudly showing on his otherwise bare chest. In his hands he held a wide strip of similarly designed cloth, with six symbols etched across it in blazing, bright blue. The seven Metian words for war, minus the fifth. *A war without bitterness.* Qor held it with all the tender care with which one might hold a newborn baby.

Walking straight up to the armored Jupiter, the bald monk bowed, holding out the strip of cloth with both hands.

After hesitating a moment, Jupiter reached out an armored hand and gingerly took the gift. Qor bowed lower, then stood up straight with a somber smile.

Mercury watched as the trayite bands of Jupiter's helmet parted, pulling back all the way until his face was entirely exposed. Taking the cloth with both hands, Mercury's brother held it up to where his eyes used to be and tied the cloth behind his head. He bowed back to Qor and the components of his helmet reformed around his head, the thick cloth with its striking, blue script now covering his eyeless sockets.

"Take care of yourself, Jup," Vera said.

"You too."

Vera turned to Mercury. He expected her to say something, but she just stood there, bright red hair tied back and staring at him intensely. She held out a gloved hand.

Holy shit, that's right. This is the leader of the Sons of Liberty. Mercury took her hand, careful not to accidentally crush it with the suit's enhanced strength. He shook it. She still did not say anything, instead just looking at him. She did not let go. Her eyes were glistening, but her expression was stern. In her eyes he saw understanding, pain, anger and hope, all swirling together before him. Past that he saw a fierce promise if her hopes in them were proven wrong.

Mercury dipped his head in respect, and she let go of his armored hand.

She blinked. "I can't believe I'm saying this, Angel, but…gods' speed."

"Thank you," he said. *I'll need it.*

***

MARS
Age 20

Mars stood at attention atop Angel Tower. Somewhere next to him was Saturn, but he could not see her. Both of them might as well be statues. Every muscle in his body was completely immobilized by the crushing grip of Sol's will. They were prisoners of their own bodies. All he could do was stare at Sol, the monster holding them captive. The man had his back turned to them, standing tall, proud and terrible. The deep blue Cloak of State was draped over the shield on his back. Mars' skin crawled just looking at the man. Past Sol, the sky was slowly turning from orange to red as the sunset and the time limit drew to a close.

Any minute now Mercury and Jupiter would arrive. Showing up was stupid, but it was in their nature. Unfortunately for all of them, no matter how much Mars and Saturn cared for their brothers, Sol could turn them against each other with one word. That was all it would take. Sol's will was absolute, and he had been teaching them to kill for every waking moment of the last ten years.

The smart thing to do would be for Mercury and Jupiter to let Sol's ultimatum run its course. Sol would command him and Saturn to fall on their swords, and then Mercury and Jupiter could fight Sol together. *Yeah…that's not going to happen.*

Mars closed his eyes and thought back to the sight of Sol killing Earth and Venus. He had knelt there, unable to move as they were each run through by Sol's blade. An empty, aching void began to open up inside him. Just like on Maracca, his family was slowly taking casualties. First with Mercury leaving, now with the death of Venus and Earth. Soon, Sol would force him and Saturn to cut down Mercury and Jupiter.

He felt tears slowly roll down his face. *I'm sorry, Sat.* He tried to reach out for her, but his arms would not respond. He knew just how much Saturn must be hurting right now. The knowledge tore his heart to pieces.

In Dabo's army, he had killed so the rest of the kids would not have to. He had done his best to keep them safe, and they still died. At least back then he had a choice. Now, it was all too obvious just how powerless he really was. He and Saturn were still breathing right now only because Sol allowed it.

"This is a fresh start," he had told Saturn all those years ago when Sol found them. *"We aren't going to lose anyone else. I promise."*

A wave of guilt washed over Mars. *I'm sorry, Sat.*

"I'm scared," she had said to him. *"I don't want to be alone."*

Even more hot, stinging tears ran down Mars' face. *I'm so, so sorry.* There was nothing he could do. He was powerless to stop this madness. He could not comfort Saturn as it unfolded. He could not even protect her after the fact.

There was one truth Mars knew with absolute certainty. If Saturn killed Mercury or Jupiter, even if it was under Sol's control, it would change her forever. He would probably never see her glowing smile again. Even if the two of them survived this, they would not emerge unscathed.

He remembered his nightmare of him strangling Mercury. He could still see Saturn's eyes, wide with fear as she backed away from him. If he killed them, there was a good chance Saturn would never look at him the same way again. If she ever looked at him like she had in that dream, Mars did not know what he would do.

I have to stop this.

Mars leveled his eyes at Sol's back. Summoning every last reservoir of strength he possessed, he willed his body to move. *Draw your sword.* His sight narrowed on the trayite covering Sol's neck. He could almost feel the blood pulsing through the man's carotid artery. Every muscle in Mars' body tensed, coiling up to strike. Sol was completely unaware of the danger he was in. *That's the problem with being the apex predator, you don't expect anyone to be stupid enough to mess with you.*

Mars could feel his whole body start to shake as he raged against the shackles on his mind. *He's a human being, damn it. He can be killed.* Mars felt his hand slowly start to open. He visualized himself drawing his weapon and slashing open Sol's throat. *I'm keeping my promise, Sat. We aren't going to lose anyone else.*

With a cry in his heart, Mars took a step towards Sol and drew his blade in a flash. Or at least, he tried to. He took a step forward and immediately dropped to one knee with a resounding clang, head bowed to the ground.

Sol must be obeyed.

All was silent. Then Mars heard Sol's armor shift. He could feel Sol's gaze on him. A cold sweat broke out all over his body. He could not see the man, but somehow, he knew Sol was looking at him. *Are you going to kill me? Do it.*

"Well done," Sol really sounded impressed. Mars heard Sol's armor shift as the man lowered himself. As Mars stared at the ground, he heard the soft ring of metal on metal and felt Sol's armored hand clasp the back of his neck. "Just remember, in the end I *always* get what I want."

CHAPTER TWENTY-EIGHT

JUPITER
Age 20

Jupiter stood just outside the *Defiant*'s LaunchTubes with Mercury. Now that his eyes were gone he was relying entirely on SmartOptics to perceive his surroundings. His entire world consisted of a bright blue holographic model. Next to him Mercury's armor shifted, each individual trayite band and plate captured in cutting detail. In fact, Jupiter was no longer limited by line of sight. From where he stood, he could "see" the entire ship, right down to the inner mechanisms of the MauKe drive. Without color, the world felt awfully cold.

The blue model representing Mercury leveled its WristGun at him. Immediately Mercury began flashing between red and blue. SmartOptics painted Mercury's firing vector red and suggested a hundred evasive vectors. Jupiter gave thumbs up and Mercury lowered his WristGun. Mercury's hue cleared up and the suggested evasive maneuvers disappeared.

"This is it," Mercury said.

He nodded. "Yeah…"

His brother slowly shook his head. "I'm sorry I left without telling you."

Jupiter put an armored hand on his brother's shoulder. "Apology accepted. But now's not the time or place to be emotional, Merc." He said that for himself just as much as Mercury.

The bright blue holographic model representing Mercury nodded.

With that, they each got into their respective LaunchTubes. The hatch above Jupiter opened. He saw a cluster of bright red bogies marked "Federation Fleet". One bogie in particular, much larger than the others was marked "*Balemore*". That was his target.

"Launch."

Space ripped past Jupiter as he shot in between the Federation fleet towards the *Balemore*. He and Mercury could never hope to defeat Sol, Mars and Saturn without first dividing the enemy forces. Sol was not stupid enough to be tricked by any of their plans, but they did not need to trick him. There was no way Sol would let a planet killer like the *Balemore* fall into their hands. Sol would send Mars and Saturn to stop him. As Jupiter approached the fleet, the red bogies turned into full holographic models of the vessels that comprised the Federation's navy.

One of the issues with having a ship as large as the *Balemore* was it was simply too expensive to put so many eggs in one basket. While no engineer would be stupid enough to make the bridge a single point of failure that could bring the entire vessel down, it was still a weakness. To work around this, the *Balemore* had not one bridge, but a hundred, each crewed by a hundred people and capable of running the vessel if all the others were destroyed. There was not much point to having a vessel capable of single handedly destroying a fleet if a single shot to a precise location would leave the machine floating dead in space. What was more, the enemy would need to have a ship with big enough guns to actually punch through the *Balemore's* impossibly thick armor to the center of the vessel in order to damage any of the hundred bridges. Anything big enough to hurt the *Balemore*, was big enough to be blown away. After all, they had to make sure the vessel would not fall prey to some random fighter.

However, none of it mattered to a man-sized trayite rocket traveling at over seventy kilometers per second.

Even worse for the *Balemore*, the lack of a centralized bridge meant that control of the vessel could be shifted from one bridge to another. Because Sol knew that such a powerful vessel must never fall into enemy hands, he had installed a backup system for diverting control of the ship to any of the other subsections manually in case of mutiny. No one knew about it or had access to it other than Sol. No one except for the Angels anyway.

Once Jupiter was close enough and had a direct line to where the currently active bridge was buried, he put all power to Boosters. Then he clapped his hands above his head and locked the joints in his armor. With a crash, the hull erupted like an ocean struck by a meteor. Jupiter did not feel a thing.

Jupiter watched as the hundred crew of the current bridge subsection were sucked out the hole he had made upon entry and into the black of space. Control of the ship would have been shifted from this subsection to another. Moving over to the main computer, Jupiter synced it to his suit and initiated the emergency procedure. "Security override code: Angel," he said. He felt his body tingle as his suit performed a full body scan to verify his identity. He had full control of the ship. Immediately, he locked out all future access via this security measure.

"Merc," he said on the comms. "I need double authorization."

"Security override code: Angel," Mercury said.

Now Jupiter had complete control over a ship powerful enough to burn planets. The thought was rather terrifying. Even if this bridge subsection was destroyed, they could not stop him. He was the bridge now. The only way to forcefully regain control of the vessel was to kill him. Next, he locked down all the doors and every comm in the ship other than his. "Attention all crew, I am an Angel. The Sons of Liberty have infiltrated the ship. You are now officially in threat level one lockdown. Remain at your stations. The threat will be resolved swiftly."

In truth, the ship probably did have some agents of the Sons on board. With over half a million crew, it just made sense. Now all he had to do was wait for Sol to send Mars and Saturn to deal with him. He sat heavily in the captain's chair and heard the sound of warping metal as the chair gave beneath the weight of his armor.

As soon as he sat down, the emotions he had been suppressing began strangling him. Every breath he drew was ragged and painful as he forced air past the rising lump in his throat. Venus and Earth were…gone. Vee was gone. Thanks to his wounds, he could not even shed tears for her. He wanted to cry out and escape this bitter anguish that consumed his very soul, but his tortured body lacked the strength.

He should be dead right now. Vera had saved him back in the El Psy, but just barely. His tether to this colorless world was fragile at best. He had frayed until a mere thread remained to keep him here. Soon he would fade away completely. His wounds were grave, beckoning him to embrace oblivion, but not yet. Not when his family needed him.

Jupiter looked at the holographic model of his armored hand. How did it all come to this? Was there any way he could have done things differently? He looked up at the hole in the ship's hull. Beyond the holographic model was just…emptiness. Could he have saved Venus and Earth? Would he be able to save Mars and Saturn? Even under Sol's control, they would not be able to bring themselves to kill him, right?

His thoughts drifted back to when they were younger. They had trusted Sol utterly. They were so sure the six of them together would protect humanity from whatever dangers threatened it. There had been no question in Jupiter's mind that his life's purpose was to be an Angel. He would have lived a happy life and when Sol passed away, he would help train the next generation of Angels to replace them.

Amidst the silence, his mind echoed with the memories of voices he would never hear again in this life.

"I'm sorry Vee," he whispered to no one.

The crisp smell of the bitter cold filled his nostrils. He thought back to Venus' Forging floor. The icy wastes of Bjornhal had been her own personal Hel that Sol, quite literally, saved her from. Now she was dead by Sol's hand. Jupiter remembered what she had looked like that day the five of them had taken her back to Forging for trying to fight on her own. Her eyes had looked up from the snow as clear and bright blue as ice.

"Together we are invincible," Earth had said that day. *"But alone we fall."*

Jupiter shook his head. *I really screwed that one up, didn't I?*

"Your team will suffer for your mistake," Saturn had said to Venus.

"I'm sorry I wasn't there for you," Jupiter said aloud. He knew Sol would have killed him with barely more than a word. Still, his heart ached with an emptiness for the two of them. He knew that emptiness would remain until his heart stopped beating.

"Six bodies," he heard Venus whisper to him.

"One soul," he whispered. The smell of fresh snow still permeated his senses.

No matter what happened, he would see this through to the end.

Since he had rerouted control of the *Balemore* to his armor, SmartOptics fed him relevant data about the vessel. He perceived in his mind's eye a camera feed of the corridor leading to his bridge subsection. There was an army of Federation soldiers in the latest models of BreakerSuits. SmartOptics counted a hundred and forty-four. He had not expected so many. Protocol dictated they get additional verification of an Angels presence, but he doubted they would respond well to the gaping hole he had made in the hull. *Besides, twelve dozen BreakerSuits? That's a bit much for a simple verification.*

He opened a channel to the leader. "What's your name soldier?"

A woman's voice answered, hard and experienced. "Captain Allison Rainnes reporting, Angel."

"Protocol override Captain Rainnes," Jupiter said. "Take your team back to your station and await further instruction. The Sons are attempting a mutiny. Any and all crew not at their stations will be treated as hostiles."

"I'm afraid I can't do that sir," she said. "Protocol dictates we must personally assess the situation." She was not buying it.

"This is an order Captain," Jupiter said forcefully. "Return to your stations."

"That isn't an order I can follow, Angel."

"Allison," Jupiter said. "If you continue, then you and your subordinates will die. Don't be stupid. Let them go back to their families."

"We made the pledge, Angel," she said simply. "We made the pledge because we believed in something greater than ourselves. With all due respect, it doesn't matter who stands against us. Not even one of you."

"Very well," Jupiter said. "Best make your peace with the gods."

After ending the call, Jupiter stood and pointed both WristGuns at the door into the room and set them to antivehicle. He heard a faint hum as he diverted all excess power to weapons. When the door started to glow orange, he was ready. As soon as the first pieces of slag fell away, Jupiter unleashed white fire upon his adversaries.

They all died like rats as they tried to make their way through the chokepoint. The hopelessness of their situation became apparent within seconds, but every one of them died fighting. Now Jupiter waited amidst the carnage for Mars and Saturn as the smell of snow mingled with the smell of blood, smoke and burning flesh. An alert from SmartOptics. The *Balemore*'s scanners showed two Angels were rapidly approaching. *Good.*

Less than a minute later Mars and Saturn were flying through the hole Jupiter had made upon entering the *Balemore*. He would have liked to be able to see them with his own eyes.

They descended slowly, touching down amidst the bloody slag. Even without his eyes, he could tell they were under Sol's control. Had they been themselves, they would have said something to him. Anything.

"I'm sorry I wasn't there for you when you needed me," Jupiter said to them over their comms.

Silence.

For a moment, Jupiter thought he could see flakes of snow floating on the edge of his holographic vision. A phantom cold sent shivers down his spine as the smell of snow once more seeped into his awareness. "Remember what Earth used to say?" he said to his unresponsive siblings. "There is no power among gods or men that can come between us. Not Sol, not anything."

Mars and Saturn drew their swords. The motion was mechanical and cold. But this time, they did not even bother to draw their shields. Each of them had two swords.

He really should not be trying to fight so soon after his injuries. Him, the weakest Angel, outnumbered and outmatched. In front of him were four very sharp reasons why this was the stupidest idea his brain had ever concocted. As the cold spread through his limbs, he drew his sword and shield. Silently, he prayed for Mercury to end Sol's life quickly. Hopefully, once Sol was dead, they would snap out of it. Jupiter knew that if they killed him here, even under Sol's influence, it would destroy them.

Tightening his grip on his sword, Jupiter shifted into his stance. Mars and Saturn stalked towards him. He changed his stance to something much more defensive. They charged.

Their attacks were a storm. High, low, thrust, feint, switch. Everything Jupiter could have possibly imagined they might do they did better and faster than he could hope to keep up with. If not for his shield, he would have died in an instant. His heart hammered in his chest and every time their blades clashed, it felt as if they were being driven right through him.

I'm sorry guys, I'll save you from this. I promise. Just hold on.

He gave ground without remorse, retreating deeper into the ship. Thanks to being in control of the vessel, opening doors could be accomplished with mere thought. Had it taken anything else, he would have been gutted like a fish.

This was mostly a scramble to keep some distance between him and them. Block a few strikes here and there, then retreat down one of the ship's many empty passageways. Mars and Saturn were just too fast though. Not only were their movements almost too fast to see, but they were in perfect synchronization with each other. Of all the Angels, they had always worked best together. Not even Venus would have been able to fight them alone.

"Save them," he heard Venus say to him.

"I don't know if I can, Vee," he answered in his mind as he continued to narrowly escape death.

"Don't give me that shit," Venus' voice rang inside his head. Memories began flashing through his mind of all the times he had watched Venus during training. He had thought he was being subtle about it, but now he saw how obvious he had been.

Mars and Saturn continued to assail him with flurry after flurry of blows, each strike more vicious than the last. Somehow, he managed to block every one without giving ground. His movements had been exactly like Venus'.

"Slow your breathing and listen to the music," she said to him. He could almost see her there beside him. *"The music is there and if you listen to it, it will guide you."*

Jupiter tried to listen, but his mind was too busy frantically trying to stay alive. Besides, he was so cold. *Fighting in my condition really is stupid.* His throat was closing up and his mind could see his end coming. He was going to die. Six moves and he would join Venus and Earth.

"Peace," she moved her hand over his heart. As she did, his ears were opened. He could hear the music. The clamorous notes of swords and his shield created a harmony set to the beat of his heart. *"Dance with me Jupiter."*

"I don't know this one," he answered.

"Don't worry," she smiled. *"Just follow my lead."*

Jupiter did not fully understand what happened next. Mars and Saturn were just as impossibly fast as ever, but he could see their moves now. He *knew* them.

Before he had thought and his body responded. Now, he was not even thinking. His entire being was pure movement. He dodged Saturn's slash and flicked his blade at Mars. When Mars shoved against his shield before sweeping at his legs, Jupiter flowed through the air like water. While flipping backwards he deflected Saturn and Mars' swords with a single strike.

Slowly he let out a breath and with it the last of his inhibitions melted away. Venus was with him, and this was their dance. Mars and Saturn looked at each other, then shifted their stances and advanced. Jupiter smiled inside his helmet. "I am the eye of the storm," he said to himself.

Blades darted and sang as Jupiter danced between his enemies. Every aspect of his being was entirely present in this moment. The rage of their battle was a lullaby to his ears. Soon he was pressing them back, the ship's corridor being carved with deep gashes as they fought.

Jupiter could feel his enemies' confusion as their weapons rang out and he continued to push them further and further back. They had expected to be fighting one opponent, but they were fighting two. Jupiter was sure the voice that whispered in his ear and the hands that seemed to hold his sword and shield were not real. They existed simply because his body was pushing itself to death's door from his earlier wounds, but he did not care. Somehow, he knew this was her.

Sparks flew and metal rasped and scraped. On more than one occasion Jupiter heard cries after their swords carved through a nearby wall. There were people on the other side after all, and he could feel their eyes on him as he continued to press his adversaries back.

Despite Jupiter's efforts, he could not land a scratch on them. However, they could not pin him down either. He knew how they were thinking and did the opposite. They were anticipating what Jupiter would do, but not what Venus would do.

The music of battle was his now. He guided it and shaped it as he desired. There was no logical reason he should still be alive right now, but he was. And he was winning.

"It's time for me to go Jupiter," Venus said to him.

"No," Jupiter thought. "Don't go. I don't want you to leave. Stay with me a little longer. Please."

"I'm sorry Jupiter," she said. *"You can't come with me where I'm going. Not yet."*

Jupiter felt her presence fading. A tear rolled down his cheek as he continued to fight.

"Give my best to Saturn and Mars, won't you?" Her voice seemed so far away.

"I will," he whispered. "I promise. I'll save them Vee; I'll save them all."

"Goodbye." Just like that, she was gone.

Jupiter gave himself over to the music.

Somewhere along the line, Jupiter's mind registered that Mars and Saturn were fighting differently now. They moved as if they were fighting Venus, not Jupiter. He could only imagine how confused they must be.

Before he could stop it, Jupiter found his sword flying out of his grip. How did that happen? In the same motion, Saturn sheathed her extra sword and caught Jupiter's sword midair. Now all he had was his shield.

"Guys, stop," he shouted while blocking their strikes frantically with his shield. "Sol has to die."

One of Mars' swords came stabbing past Jupiter's shield out of nowhere. A quick dodge just barely kept the strike from landing. Jupiter retreated several meters. Mars and Saturn each slid one of their swords back into their shields. If he let either of them grab his shield, he was a dead man.

"Wake up guys!" Jupiter let his helmet retract from his face. "It's me."

Instantly Mars raised his WristGun and fired at Jupiter's exposed face, but he blocked it with his shield. Jupiter saw Saturn flinch. *Yes! Fight him, Sat!* As they walked towards him, he backed away.

"Mars! Saturn!" he cried out. "You're stronger than this."

This time Saturn fired a shot.

Jupiter lowered his shield. "Are you going to let him use you like this? To kill me? Just like he killed Venus and Earth?"

Mars and Saturn each fired. Jupiter was barely able to bring his shield up in time. This time, he let his helmet cover his face again before lowering his shield. SmartOptics showed the blue images of Mars and Saturn advancing slow and steady. Their WristGuns were raised and swords ready to cut him in half if he got too close.

"You guys are my family," Jupiter said with conviction as he felt the cold work its way into his chest. His thoughts grew murky. "No matter what happens here, that won't change. Understand?"

Mars charged, and Saturn followed. This was not working. His words could not reach them. A thought struck him. Jupiter tried to back away, but he was so cold. His arms and legs were not responding as fast as they usually did. Mars' giant hand seized his shield and pulled him off balance, sword darting towards him like a snake.

Summoning every last reserve of energy, Jupiter caught his footing and pulled at his shield, even against Mars' superior strength. The point of Mars' sword glanced off the shield's rim. Letting the shield go, he leapt away just as Saturn's sword whistled through the air where he had been.

As the last of Jupiter's strength faded, time seemed to slow. He knew how this fight would end. His vision started to go black. "I promised her I'd save you," he said as his helmet retracted into the rest of his armor. Saturn was already charging, sword ready to skewer him. If she killed him, his face would be etched into her memory forever.

Words won't reach them.

Jupiter raised his WristGun to his exposed head. He prayed to the gods that Mercury would kill Sol before Mars and Saturn arrived. "Six bodies, one soul."

He fired.

CHAPTER TWENTY-NINE

MERCURY
Age 20

Mercury thundered to a stop in a three-point landing atop Angel Tower. The ground cracked underneath him and he felt the tremors as he looked up to see his enemy waiting for him. Sol stood near the edge of the tower's roof, the imperial blue Cloak of State whipping to the side in the high-altitude winds. Behind his old mentor the setting suns cast the world in blood. The clouds, infused with crimson, spread out behind Sol like the wings of some horrific monster.

Surrounding them in the sky were hundreds of military and news aircraft. All the worlds would bear witness to this duel. Even though Mercury could not see Sol's face, he could feel the man staring. That glowing blue visor threatened to snuff the life out of him through will alone. Every fiber of his being screamed to run. This was the man who made him. He could unmake him just as easily.

Mercury swallowed. Then, Mercury slowly let out a single breath, expelling the fear. He was not scared. He was determined. This was the bastard that killed Venus and Earth. This was the lunatic that fancied himself a god. He was this man's executioner. Mercury held out his arm and felt a reassuring pressure as his shield left his back and latched on. He drew the blade.

"I commend your decision to use Jupiter as bait," Sol said so calmly it made Mercury's skin crawl. "At least you have the foresight to know such sacrifices are necessary."

Mercury said nothing. He was already fighting Sol in his mind.

"I had such high hopes for you Mercury," Sol shook his head. "This entire time, I wanted nothing more than to pass what I built on to you." His voice dripped with disappointment. "Yet for all your training, you could not see what was right in front of you. What a shame."

"Why Sol?" Mercury shook his head. "Why do all this?"

He could hear the smile in Sol's voice. "Because I actually can." He spread his arms wide. In that moment, with the setting sun and the fiery clouds behind him, Mercury imagined a god might actually look like that. A dark god. Sol's thunderous voice echoed out, "My rule will bring peace for a thousand generations. Only a madman would let such a glorious future slip through his grasp!"

Mercury let out a weary breath as he beheld the monster before him. "To think I once looked up to you."

Sol laughed. A tortured, twisted laugh of victory without any semblance of sanity. He drew his sword and shield, then casually twirled the sword in his hand. "Please don't disappoint me again."

The moment of truth. Mercury slowly circled around Sol. He was almost unaware of his weapons; they were a part of him. He stopped when the suns were out of the way and shifted into a stance that should counter Sol's fighting style. In response, Sol shifted into a stance Mercury had never seen before. Mercury nodded. Carefully shifting his stance again, Mercury waited. Sol shifted his position by a few steps, but his stance did not change. Mercury calmly adjusted his grip.

Neither of them moved. Mercury's heart thumped in his chest. He could feel Sol waiting for him to close the distance. The silence taunted Mercury to action, but he stilled his mind. The wind whistled off his armor. Somewhere off in space a fleet was hurrying here to start the war to end all wars.

Sol charged. His strikes were perfect. Mercury could barely see the man's sword and shield as they swarmed Mercury in their deadly dance.

Mercury blocked and countered at a speed he had not known himself to be capable of. He tried to gain the upper hand by using his Boosters in spurts for speed, but Sol anticipated his every move. Sol drove him towards the tower's edge. Mercury used his Boosters to get on the other side. Sol swept his legs out from under him. Mercury Boosted away, but Sol was right on his tail.

Slash and parry. Mercury retaliated. Sol caught it on his shield and thrust. Mercury dodged and saw his reflection as the weapon darted before his eyes. Mercury hacked and slashed. Sol pirouetted in an overhead strike. Mercury blocked and shifted low for Sol's legs. Sol used his Boosters to twist in midair. Mercury used his shield to block a sweep of Sol's sword and leapt back with his own Boosters.

The two of them stood a good ten meters apart and watched each other. Sol had no weaknesses. His technique was the definition of flawless. But Mercury could not wait. Not while Jupiter was buying him time. He instinctively glanced up towards the *Balemore*.

Instantly Sol was upon him. Mercury stepped back just as Sol's sword came raining down on him from seemingly all directions at once. Strike after strike. Blinding speed. Then Sol was behind him. Mercury caught a thrust on his shield and retaliated. Sol's shield shoved his sword arm. Mercury was unbalanced. He took to the air. Sol's blade whistled just under his feet.

Midair one-eighty. Mercury rocketed back towards Sol. His sword scraped harmlessly off Sol's shield. Mercury spun. His shield connected with Sol's helmet. Sol's sword stabbed from underneath. Mercury rotated on his Boosters and slashed. Sol fell back and buried his sword in the tower roof. Sword as an anchor, Sol kicked Mercury's shield, forcing him away. Sol flipped up and fired his Boosters, smashing through the roof and out of sight.

Skidding to a stop, Mercury frantically looked around for where Sol would emerge. An explosion of concrete at his feet. He rocketed back on his Boosters. Sol was not there. Mercury spun just as Sol exploded through the concrete behind him.

Just barely able to block with his shield, Mercury brought his weapon around to counter. An armored hand seized his shield. Mercury was yanked forward as a blue visor peered through the shower of still falling concrete. The sound of their swords rang in Mercury's ears. Again and again and again. Faster and faster.

They soared into the sky. Mercury shoved him off and slashed. Sol twisted and held on. A blade darted for Mercury's throat. Abandoning his shield, Mercury flicked his sword towards Sol's visor as he rocketed away. Sparks. No blood.

The two of them circled each other in the air. Sol had given up his own shield and acquired Mercury's. *Shit*. Suddenly, Sol cast the shield aside like a disc down towards Angel Tower. *Why would he give up the advantage?*

Sol straightened and Mercury saw the metal bands of his mentor's armor shift. From his back Sol pulled out a second sword. Not just any sword either. The weapon their trayite swords were based off of. The weapon found long ago in Bjornish mines by a young girl. The Balemore's Blade. The Sword of Morning.

Mercury's brain registered pain in his shoulder and he felt blood. *When had Sol cut him?* Grimacing, Mercury twirled his blade and beckoned him forward. Sol obliged.

If Sol had been impossibly fast before, Mercury did not want to know what he would be like with two blades. Mercury met his charge, but just before Sol was in range, he shot him square in the chest with his WristGun's highest setting. No damage, but it slowed his enemy's advance. Mercury blocked one blade and caught the wrist holding the other. This was now a contest of raw strength.

Their swords scraped ominously off each other as each one attempted to skewer their opponent. Sol had the Federation's medicine to keep him in a state similar to youth, but it could not beat the real thing. Their mechanized suits were equal and Mercury was stronger. In a few moments this fight would be over.

A jolt of pain slashed Mercury's foot and one of his Boosters sputtered out. Aerial stability was gone. Sol's gauntlet clamped behind his neck. The man loomed over Mercury as the bloody sky spun behind him. Their crossed blades inched further away from Sol and closer to Mercury's throat.

With his free hand, Mercury broke off Sol's vicelike grip. Using the force behind Sol's sword and his one remaining Booster, he shot down towards Angel Tower.

Mercury crashed onto the roof and rolled to his feet none too soon. Sol was almost upon him, blade bloodthirsty and gleaming in the light of the setting suns. Mercury blocked the strike as Sol flew past. His enemy rolled to his feet, skidding across the roof before charging once more. Mercury blasted the roof under his enemy's feet. As his enemy fell, he saw the barest opportunity. *One, two.* Sol's sword went flying. The man used an armored fist to smash through the next floor, falling out of sight. Mercury caught Sol's lost weapon and pursued.

When he emerged through the last hole Sol had made, it was in a place Mercury had never seen before.

He was on Taurus, but not the Taurus he knew. Scorched desolation as far as the eye could see. A mountain of bodies reached for the burning heavens and the sparking, cracked hole in the sky. Water from ruptured pipes rained down on the Helish landscape. Never before had he laid eyes on Sol's Forging floor.

Landing atop the sea of corpses, Mercury drove a sword into one of the bodies to brace himself. Water had made the footing treacherous. He scanned the corpses. Solid steel with holographic overlays to look like corpses. All except one. Somewhere amidst these bodies Sol was hiding.

There he was. Playing dead near the top of the corpse mountain. Bounding up with his remaining Booster, Mercury cut the body in half from hip to shoulder. The hologram flickered off and a chunk of steel tumbled down the slope. *A fake?* Mercury once more plunged a sword into a nearby "body" for support and looked around. He saw them. The rest of the Angels, strewn about in this fictional world Sol had created for himself. Four, five, six, seven. Eight counting the one he had just cut in half. One of them was definitely Sol.

He shot two of the bodies, turning them to slag. *Wait a minute.* These bodies had shields on their backs. Where was the body without a shield? He counted four with shields, and one body lying on its back. Smiling underneath his helmet, Mercury dove forward. *Just hold on, Jupiter. I'm coming.* At the last moment, Mercury pirouetted over Sol, lopping off the man's head in one clean strike.

A lump of steel fell away as the hologram died. He could already hear Sol moving behind him, too fast for Mercury to react.

With overwhelming force, an armored fist knocked one sword out of his grip, sending it high into the air. Mercury lashed out to disembowel Sol. His strike went high as Sol bent back at the knees. The sword above them reached the peak of its arc and began to descend. Mercury brought his own sword down in a two-handed strike powerful enough to bisect his old mentor.

Sol clapped Mercury's sword between his hands and wrenched it from his grasp. Mercury scrambled towards the top of the mountain on his one remaining Booster. Sol was right behind him. Upon landing, he slipped on the slick metal. A sword came whistling towards him. Mercury raised his arms. A stab of pain as the blade plunged into his left arm. As Mercury leapt for the hole in the sky, he noticed Sol casually catch the still falling sword and rocket after him.

Jumping from floor to floor with his one working Booster, Mercury dared not even look back. The sound of Sol's blade carving concrete erupted behind him. Too close. He leapt again.

Gritting his teeth, Mercury tore the sword from his arm mid-jump as he emerged back out onto the roof. He rolled to his feet. Suddenly Sol was there, blue visor thirsting for blood. Sword in both hands, he advanced for his final clash with the monster.

Metal rang against metal. Once. Twice. Three times. Sol was inhumanly fast. Faster even than he had been at the beginning. Or was that just because Mercury was slower? A slash of pain and Mercury felt his sword slip from his grasp. A follow up strike at his neck. Mercury dove back. Sol's hand lunged forward and caught him by the throat, holding him in place.

This was the end. As Sol raised his sword high, Mercury saw above him Mars and Saturn re-entering atmosphere as blazing streaks of fire. *I'm sorry, Jup. You sacrificed everything and I failed you.*

Mercury blinked. *Wait a minute…Why are there three of them?*

Sol looked up. He saw them too. Definitely three Angels, with swords drawn and screaming towards them. The hand around Mercury's throat shifted, and he was tossed towards Mars and Saturn. They quickly switched grips on their swords and caught him.

"You alright?" Mars asked, still holding him.

"…How?" Mercury looked at Jupiter.

"Reverse psychology," Saturn answered.

They all landed, wary of Sol. But the man kept his distance, his visor studying them. Mars handed Mercury one of his swords, then grabbed Saturn's shield from her back and offered that to him as well. Mercury gladly accepted. *They're back.*

"Jup," Mercury took a staggered step towards him, all the while not letting Sol out of his sight. "You…you did it."

"You're damn right he did," Saturn nodded. Mercury could hear the all-too familiar smile in her voice. "And it'll be one Hel of a story for when this is all over." She pointed a sword at Sol. "For now, let's shish kebab this asshole."

***

SOL
Age: 62

Sol felt a strange catharsis overtake him as he saw the four Angels standing there together. A smile crept into the corners of his mouth underneath his helmet. Was this finally his end? He turned his head to look at the twin suns as they set. He was never going to see them rise again. What a shame.

"It's over Sol," Mercury said as the four of them drew up their formation. "There's no way you can take all of us."

He did not answer. All he could do was stare at the buildings of New Tarence stretched out beneath him, stained blood red by the fading light. Back in the slums, he had looked up at the sky and wondered. Now here he stood. Lifting his face to the sky, he beheld the numerous fleets under his command. He thought of the worlds that rose and fell by his choices. Is this how far his dream would take him? He raised his sword and stared at it. Apart from a little blood, the tool bore no sign it had ever been used.

Blue skies barely visible above narrow alleyways flashed through his memory. Everything had seemed so big back then. He felt a tear run down his cheek.

What a wonderful world.

Turning back to the Angels, he looked at each of them in turn. His control over them was gone. With a nod, he held his sword in both hands and shifted his stance. They responded by raising their swords and shields. Sol blinked, and suddenly all four of them were kids again. His heart held no regrets. He blinked again and the kids were gone.

"Yuki?" Sol said on a private comm channel.

"Yes, sir?"

"They've grown up."

"Yes, sir," she answered. After a moment she continued in an unsteady voice, "Sir?"

"Yes, Yuki?"

"It's been an honor, sir."

Sol smiled. "The honor is mine." He charged.

He managed to block six strikes before the first sword plunged through his chest. Then two more. Then another. And another. As his children lowered him to the ground and Sol drew his last breath, he felt no pain. Just pride.

"Well done."

CHAPTER THIRTY

MERCURY
Age 20

Sol's body slumped where it stood, impaled by five separate swords at varying angles. Mercury's hands started shaking on the hilt of his weapon. Sol's armor did not move. Was he really dead? As one, the four of them withdrew their weapons from their dead mentor. Catching the body in one arm, Mercury gingerly lowered Sol's corpse to the ground. While he lowered the body, Mercury pondered how Sol was now an inanimate object. He had always been familiar with death, so why was he thinking of this now? Once the universe had seemed to dance at Sol's every whim, but now the man was gone. Because after all he was just that…a man. *Memento Mori.*

Mercury blinked as tears ran down his face. He shook his head. Why was he crying? He hated the man. The man was a monster. Now, at long last, he was gone from this world. Mercury sheathed his sword and returned his shield to his back. The other Angels did the same. From the way they stared down at Sol's corpse, Mercury figured they must be just as confused as he was.

With a beep, Mercury was alerted to an incoming call to all four of them. A call from Yuki. "Ma," Mercury began to say. "I'm sorry."

"What's done is done Merc," she said. "Archangel left orders that in the event of his death the military was to be turned over to you. You're Archangel now. We'll see this plan of yours through to the end. What are your orders?"

"Tell the fleet to stand down," Mercury said. "Under no circumstances are they to engage when the Sons arrive."

"Yes sir," Ma ended the call.

Mercury took a breath and watched as one of the nearby aircraft approached and landed on the roof of the Tower. Out stepped Vera with Qor D'Rhal and two others in tactical gear.

Vera shook her head somberly as she approached. "I never imagined you guys would be the ones to put him down." Her eyes thoroughly swept the armored body before her. Once she was satisfied, she looked at Mercury and the others. "Thank you."

"All we want is peace," Mercury said.

"You have it," Vera said. She gestured at the ships surrounding them. "Each of those ships is broadcasting this to every news station, every screen and every Son of Liberty in the entire system. You did it." Qor knelt by Sol's body, reverently placing his copy of *The Metian Way* atop the man's bloodied chest.

Vera watched Qor a moment, then turned back to Mercury. "You held up your end of the bargain, and we'll hold up ours. I already sent word to the other leaders to stand down."

Mercury could feel the cortisol in his brain dissipating. He let out a breath. "You're sure they'll listen?"

"Yeah," Vera nodded. "They're still going to hold onto the bullets though, just in case."

"Completely understandable," Mercury smiled underneath his helmet. If he were in their shoes, he would hold onto the bullets too.

"Vera," Jupiter held out a hand. "Thank you for everything." His brother's voice was weary, but Mercury could tell he was smiling.

She shook it. "You saved my life, Jup; I saved yours. Don't read too much into it."

"Archangel," Ma said to the four Angels on a comm channel. She sounded worried. "Something's wrong."

Mercury's senses shifted into overdrive to detect the danger, but all he could see was one of the nearby military craft, a gunship, landing on the rooftop. The other Angels drew their shields. Vera's hands twitched for her pistols.

"Vera," Mercury said slowly. "What's going on?"

But she looked just as confused as he was. The gunship's side doors opened and roughly two dozen people in black tactical gear with pistols poured out. Pistols designed to fire bullets. The soldiers had three hostages with them, bound and gagged.

"What the Hel is this?" Vera demanded. She did not seem to immediately recognize the hostages, but Mercury did. Mars, Jupiter and Saturn had only seen them once before, but they would remember them well. Perfectly, in fact.

Mercury had left his biological family at a very young age to be an Angel. If not for the PerfectMemory Sol had given the Angels during their MemoryShare, he might not have recognized them. Over ten years had passed since he last saw them, but he knew them. They looked so much older than he remembered. His parents' hair was completely gray and their eyes were wide with fear. His sister's face was stern, staring daggers at him. There was no trace of the kind younger sister he remembered.

The soldiers leveled their weapons at the four Angels. Mercury would bet anything the two remaining trayite bullets were somewhere among them.

One of the soldiers, a man by the sound of it, spoke up. "Remove your helmet, Ilyas, or they die."

Mercury had not heard that name used in a very long time.

"Who sent you?" Vera demanded in a voice full of anger.

The figure glanced at Vera. "We won't sit by while you make your deal with the devil, Valkyrie."

"Mercury," Jupiter said nervously over the comms. "What do we do?"

"They only have two bullets," Mars said. "We can win."

"If we fight now," Saturn warned. "It won't ever stop."

"Archangel," Ma said. "I have shots lined up on all of them. Just say the word."

Everything was spiraling out of control. The Sons wanted blood, not peace. He had done what Erithian's Eye said, but the machine was not perfect. Even with all its data, Erithian's Eye could not totally account for human will. Had all of this been for nothing? His family bled and died to give humanity a chance at peace and now they were rejecting it. Was Sol right all along? Was his way better?

"Archangel," Ma said. "The Sons' fleet is approaching. They will be within firing range of the navy in minutes."

In a twisted way, Mercury wished Sol was still alive. Monster that he was, the man had been able to make tough calls without hesitation. "Battles are first won in the mind." That was the Metian way and it had been Sol's way. The answer was here, but Mercury could not see it. There were too many variables.

"We won't wait forever," the man said.

Mercury looked at the three hostages. They had been his family at one point, but not anymore. His family was the people beside him. But the three hostages were people just the same. Everything he did, he did for people like them, for people like the Titors.

"Don't do it Merc," Jupiter said over the comms. "You know you can't."

"I'm not going to sacrifice others anymore," Mercury said.

"You can't save them Merc," Mars said. "They're as good as dead already."

"Mercury," Saturn said. "Now isn't the time to gamble."

The man spoke up again. "I'm going to count to three. If your helmet is not off by then, they die."

"Don't do it, Angel." Vera shook her head.

"I'm sorry guys," Mercury said to his family. "I hate to leave you again."

His armor was too damaged from his fight with Sol to allow the helmet to retract into the rest of the armor like it normally would. Thankfully, the armor could separate into physical pieces in times like these. Slowly grabbing his helmet, he heard numerous clicks and a hiss.

He removed it. The world looked so different without this thing on. He let go. The helmet dropped to the ground with a resounding thud.

"I'm glad you saw reason," the soldier said. Mercury knew there were most likely several snipers ready to blow his brains out. "Now, the rest of you remove your helmets or your friend dies."

"If you don't mind," Mercury began removing the other pieces of his armor. "I have something to say."

That confused the man. *Good.* "Most of you know me as the Fallen Angel," Mercury began as he continued taking off his armor. First came the arm pieces. As he removed them, the wounds Sol gave him began oozing blood. He dropped them with more loud thuds. "But I'm just a man. My only motive in coming here today is this. Someone once told me one resolute person can make a difference."

Next Mercury removed the breastplate and let it fall with a crash that made his ears hurt. "This belief drove me, my brothers and my sisters to do the things we have done." Stepping out of the leg pieces, Mercury flinched as his wounded foot found purchase on the concrete. He refused to look down, but he knew he was bleeding dangerously fast. He looked at the surrounding aircraft that were sure to be recording him. "This belief drove a small Bjornish girl to stand up to parents who beat her. This belief spurred three child Zeroes to survive, even when their homes were burned and everyone they knew were killed." He could not help blinking away tears, and it was not because of his wounds. "This belief compelled Liberty Tormen to cry out for peaceful protests when her peers desired violence." He let his words linger. "And this belief was the catalyst for all of you to risk life and limb for your liberty and the liberties of your people."

He clenched his hand into a bloody fist. "The present danger is very real. If we go to war," he shook his head. "No one wins. Instead billions will die on both sides," his face twisted in pain as he imagined that future. A tear ran down his face. "Down to babes in their mother's arms. We have to see this is as a battle against the basest and most brutish of our natures." He slashed the air with one hand, sending droplets of blood flying and pain shooting up his arm. "If we do not stop this madness today, we doom ourselves, our children, and our future to a war deadlier and more devastating than any in humanity's history."

Mercury paused a moment. "I did not come here to curry favor; I ask no forgiveness for my sins. I am convinced that we are at a crossroads. I believe we can build a better world for ourselves and our children's children." He opened his hands. "I believe that we are tied together by bonds that go beyond where we were born. I believe in a world where there are no Angels, where there are no Sons, where there are no Bjornish, Taurusians, Tarencians or Maraccans. I believe in a world where there are only people. For this reason," he pointed at Sol's body with a bloodied hand. "I killed the closest thing I have to a father."

"I have taken the first steps; Rauss is dead. The old regime is gone. Let us lay down weapons, rebuild our world, and seek a lasting peace." He looked at the soldiers. "You can kill me if you wish, but make no mistake," he pointed at the *Balemore* in orbit. "Our worlds will burn. The choice is up to you." He spread his hands. "Will we have peace, or war?"

The soldiers did not lower their weapons. Mercury did not expect them to. Not yet. They were acting on someone's orders. Mercury had no idea who they answered to, and in a way, it didn't matter. If one resolute person can make a difference, that was true on both ends of the scale. All it took was one decision. One command. Then life as everyone knew it would end.

"Copy that," the lead soldier said. His weapon lowered. He looked at his comrades. "Stand down."

One by one, all the soldiers present lowered their weapons. The leader approached Mercury and held out a gloved hand. "On behalf of my commander and the rest of the Sons of Liberty, we shall have peace."

Mercury looked around at the others present, then took the man's hand. He had no idea what to say, so he said nothing.

"My commander would like to begin peace talks as soon as possible."

"Of course," Mercury nodded.

Instantly, every muscle in Mercury's body relaxed. A wave of dizziness washed over him. He was not sure if that was from blood loss or the fact that he had just stopped the war to end all wars. Little by little the tension in the air started to fade. Mercury looked back at the three Angels and smiled, "We did it."

At that instant, Mercury felt a sniper shot rip through his heart. Then another. His legs buckled underneath him and he fell. *Why? Who?* But really, what did any of that matter? After all, all it takes is one resolute person to make a difference.

Then everything went to madness.

Mercury's mind vaguely registered his family calling out his name as the shots started firing. Two of the Sons raised their pistols and were immediately shot through the head, one by Ma's sniper and the other by Vera's pistols. The leader sprang back from Mercury. Vera fell with a sniper shot between the eyes. Qor was riddled with shots before he could reach any of the soldiers.

As the edges of Mercury's vision started to go black, he saw Mars, Jupiter and Saturn flying up to the Federation fleet as it began firing on itself and the approaching Sons' fleet. The only ship he could identify at this distance was the *Balemore* and the misty light of ten thousand missiles being simultaneously launched.

***

All at once, Mercury snapped back to the present time. He was not dead and war had not broken out. He was still in his armor and the soldier was still standing in front of him. Nearby were his biological mother, father and sister.

"I'm going to count to three," the soldier said. "If your helmet is not off by then, they die."

The Metians believed all battles are first won in the mind. What he had seen was one possible future. A very likely future. No matter what Mercury did, there was no guaranteed outcome. All it took was one hateful person to light the fuse that would send humanity back to the Stone Age.

"One," the soldier said.

No matter what Mercury did, it was a gamble. There was no stopping that. In the end, everything came down to choice. He made his choice a long time ago, now he would let them make theirs.

"Two."

Slowly letting out a breath, Mercury removed his helmet.

THE END

EPILOGUE

One Week Ago...

SOL
Age 62

The reinforced steel doors opened and Sol entered Erithian's Eye. He was still wearing the clothes he had been sleeping in when Mercury tried to kill him. The machine's holographic avatar appeared. A child. He had always found it fascinating that of all the appearances the artificial intelligence could have chosen, it chose one that implied a lack of experience. For all the prodigious computing power and knowledge the machine possessed, it was so unsure.

Sol was silent, waiting for the doors to close behind him...Only after Sol heard the faint sound of the doors locking did he move forward to the waiting child. For the sake of the entire human race, no one could ever know this conversation took place.

"I'm sorry Sol," Erithian said. "I tried to convince Mercury to wait to kill you until after you overthrew the government, but he wasn't willing to sacrifice those who would die in the coup."

Sol raised a hand. "Don't worry. Neither of us can account for the human will. We knew it was a possibility and we will adapt the plan accordingly. Is everything else still on schedule?"

The hologram nodded. "For the most part. Mass production of the MauKe drive and terraforming equipment is right on schedule for the Expansion Event to go critical. Assuming Mercury is able to make peace with the Sons of Liberty after killing you, the Event should go smoothly. They will be busy for the next ten thousand years expanding to the farthest reaches of our galaxy and beyond."

"Good." Sol took in a deep breath. The air in the room smelled perfect and clean. After so many years, the end was finally in sight. Sol breathed out and his shoulders relaxed.

An alliance forged by the Angels and the Sons would not last long. Not normally anyway. However, thanks to the MauKe drive, humanity was about to experience an Expansion Event on the same scale as the universe's birth. Overnight the known universe would go from being unbelievably vast to something mankind could traverse instantly. The infinite would become finite. There were trillions of galaxies out there, each with billions of planets. Humanity would not stop until they had subdued them all; it was their nature. And if mankind discovered they were not alone in the universe, even better. Humanity tended to work best under pressure.

Ten thousand years from now, humanity would have only scratched the surface of the near infinite worlds to explore. Erithian theorized the Event might go on forever. If in some far-flung future humanity finally lay claim to the universe in entirety, they would be living in a reality utterly beyond his ability to comprehend or imagine. By that point, Erithian would have surpassed organic life in every conceivable way.

After all, humanity would only get to such a far-flung future if the artificial intelligence continued to manage them properly. If the Event took too long to become self-sustaining, humanity would tear itself apart.

"By the way," Erithian said. "You should do something to throw off the public. We've got enough equipment to terraform and colonize a dozen worlds, with far more on the way. Inevitably they will ask why all that equipment exists."

"Don't worry," Sol waved a hand. "I'll just make some sadistic speech about building an empire that will span the known universe. The masses will eat it up."

"I mean, that is *exactly* what we're doing. You just won't be alive to see it."

"I know," Sol said. The thought stirred up bittersweet feelings inside him. What he would give to see that world with his own eyes. "What about the Angels? How are they responding to Mercury's attempt on my life?"

If the two of them had not ensured Yuki would be in the armory to intercept Mercury, the boy might have actually succeeded in killing him just now.

Erithian raised an eyebrow. "About as well as you can expect." Live feeds of the five sleeping Angels' physical and mental states appeared in the air before Sol. An inordinate amount of data was necessary to represent the human psyche, but at this point he did not even see the numbers.

"Even now," Erithian said. "They're still loyal to you. It will really take some work to convince them to turn on you."

Even though the Angels' loyalty was an obstacle in the way of their plans, Sol still felt pride in their dedication. "Feed their doubts whenever they are in the DreamTanks, but keep it subtle."

"Don't worry Sol," Erithian shook his head. "They won't suspect a thing."

"Good," Sol nodded. "And the list?"

"Fully compiled," Erithian said. "Every member of the Sons who is at least two standard deviations more prone to violence or inciting violence than the mean. I have their homes and daily patterns. We'll be able to take them all out from orbit. It's a crude plan, but it will improve Mercury's chances of getting the Sons to agree to peace."

"What about collateral damage?" Sol asked.

Erithian exhaled with a distant look in his eyes. "Between one and one-point-one billion deaths."

Sol smiled grimly and raised his eyebrows. "If that doesn't get humanity to unite against me, I don't know what will."

"Oh," Erithian bobbed his head up and down. "They'll turn against you alright. Although, stoking their hatred too much could cause problems after you're gone. I suggest you give the Angels a much more personal reason to want you dead. Something the masses can sympathize with."

Sol stroked his chin and stared at the data of the five sleeping Angels. Something in Venus' biological readings captured his attention. *She's pregnant. That…changes things.* He didn't need to look at her psych data to know she would choose the child in a heartbeat. But Angels could not lead peaceful lives among humans. Not as Angels anyway.

As Sol formulated a plan to account for this new information, a fond smile spread across his face. *I must be growing soft.* Considering Venus had been working to undo the behavioral conditioning, defeating her in a convincing way without harming her or the baby would prove difficult. Even for him. *My last gift to you.*

"What if I killed two of them and made a public display of it?"

Erithian's eyebrows went up in shock. "I mean…yeah, that would work." The machine hesitated. "…Are you sure you want to do that?"

Two clean strikes are all I need. "I'm sure."

Erithian's eyes flicked from Venus' data, to Sol, and back again. Sol caught a glimmer of realization in the machine's eyes as it clued in to his plan. "…To alleviate their suspicions, I recommend making them think Agent Matsuri patched up their wounds without your knowledge."

"That's exactly what I was thinking."

Erithian's eyes flickered back and forth as he crunched the numbers. "Then it should work."

"Good. Anything else?"

"No…" Erithian paused. "Your death at the hands of the Angels should galvanize humanity and give them a chance at peace. But it's only a chance Sol. I can't say for sure whether humanity will choose peace, and if they don't, then it's over. Everything…gone. There might not even be a male and female to rub together. Are you sure your life is worth giving humanity that chance? If you ruled over them instead, you could make sure they expand."

"Erithian," Sol looked at the machine. "You know that's not best."

"Yes, yes," Erithian brushed him off. "I've run the numbers. 'How this new era begins sets the precedent for future generations.' But what if there was a way around it? Eventually humanity would forget you and all you did."

Sol shook his head. "Humans won't be controlled Erithian. You know this. If they believe they are being controlled, they *will* fight back. The only way for this to work is for everyone involved to think they beat me."

"Even Mercury?" Erithian asked. "You could at least let me tell him after you're gone."

"No. None of the Angels must ever know." Sol focused his stern gaze on the computer's avatar. "That is the whole point of this final test. If they can stand against me for the sake of humanity, then they can stand against anyone. They must never know I was guiding them the whole way. It must be their choice, and they must know it was their choice. Understood?"

The hologram's head drooped. "I know. I just…"

"What?"

The hologram looked up with tears in its eyes. "I don't want you to go."

Sol smiled at the machine. "I know."

The machine sniffed and took a step back. "You're throwing your life away to give humanity a chance at peace, but you don't know if they'll take it. You have the entire history of the human race as evidence that they won't…so why?"

"Ever since I was a boy, I dreamed of a world without war."

"But why?" Erithian pressed. "You don't know if it will work."

"Because I believe in them."

"In the Angels?" Erithian asked.

He spread his hands. "In all of them."

Erithian sighed. Silence slowly filled the room. "Any regrets?"

Sol thought a moment and nodded. "A few. But too few to mention."

The child's countenance fell. The hologram opened its mouth, then hesitated. After shifting in place, it eventually looked away. "It's too bad you won't be alive to see what happens."

"Humanity's Golden Age, or a new Stone Age."

"The things humans do for a dream," Erithian shook his head, his voice filled with equal parts awe and confusion.

"Dreams can be powerful things," Sol said.

Erithian looked around the room they were in. "Maybe I'll find a dream someday."

"You have plenty of time."

Erithian laughed. "Yes. Yes, I do. Assuming of course we're lucky and your plan works."

"I believe you'll find that humanity is full of surprises."

"Well," the machine raised its eyebrows and shook its head. "You certainly surprised me."

"...Goodbye Erithian," Sol said. "Thank you for everything."

"They may forget you," the machine said in a voice that threatened to crack. "But I won't. I promise."

"I know," Sol smiled. "Watch over them, won't you?"

"Always."

CPSIA information can be obtained
at www.ICGtesting.com
Printed in the USA
BVHW080437160419
545599BV00002B/4/P